MW00774434

CHANCEY JOBS

CHANCEY JOBS

4

KAY DEW SHOSTAK

August South
PUBLISHING

ISBN: 978-0-9962430-6-3

Library of Congress Control Number: 2016912302

SOUTHERN FICTION: Women's Fiction / Small Town /
Railroad / Bed & Breakfast / Mountains / Georgia / Family

Text Layout and Cover Design by Roseanna White Designs
Cover Images from www.Shutterstock.com

Published by August South Publishing. You may contact the
publisher at:
AugustSouthPublisher@gmail.com

To my Fernandina Beach Friends

You weren't there when I began writing. That was in Illinois.
You weren't there when I began searching for agents and
publishers. That was in Georgia.
You met me when my dreams were at their lowest,
and you splashed me with saltwater, sunshine, and laughter
and encouraged me to try again.

So I did.

CHAPTER 1

"For crying out loud, it's not that heavy. Lift up your end."

"Can't believe you had to do this before school. I better not break a nail."

My end of the big laundry basket dips as my teenage daughter, Savannah, removes one hand from her end to look at her nails.

"Hey, pay attention," I say. "Anyway, you were already coming to Ruby's, you can't help your mother with one little thing?" Then we both stop, set the laundry basket full of paperback books on the sidewalk, and stare at the brown paper slowly being eased off the plate glass window beside us.

Savannah cocks her head and takes a step closer, but when a woman's head appears, she jumps back. She looks at me across the laundry basket full of books and asks, "Who's that?"

Someone new in Chancey? Someone we don't know?

Not that we exactly know everyone here, but if she belonged here, we would've noticed her. As the piece of paper from the window falls to the floor, I can see we'd definitely have noticed her in our small Georgia town. Her black dress is tight but in a business kind of way, since the long sleeves and a turtleneck cover everything. She's so slim the tightness doesn't look too tight. Her shiny white-blonde hair swings along her jawline, and she smiles and waves at us as she removes the next panel of brown paper from inside the corner store.

As the next piece of paper falls, the woman loses our attention and our mouths fall open, mimicking the brown sheets of paper.

"OMG, look at that place. Where's all the junk?" Savannah says as she steps to the window.

I can only shake my head. Since long before we moved here, the corner building has housed Mac McCartney's junk shop. Not that he ever sold any of the junk, so the shop label might not have been accurate, but his family had owned the building since Chancey was built and he stored his junk there. No one thought much about it because it was so full and so dark you couldn't see past the filthy windows.

"Who would've imagined they could shine like this?" I say. Savannah and I stand right up at the windows and finally we look through them, past them. Lights encased in modern, brushed nickel hang from the ceiling, and the floor is made of wide-planked, old wood boards, sanded and varnished to a high sheen. The brick walls are glossy white and shine like the paint is still wet, and then at almost the same time we realize what we are looking at. Our wide open mouths widen further and then close in grins. A wonderful, fancy coffee machine. Navy blue mugs with bright yellow moons on their sides.

"Welcome to Moonshots #34," the lady in black says from the door she's cracked open.

"We love Moonshots. The one in Marietta is our favorite place in the world," Savannah sighs. "Are you open?" She walks away from the basket of books and me.

"So glad you're familiar with Moonshots," the woman says as she opens the door wider and steps forward. "But, no, we're not open yet. Monday is the grand opening. I'm Jordan."

Savannah shakes her hand and tries to look around her. "Savannah, and this is my mom. Can I go in and look?"

"No, the guys have wires laying everywhere." She sticks her

hand out at me. "Hi, I'm Jordan Moon. Where are you taking the books?"

"Hi, I'm Carolina, and I'm getting ready to start, well help start, a business next door to you here. In the florist shop."

"Oh, lovely, books and coffee go perfectly together."

Savannah, ever on the stakeout for potential drama, asks, "So does Ruby know?"

I close my eyes. *Ruby.*

Jordan's sheet of hair swings back and forth. "I don't believe I know a Ruby."

My innocent daughter with the wide-stretched, blue eyes takes a step back on the sidewalk and points past the florist. "There on the corner, with the lights and the people. That's Ruby's coffee shop."

Jordan shrugs as she looks down the street, "So we do have some competition. Unusual for Diego to have missed that."

"Diego?" I ask as I reach down for my end of the basket and motion for Savannah to get her end. "Is he the owner?"

Jordan nods. "So this Ruby's is open? Maybe I should go introduce myself."

"What a great idea. Mom and I were just headed there." Savannah pushes me ahead, but at the door to the florist slash bookstore, when I drop my end of the basket and start looking in my purse for the door key, she grabs my arm and steps behind Jordan, whispering, "Get it later. Like someone would steal a bunch of old books in Chancey."

Retro may be a chosen look for some places. For Ruby's, she'd have had to let something go in the past for it to come back around. The chairs with red and yellow leatherette seats surround white and chrome tables with sparkles imbedded in the Formica tops. The booths are flanked with high-backed, turquoise benches, made higher as the springs in the seats sag and leave you sitting closer to the ground each time you visit. Country music blasts from an old boom box sitting on top of a glass display case, which is crammed full of local peewee baseball teams wearing Ruby's Cafe t-shirts.

At the door, with a slow look around the cafe, Jordan displays an interesting superpower. Suddenly, like magic, one glance from Jordan and quaint turns to weird. Cozy becomes junky. Colorful is just plain tacky... and when did Ruby stop dusting?

Even in my darkest moments, when Jackson had just moved our family to this sleepy small town, when I loathed Chancey with every fiber of my being, Ruby's had maintained a certain charm. A charm I can't begin to conjure up now. Savannah's wrinkled nose mimics Jordan's wrinkled nose, and a second too late, I smooth my nose from its tilted, scrunched position. Oops.

"Hey, Libby," I greet the waitress pouring coffee at a near table.

"Carolina! Savannah, too! Out for a morning mother-daughter coffee and chat? Hey, darlin', I'm Libby and don't think we've met."

Jordan's eyebrows shove down to meet her upturned nose. "Oh, no, we haven't. I'm Jordan." And as her hand stretches out her face smooths out into a smile. "I'm opening, well, the new shop on the corner. Hope—"

I interrupt. "Libby, where's Ruby?"

"Bathroom. Should be out in a speck. Y'all want that table yonder?"

Jordan pulls back. "I can't stay."

"Carolina," Ruby hollers at the door of the bathroom and then leans back in. "Wait a minute, forgot to flush."

Wow, how did I ever miss that you can see the toilet from practically every table?

A quick glance at Jordan tells me she didn't miss it.

Ruby pulls the unvarnished door with the brass knob closed behind her. "You here to pick up muffins for your place?" She pushes past the chairs to us. "If you are, ain't got 'em. Been busy, and I sold 'em. Told you if y'all didn't get here early enough I'd

sell 'em. And I did. Y'all sit down. You're blocking the door."
With a smile at Jordan, I say, "We have a B&B. We get
muffins here for our guests."
Jordan leans around me. "Ah, Ruby. I can't stay—we're
in the process of opening. I did want to stop in and introduce
myself, though." She sways around me, you know, how tall,
skinny people do displacing no air, using little motion, and
making everyone else look like klutzes. "I'm Jordan, manager
of the Moonshots #34, opening on the corner."
Law, crowd control at its finest. Barely a muscle moves, and
every conversation stops on a dime. Superpower #2.
Now Ruby's eyebrows slide down, and *her* mouth puckers
up. "Here?"
Just then the door behind us slams open, and my friend
Laney barrels right into me. "Did you see it? We're getting
a Moonshots. No more of this dumpy coffee! Oh, hey, Ruby.
Guess you do know."
Confusion leaves Ruby's face as she glares at Laney. Ever
since Laney stole Ruby's daughter's boyfriend in high school,
Ruby and Laney have fought. Even though Laney has now been
married to the stolen boyfriend for over twenty years and has
two daughters. "Out!" Ruby shouts at Laney. "Guess I'm finally
rid of you, Laney Connor. Go drink your coffee with this sack
of skin and bones Yankee and her shower curtain hair."
Jordan pulls up and squares her shoulders. Her high heeled
boots make a very satisfying sound on the worn linoleum as she
walks to the door. Laney holds the door for her as she mouths
to me, "Who is she?"
I mouth back, "Moonshots," just as Jordan stops and turns
toward us all. She once again displays her superpowers. With a
sweep of her eyes, Ruby's is laid open, exposed for our innocent,
unsuspecting eyes. She doesn't roll her eyes, but with only a tiny
shake of her head and a slow closing of her eyelids, she leaves
no doubt that she was a major league eye-roller back in the day.

"Good luck," she says and turns to stride up the sidewalk, Laney by her side. The door shuts, the bell above it sounds once, twice, then holds still along with every tongue in the room. Until...

Savannah cocks her head at me and asks, "Wonder if she's hiring?"

Chapter 2

"So, the bookshelves?"

"Oh, hey, Carolina. You brought some more books," Patty, my partner in the bookstore says. She descends from the last step on the staircase from her upstairs apartment at the back of the cavernous room. Our building, which her mother owns, is one in a two-block row of old, attached red-brick buildings that make up downtown Chancey. About half are empty or holding junk left from some past, failed business venture. Ruby's and the newspaper occupy the two that are active. Ours is some of both, half-empty, half-active. The active half is Chancey Florist. The other half is what Patty and I are supposed to be making active.

We might not have been the best choice for that.

Patty's family has history here, but she only came on the scene this past spring. Her mountain of a mother had plans to marry her off, sight unseen. Yeah, that didn't work out. Patty's only a few years older than my oldest son, Will who's a senior at the University of Georgia. But Patty often seems as old as me and she and I get along pretty well. Or did until we started into business together.

"Yep, just need something to put them on." Opening my arms and pointing out the still-empty space hopefully stirs something in the girl. "When's the guy delivering the shelves?"

Patty tucks a piece of lank brown hair behind her ear and folds her arms over herself. Between her hair, pale skin, and huge, faded purple tee shirt, she's about as non-descript as you can get. And when you add the monotone, mushy way she talks, you just wouldn't be surprised if she melted into the floor like a scoop of ice cream falling off a cone in the middle of July. Cheap vanilla ice cream.

She makes me look like a ball of fire.

"Well, I didn't call him. Thought you'd want to."

"You met him. You talked to him at the flea market. What's his name?"

"Andy."

"Why should I call him? You call him. Now." Lord, this is like dragging a big old rug through a field of mud. I turn around so I don't have to watch her, but her sigh lets me know what I can't see. Finally, after two more sighs, I hear the buttons on her phone being mashed.

"Hey, Andy? Yeah, this is Patty Samson over in Chancey... yeah, with the bookstore. Except we don't have any shelves." Loud laughter coming through the phone makes me turn around and the surprise smile on Patty's face surprises me. "You probably done sold them, right?"

More laughter on the phone and bits of color show up on her face as she listens. Rapid blinking with her mouth hanging open tells me she's trying to come up with some answer. Okay, I'll give her a little help. "What is it?" I whisper.

She pulls the phone away from her face. "Today, he wants to bring them today."

"Good. Right? Tell him." I lift her hand with the phone back toward her face.

"Okay," she says into her phone. She listens, then finishes off with two more "okays," and hangs up.

"He's bringing them this afternoon."

"Six of them, right? Where do you think we should put

them?"

We look at each other and sigh at the same time. This isn't going to work.

Patty sits down on the window ledge. "You want some coffee?"

"Yes, but I'm kinda scared to go up to Ruby's right now. Did you know it's a Moonshots going in next door? Savannah and I met the manager this morning."

"You met Jordan? Isn't she beautiful?" Patty stands up. "I have instant coffee upstairs."

With a look around at the laundry baskets, boxes, and stacks of books, I make an executive decision. (Quit laughing, I can do that.) "Coffee it is." We cross the concrete floor past the flower coolers and work bench and walk upstairs. "Besides, I want to see what you've done with your apartment."

Patty stops on the step ahead of me and turns to look at me. Wonder if the term 'hangdog expression' comes from what a dog about to be hung would look like? I shake my head and push her on up. "I know, I know, you've done nothing with the apartment."

And we sigh.

"This is a huge mistake, Laney. She's driving me crazy. And her apartment? Might as well be a storage unit down on the highway. There's a closet, but no hangers, so everything is still in boxes and one old suitcase. Her kitchen is left over from World War II, I'm sure."

After a couple hours working with Patty, escape was needed, and Laney walking across the park provided it. While I've been getting the bookstore ready, Laney has been taking over more duties with Crossings, the B&B Jackson and I opened last Labor Day. Specializes in railroad enthusiasts (read "nuts") ,since we are right beside the busy train bridge. I don't know why she's away from the B&B, but I don't care. I have to talk to someone. Now!

Shockingly, Laney has barely gotten a word in edgewise, because I have barely stopped talking to breathe. "Rusted metal cabinet, a two-burner stove crusted with either food or rust, I couldn't tell, it just looked gross. And the refrigerator door has to be propped up with a can of food for it to even close. And there's no air conditioner. What are you looking at?" I'm sitting on the steps of the gazebo in the park, and she's standing in front of me and staring behind me. Before I can turn, Missus beckons.

"Ladies, isn't it a beautiful day!"

Wait, that can't be Missus, sounds too, uh, nice. And happy. Missus is talking in a singsong manner. And smiling. "So beautiful! And the azaleas are magnificent, aren't they? I had to come over to stroll in the park and see them up close. Gazing at them through my front window no longer sufficed."

Laney meets my eyes while our mouths form the words: *Stroll? Gazing?* Missus never strolls, and her gazing is more like glaring.

"Carolina, what a pretty sweater! Is that cotton? Peach looks good on you. May I sit with you?"

She settles on the step next to me and weaves her arm through mine then pulls me to her in like, well, a sideways hug. Laney's big, purple-blue eyes express her disbelief. "Missus, you're sure in a good mood. Or high. Are you high?"

There, that should do it. Missus' back will stiffen, and her jaw tighten, but instead—she laughs. Laughs and waves her free hand at Laney. "Sweetie, you are just delightful. And so pretty this morning. I've always said you have the prettiest eyes in town."

For a moment, we sit and take in the quietness of a spring

morning. Birds provide a bit of background music, and every so often a breeze sets the boughs of pink azaleas to swaying. Overhead, the layers of white that form the dogwood trees barely block the morning sun. Of course, the only one paying attention to all that is Missus. Laney and I are staring at her.

With a deep breath, she pushes herself up from the step and groans a bit. "Oh, well, guess my age is showing," she says with a chuckle. "Best be getting back over to the house. Have a beautiful day, y'all."

She saunters across the park towards her huge house. One in a row of restored homes from days when Chancey was a center of commerce and railroad activity. Her home, which she shares with her husband, FM, is the loveliest and biggest in the row.

"She's walking slow, actually, well, actually strolling," I say to Laney as we watch her go.

"And did you see what she had on?" Laney shakes her head. "She's always so put together, she never looks like... well, like my mom.

I stand up. "She looked softer, almost happy." Dusting off my jeans, I pull to lengthen the soft cotton sweater Missus complimented me on. "And she complimented me. She never does that."

Laney nods. "You know, it's cute, but that's not *that* great a color on you. Wonder what she's up to?"

"Who knows? I mean, she also said you have the prettiest eyes in town. She must be up to something, right?"

Laney puts her hands in the pockets of her blue jean dress and tilts her head to the side. "But that's true, so it doesn't tell us anything. Anyway, want some help with the bookstore?"

"No," I blurt out. Half-due to being hurt by my friend's insinuation that my compliment from Missus means evil and hers is just accepted fact; half because if I ask for her help, she'll take over. Been there, done that. "Our shelving is coming today. Maybe that'll help get Patty in gear."

"Good luck with that," Laney calls as she heads toward her car, and I cross the sidewalk and street toward the store. Compared to the brightly lit, shiny windows of Moonshots, all the rest of the block looks dark and gloomy. Even Shannon's bright flowers in her half of our building look drab. Must be the lighting, but we can't afford those fancy lights. At Ruby's, the windows are blocked by the booths at the bottom and ancient blinds all catawampus at the top. Maybe Moonshots should put us all out of business, I think, as I push open our door and the little bell above it jingles.

"Hey, Shannon."

"Morning, Carolina. You saw the Moonshots? Isn't that awesome to have right next door to us? That Jordan is a treasure. She's already set up a standing order for flowers. She wants stems of whatever's in season on *each* of the tables *each* week, and she has ten tables. Ten!" Shannon draws in a deep breath, then blows it out. "This is the best day of my life."

Shannon isn't exactly cute, but you think she is when you first meet her. She's short, got a big bosom, little waist and behind, but since she always wears dresses you can't really tell that right away. Her hair is jet black and cut in a pixie style. At first you think she's twenty and cute, like I said. Then you realize she's over thirty, and her face isn't pixie-ish, just kind of pinched. Like she's always trying to solve a really hard math problem. Oh, and she's constantly in motion so it's hard to get a true reading. I like her, but she talks an awful lot. Mostly about herself, which is kinda refreshing in Chancey.

"Where's Patty?" Everything looks the same in the bookstore as it did earlier. "I thought she was going to mop the floor."

Shannon shrugs. She doesn't even look up from the order she's writing. "She's out back where the utility sink is. She's been out there forever."

Deeper in the building, away from the front windows, the darker it gets. At the bottom of the staircase that leads up to

Patty's apartment, there is also a door leading outside. We rarely use it because the back lot is full of broken concrete, gravel, and weeds. There's a small room with a wooden door where junk is stored, along with the mops, brooms, and bucket. Patty's mom owns the building, and slumlord would be an apt and generous title.

As I push open the door I hear crying, but I can tell it's not Patty. I push on out and realize it's coming from above me. To my right, behind the Moonshots, there is a metal grating decking area at the rear of the second floor, like an extra-large fire escape. Its stairs come down right in front of me where another set of metal steps goes up to Patty's apartment door. Patty's apartment doesn't have any decking or balcony.

Looking up through the metal grating, I can see chairs and a table, pillows, and even some rugs. Looks like Patty's flip flops on the person sitting in one corner, and then I see where the crying is coming from. Jordan's black, high-heeled boots are in that corner.

"He won't even let me talk to them. His mother has them with her at her condo, with a heated swimming pool and daily trips to FAO Swartz. She spoils them rotten and she hates me." Jordan pulls in a broken breath. "How can she love them so much and hate me? They came from me."

"What are their names?" Patty asks.

Jordan takes a deep breath. "Carly is the two-year-old, and Francie is three." The metal flooring creaks as she stands up. "I should get back downstairs."

She continues talking to Patty, but as they move for the stairs, I slip back inside. She has two children? Wonder why she's here without them?

"Did you find her?" Shannon yells from the front.

I scurry away from the door. "No. Oh, here she is! Hey Patty, where you been?"

She tucks a hank of hair behind her ears and shrugs.

19

"Nowhere," she says as she lumbers past me.
Without the mop.

CHAPTER 3

"Susan, do you know if there's an apartment above McCartney's junk shop?" I've stepped out to the sidewalk to make my call.

"I believe so. A couple of Mac's sons lived up there at different times. Why?"

"Just wondering if that's where the lady, Jordan, who's running the Moonshots is living."

"You've met her? I hear she's glamorous and beautiful."

"She is and apparently she and Patty have stuck up some kind of friendship. How weird is that? So if she's living up there and new to town..." *Come on, Susan,* I think. *Don't let me down.*

"We should fix her some food and take it over to welcome her. I'm at the Piggly Wiggly now, so I'll get fixings for chicken and dumplings and a salad. You can take her some, well, some tea."

I roll my eyes, but agree. "Can I borrow your tea jug?"

"Sure, Laney always brings cookies. Now, I want to know if you've talked to Missus today? What's up with her?"

"All sweetness and light? She wore an old pair of cotton gardening pants and frumpy sweater to the gazebo earlier. Her hair was soft, like she hadn't even used hair spray today."

"She wore the same outfit up to the church."

"No way."

"And stood there, soft hair and all, talking to the pastor. Didn't faze her a bit. She kept smiling and talking. You think she's drinking?"

"Laney asked her if she was high."

"Lord, I bet that got her mad."

"Nope, not a bit. She laughed. Wonder what's going on. Hey, wait, FM is headed toward Ruby's. I'll head him off and see what I can find out. I'll call you back."

"Hey, FM," I say as I wave my hand. I turn my head to look both ways crossing the intersection between our block of storefronts and the corner where Ruby's sits, and then jog across the narrow street. On the other side, I look up just in time to see FM double-timing it back up his sidewalk. He bounds up the porch steps, enters his and Missus' front door, and shuts it behind him.

This leaves me with my mouth hanging open on the corner, so I tuck my phone in my pocket and move to Ruby's front door. Might as well have a muffin while I work this thing out.

"Hey Libby, any muffins left?"

She motions for me to sit at the counter that faces the back. We're the only ones in Ruby's as it's almost lunch time, and everyone knows Ruby doesn't do lunch on Fridays. Well, most Fridays, unless it's raining, in which case she makes chili. Only on rainy Fridays. Makes me think of the detailed schedule of hours on the shiny, glass doors at Moonshots. No wondering or guessing there; the schedule makes perfect, logical sense. It also makes me kind of sad.

Libby pours me a cup of steaming coffee and pours herself one, too. Then she sits down beside me. "Nope, no more muffins. Been crazy here all morning. We could've sold a blue million muffins, but after that woman from that moon place showed herself to Ruby and all, well, Ruby didn't feel like baking. Left here saying she might never bake another muffin." Libby blows on her coffee and shakes her head. "It's a tragedy. Pure tragedy."

"I'm sorry. So Ruby's gone home?"

"Yep, first time in the eighteen years I've worked here that she left before I did. You know if she wants to close, she just closes and we go home. Today she said she didn't trust herself to make sure the ovens and coffee pots were turned off and the door locked. I've just been cleaning up and wandering around, thinking about what we're going to do."

"Aww, Ruby'll come around and this place will be full of people. Wait til folks find out how much a coffee at Moonshots costs. We can have the best of both worlds."

"Maybe." She shrugs. "So how's your shop coming along? I hear you're getting shelves today."

"Yeah, then we can get some books set up and actually start to look like a bookstore. Well, I better go. See if I can light a fire under Patty to get some cleaning done." I take another sip of the coffee, which is bitter from sitting on a hot burner too long, and then stand up and thread through the tables and chairs.

"Well," Libby says, "come over tomorrow morning and maybe we'll have some muffins."

"Can't tomorrow. We'll all be going to Athens early. Will graduates from the University of Georgia tomorrow!"

"Congratulations, I can't believe it's already time for graduations to start. What's he going to do after graduation?"

"He's headed straight off to Washington, D.C. for an internship one of his professors helped him get there, and then he'll begin law school in August. And he got a teaching assistant job with a good salary. Two more years at UGA."

"Law, you must be so proud of him. He's a good boy. Y'all have a real good time tomorrow."

"We will!" I practically shout as I leave. It's hard for me to believe Will is done with his undergrad. Tomorrow will be a fun family day, and maybe being on campus will get Savannah excited about her senior year and help her get a move on filling out college applications. She's been dragging her feet there in a way that makes Patty look like a jackrabbit.

With one eye open for FM or Missus, I follow the sidewalk to the florist. Even in the shadows of the tall buildings, it's warm. I've been warned how hot graduation will be tomorrow in the stadium, with no shade from the intense May sun. Athens isn't really in the mountains, so this time of year it feels a lot hotter. My dress for tomorrow has short sleeves, and I have an assortment of visors packed to shield our eyes so we can see the grand moment Will crosses the stage. He's loved University of Georgia, and even though he applied to some law schools out of state, I know he made the right decision to stay there. At least, it was the right decision as far as his mother is concerned.

At our shop window, I stop and watch Patty mopping the old wooden floor in our half of the business for a moment.

With the opening of the door and the bell dinging above my head, Patty looks up.

"Patty! This looks wonderful. You've taken away years, decades of dirt. I never thought the wood could show through like this."

Shannon comes out from behind her counter, and with her arms crossed examines the floor of her business. "Yeah, guess I should've worked harder on my side. Think it could look like that?"

Patty's face turns pink and she nods. "I can do yours next. I'm good at cleaning."

"No," I interject. "Shannon can clean her own floor, or you can do it sometime after the shelves are in place. When are they getting here anyway?"

She shrugs. "Don't know. He said afternoon." She goes back to finishing up the last corner.

Just then the front door bangs open, and a man bellows, "Someone order some shelves? Heard there's a bookstore with no books 'cause it's got no shelves." A tall man with frizzy red hair holds back the heavy glass door with one ample shoulder.

"Hey, Patty!" he shouts and waves at her, and then waves at me and Shannon. "Howdy do, ladies. I'm Andy, Andy Taylor, and nope, I don't live in Mayberry. Here's the box with some extra brackets, if you want to add shelves. I've got the extra shelves for you, too." He drops a cardboard box onto Shannon's counter. "Can I set it there for a minute?" He turns back to the door. "Will this stay open, or do I need someone to hold it open?"

Shannon bounces toward him. "I'll show you how to prop it open." Her boobs seem larger and her dress shorter as she leans over to set the piece on the door that most people would engage with their foot. But what's the fun in that when a lean just a bit too far means showing your panties? Purple with lace trim, in case you're wondering.

Andy nods at her and breezes past. I watch her watch him stride up the sidewalk.

Patty finishes with the last corner of the store and pushes the mop and bucket against the back wall just in time to watch Andy cart a tall metal bookshelf in on his dolly.

As he sits it down, I shake my head and say, "These are huge. Look how tall."

"That's why I brought the extra brackets, figured you might want to add some shelves to each unit since you'll probably sell a lot of paperbacks. You can get an awful lot of books on six of these shelves."

He whips the dolly around and heads back out the front door. By the time he's bringing in the sixth, and final, shelf, we've figured out how to place them.

"Some couches and a couple tables by the front windows, right?" I say to Patty, who has gained more color in her cheeks, and words in her answers, since Andy has been here. Somewhere around the third shelf, Shannon quit bending and displaying her flowery parts as it became evident Andy is more interested in Patty. It's like he's enjoying getting her to come out of her shell, but maybe he's trying a little too hard. Something has red flags

25

springing up in my head. Maybe it's just that I can see Patty has lost her head already. She's acting kind of goofy, but she's moving at a speed above turtle, so I'm not gonna complain.

Andy eases the last shelf in place and pulls the dolly away. "It's kind of a wall between the florist and the bookstore, but a wall you can see and walk through." Like dominos, the shelves stand down the center of the large space, spread far enough apart for two people to walk through side by side. "Maybe a counter there towards the back, and your seating area in the light from the window?"

He stands surveying the space with his hands on his hips, his feet spread wide and every kink in his flame colored hair standing on end. His shoulders are wide, his waist a little narrower, and his hips and behind almost non-existent for such a big guy. He wipes his forehead on his sleeve and nods. "Yep, I have some furniture that would work great, and even a big old wooden counter. Nothing fancy, got it out of an old shoe store being torn down. I think it's plywood. But with some paint, it would work just right. Patty, how about we go grab some dinner and then I can show you the furniture at my warehouse? Well, my old garage actually."

"Can I, Carolina?" Patty looks at me, asking permission, but also not really sure she can *actually* go with him. And really, maybe she shouldn't. Maybe her instinct says she won't be safe. What do we know about him? Maybe it's not a good idea.

Shannon tilts her head, leans on her counter so her blossoms bloom for all to see and says, "I'm free. I could go check it out. It *is* Friday night, you know."

"It's Patty's store. She's going. Truck would be too crowded." I turn my back on Shannon's blossoms and walk over to put my arm around Patty. "Just change your shirt and come right back down. I have to leave, too." Nearing her stairs, I whisper, "You're a grown woman with good judgment. If you like the furniture and counter, we'll buy it." Then add a little louder,

"As long as it's a good deal."

Andy laughs. "Oh, it'll be a good deal."

I push Patty up the stairs and turn to look at him. Shannon is actively pining for him from her side of the store, and I can't help but wonder what he sees in Patty. Compared to Shannon, she's no, well, no comparison. Alarms go off in my head and the red flags re-wave, but still I ask, "Where do you live, Andy?"

"Outside Cartersville. I'll take good care of Patty, I promise."

"Good, I'll hold you to that."

I fold up the red flags, turn off the alarms, and remind myself Patty is a grown woman. Besides, I have a graduation to get ready for.

On the sidewalk, as I lock the door, I turn my head to watch Patty and Andy walk to his truck. They look pretty good together. He's taller than her, which can't be said for many guys around here, and the black shirt she put on isn't a T-shirt. (Who knew she owned something not a T-shirt?) It's a silky polyester, but thin and while it falls straight, it kind of floats. Even better, she's laughing.

"Who's that?" a voice says in my ear and I jump.

"Oh, hi, Peter. That's Andy. He sold us our shelves." I point through the front window and step away from Missus' son, my once-good friend. Well, not too good, you understand. Just friends, really, just friends.

He glances in the window and mimics my step so that he's back beside me. "Hey, we have to talk." He looks past me, like he's seeing who's around, then bends his head to me. "Unlock the door and we can step inside the store. Shannon's gone, right?"

"I have to go home. I do. I have to go home." All these weeks I've flirted and played, and now here Peter is wanting me to be alone with him. But, no. "No, Peter, Jackson and I are good. We're good, real good."

He touches my arm and licks his lips. "Okay, but we need to talk. You need…"

"I need to go." I pull away and dart across the street to my van. My heart is racing, and my mouth is dry. In my car, I stop to take a breath. Darn, Chancey gossips let me down. I figured they would've informed Peter about me and Jackson. I chance a look out the side window and see him still standing where I left him. He raises his hands into the air and shrugs at me.

Starting the car, my eyes stay straight ahead. Straight ahead to home. Where Jackson is.

Chapter 4

Just when my dress starts to come unstuck from my back. "What? You're not taking the internship in DC?"

We sat for an hour waiting for the ceremony to start and then it was forever watching the thousand or so graduates file into their seats. Seats in the full sun on the football field. They did have their mortar boards for shade, but those black gowns can't be comfortable. Not that our metal stadium bleachers are comfortable, but at least we weren't wrapped up in those gowns. The ceremony lasted another forever and then there was the scramble to find Will. I think I'd be more teary if I had any moisture left in my body to form tears. One good thing, sweating this much means I didn't have to find a restroom all morning.

Walking away from the stadium in the throngs of people, Will speaks to several other graduates, and when one similarly robed young woman grabs his arm, he bends down to hug her. The girl says, "Can't believe you're not going to DC, Will. It was going to be a blast."

The girl gets pulled away by her crowd of smiling friends and family, leaving me and Jackson to clog up our side of the closed street. "Will?" Jackson asks as our son keeps walking with his brother and sister.

"You're not taking the internship in DC?" I ask again. I take a couple steps toward him and he slows and turns. Bryan has his head tilted back as he squints up at his brother. Savannah, however, is studying her wedge heels tied with black ribbons around her ankles. Her arms encase her waist and hold the black and white sundress against her body. Uh oh, she knows something. Something we're not going to like. The girl who's perfected the "never show guilt" look, for once, looks guilty.

Jackson walks up behind Will and puts a hand on his shoulder. "Son, did you get a better offer?" When Will doesn't answer, Jackson looks at me and I look at Savannah. Jackson follows my eyes and grimaces. "What's going on?"

"There they are!" Missus exclaims as she steps between Savannah and Will, threads her arms through theirs, and pulls them to her. "What a marvelous day!" FM and Anna follow up behind her, and their smiles are as weak as Missus' is exuberant.

Jackson and I join Bryan in his head-tilted squint. *What are they doing here?*

People attempt to flow around us in the street, but not without looks that say, "Can't you see you are stopped in the middle of traffic?" Will clears his throat and says, "Let's move out of the way." We try to move to first one side, then the other, but there's nowhere to move to as a group.

Missus folds her hands on her purse. "Then let's just meet at the restaurant. See you there." FM puts a hand on her back, and they weave off to the side a couple steps, but Anna doesn't move.

"Anna, aren't you going with them?" I ask.

Her soft gray eyes look up at Will, and he steps to her. He wraps one black clad arm around her. "Anna and I got married last night."

"Married?" I gasp, but before I can ask why or anything else all I can see in my head is Missus is smiling, no beaming, at me. And my eyes dart down. Down to Anna's stomach.

Jackson explodes. "What is wrong with you two? Is this why you're not going to DC? Do you know how much harder this is going to make law school?"

Savannah and I meet eyes, and it's true. She smiles sideways at me, and shrugs a little. She steps to me and hugs me. In my ear, she whispers, "It'll be okay. They really love each other."

Jackson and Bryan are the only ones still squinting, but Jackson's eyes slowly uncrinkle and his jaw softens the longer I hold his eyes over our daughter's shoulder. He mouths silently, "A baby", then looks up at his son.

Will nods and says, "Yep, you're going to be a grandpa."

And standing in the middle of the campus on a busy street, throngs of people pushing around us, I think there is nothing more to be said. Until Will takes a deep breath, grins, and says, "And no more school. I'm getting a job, and we're going to live in Chancey."

CHAPTER 5

"If my head falls off, don't pick it up," I say as I dump myself into the hot car.

"That was the best chicken ever," Bryan says while buckling his seat belt. "Can you make chicken like that, Mom?"

"No."

A slap and a yell come from the back seat accompanied by Savannah's "Shut up."

"What?!" Bryan asks in outrage.

This is followed by an eye roll big enough to hear, and his sister saying, "You're so clueless."

Jackson pulls open his door. "Okay, the rest of the cake is in the back, so don't throw anything on it or mess it up when we get home." Settled in, he looks at me. "How are you?"

I close my eyes to keep the tears in and shake my head. My mouth is clamped tight, but my chin quivers anyway. The bones in my jaw feel ready to shatter, and the muscles in my neck have gone from tight to knots to pulsating hot coals. The heat from the closed-up car is nothing compared to the heat radiating off my neck, shoulders, and back. And now my face, as the tears start leaking, hot and heavy drops.

"Just breathe and relax. Take a nap on the ride home," Jackson says as he starts the car and directs the air vents toward me.

"Savannah, can you hand me my purse? I left it back there under my jacket."

She leans up and hands me the cute lavender purse I bought to go with my new dress. Just seeing it makes me tear up again. I was so happy about this day. A real family day with just the kids. A day of celebration, a family milestone.

It's just not fair. They took it all away from me, the day I thought we were going to have. And the supposed-to-be joyful and years-away day of finding out Will's getting married— and the joy of planning for, getting ready for, and enjoying the first wedding of any of my children. Even the much-farther-down-the-road joy of finding out I'm going to be a grandma. These have all been wiped out and replaced with a sweaty confab in a crowd of strangers, in the middle of the street. I feel like Sally from Charlie Brown when she realizes she missed Halloween and shouts, "I've been robbed!"

I touch the button on my phone, and the screen is covered with texts. Blinking, I try to focus, but realize that's probably not a good idea. "Everyone knows. They all know everything!" I hold up my phone for Jackson to see. "That place is amazing. We're not even back in town, and they know it all." Scrolling through congratulation after congratulation and question after question makes my head pound and voice raise. "Yep, the baby, that they're going to live with Missus and FM, about his job, even what we had for lunch. Unbelievable. I'm never speaking to Missus again. You know this has to be her. She's out of her mind with happiness. Did you hear her at lunch?"

Jackson takes his right hand off the steering wheel and lays it on my thigh. "Honey, you need to calm down." He motions with his head to the back seat.

"Calm down? Wasn't I calm enough in the restaurant? Between Missus crowing and Will drinking too much and you sitting there with your arms folded all mad, and FM chattering like a fool, I was the *only* calm one."

Savannah, of course, chimes in. "Not sure you were actually calm, Mom. You looked more stunned. Kind of frozen."

"I didn't stab anyone with my steak knife, did I?"

Bryan laughs. "That's funny, Mom. I think it'll be cool to have Will living in Chancey."

"No it won't," I say. "It's a hellhole full of gossips and small-minded people and, and, he was going to live in D.C. He was going to be a lawyer. He..."

I crush my teeth together keeps the sobs back. I turn to the window and lay my head against it and close my eyes. No more. I'm saying no more.

And I'm going to try and keep from opening the door and jumping out of the car while we're on the interstate.

"Kids, go on inside," Jackson says as I come awake. "Hey, sleepyhead. Have a good rest?"

"Wow, I was dead asleep." Sitting up straighter, I feel the knots reforming in my neck, but the pulsating is gone and my head has a mild ache instead of being on the verge of explosion.

Avoiding Jackson's eyes, I watch Savannah and Bryan walk up the porch steps. "Did they say anything while I was sleeping? Guess I went a little crazy."

He rubs my neck with his hand and grasps my left hand in his. "Honey, it was a horrible day. That's all there is to it. Our son left us in the dark to get blindsided. Kids fell asleep pretty much about the same time you did."

I shake my head. "I can't believe Will is going to wind up here. In Chancey. You know Missus will never let Anna go. And her great-grandchild? Well, you heard her. She's talking about the nursery and how they'll put up a play fort in the back yard and how easy it'll be to walk down to the library to do schoolwork and getting an afterschool job when her heir is a teenager, since they'll live right next to town." I lay my head on his shoulder. "We just found out the baby exists, and she already has its life planned."

"Honey, it's all a long way off. Will and Anna are going to have this week in Athens and that will let us get used to the idea. Then we'll deal with everything else. Let's go inside and change. Get comfortable. Okay?"

Lifting my head, I look into his eyes. No one has ever loved me like this man, and a shudder goes through me when I think of how far we drifted apart over the winter. "Thank goodness this happened *after* we figured our weirdness out. I wouldn't have made it through today without you."

"Me either." He laughs and opens his car door. "If this kind of day happened to someone in a movie, I'd swear they made it up."

That actually makes me chuckle while walking around the car. "Well, in case I haven't told you lately…" I pause and take his arm.

"What? Haven't told me lately that you love me?" He winks. "I believe you've told me *and* shown me, Mrs. Jessup."

"No, not that."

"What then?"

Up the steps, I turn on the last one and look down at him. "I hate small towns."

Chapter 6

"Jackson, please don't go. Don't get out from under the covers. Come here." Soft light through the blinds, and the birds all excited about the novelty of the sun rising, say it's morning. Under the covers, it's darker, quieter, and decidedly more fun, but apparently it doesn't last long enough as my husband pulls away from me with still enough time to get up, get dressed, and go to church.

"Stay here with me," I say.

He laughs and pulls on his dark green robe. "I did! Remember that guy a minute ago? That was me. Now I'm getting up, well, out of bed." He laughs again and tosses his pillow at me. "You've got plenty of time if you want to come with us."

"But all the questions. All the gossip. I can't face it."

Jackson stops before opening the door to leave our room. "Oh, I think you can. It's just talk. Normal talk about something happening. Nobody hates you or is plotting against our family. You didn't mind last Sunday when everyone was talking about Will graduating, moving to DC, going to law school, did you?"

"That's different."

"Not really. It's all just talk, and actually, true. I'm making coffee and having a cup on the deck. Come join me. I like coffee and church and, well, everything better with you."

He smiles, not that I can see him that clearly in the darkness, but I kind of heard his face crinkle. It's been less than a month since I decided to go to church with the rest of my family. It was nice, but a little claustrophobic, and that was before I made center stage again. Maybe I'll take a quick shower and go down for coffee. Yeah, maybe that. Maybe...

Something won't let me stay in bed. Something tells me all those weeks of staying in bed, waiting to hear my family leave on Sunday mornings without me, might have had something to do with mine and Jackson's problems. Something, but probably not. I'm just ready to get up. That's all.

The cucumber melon smell of my shower gel and shampoo keeps my nose happy until I'm halfway down the stairs, when fresh coffee and baking cinnamon rolls enter the competition.

"Hey, Mom. I made that can of cinnamon rolls. They'll be ready in three minutes." Savannah has on a short blue dress with wide straps on her shoulders. Her long hair hangs flat and shiny and wet.

"Your hair is getting your dress wet," I say as I scrunch my short mop with my fingers to keep the kinky curls in place.

She shrugs. "It'll dry. Dad has the coffee outside. Cups, too. I'll bring the rolls out there to ice them."

Bryan is out in the backyard, running in the sunlight spilling over the tall trees, down the hill, and beside the river.

"Oh, his shoes will get wet," I fret to myself. "Bryan, get out of the grass! Your feet are all wet," I yell over the railing.

He stops, looks down at his wet tennis shoes, and then back up at me. "Okay." Then he continues running around, but with a weird tiptoeing motion.

With a sigh, I turn around to his father who is reading a paper lifted up in front of his whole upper body. "Jackson."

Over the paper, he looks at me, then at his son, then back at me. "So?"

"Fine. I don't care." I flounce—yes, flounce—into the patio

37

chair across from Jackson.

"Honey, it's not like its cold or he's sick or they're dress shoes. So, they get wet. So?"

"Never mind," I say. "Can you pour me some coffee?"

"You going to church?"

"You still want me to?"

He looks up from where the steamy liquid is filling my cup. "Of course. It's so much better when we're all there together." Then he gets a sappy grin and adds, "Especially when we're all so happy."

I stick my tongue out at him then take a tiny sip and lean back, propping my feet on the rails of the chair beside me. My skin feels scratchy, irritated. Nothing I can actually scratch, just like I want to yell or kick something or eat six cinnamon rolls all at once. Yeah, then I could lay down on the couch, all full and warm and happy. Yep, that should do it.

I yelp when my daughter pushes open the French doors and bangs into my shoulder with them. "Ow, Savannah! I'm sitting here, you know."

"Sorry," she says. "Here, hold this." She hands me the little plastic cup of icing with a knife stuck in it.

As soon as she lets go of the knife, it balances itself out by flipping right into my lap with a dollop of white icing. "Savannah!"

"Mom, just hold it. For like a minute, okay?" She says something else under her breath when she steps back into the kitchen. I bet it's a good thing I couldn't quite hear her, since my need to kick something is still in high gear, despite getting to yell a bit.

Jackson hasn't moved, and his paper is still up high. I sit the icing cup on the table, lay the knife beside it and rake the glob of glistening white off my shirt. After I sling most of it back into the container, I stick my finger in my mouth. It's good, but I'm going to need to eat the rest of the cup to feel even a little bit better.

Savannah comes out with the hot pan in one hand, plates in the other, and shoves the door closed with her foot. She puts it all down and then starts plopping my icing on all the rolls. Guess it's not really *my* icing.

Reaching across the table, I pour coffee into one of the waiting cups. "So, how long have you known about Will and Anna?" I ask my daughter. Oh, did I see the newspaper move? Her eyebrows raise, and she twitches her mouth to the side. "Um, last week sometime, I guess."

"Did you know they were getting married Friday?"

"No. I swear, Mom. I didn't know that. It wasn't supposed to happen like it did."

Now the paper falls to the table. "No, duh," Jackson says. "He was supposed to go to DC, supposed to go to law school."

Oh, an eye roll for dad. "Not that, Daddy. The whole telling you guys thing, but Missus, well, she—"

"Yeah, how did Missus find out about all this before me, before us?" I want to know.

Savannah puts a cinnamon roll on a plate and hands it to her dad. "Anna told her grandmother, which made sense, but then," she shrugs. "You know Missus. She kinda took over."

With my mouth full of cinnamon roll to calm me down, I growl. "And ran right over Will and Anna in the process. Well, we know now, and she's met her match. She's not railroading my son into living here in Chancey."

Savannah flips her wet flap of hair over her shoulder. "I don't know what happened. Anna was supposed to go with us to graduation and then they were going to tell you at lunch. But yesterday morning Anna texted me to say I shouldn't ask y'all if she could come, like I was supposed to. I thought maybe she'd backed out of going."

Popping the last bite of my roll in my mouth, I exclaim, "Then there they were. Bryan! If you want a cinnamon roll you better get up here." I push back, clutching my coffee cup in both hands to keep myself from grabbing another roll. "And he's been just too secretive about this so-called job he has here. I bet Missus is paying him to sweep her front porch, just so they'll stay."

"Now, honey," Jackson says with a deep breath. He's just as worried as I am. He's just choosing not to show it. Coward. "He said he has one more interview and then he'll tell us. Maybe it's a good job."

"In Chancey? This is the last place a young person with a college degree would find a good job. Over my dead body is she going to run his life. She as in Missus, not Anna." Hey, I'm not stupid, I know which side my grandbaby is buttered on.

Bryan grabs two cinnamon rolls, one in each hand and walks off licking both arms as the icing drips. His father and his sister don't even notice, so I don't either. I always made sure Will had a plate and a napkin and a fork, and look where it got him. With a pregnant wife in a dead-end town with no future.

"I'll be ready in a few minutes," I say and stand up.

Jackson smiles. "So you *are* going?"

"Yep, can't give Missus a piece of my mind sitting up here." I pinch off a hunk of another cinnamon roll and shove most of it in my mouth. Plates are for sissies.

Everyone is staring at me. Even the preacher can't concentrate for checking every couple seconds what's going on with me. The tears just won't stop.

We parked in the side parking lot and walked around the church to the front doors. The deep blue of the sky sparked the fresh leaves into neon green on the tree branches above us. As the leaves bounced in the breeze, morning sunlight sparkled. Grass—fresh, thick, and smelling of a recent cutting—stretched all around the sidewalk as the last of the dogwood petals snowed down on us. And while all that was moving and heart-squeezing, where did all these beautiful babies come from? Everyone seems to be carrying a baby or a toddler into church. I can't remember the last time I really paid attention to a baby. The smooth skin, fine hair, wide eyes... and look how tiny their fingers are! Oh, and each perfect fingernail. Babies have never really been my thing, but they've never simply been everywhere I looked.

So even before we got up the front steps, I was blinking abnormally. Had to hold onto Jackson to make it up the steps, and then walking inside, leaving the noise and breeze and sunlight behind, a hushed feeling wrapped around me. The old wood and wax smell mixed with the organ music, and blinking back tears no longer did its job.

I followed Jackson into a pew, keeping my head down. The stained glass made me catch my breath. Had I ever really noticed the pictures? The faces? Even the way people talked quieter, laughed in a deeper register, smiled, and waved at each other across the room. There is no reason at all, none, for all that to make me cry and yet it did. It and everything else that's happened. Jackson just keeps patting my arm. He has no idea what to do either. So much for giving Missus a piece of my mind. I'd probably just hug her and ask if I could move in with her, too.

And then Ruby stands up when the minister asks for prayer requests.

"Preacher, I want to say something. I mean, I want to ask y'all's prayers for something. For me. Just 'cause something is big, don't mean it's better. Every lady in here can tell you that. Ain't I right, ladies?"

And my tears dried up just like that. Ruby wears blue jeans with either a T-shirt or sweatshirt every day, everywhere.

Today—I'm assuming in honor of going to church, which she rarely does (but no judgment coming from this pew)—she has on a denim skirt. Her t shirt is black and has a big yellow ball on the front with a red line and circle over it. Last winter she had a bunch of bright green shirts made with the same red line and circle to protest the power plant she later became a big proponent of. However, as she turns to address the congregation behind her, I see the yellow ball isn't the only enhancement, this shirt has writing on the back.

"NO MOONS."

"Ladies? Ain't I right? Sometimes big just means big and that's all. Small can be good!" She emphasizes this with a shove of her fist high into the air, and some of the smiles turn into chuckles.

The preacher realizes he needs to get this back in control, so he clears his throat next to the microphone. "Thank you, Ruby. We'll keep that in mind. Any other prayer requests?"

"Me!" Ruby shouts. "Me, I need prayers that I don't go hungry. That I don't lose my business. That woman has moved in here to ruin me, and so I need prayers. Prayers and, well, customers. Thank you, Preacher, that's all I got to say." She plops down and nods at the people sitting near her.

This time the preacher not only doesn't ask for more requests, he turns to the choir leader and rolls his hand at her like, hurry up, no telling who'll stand up next. I remember Laney telling me that every time a new preacher comes, he or she tries to get the prayer requests from the congregation cut out of the service, but she says it'll never happen. She says that's why half the people are here. Gossip update.

Listening to the choir sing, I feel a poke in my shoulder and a piece of paper the same buff color of my bulletin falls beside me. Bryan picks it up, but I grab it before he can open it, since who knows what it could say about Will and Anna.

"We're taking food over to Jordan's this afternoon. You

42

coming?" Over my shoulder, and a couple rows back, Laney is looking at me with her head cocked, eyebrows lifted, and eyes questioning. I nod and then crumple the note in my hand as I look down at my lap. Well, it's probably just a ruse to find out what's happening with Will. Guess I might as well get it over with this afternoon. Plus, if we go out to the barbeque place for lunch I can just buy a gallon of sweet tea and not have to cook at all.

Because yes, making tea is cooking.

CHAPTER 7

"Ruby goes out to the nursing home to see her Aunt Meredith every Sunday, so I figured we're good going to see Jordan today," Susan explains as she waits for me to unlock the bookstore. "Sure don't want to run into Ruby while carrying food to the enemy."

"Oh, wait, the door's unlocked." I push it open and stick my head in. Music comes from near the back. "Hello?"

"I'm not open," Shannon calls from behind one of her displays. "Oh, it's you," she says when she sees us. "Meant to lock that behind me."

"What are you doing here?" I ask as I hold the door open for Susan. She has a cardboard box full of food which she carries in and sits on the florist's counter.

"Filling Jordan's order. She says she has to have the table flowers by 6 a.m. opening on Monday mornings. So I guess I'll have to work Sunday afternoons now. She was shocked when I said we weren't open on Sundays."

Susan asks, "She's going to be open on Sundays?"

"Yep, not until 7 a.m., though, instead of 6 like during the week."

"Hmm, wonder who she'll find to work. Nothing's open here on Sunday mornings." Susan walks back to Shannon's work

44

table. "These look great. Where did you get the black vases?"

"Jordan. Apparently they are the same in every MoonShots. And there's a chart on how high the flowers need to be and how wide. I have these gorgeous hydrangeas, but nope, they don't fit the chart. Hey, what smells so good?"

"We're taking some food up to Jordan. Figured it was just as easy to come through here to do it. Besides, I wanted to show Susan the bookshelves."

Susan had walked over to the bookstore side. "This setup is great. You going to paint the shelves? What color you thinking?"

"Shoot, you're right," I say. "They would look better painted. Why can't anything be easy?" I turn to Shannon. "You seen Patty?"

Shannon shrugs. "Maybe."

"What does that mean? Is Patty here?"

"Yes, she is here. She most definitely is here. Now."

Laney had walked in the front door and heard what Shannon said. "Now? As in 'now she's here,' but she wasn't here earlier? And if that *Now* was because she was at church, then it would have been just a plain old *Now* and not a full-of-double-meaning *Now*. So, she's here *Now*, wasn't here earlier. Shannon thinks there's something we might want to know, but something she shouldn't tell. I'd say it involved a walk of shame for Patty, but Lord knows there ain't no man involved." Shannon grins, and I catch my breath, causing Laney to step towards me, her plate of cookies still in hand. "Or is there?"

"Shannon, no. All night?"

Her pinched up face pinches further. "Good thing I didn't go to look at the furniture. I'm just not that kind of girl."

"And you weren't invited," I mumble as I head to Patty's stairs. However, at the bottom I pause, with my hand on the railing. She's a grown woman. What am I going to say or do? But if he dropped her off right here in town on a Sunday morning, oh law, everybody's going to know it.

Laney shouts back at me. "Are we going to take this food to the MoonShots lady or not? I've got things to do."

I walk back to the front and pick up my jug of sweet tea from where I'd set it on a window ledge. Shannon is collecting the vases and putting them in a box. "I'm going to deliver these next door while the workmen are still there. Jordan said she was going upstairs for a bit, earlier. Patty may, or may not, be upstairs also. But I think she has more company than Jordan."

"He came back with her? What in the world is she thinking?" I shake my head.

Shannon grins and nods to the panel truck sitting in front of the shop. "That's his truck. Guess we better get used to it."

"Lord help us," I say, still shaking my head, "Patty has a boyfriend."

"And more power to the big ol' girl if she found a guy who can get her some furniture. This place needs some, and furniture ain't cheap," Laney opines as we walk to the back door.

We push it open, and I hold it while the two sisters walk out. Susan leads the way, but Laney balks at the bottom step. "These metal steps are impossible in heels. Here, hold this." She hands me her plate of cookies, which I balance on my free hand while she takes off her beige heels. She threads the straps on her fingers and takes back her plate. "Give me that. Don't want you getting credit for both the cookies and tea."

Susan is already standing on the deck by time we get up there, and her mouth has dropped open. "Look at this place."

Olive green gauze curtains are held back with black cords on each side of the decking. They hang from brass rings, threaded on a brass rod that circles the outside edges of the deck roof. Two square, black woven chairs with olive cushions sit beside a matching table. Right at the top of the steps is a small cabinet with glass doors, containing glasses and small plates. Fat white candles sit on pedestals, and tinkling from a wooden wind chime makes us look up to see the fan overhead with wide paddles of black wicker turning slowly. Susan rests the box on her thigh. "I could live here. Here, just on this porch."

Laney pads in her bare feet to the French doors painted in glossy black and knocks on one of the panes. "Jordan?" she calls out. "We brought you some welcome goodies."

Already through the door I can see this is nothing like Patty's apartment. Silhouetted by the light from the big front windows, Jordan makes her way to the door and opens it. A crack.

"We've brought you some food to say, 'Welcome to Chancey.'" Laney actually lifts one foot to step inside, but Jordan doesn't budge.

"I'm kind of busy right now," she says and doesn't give an inch.

Pure Southern panic sweat breaks out on those of us on the porch. My eyelids start jerking. How many times have I wanted to not let someone in my front door when they just show up, but have I ever? Well, nooo. And she doesn't even look bothered. This is a whole new superpower I've never even heard of. Fend off nosy, unannounced Southerners carrying food surrounding your front door with one, just one, sentence. Amazing.

Then Laney shakes off any panic and fights back with a dose of shame. "Kinda hot out here, and I'd hate for this food to spoil if we just leave it on your porch."

I can't see Laney's face, but I believe that's fluttering eye lashes I hear. There, that should make Jordan melt and let us in.

But melt is hardly the correct word. Maybe concede? Cave? Retreat? She sets her mouth in a straight line and steps back. "Okay, come in."

Sleek wood floors reflect muted sunlight coming in the front windows. The trees of the park provide a background of green, and I realize just how dirty Patty's windows are. I don't remember even seeing any trees at her place. Jordan's low, wide bed with a tall head board of ebony is half-hidden behind free standing screens. The walls are painted white, and her couch and chairs are a dark brown leather set atop a cream rug. When I turn to set the jug of tea down, I notice the kitchen for the first time. Laid out just like Patty's, it couldn't be any more different if Patty didn't have a kitchen.

Granite countertops, steel appliances, tall white cabinets. Susan can have the porch; I want to live here.

Susan puts down the box of food. "This place is beautiful. I can't believe it's in Chancey."

"You must be planning on staying here for a long time if you spent this much money fixing this up," Laney adds. "Here's some cookies."

"Oh, thanks." Jordan takes the plate, sets it down on the counter, and then picks up her glass of wine. As she takes a sip, it's as if her manners get jump-started, well, a little bit. "Would you like something to drink? Wine or, ah, that." She points to the jug of iced tea. Every fiber of her body is saying, "No, say no". Of course, we ignore that and act like she meant it.

"Sure, wine would be great."

Jordan pours us all half glasses of wine. We try to appear casual, rather than awkward, for a few moments. Then Laney spots a couple of folding wooden chairs. "Hey, why don't we take those out to the porch?" She picks them up in her unoccupied hand and nods at Susan to open the door. Jordan and I follow. We sit in the two cushioned chairs and watch the sisters get settled into theirs.

Laney tries again. "So, you must plan on being here a long time since you put so much money into the apartment."

Jordan sighs and resignation flows over her. "It wasn't my money. Diego did that when they were fixing the shop."

"Diego?" Susan asks.

"Yes, Diego Moon, the owner." And she waits a moment while I make the connection.

"Wait, your last name is Moon. Are you…"

"Yes, Diego is my husband."

Like filling in a long word in a crossword puzzle, things start clicking. "Oh, you're the owner. Of MoonShots. Oh."

And the more words we fill in, the more questions we get. "Do you often open stores for the company?" "Will your husband be joining you here?" "How did you pick Chancey?" Weariness replaces the resignation, and she softens her tone and body language. "I haven't opened a store for the past several years, but at the beginning, yes, I opened several stores. No, Diego is busy in New York, and well, I don't know how he picked Chancey. I haven't been involved with the business since, well, for a few years now."

When tears fill her eyes, we all hush. She licks her bottom lip and tries to smile. "I'm sorry, but I really do have work to do. We *are* opening in the morning." She stands up, and we do, too.

I collect our three glasses, so Laney and Susan can fold up their chairs. Back inside, I set the glasses in the sink and on a small shelf above the sink, I notice pictures. In one of them, there are two little girls and a very handsome man. The other two pictures are individual ones of the girls from the first picture. They are beautiful, one with dark hair like the man, and one with blonde hair like Jordan. "What beautiful children," I say.

Jordan nods and smiles.

Laney cranes her neck to look. "Oh, are they yours?"

Jordan only nods again and presses her lips tight. Her eyes shine, and again we are all left standing awkwardly silent. Laney and I make moves toward the door, and then leave it to Susan. She covers the few steps between herself and our host and wraps the tall woman in a hug.

Jordan's shoulders stiffen at first, and then they bow into Susan. Susan says in a low voice, "I know we seem like just nosy old women, but we do care about you and want you to be happy. Your girls are beautiful and missing them is normal. Maybe they'll be able to come see you here, and play right over there in the park."

Jordan takes a deep breath and then steps back. "Thank you. Maybe they will, but probably not. No, probably not. Thank you for the food."

Susan reaches into the box she'd sat on the counter earlier. "This is green salad and should probably go in the fridge." As she lifts it out, Laney takes the lid off the larger glass bowl and releases a smell which causes her and me to breath deep and smile.

Jordan looks over into the bowl, but wrinkles her nose and visibly recoils. "What is that?"

"Chicken and dumplings. Susan's are the best in town," I say. However her face remains contorted. So I take a better looks. Hmmm, never really thought about it, but looks pretty unappetizing. Beige lumps in beige gravy. Hmmm.

Swallowing, or almost gagging, Jordan takes a step away and reaches to take the salad container out of Susan's hand, as she says, "A salad will be perfect." She lifts the lid for a peek, then peels the lid completely off. "What's this? A green salad?"

Susan says tersely, "Not just 'a' green salad. Green salad."

"One of her specialties," Laney adds. "I tried making it, but my marshmallows stayed hard and the pudding mix seemed grainy. It's the pistachio pudding mix that makes it green. Isn't it pretty?"

I try to help. "There's a whole can of crushed pineapple in it." I don't think that helped.

Jordan takes a big swallow of wine, and then takes a deep breath. She straightens her back, and with the settling of her shoulders, neck, and then chin, she dismisses us.

Quietly, we walk down the steps and pause at the bottom for Laney to put on her shoes. We wait until we are through the back door inside the bookstore, and we all look at each other.

"What is going on with her?" I ask.

With shaking heads, and thoughts circling, we walk up to the front where stretched out on what must be our new couch is a topless Patty and a big, red-haired man who is between us and seeing all of Patty's chest.

He has his clothes on.

"Patty! What in the world?"

Andy starts to get up, but Patty pulls him back to her. "No! I don't have my shirt on."

Susan pushes a laughing Laney toward the door. "We're leaving."

I follow them to the door, and don't look back. But at the door I stop and say loudly, "You need to take this, whatever this is, upstairs." I slam the door behind me and storm right into Laney and Susan waiting on the sidewalk. Do I even need to mention they are doubled over laughing?

"Who was that?" Susan asks.

"Andy, the furniture guy."

Laney tips her head. "Well, from what I could see the couch looks nice. Not many folks these days will deliver furniture *and* give it a test drive for you. He should hand out cards."

CHAPTER 8

"Right there in the front window for anyone walking by to see! What is wrong with her?"

Jackson hasn't stopped whatever he's doing with the back tire of the lawn mower, but he's laughing while he does it.

Banging my hand on the hood of the riding mower I'm leaning against, I demand, "Why does everyone think this is so funny? She's kind of like under our care, or something. Least it feels that way."

Grass stains mark the knees of his faded jeans when Jackson stands up. We are close to the river and the bottom of the hill has been mowed. Between the smell of lake water and freshly mown grass, I can't breathe deep enough. "I need to get some chairs to put down here. I don't ever come down here anymore."

Jackson stands in front of me. "Not scared of ghosts down here, now?"

"Nope," I say and pull him to me. "You smell like cut grass and gasoline. We should bottle that and make our fortune." We nuzzle for a moment and about the time I'm feeling all good, Jackson pulls away. I pout and ask, "Hey, where you going?"

"I've got mowing to do before it gets dark."

I straighten up from leaning and look around at the purpling air. Bats and swallows are darting here and there, catching dinner, and just as I look up at the house, I see lights way at the top come on. Savannah must be home from youth group. "Okay, one more kiss before I let you get back to work." When I kiss him, and I really do kiss him, he breaks it up by grinning and pulling back to look at me.

"Guess seeing your business partner getting busy with her boyfriend got your motor running."

"What? No. Not at all. You're crazy." I step away and turn to walk up the hill as he sits down on the mower. However, instead of hearing the roaring of the engine, I hear him call me.

"Hey, Carolina, so what did Laney and Susan have to say about Will and Anna and all that?" His light voice doesn't betray the concern I see in his eyes when I turn toward him.

"Um, you know, it didn't come up. At all."

His smile is lopsided, and then he turns the key and the machine comes to life. He drives away, and as I walk up the hill, I wonder why Will and Anna didn't come up. Were we just preoccupied with Jordan, and then Patty? Do they not care? Or are they embarrassed to bring it up? Wait, Laney embarrassed? I don't think so, but then why wasn't it mentioned?

The back door on the porch swings opens and Bryan walks out.

"Mom, what's for dinner? They only had baked potatoes at youth group, and I'm starving."

"Okay, did you have fun?"

"Sure, I guess. What are you cooking?"

"Hold on, you won't starve."

"I might. Those baked potatoes were gross."

I close the door behind me and flip on the kitchen light. "Gross? You like baked potatoes."

"Not when they're the only thing to eat. If you have steak or something, but just a baked potato? Gross."

"They didn't have cheese or bacon bits?"

"Yeah, but just baked potatoes. Weird."

"You're like your daddy. If there's not a meat on the plate, it's not a meal. Frozen pizza? Pepperoni or everything?"

He thinks for a minute. "Pepperoni. I'll get the pan."

While I turn on the oven and collect dishes from around the kitchen to load into the dishwasher, he unwraps the pizza and puts it on the pan.

Maybe if he's hungry, and I don't look at him, he'll talk. "So, was Brittani there?" Brittani is a high school girl my little boy started hanging out with in the winter. I'm still having trouble calling her his girlfriend.

From the corner of my eye, I catch him as he shrugs. Then he walks out of the kitchen.

Okay, guess he's not *that* hungry. We've not seen the little redhead for a week or two, and he won't give me any information. Savannah says she doesn't know if they are still dating (like they can date when they can't even drive) and says she doesn't want to know, and then she launches into how much she hates Brittani, so I can't ask her anymore.

And Savannah's resentment has nothing to do with sisterly love, but teen-girl vengeance and drama. Brittani stole Savannah's lead role in the spring play, then caused Savannah to trip during a cheerleading stunt - The world according to Savannah Jessup.

Soft light fills the living room when I leave the brightly lit kitchen. I reach back in to turn off the kitchen light, and then walk in the liquid light from the front windows to the front door. I slide the glass top panel down to expose the screen window, and the smell of mown grass falls in on a cool breeze. The sun is gone from the sky, and there are no clouds to reflect its setting behind the mountains. Just clear air taking on depth as the shadows lengthen. The heat of the early May day required the air conditioner earlier, but the heat slipped through our fingers with promises of a more stalwart return.

Turning from the windows, the stillness of the house is

accentuated by the creeping darkness, but now that we are headed towards summer, even the darkness seems soft. Maybe it's the smell of the grass, or the chirp of grasshoppers outside, or the birds calling good night to each other, but this darkening contains hope. Summer is coming, and even the night knows it.

"What are you doing?" Savannah asks from the top of the stairs. "Buzzer is going off. What are you cooking?"

"Oh, nothing. I mean, I'm doing nothing. Pizza. Pizza must be done. Holler for Bryan." This time when I flip the kitchen light on, the windows are black. That in-between time is gone, and night has fallen.

Before the pizza is fully cut, Savannah and Bryan are waiting for a piece. Bryan takes the first two pieces and heads to the living room. He has the lights and TV on before I can get Savannah's slice onto her plate. How quickly the magic of twilight evaporates into light and noise. "So, you didn't like the baked potato at youth group either?"

"It's was okay. I just forgot to eat it. Jenna got my application and hers from MoonShots, so we were filling them out. We're going to take them in tomorrow before school. It was closed when we went by after church. Hey, who's Patty's boyfriend?"

"Why? What did you see?" Apparently my flipping around to face her with melted cheese stringing from the pizza cutter was a little abrupt.

My middle child wrinkles her nose. "Chill. They were kissing at the door to your shop. He's even bigger than she is. Kinda hard to miss 'em."

"Oh, yeah," I say, bending down to wipe up cheese off the floor. "He's Andy. We bought some furniture from him. I think they're moving kind of fast."

Savannah shrugs. "She's old. Guess she doesn't want to waste time." She grabs a bottle of water out of the refrigerator, then she joins her brother in the living room.

At the back door, Jackson steps in just as I was getting ready to step out and tell him about the pizza. "Oh, here you are. I made a pizza. Kids are in the living room."

He washes his hand in the sink. "Want to eat it on the deck? Sounds like the kids have taken over in there."

With two bottled waters and my slice, I get settled on the deck. Jackson joins me with a bigger plate and a couple pieces on it. Light from the kitchen window spills across the deck, and in the black sky, the brighter stars make their appearances. "Hey, turn off that light over the sink, okay?" I ask before he sits down. When he turns it off, the stars start popping out. We still have enough light from the stove hood, but it's muted.

"So you have folks in the B&B this week?" he asks.

"Not until Wednesday night, but they'll be here through the weekend. Then I think there's a couple coming just for Friday and Saturday. Laney's handling the reservations, but I caught a peek at the book earlier."

"How about the bookstore? When do you plan on opening that? Laney's still good with taking over the B&B?"

"Yes. You know she's itching for me to get out of the way." Keeping annoyance out of my voice is hard. Venting my unhappiness through tone, if not words, became a habit over the past couple months, and it feels so good to let it out. But I know, I know, it doesn't help. He's annoyed at me for not wanting to do the B&B, and I'm annoyed at him for being annoyed. This B&B thing was never my idea.

We eat in silence, and now I'm getting annoyed because he has no idea I'm annoyed. He's just sitting there eating and smiling. I close my eyes and take a deep breath. Then out of nowhere a thought enters my head. *I'm jealous of Laney taking over the B&B.*

My eyes pop open. Where did that come from? Well, that's a little more truth than I want on a Sunday night. "I've got some laundry to do, so I'll be downstairs," I say as I stand up.

Jackson just smiles and gives a little nod toward his plate.

"Okay, I'm going to finish eating out here and then take a shower and pack. I should be home by Thursday night."

"Fine," I say as I pull the door closed behind me.

I put my saucer in the sink and head down the basement stairs. As the smell of dryer sheets, musty concrete floors and walls, and cardboard from the stacks of boxes we've yet to unpack greets me, all I can think is, "What do you mean you're jealous of Laney? You hate the B&B."

Forget that. Once I get the bookstore open, it'll be great. Absolutely great.

CHAPTER 9

"Thought I heard someone down here. Why are you here so early?" Patty asks from the bottom stair from her apartment. Turning to look at her, I want to tell her no need to clutch her robe around her like that 'cause I've seen it all already.

"We've got to get this place open. No more playing around with it. Graduation weekend is behind me and I'm ready to get the bookstore open. It's already May 3rd. Go get dressed, and I'll get a couple coffees, okay?"

She nods, turns, and lumbers up the stairs. A sigh can't help coming out as I bend over to pick up my purse, and with a quick look around, I realize I left my pink ceramic travel mug in the car. Ruby doesn't do to-go cups, so everyone carries around their own if they want to drink their coffee anywhere other than inside Ruby's. Oh, wow, until now.

My hand actually warms and tingles a bit at the idea of a MoonShots to-go cup. Deep purple, with the yellow moon and the white cardboard sleeve. Every so often a jolt of suburban envy hits me; this time, though, it leaves me with weakened knees.

I can actually go get a coffee from MoonShots.

Unless Ruby is sitting in the park gazebo with a gun, which is not entirely out of the question. I grab my wallet out of my purse, check through the front window for the glint of early morning sun off a gun scope in the park, and slip out the door. The sun sits just above the mountains in front of me, hitting the store windows and turning them into sheets of light. Good cover, I figure, but I hurry anyway, hugging the front of the building and keeping my head down.

When I open the door, my knees weaken again. This smells like home, our old home. Like new floors, granite counters, sparkling bathrooms, new paint, strong coffee. Ruby's smells good, but good like your grandma's house. Worn floors, muffins baking, a touch of Lysol or mothballs, and coffee. Not strong coffee, not dark coffee, grandma coffee. Nice, brown coffee.

"Good morning! Welcome to MoonShots!" A young man calls out. "What can I get you this morning?" What? No insult upon walking in the door? Ruby's is in serious trouble.

"Good morning. You know, it'll take me some time to get used to your menu again. How about just two medium coffees." I pause to savor it before I say, "To go."

As he rings me up I glance at his nametag. "So Matt, are you from around here?"

"Nope. I'm from the Boston store. When a new MoonShots opens, there's a contest for who gets to go open it and run it for two weeks. We train the new staff."

"Wow, I bet this is different from Boston."

Matt pulls two cups off the stack to his left, and all I can see from his turned down head are his eyebrows raising. Then he looks at me and tries to smile. "Sure is. When we heard of a Georgia store opening, we all thought it would be Atlanta."

The girl behind him laughs and asks, "Who ever heard of a MoonShots in such a small town?"

"Really," I agree. "Where are you from?"

She smiles and takes the cups from Matt. "I'm from Seattle, but I currently work in the Dallas store." She fills the first cup and sits it on the counter.

"Where are y'all staying?"

She can't help but sigh with her whole body as she watches the steaming coffee fill the second cup. "Out at the interstate. Not quite the experience we all competed for."

"Yeah, I guess not. How many of you are here?"

Matt answers, "Six of us. Seven with Jordan."

I pick up two cardboard sleeves. "But Jordan must be here for longer. Her apartment upstairs is quite nice."

Matt and the girl meet eyes, and she turns back to the sink. Matt pushes the cups toward me. "Yeah, well, not sure what's going on there."

Focusing on putting the lids on and acting all nonchalant, I say, "So, it's not usual for Mrs. Moon to open stores."

Matt laughs a bit in the back of his throat. "After the mess last winter, I guess she figures it's the only way to keep being called *Mrs.* Moon." His emphasis on the word "missus" causes his coworker to snicker. When I look up, he shrugs. "Enjoy your coffee."

Before I push through the door, I take a careful sip. It's hot, rich, strong but not bitter. Which is more than I can say for the employees. Holding the cups low, I scoot back to our shop, and make it without being seen. Patty opens the door for me.

She has on jeans, a shapeless blue shirt and house shoes. "Why are you wearing house shoes?" I ask, as I hand her her coffee.

Her lank hair barely moves as she looks down at her feet. When she looks back up, there's no answer on her face or in her mouth.

Never mind.

I sit my coffee on the counter for the flower shop, and pull the notepad I laid there earlier towards me. "I started working on a list of things we need to do. I think we should plan on opening Monday, ready or not."

"Next Monday? In just a week?"

"Why not? We have to open up sometime, and I have a feeling if I left it to you we'd never open." And wow, did that sound mean. "I'm sorry, Patty, I didn't mean that."

She shuffles to the couch and sits down. "Just tell me what you want me to do."

Drawing in a deep breath, I let it out through a big smile. "We're partners. We decide together what to do. Like, should we paint the bookshelves? Do we need more furniture? How will we do book trade-ins, and how much will we charge for books?"

"Andy is bringing two more chairs this afternoon. He also found us that counter he talked about. Mother is bringing us a computer this weekend."

"See, you've gotten a lot done. So, your mother is coming for Mother's Day?"

"Yeah. She may stay for a while, too. Laney reserved the Chessie Room where I stayed last fall."

Gertie Samson in my house for an extended period of time? I'm going to kill Laney. Sucking in a deep breath through my nose, I tamp down the screaming and ask, "Really? At the B&B? Why is she staying so long?"

My partner drinks her coffee and shrugs.

"Does she know about Andy?"

Patty grins and actually bites her lower lip. "Not yet, but she'll meet him Sunday. We made reservations for a Mother's Day brunch."

"That sounds nice. Where is that? Maybe I can talk Jackson into taking me."

She laughs, "Up at Crossings. On the deck. Laney said it's for those staying there and their guests. Maybe she could find a place for you and Jackson."

Okay, maybe I won't kill Laney, because then I'd have to fix the brunch. But as soon as the last mimosa is drunk, she's dead.
#####

"And just who is cooking this brunch?" With my cell phone

tucked between my ear and shoulder, I talk loudly over the sound of sanding. Andy arrived armed with sandpaper, since we "obviously" were going to paint the shelves. He also arrived with paint. Apparently we're going with a wine red and navy blue color scheme. Cream will be our accent color. Someone must've slipped mine and Patty's lack of decision making on the church prayer list, and it looks like Andy is the answer. He loves making decisions. Just ask him.

"When I saw you ladies were having trouble deciding, I decided to decide for you." He talks as big as he is. "Doesn't that look good?"

Patty nods, like a bobble head dog in the back of a car window driving down a dirt road. Guess I should be grateful her tongue isn't hanging out. And I have to keep my head from bobbing, 'cause it does look good. I'm hand-sanding the rusted places the sander can't reach, Patty is painting the shelves, and Andy is painting the counter he brought over this morning. It's old and pretty basic, but he's painting it to look like something you'd see in a furniture shop. The top is deep red, and the sides he painted navy blue. Now he's covering the trim with the thick ivory cream, and I can't believe how good it looks. I also didn't notice last night that the couch is leather, oxblood red, and matches the shelves perfectly. The chairs he brought are high-back and a muted plaid of navy, cream, and a lighter blue. Patty is painting the shelves the cream, and they stand out in the huge dark space. I had thought we should paint them the blue so they wouldn't show dirt from people looking at the books, but Andy said, "No." And he was right again.

This is getting old.

Figured I could take out some of my frustration by yelling at Laney about the B&B stuff, but that isn't working either.

"Why do you care who's cooking? You just worry about the bookstore. That was the deal, right?"

"What if we don't want a brunch on *our* deck this Sunday?

What if we had family plans for Sunday that don't include a crowd of strangers?"

Hard to be indignant when the person who should be cowering and apologizing keeps laughing. "Be serious, Carolina. You don't plan things like that. I did want to ask you something, though."

Finally. "Okay, what do you need?"

"How many seats do you want to reserve? Is Will coming home?"

"I don't know, go ahead and put us down for five."

"Six? Remember you have a daughter-in-law now, and it's kind of her first Mother's Day."

"Oh, Lord. You think Missus will want to come, too?" Now I'm feeling sick, and it's not from the paint fumes.

"I don't know, let me ask. Hey, Missus, Carolina wants to invite y'all to sit with them at the Mother's Day brunch. One big happy family." She speaks back into the phone. "Aww, so great to see families getting along. I think you made Missus tear up. She's thrilled."

"Laney, I'm trying real hard to not kill you before Sunday, but you're making it downright impossible." I take the phone in my dust-covered hand and push the end button. I tuck it into my jeans pocket, lay down the sand paper, and pick up the damp rag for wiping off the dust. "Last shelf is done," I say as I step away from it. "What in the world?" I mutter with a shake of my head.

Andy is pressed up against Patty's back, and his head is buried in her neck. His saggy jeans and faded tee and big ol' head of red hair is all I can see, but I hear her giggles.

"Cut it out, you two."

Patty turns around, paintbrush still in hand, and now Andy's big ol' head is laying on her shoulder looking at me. He looks drunk. Is he really besotted with her? I learned that term from years of reading romances, but it fits his look. And she, well, another romance term comes to mind. She's, yeah, she's *blossoming.* Pink cheeks, eyes wide and dilated, light changing them from flat to glowing. Heck, even her hair looks fuller.

He unwraps his arms from her middle and stands straight. "We've really gotten a lot done today. I'm going to go upstairs and get started on our dinner. I'm cooking for Patty tonight." He jogs toward the stairs as Patty turns back to the shelf and continues painting.

"So, he's cooking in your apartment tonight?" I ask as I wipe my hands off on a wet wipe.

"Yeah," she answers.

"You must really like him."

"Yeah."

"Seems like you two are moving pretty fast. And don't you dare say, 'yeah.'"

So she says nothing.

"I'm worried about you. You haven't really dated much and well, he. . ."

"He likes me."

"Well, of course he likes you, but you need to be careful."

She flips around to face me, and her eyes are still wide, her cheeks still pink and her hair actually flew a bit, but this time she doesn't look happy. She looks mad. "Careful? I need to be careful? Careful so I don't actually have some fun? Careful so I don't accidentally end up with a boyfriend? Careful so I don't go to my grave a virgin?"

Now my eyes are stretched wide in surprise. "Hey, sorry. Um, no. I mean, just careful. He might, well, break your heart."

She shakes her head and walks over to the paint can to lay the brush across the lid lying beside it.

No idea how that blew up so fast. She never gets agitated or angry. I pick up my purse and look around. She's putting away her brush and closing the paint can, facing away from me. Pulling out my car keys, I take a couple steps toward the front door. "Have a good night. See you tomorrow."

"Carolina?"

I turn, and smile and shrug as I turn, but before I can say "sorry," she holds her hand up to stop me.

"You're right. He might break my heart. But isn't that what having a heart is all about?"

Oh, mercy. I'll take old and tired, over young and hopeful, pretty much any day.

CHAPTER 10

And let the Twenty Questions begin…

Sitting in one of the rocking chairs on the front porch, waiting for me to pull in, is Bryan. Just rocking. Just hanging out. Nothing going on. But this ain't my first rodeo. He wants to talk. No, not exactly talk, he wants me to ask questions until I hit what's on his mind. Like an old party trick of mind-reading. No self-respecting teenage boy wants to think he needs to talk to his mother, so he just hangs around waiting for her to talk to him, and he will tolerate it long enough to hear what he wants.

"Hey, sweetie. You're not chilly out here?" I cross my arms and shiver a bit. The warm morning sun reset my internal thermostat. I'm ready for summer.

"Naw," he says.

"You waiting on somebody?"

"Naw. Not really."

"Maybe I'll sit with you for a minute?" If he's not wanting to be questioned, he will immediately get up and move along.

He stops rocking by setting his feet solidly on the porch in front of him. Maybe I was wrong. Maybe he's going inside.

Instead, he looks up and asks, "Want me to get you a blanket? Or a sweater?"

See? Knew it. "I'm okay for now with my sweatshirt," I say,

managing to keep a sigh out of my voice. "So, what's going on with you?" I ask.

"Nothing."

"School good?"

"Yeah."

"Can't believe you only have a month left of middle school. Only 3 more Monday's after today. Orientation for high school is next week, right?"

"Yeah, Thursday."

I try to peer into his face. "How you feeling about high school? You nervous at all?"

"Not really. Kinda excited. Be glad to get out of junior high."

We rock side by side for a few minutes. As I move, the setting sun through the trees on the hill across from us causes the light to shift back and forth. The trees are covered with new leaves, but the leaves aren't big enough to block out the light like they will in a few weeks.

"Are you looking forward to summer?"

"Not really."

Okay, now we're getting somewhere. "Why?"

"I don't know. Just 'cause."

"The swimming area at the lake should be open this summer. You and the guys had a lot of fun last year, and you have so many more friends now. You'll like the new docks they're putting in."

He doesn't say anything, but his head bends a little further down. His closed mouth moves around like the words are working themselves up to escape. Finally they do. "Brittani says Grant acts like a little kid."

Now there are words stuck in my closed mouth, but they have to stay there. "Really? I've always thought Grant acts fine for a fourteen-year-old…" Since I couldn't add "kid" without risking upsetting Bryan, I leave the sentence hanging.

He notices and looks at me. "What else were you going to

say?"

"Oh, nothing. Just that sometimes girls mature a bit before boys."

"So Brittani's right when she says he's immature?"

"No, it's not just Grant, all boys."

"Brittani says I'm more mature than my friends. That's why we're dating, she says."

Oh, for crying out loud. I swallow and take a deep breath. "So, do you feel you're too, uh, mature for your friends?"

He doesn't answer, and his rocker slows down as he stills his feet again. "Sometimes. Not really. Just…"

"Does having a girlfriend kind of set you apart from them?"

He nods. "Well, an older girlfriend. James is going out with Zoe, but they just hang out with the same group. Zoe's in our grade. Brittani says we should do more couple things."

"Really? Like what?" More swallowing, more breathing through my nose.

He shrugs, then stands up. "I've got homework. When are we eating?"

He's already heading for the door, and his talking itch has been scratched. For now.

"About thirty minutes. Oh, Savannah got a job at MoonShots."

"Good." As he opens the screen door, he smiles at me. "Talk to you later, Mom." The door bounces softly closed behind him. I lay my head back against the rocker.

And I thought I was tired after talking to Patty.

Strong winds push at me as I leave the porch. Spring storms are forecasted for this week. Maybe they'll last into the weekend, and the Mother's Day brunch will have to be cancelled.

And Gertie won't stay here.

And Jordan will send Savannah home with Susan's chicken and dumplings.

And Will will go to law school.

And Anna won't be pregnant.

And if a frog had wings, he wouldn't bump his behind on the ground when he hops.

CHAPTER 11

Our house has stood on this hill for over one hundred and thirty years. Or maybe it's only one hundred and ten years. As with pretty much everything else in Chancey, the facts depend on who you're talking to. So exactly when our home was built is up for discussion, and if you think this is strange, you've never lived in an old, small town.

So, for a long, long time our house has stood on this hill, but tonight feels like it might be its last. At least its last with a roof. Our power's been out for a couple hours, and Savannah never made it to her tower room on the third floor once the storm hit, right before bedtime. No, instead, she is dead asleep and taking up most of my bed. Bryan is keeping vigil over the storm at his window. Only because I won't let him watch it from outside on the porch. His daddy loves storms and can't stay inside when one is raging. But his daddy's not here, is he?

Of course, Jackson is out of town when anything happens. So when the house gets swept into the river, why would I expect him to be here? My love of the suburbs wasn't just for the privacy and convenience and stores and, well, just everything. But our move to the Atlanta suburbs had been in conjunction with Jackson's new job. In an office. Not traveling. No more sick children on my own. No more water heaters, microwaves, toilets breaking on my lonely watch. No more hamster burials, where I alone made the casket, dug the grave, and officiated the service. Obviously, I took that to be my due when I got married—two-person parenthood. And in what I thought was the eternal security of that agreement, I neglected to stress strongly enough how I planned to never go back to him traveling again. Never.

But I did let it happen, didn't I? Like everything else. With a sigh loud enough to wake up a dead hamster, I roll off my little slice of bed and onto the floor. No fear of my sigh waking up my sprawled daughter, I've been trying all night to make her feel guilty for encroaching on *my* space in *my* bed. I may, or may not, have even pushed and poked her. Maybe.

With the flashes of lightning, I find my robe and pull it on. The thunder is actually shaking the window panes. Outside, the trees pull back and forth, bending to the wind's will. The rain also follows the wind's bidding and slashes in waves against the house, then follows in a different direction, only to startle me anew with each assault.

In the hallway, I push open Bryan's door and see him still leaning against the window glass. With a flash of lightning, however, I see his eyes are closed. I gently push him down on his bed, and he grabs onto the covers, pulling them over himself, and then he's still.

Out in the hallway again, I debate going downstairs, but the storm seems less violent now. Less noisy. And there is Will's room. We call it his room, but it's really just a spare room. It doesn't look like Will's room. He'd already been away at school for three years when we moved here. Actually, Jackson has spent more nights in it than Will. As much as I hate Jackson's traveling, it's hard to believe how many nights he didn't sleep in our bed when he was home. Only in the dead of the night, when I'm all alone can I even begin to think of how close we came to falling apart.

Marriage can be so hard, and now, now Will is married. And having a baby. This really is a spare room, and I can't call it Will's room anymore. He no longer has a room here. He and Anna have a room at Missus' and FM's. And the baby has a room there.

A baby. The thought makes my stomach churn, and I sit on the bed. Then, with just a little lean, I'm laying down on the green floral bedspread from our old master bedroom in Marietta.

This bedspread was a gift at our wedding shower. I think about Jackson and me on that day. How young we were and so stupid about so much. I try to remember how that unconscious joy in the future felt. The joy I saw on Will and Anna's faces on Saturday. No fear. No understanding. What's to understand? You're in love, you get married, have babies. No big deal.

And then one day you have pre-adults in your care in a big, old house with so many windows and doors and shingles. People think you know what you're doing, and actually ask you for help or advice. And you have no idea how you got there. No idea why people act like you should know what you're doing. I flop over onto my back and notice the lengthened space between lightning flash to thunder roll. So, no blowing of the house into the river tonight. No dash to the basement because the sound of a train barreling down isn't actually a train barreling down, but a tornado.

In the quiet space of soft rain and leftover wind blowing itself out, my words seem loud. "I just hope Will and Anna know what they're doing." Before my sigh can finish, I'm laughing. Why should they be different from the rest of us and *know* what they are doing?

"Shoot," I say with a sigh as I close my eyes. "If people ever fully start realizing what they are doing there will be no more weddings *or* babies."

Waking up to a flashing clock beside the bed doesn't tell me much about what time it is. A steady rain is the only sound, and that could explain why there's no light coming around the curtains, or it could just be too early. I sit up and realize my phone is back in my bedroom. Dead. And of course, I should've plugged it in so it would charge if the power came back on. But seeing as I was busy planning all of us dying in a tornado, I forgot. Of course, late at night with all the weather forecaster's panic materializing into the storm outside, I might've been a tad dramatic. Harsh spring storms are common across the south, but they rarely result in death.

A peek in Bryan's room shows he hasn't moved since he rolled himself up in his covers last night. In Jackson's and my room, Savannah still claims the whole bed. Hair and limbs splayed out to cover the most possible space. Her phone is in bed with her and is lighting up, but not making any noise. I take mine off the dresser and shuffle out of the room and downstairs, still with no idea of the time since my phone is completely black. Downstairs is that murky gray and although the clock's hands point to 4:20, I don't know how correct that is. I plug my phone in and fill the coffeepot with water. Finally my phone makes a sound and shows the time as 6:42. Then the face of my phone fills up with a list of missed calls and texts. Trying to read them while I spoon coffee into the filter proves too hard, so I finish preparing the coffee and press the brew button. Then I leaned on the counter and look down the impressive list of people wanting to know if we're okay. Jackson has called and called and called, and his last text says he's headed home. What?

Then the phone rings in my hand and scares me to death.
"Hello?"

"Carolina? Oh my God. Are you okay? The kids? I'm headed that direction."

Jackson's practically screaming, and my heart starts racing. "What's wrong? I just got up."

"You were asleep? The kids are with you?"

"Of course, they're still asleep. The storm was really bad here. Power was out, and my phone died."

"Carolina, there was a tornado. It's been all over the news. I've talked to Susan and Laney. Tree fell on Missus' house. Some branches down, so they can't get around. Griffin was going to check on y'all, but they're telling people to stay put because of downed power lines, at least until first light. You need to call Susan and tell her you're fine."

"Yeah, the phone keeps beeping. Where are you?" I move to the window and look out. Just a few small branches and lots of leaves lie around the yard.

"Still out near the Alabama line. But you're okay? What about the house?"

"It all seems fine, but let me go check and then call Susan. I don't want Griffin to be out trying to get here. I'll call you right back."

I hit Susan's name on recent calls, and she answers almost immediately. "Carolina! Are you okay?"

"Listen, I just talked to Jackson, and we're good. Fine. I just woke up. He said Missus' house was hit?"

"Oh, wait." She shouts, "Honey, Carolina's fine! Slept through it." She speaks back into the phone. "He's been just so afraid y'all needed help up there, but fire and police are saying there are too many wires down to go out in the dark. Apparently, there were a couple tornados, and they hit here and there. Downtown got messed up quite a bit, but so far they don't have anybody seriously hurt. Missus and FM are good, just have a big tree on their roof. Over in Jasper, though, a tornado went right up the highway, and some folks in the cars there were hurt."

"Oh, my goodness. That's awful," I say. "Our power came back on. Do you have power?"

"It's come on and gone off a couple times. Off right now. Listen, I need to get off the phone. Mother is calling again. I'm just glad you're okay. Jackson was frantic when he couldn't get you or the kids."

I turn on the TV and sip coffee while watching the breaking news of the line of spring storms across Georgia. I watch as I call back and talk to Jackson, who's stopped at a QuikTrip getting coffee and regrouping since he knows we're okay. We hang up after he decides to go back to his hotel at the job site to get some sleep. We're fine, so he might as well go back to Alabama. As the sun rises, news crews report on the worst damage. So far, the injuries on the highway in Jasper are the only ones known. One by one, I answer the texts from our family and friends and answer when the phone rings again, which is now plugged in beside the couch in the living room. "Hey, Will," I greet my eldest son. "We're fine. Slept through it."

"Yeah, that's what Dad said. We've been talking through the night."

"You and Anna okay? Did it storm there?" The quickly planned honeymoon was in a lake house on the east side of Georgia, loaned by some friends of FM's family.

"No, just rain. Did you hear Missus and FM's house got hit by a tree? They're okay, though."

"Yeah, I heard. Wonder what the rest of downtown looks like. It's getting light, so we should know soon."

"Turn to channel five 'cause they have a crew headed to Chancey specifically. I'll let you go. My wife wants me." He laughs. "That's a trip, isn't it? 'My wife.'"

I grudgingly smile. "Yes, it is. Tell Anna I said 'hi.' Love you."

"I will. Love you, too, Mom."

From the stairs, Savannah asks, "You on the phone? Can

you believe all this? School's cancelled. There was a tornado."

He eyes are huge, and she slides next to me on the couch. I pull her close, and she shows me her phone. "Look. I rolled over and felt my phone, and I was going to just put it back on the nightstand, but then I saw all the calls and stuff."

"Well, everyone we know seems to be okay. Daddy called. He was worried about us." I bend my head to look in her eyes. "Are you okay?"

She smiles at me and snuggles closer. "Yeah."

For few moments we just enjoy sitting close, and this feels as familiar as it does strange. But most of all—it feels good.

She's still and I wonder if she's fallen back asleep until she asks, "Missus' house got hit by a tree. Can we go see it?"

"Not yet. Power lines are down, and we need to stay out of the way of the police and firefighters. Luckily, we have power."

The news comes back from a commercial break, and I unmute it. We pull an afghan off the back of the couch to cover us and watch as the news crews and the rising sun uncover the damage.

Bryan joins us just as the Atlanta news crew shows downtown Chancey. Shingles and lots of little, and not-so-little, branches litter the streets, sidewalks, and everywhere. Thousands of leaves were ripped from the trees and plastered around town by the wind and rain. The fresh new leaves cover cars and store windows.

The fact there are store windows to be plastered, though, is a good thing. The row of businesses is intact and seems to have power. Moonshots is fully lit, giving off the effect that a spaceship has landed in the dark, little mountain town. Everyone seems to have a Moonshots cup in their hands, apparently because the door is propped open with a hand-lettered sign advertising free coffee. Through the window, Jordan's blond hair is easily spotted.

Leaving the row of businesses, the camera finds the damage done to the row of old homes on the other side of the square.

The tree lying on Missus' and FM's house is huge, and when the roots came up, they destroyed the side of the neighboring home. Blue tarps cover the roofs, and under a huddle of umbrellas, I see familiar faces. Peter has his arm around his mother. When the reporter pushes the microphone in her face, she turns away. Peter steps forward.

"Yes, everyone in these houses has been accounted for. Just property damage. Pretty severe, but nobody was hurt." He turns his back, and the camera pans for a closer look at the row of homes, seen through the curtain of tree branches.

"Poor Missus. Poor FM," Savannah says.

I scroll through my phone. "Patty and I have been texting, she's okay and so is our store, but she says it's crazy down there. Moonshots is giving out free coffee, and Ruby's isn't even open. Some of the little roads getting to town are pretty much blocked, so Ruby's probably stuck out at her farm. The highway is open, which is good for the police and firemen and news crews, but not for anyone not already living downtown that might want to get there."

A loud knocking at the door causes us all to jump, then Bryan gets up and runs to it. He jerks it open, and Griffin comes inside, carrying with him a gust of warm, humid air.

"Hey guys, the road to our house is fine, and Georgia Power crew has okayed our whole neighborhood. I just wanted to stop in before I go downtown."

I stand up. "Thanks, Griffin. You want some coffee?"

"Did you see us on TV?" Bryan asks. "They're right downtown."

He grimaces. "Yeah, you're not the only ones watching it. Apparently Ruby has electricity, but also a tree across her driveway 'cause she's been calling me constantly ever since that news crew talked about Moonshots giving away free coffee. And, thanks, but no coffee. I've been up drinking it all night." He steps to the door. "So y'all are good and the roads are clear

77

down the hill, but I'd stay put for a while until they get things more settled."

Bryan follows him to the door. "Is Grant up? What's he doing?"

"Yeah, Grant's up. He's doing what you're probably getting ready to do—driving his mom crazy wanting to go downtown. Head over to the house in a bit and distract him if you want." As the screen door shuts, Griffin pulls it back open. "But no wandering off downtown, you boys will see it all soon enough."

Of course, Bryan doesn't hear him because he's already halfway up the stairs to get dressed.

I smile, watching my son bound up the stairs. "I'll tell him," I say. "Is there anything anybody needs?"

Griffin shrugs. "Council folks that can get there are meeting downtown. If I find out anything, I'll be sure to let Susan know, so just keep in touch with her." He lets the screen door close completely this time, and he's gone.

"I'm going back to bed," Savannah says, stretching. "I couldn't sleep in your bed. It's not very comfortable."

I cross my arms. "You sure looked comfortable stretched out like you were dead, while pushing me out of my own bed. Wish I'd known how much you were suffering."

"Whatever." She's too busy looking at her phone to roll her eyes at me, but I felt it anyway.

As she walks up the three stairs to the landing, something catches her eye outside. As she looks back down at her phone and makes the turn on the landing, she says, "Your friend is here."

Outside I see Griffin talking to someone and then he steps toward his car, and I see its Laney. How in the world did she get here? She lives clear on the other side of town, at least a mile off the highway.

She has on cute, bright pink rain boots with green hearts on them. Her rain jacket is green with pink hearts on it. The hood is up, and she scurries up the sidewalk with her head down. On the porch, she shakes off and pushes her hood back as I open the door.

"What are you doing out?" I ask. "Didn't you hear you're not supposed to be out?"

She unsnaps her coat, pulls it off, and lays it on one of the porch rocking chairs. "They didn't mean me. Just people that don't know what they're doing." She scoots past me. "Besides, I needed to check on the B&B, didn't I? I have a lot riding on this, you know." From the kitchen she asks, "You need a refill on coffee?"

Cup in hand, I follow her. "I'll get it. So, guess there weren't any trees down on your road?"

She flits bright pink fingernails at me. "I just drove around them. Be stuck at home all day with Angie and Jenna? There isn't a tornado made that can stop me from getting out when I want to get out."

I cluck knowingly as I pour more coffee. "Savannah went back to bed."

"That's 'cause she doesn't have a sister to fight with. Those two are driving me crazy. It was so much better when they just ignored each other. And glad to see thing look good here. Should be no problem having the Mother's Day brunch Sunday. Griffin says the roads will all be cleared by tonight."

Tornados in the mountains don't usually leave those large swaths of destruction seen in the Midwest. It's spotty, and usually has to do with fallen trees and branches.

"Mom, I'm going to Grant's," Bryan yells from the living room.

"Wait!" I instruct from the kitchen door. "No going downtown. You do just as Susan says, understand?"

"Sure," he says as he bangs open the screen door and runs across the porch.

Laney has sat down at the kitchen table, and when I turn

toward her, she grins, but not a happy grin. A closed-mouth flounce of a grin.

"What is it?" I ask as I join her. Looking past her out the French doors, the dark clouds racing across the sky catches my attention.

"Um," Laney says and then nothing.

Now she has my full attention. Laney not knowing what to say is not a good thing, I'm guessing. I've never actually experienced it, but I'm guessing it's not good.

"What? Is everyone okay?"

"Well, you saw the news, right? It's like an emergency, right?"

"Yeah, yeah, I guess."

"So we have to do our parts, right?"

"What exactly is our part? Laney, what is going on?"

Her eyebrows raise, and her eyes widen along with her smile. "I've booked the B&B solid. Isn't that great?"

"Why do I think it's not so great? And what does it have to do with the storm?"

"Well, you know we have two of the rooms full this weekend with those two couples who are coming all the way from Chicago. They're train people."

"Okay, I remember. They'll be here three nights, right?"

"Right, and Gertie Samson gets here Friday for an indefinite stay. Patty says she told you."

"Yeah," I frown. "How could you do that to me? That woman is a royal pain."

"Hey," Laney shrugs. "Business is business. And so that's all the rooms full for the weekend, but with the emergency and all… well, well." She pauses to lick her bottom lip and then her eyebrows jump again. "Yes, Missus and FM are going to be staying in Will's room through the weekend. Then, when Will and Anna get back Sunday from their honeymoon, they'll need Will's room, and FM and Missus will move into the Orange

Blossom room until they can move back into their house."
My eyebrows have joined hers on the ceiling, and they only
start coming down when I find a way to talk. "No way. Uh, no,
this won't work."
She picks up her mug and takes a sip. "Oh, Carolina, you
should've expected this. Where in the world did you think they
were all going to stay?"
Now that she's delivered her news, she's all matter of fact.
"I hadn't thought about it," I say. "Missus' house didn't look
that badly damaged. I mean, I can see Will and Anna needing
to stay here, but Missus is just causing trouble."
"It's a done deal. Peter and I have it all worked out. Insurance
will be paying for Missus and FM, so we can charge them our
full rate. Gertie, of course, is paying the full rate since she's, as
you said, such a pain. And that leaves us a room for real guests.
If we need more than one room, we'll move Missus and FM into
Bryan's room, and he can stay at Grant's. See? No problems."
She switches tacks. "So, how's the bookstore coming along?
Looks real nice from what I could see through the windows.
I always check your windows now to see if there's something
happening on the couch." She laughs and then goes on and on
about something else.
I can't hear her because I'm busy picturing our house, caught
up in a tornado like Auntie Em's in *The Wizard of Oz*, being
flung to kingdom come.
Ah, why can't life be like the movies?

CHAPTER 12

"Peter Bedwell! Get in here." I pull my head inside the door of our shop and yank my arm back to open the door further.

Peter turns around on the sidewalk, retraces his footsteps past our front window, and comes inside. He stops next to me, his arms crossed and eyes looking over the store. "Hey, Carolina. So good to hear things were okay with y'all in the storm. Store looks fine, too."

"I bet you were happy things were fine with us, since you needed a place for your mother and father to live. Why can't they stay with you?"

His head pops back toward me, and his eyes squint. "With me? Where?" Then his eyes relax and he nods. "That's right, you haven't seen my house. I'm remodeling, remember? That's why Anna had moved to Mother's."

"You're not done with that yet?" I release the door and walk toward our newly painted desk.

He follows. "The kitchen and dining room, but we just tore the bedrooms apart last month. I'm sleeping on a couch in the living room with everything from the bedrooms piled around it."

Behind the work desk and checkout counter, I place my hands on its top and look down at them. Now that he's here and we're alone, I remember why I've avoided him. We got too close. Too close.

"Feeling safer behind there?" he asks, and my eyes dart to his, which are darker in here. He's leaning on the counter across from my hands, so I retract them back to me and shove them in my pockets.

"Okay, never mind," I say. "I did forget about your remodeling. You can go on, wherever, go on to finish whatever you were doing. I didn't mean to yell at you, I just thought that this was some scheme of Missus' and, well, yours."

He plants his elbows on the counter and leans his chin on his folded hands. "No, Caro, I told you playing the ghost up at your house was the end of my games. And I am glad you and Jackson are doing well. However, you can't keep me at arm's-length, you know. Nothing gets small town tongues a-wagging like two people avoiding each other."

"Okay, whatever you want. You just need to leave before Shannon or Patty comes back."

Peter sighs and pushes away from the counter. "People are attracted to people they aren't married to all the time. It doesn't have to mean anything. We're friends, that's all. You're not dead, and I'm not going to just disappear. I live here now. You live here. It's a small town."

"I know. I know exactly how small towns are. That's why you need to leave."

"All right." He walks toward the door. "I'll bring the rest of Mother and Dad's stuff up later. The insurance adjustor has been in town all morning, and he's at their house now." He looks around before he opens the door. "So no damage here at all?"

I've laid my hands back on the counter, and I see him notice that before he looks up towards the high ceiling.

"No, at least not inside, Patty says. Adjustor is going to get up on the roof, though. Gertie Samson, Patty's mom, is coming this weekend, so she can make decisions about the building and the roof. Apparently she owns several places in the area."

"Yep, I've heard that," he says as he yanks on the door. He opens his mouth as if to say something but then closes it, shakes his head, and leaves.

I breathe a sigh of relief.

He thinks he knows small towns, but I haven't met the man yet who really understands them. But he could be right about not avoiding him. He has been a good friend, and he does understand all life doesn't begin and end in Chancey. We just have to hold off the flirting. Leaning on the counter, I watch the activity out on the square and daydream about, well, about stuff.

"What ya thinking about? You look awful happy for such a bad morning."

A deep breath brings me standing upright at Patty's question as she comes down the back stairs. "Nothing. I wasn't thinking about anything really." Lord, I'm blushing. "What are these?" I look down and wave my hand at stacks of boxes behind the counter area.

"Books. Andrew knew a vendor at the flea market who'd bought out a bookstore when it closed. The guy forgot books would be a pain to keep dry since he has an outdoor spot, and they wouldn't sell closed up in boxes. Andrew bought the whole bunch for only seventy-five bucks."

I'm disappointed to be left out of business decisions. "Don't you think you should've asked me first?"

"I did think that."

"And…?" I probe, hoping to get a little more. She comes to stand beside me and look at the boxes.

"Well, I remember thinking that, and then I remember thinking about other stuff."

"What?" When I turn to her she's looking at me with a big grin.

"Me and Andrew. I had other things to think about than books."

She's beaming, and I can't help but smile back at her. "So,

you're happy with Andrew?"

"Real happy. We didn't even hear the storm last night. We were..."

"Nope," I interrupt. "Don't want to hear any details. And guess we had to get some books somehow. I don't own nearly enough to fill all these shelves. So, we'll say the books I've brought were worth 75 dollars, and we have somewhere to start for our records." Pulling up tape off the top of one box, I chance a peek at her, peeling tape off another box. She is still wearing baggy jeans and a faded tee shirt. Her hair hangs over her face and has no style or body to it. But I find I'm happy for her. I'm not sure what I think of Andrew, but he's opened her up to life. She's always felt like a closed book, now it's like she's breathing.

I pull out a couple books. "These don't look bad. Fairly new, but used. Must've been a used book store."

"So we just pile these on the shelves anywhere?"

"No, we need to write them each down probably. Guess we need to decide how to mark the shelves and how to divide them up."

Patty reaches under the counter and hands me a pad of paper. "There's pens on Shannon's counter. I'll start listing the books, and you can decide about the categories."

Now that was a bit more than being happy, she actually gave me an order. At Shannon's florist counter, I take out two pens and then walk back to our side. At least, she's taking a real interest, and we're getting something done.

We work for a couple hours, and our only interruption is a call from Shannon saying her road had finally been cleared, and she'd be coming to the shop around four.

When she pushed open the door, I saw it was closer to four-thirty. Looking at our shelves you could see the progress.

"Did y'all see what's going on out there? Atlanta news crew is grilling Jordan. Something about kids and her husband? Did you know her husband is the owner of Moonshots?"

Patty drops her pad and pen on the counter as she rushes past us. "Oh, no! They found out."

"No idea she could move that fast," I say as I follow her out the door and into the crowd in front of Moonshots.

Jordan is no longer outside, and the newscasters are all talking at their cameras. The sign is turned to "closed" on her front door, but after Patty knocks on it, one of the employees lets her in. All I can overhear from the reporters are bits about South Beach, Diego, Catalina. It looks like most any channel will have it covered on their newscasts tonight, so I can get the details then.

Back in front of our store, I pause to look down the street. Ruby's is still dark, so I guess her road isn't open yet. Peter, Missus, and FM are standing on their front lawn talking to another man. Insurance adjustor, probably.

The air feels clean, and the breeze has dried up the last of the puddles. Storms, even tornados, are part and parcel of living in the South. I love how they clear the air. Of course, I don't want anyone to get hurt, and usually no one does. Storms spin off a small tornado that darts down, and trees fall or a roof is messed up. But then another one pops out down the road to take out a gas station canopy, leaving lots of aluminum and plastic scattered around.

Most of the damage to Missus' house is toward the back and side, and if you don't look past the front yard, the property looks fine. Branches and shingles have been cleaned up, and the plastered leaves fell off the windows and cars once they dried. "Everything is almost back to normal," I say out loud and then groan when I remember. Missus and FM are coming to live with me.

"Wait'll you see this," Shannon says before the door even closes behind me. "Jordan is all over the news. She's like a big deal in New York, and she's even been on TMZ. How did we not know we had a celebrity right here next door?"

"TMZ? Isn't that the, um teen-age TV channel newsie thing or something?"

Shannon rolls her eyes. "It's not just for teenagers; its news. Celebrity news." She steps up and turns her phone to me. "See? From January. Jordan and her friends got drunk somewhere, and there's video of them in some crazy bar. Watch."

On the small screen it's hard to see, but I do see blond hair that looks like Jordan's. There's lots of whooping and hollering, and they all have drinks. Then a guy dancing on the stage reaches down and one of the women with Jordan goes up on the stage with him and the other men. Men who are very good-looking and barely wearing any clothes.

"That's a woman from one of the soap operas. I don't know her, but she's apparently famous and a friend of Jordan's. Can you believe it?"

"No, but they do look pretty out of control."

Shannon rolls her eyes at me again. "That's not what I meant! Can you believe we know celebrities now? This is amazing." She pulls the phone around to see it better. "Apparently this video went viral and, like I said, was on TMZ. The guy that made the video then followed the women and took more video of them on the beach with the guys from the club."

I walk around our shelves, admiring the work we've done. The shelves are only a little over half full, but it all looks great, and I have to admit it's due to Andy. From the shelves to the furniture to the books, and even the decorating, he's saved us. Pulling my purse over my shoulder, I ask, "But why is all that of interest to the Atlanta stations? Not like its real news." I don't want to encourage the drama, so I'm acting uninterested, but wonder what this has to do with Jordan not being with her children?

Shannon finally looks up from her phone and tilts her head at me. "Yeah, you're right." She looks back down and pushes buttons. "And there's nothing new online yet. All this is old stuff. Guess we'll have to wait to see it on the news tonight."

"That's good, 'cause I'm headed home now. Patty is next door with Jordan. If you have to leave, make sure the back door is unlocked in case she doesn't have her keys."

She does it again. Her eyes roll up, and she laughs. "Like I'm leaving before she comes back and tells me what's going on!"

On the sidewalk, I look up at the cloudless sky. "So, you don't think I get enough eye-rolling at home? I'm getting it at work now? Not funny, God."

CHAPTER 13

Of course, the tornado and its damage led the early Atlanta news programs, and I have the TV in our bedroom turned up all the way so I can hear it down the hall in Will's room. I can't believe Laney rented this room out to Missus and FM without lifting a finger to clean it up. Since Jackson moved back in with me, this room has become a catch-all for winter clothes I planned on putting away.

I'm boxing them up and stacking them in Bryan's room until Jackson gets home and can put them in the attic. When I hear the newscaster say "Chancey," I run to my bedroom. I have it recording downstairs, but I don't want to miss it.

The camera pans over the square, and the limbs are still strewn about. Folks walking around are in hastily thrown on clothes or robes, and everyone looks shell-shocked. Peter has his arm around his mother in front of her home, and FM is at the corner of the house pointing to the back. While the picture focuses on the downed tree behind the house, the reporter talks about Chancey being awakened by the storm and that many feel the damage is light for how loud the storm was.

And, of course, they find Hughie. They should have sub-titles, because even people who have lived in these mountains all their lives and talked to Hughie for all of his eighty some-odd years can't understand him. Do they talk to educated, worldly Peter, standing right there? Or any of the people I can see who wouldn't make us look like we just crawled out of the woods after tending to our stills? No. Hughie tells his story, shows off his couple teeth, and shoves his hands in the chest pockets of his bib overalls as he watches the reporter walk down the sidewalk.

"Chancey's newest business opened this week and may be a surprise to our viewers. Only last year, Moonshots opened up its first Georgia store in the upscale Avenues outdoor mall in Cobb County. Now, apparently with no fanfare or even PR, Moonshots has opened a store in this tiny town, miles off the interstate."

No longer does concern etch the reporter's downturned mouth and sad eyes. He's on full alert, eyes bright, nostrils flared, and as he makes his way to the window, he points inside. "And where you might ask would Diego Moon find a manager for this store tucked in the Georgia mountains? Turns out, right in his own home."

The camera swings to show Jordan behind the counter. "Jordan Moon once worked for Diego Moon's fledging enterprise, MoonShots, beginning as a barista, much like the young people you see here. She moved up in the organization and began opening new stores, continuing in that position after they were married four years ago. With the birth of their daughters, however, she stepped down." While he's talking, we see a picture of Jordan and the gorgeous man from the picture in her apartment. Jordan is holding an infant wrapped in a pink blanket and a toddler is held securely in her father's arms. They all four look like models. The pictures fade and the camera comes back to the reporter, and his eyes glitter. "However, since January, Jordan Moon has been in the headlines, for a couple more interesting reasons, as Tina Fox tells us."

Here, older footage begins showing more pictures of the

happy couple, evolving into a family of four, living the high life in New York City. Jordan wearing evening gowns and high heels, on the arm of the man I learn is her husband, Diego. There are several pictures of an elegant older woman who turns out to be Francesca Moon Sentora, mother of Diego and wife to one of the best known billionaires in the world. We're further told that her first husband, Diego Moon, Sr., died twenty years ago in his home country of Columbia, where he ran his family's coffee plantation.

"This past New Year's Eve the perfect family exploded when these videos turned up on TMZ of actress Betsie Steger, Jordan Moon, and daughter of New York governor Michael Manchester, Alison Manchester, apparently having sex on the beach in Miami with some unidentified men."

Clutching the pillow from my bed, I lean toward the TV. Even with things blocked out, the pictures are nearly pornographic. I recognize the governor's daughter and the actress from one of the kid shows Bryan used to watch, and I vaguely remember this story from back at the first of the year. Of course, then I didn't recognize Jordan, and I'm not sure they even talked much about her. And then the reporter says just that.

"Mrs. Moon wasn't focused on much at the time as Ms. Steger was in negotiations with Disney for a major picture, which fell through after the videos were made public. But the biggest story was Governor Manchester's inauguration being the next day, January second. Stories filled the New York papers and media as Alison joined her parents on the dais." Side by side pictures of the young woman on the beach and then gazing at her father taking his oath of office were too good to pass up, obviously. "However, in recent weeks, Jordan Moon's location became a topic of discussion when New York tabloids noticed her missing from her usual routines, her daughters being seen mostly with their grandmother, and less often with their father. Further speculation swirled when her parents, Jim and Marilyn

Holmes of Peotone, Illinois, contacted by TMZ, said they were
worried about their daughter as they had not heard from her.
And their son-in-law wouldn't take their phone calls."

Footage from Jordan handing out free coffee in front of her
store crossed the screen while Tina in the studio tossed the report
back to the reporter in Chancey. "So, Jim, looks like today's
tornado solved one mystery, but I bet there are a lot of whole
new questions today."

"Trash," Missus announces from my bedroom door. "That's
not news, that's gossip and trash and should not be anyone's
focus when lives have been turned upside down by Mother
Nature. Where's our room?"

"Next door," I say as I stand up. "I just have one more box
to bring out of there, and it should be ready." Seems someone
has forgotten that she had a baby with someone other than her
husband, gave the baby girl up for adoption, then refused to
acknowledge her own granddaughter. Yep, some folks give
themselves a clean slate, and we all just let 'em do it. Squeezing
around her, I step into the room. "Here you go. Hope it'll be
comfortable."

Missus sniffs and steps back out in the hall to let me back
out through the door with the box. "It'll have to do, I suppose,
until we move downstairs after the weekend." She goes into the
room. "FM is bringing . Where should we put them?"

I look around the room. "Wherever you like. The only empty
drawer is the top one and the closet has things hanging in it, but
there's a bit of room."

"Oh, no, there is not enough space for all our suitcases. We
had to pack for several weeks, you understand. When will
Jackson be home? He'll have a solution, I'm sure."

"You think I'm holding out on you? That there's some empty
closet I'm hiding?" I deposit the box in Bryan's room and come
to lean on the door jamb. "Leave some of your clothes in your
car, or store them at Peter's house."

"Carolina, you just don't understand. Leave me alone now. Go downstairs and direct FM up here when he comes in."

I take a deep breath and try to think of something kind to say. But, well, really? I'm supposed to try and understand her? So I let go the deep breath, turn around, and walk down the stairs. At the bottom, I hear my phone ringing from my purse in the kitchen.

I miss the call, but see it's from Laney, so I call her back.

"Hey, did you see the news?"

"Oh my word!" Laney chirps. "I remember it all now, but I'd never put it together with our Jordan. No wonder she doesn't think her mother-in-law will bring the children to see her."

"You think her husband opened up our Moonshots just to hide her away?"

"Looks that way. And putting together everything we've heard, it makes sense. Wonder what'll happen now. Hey, Missus there yet?"

I lean against the door frame. "Oh, yes, her highness is here and highly displeased. Glad I have the bookstore to escape to everyday. Gotta go, FM's coming up the front walk, loaded down with the royal garments, I suppose. I better go help him. Talk to you later."

Someone had attempted to call while we were talking, and while checking, I see both Susan and Savannah had called me this afternoon. Apparently a couple times each since I went upstairs earlier. Tucking my phone in my jeans pocket, I hurry to open the front door for FM.

"Hey there, not sure where you're going to put all that. Will's room is pretty small."

He stops at the bottom of the porch steps and looks up at me. His gaze is so sad and so tired.

I smile and say, "Aw, bless your heart. It's been a horrible day, hasn't it? Here, let me help you."

With the door held open, I lift a roller bag up the steps and set it just inside the living room, then reach for one of the shoulder bags hanging from his arm. "How you doing, FM?"

He shakes his head, sits his bags next to mine behind the couch, then steps back onto the porch to pick up another bag. We settle both bags on top of the pile of luggage and go back on to the porch.

"Let's have a sit for a moment. I'm about plum worn out," he says as he lowers himself into one of the rocking chairs on the front porch.

The brisk wind had swept the leaves, torn off in the storm, out of our yard. Small, fluffy white clouds, gathering tinges of pink, rush across the sky and river and on the breeze a chill sweeps across the porch and us.

FM chuckles as he lays his head back. "Hard to believe y'all sitting here on top of the hill, and the tornado plum misses ya and finds us buried down in town."

"Were you and Missus asleep when it hit?"

"Not really. First of all, sleeping well belongs to young people. Me and her are up and about through the night anyway, but then with the weather alerts on the radio and the howling of the wind, we never did completely conk out. But even still, we hardly knew what was happening until it was over. Wind picked up, tree fell down, and everything got quiet again."

"Yeah, apparently we slept right through it up there on the second floor. It never sounded bad enough to come downstairs."

We continue to rock, and in a minute, I hear him snore. I keep rocking beside him and think about how life turns on a dime. So much has changed since this time last night. For Jordan and her family. For those whose homes got hit, and for those who didn't, like us having Missus and FM and Will and Anna moving in.

Will and Anna. A couple. A married couple living here with us. My head just keeps shaking. I didn't even realize they were still dating. He was courting her during Spring Break, but I never saw them together much. Then she went to Athens for a long weekend, but I thought it was to see friends. Okay, so, I guess he was the friend. The whole things just makes me so sad, and honestly, it would've been easier to have them living with Missus and FM, so I wouldn't have to act all happy and excited all the time. Aren't you supposed to get a break from your own kids long enough to make you excited about grandkids? Of course, I'll love the baby. And it's not that I think I'm too young to be a grandmother. I'm just still in full mother mode. Oh well, guess that's just too bad. Ready or not, it's coming.

My eyes drift shut, but before I fully fall asleep, car doors slamming cause me to lift my head and pull my eyelids open. Savannah and Angie never stop talking as they walk up the dirt driveway. I put my finger to my lips and point with my other hand at FM.

They nod and smile and tiptoe up the three small steps.

"Oh, hey girls," FM mumbles. "Guess I drifted off. Been a long day."

"Yeah, sorry to hear about your house, Mr. FM," Angie says. Her voice is soft and tired. She hides a yawn behind her hand and with her black fingernails, black-rimmed eyes, pale skin, and long, dyed-black hair, she looks like a vampire returning from a full night of hunting.

"Things busy at the store today?" I ask. She's a cashier at the Piggly Wiggly and works an amazing number of hours. No way am I letting Savannah work that much at MoonShots. I know Laney and Shaw provide everything their twins need and want, and Jenna hasn't had a job until this new one at Moonshots. Guess Angie just likes being at the Pig more than school or home. Knowing Laney, Jenna, and Shaw—I can buy that.

"Yeah, once power came back on we were busy all day. Lots of folks stocking up on supplies in case another storm hits. But, really, like we're going to get another tornado. I think people just wanted to drive around and see things and for that, they needed an excuse."

Savannah cocks her head. "So Mr. FM, you and Missus are staying here, Peter said. And Will and Anna, too."

He nods. "Looks thataway. Paying customers, too. So, I expect to be treated real special now," he says with a laugh and a wink. He pushes up out of the chair. "Guess I better get moving. Missus will be wanting to get settled in."

"Girls, help him carry his stuff upstairs. They are in Will's old room through the weekend," I say and they begin loading up.

"Oh, and Carolina, I have a pot of beef stew all made up we can heat for dinner. It's in the car. I'd put it together yesterday, hated to see it go to waste. Luckily, our power wasn't out long. Didn't lose any food, but I'll go down and get more to cook this week. You don't need to worry about feeding all of us, too. You know I enjoy messing around in the kitchen."

"You are a godsend," I say as I get up. "Car unlocked? I'll get it and put it on to warm."

He nods yes, and I walk down the steps and the sidewalk. At the car, I hold my face to the driver's window and see a pot sitting in the back floorboard, nestled in towels. I walk around the car and open the door.

"Hey, Mom," Bryan calls as he and Grant walk across the railroad crossing. "What ya doing?"

"Oh, hey there. I'm getting some beef stew FM brought. He and Missus are going to be staying with us until their house is ready. Will and Anna will be here next week to stay, too."

"Cool. Did you hear we have school tomorrow?" Both boys frown and shake their heads.

Grant raises his hands in frustration. "What's the good of a tornado if you only get one day off school?"

I shake my head in mock sympathy. "Tough break, guys. Here, give me a hand, and let's take this stuff inside. Grant, you

want to stay for dinner? This pot of stew is huge."
He lifts a box out of the car and juggles to get a better grip.
"Thanks, but I can't."
Bryan laughs, and he stretches to put the handles of two big
shopping bags over his shoulder. "He's failing English. He's
grounded from anything fun. He only got to come up here for
a minute 'cause his mom said she couldn't stand the sight of
him right now."
Grant sheepishly grins as I slam the car door shut with my
hip. "Grant. You're smart. How are you failing English?"
Bryan laughs again. "He's in love with Miss Wasser, the
English teacher."
"No, I'm not."
"Yes, you are. You just sit and stare at her all class."
Grant playfully kicks out at Bryan, but my son dances away.
"See, Mom, you thought it was bad my girlfriend is a year older
than me. What if I was in love with some teacher?"
Grant's good humor begins to evaporate, and his face is
flushed red when he says, "You wish Brittani was *just* your
girlfriend. She's lots of guys' girlfriend."
"Grant! That's not nice to say," I interject before Bryan
launches at his friend. Stepping between them on the porch, I
nudge Grant on inside and pause on the threshold so I can turn
around and look at my son. "Bryan, what's going on?"
"Nothing. Grant's just jealous. Where do you want this
stuff?"
Still not letting him pass, I try to catch his eye, but he's not
having it. "Okay, we'll talk later. Take it upstairs to Will's room."
I let him pass, but he shoots a dark look at Grant before going
up the stairs.
"Grant, you can set that box down on the kitchen table.
Looked like more food. Then you'd better get on home."
"Yes, ma'am," he says, and he's gone before I can get the
pot into the kitchen.

I turn the stove burner on low and stir the stew a bit. I knew that Brittani was trouble. Just knew it.

Okay, so that makes me a little happy. And mad. Mostly mad, now that I think about it. I knew he was too young for a girlfriend.

CHAPTER 14

"What is wrong with you two?" I slam the glass door behind me and scurry across the florist shop to stand in front of Jordan and block her from view of any prying eyes on the sidewalk. "People can see right in here."

Patty holds up her coffee cup and says, "I tried to tell her, but she said I was crazy."

"Give it here," I say, grabbing the cool blonde's wine glass. I take it to the coffeepot in the back of the florist shop and dump the wine in a Bank of North Georgia mug. I also grab an empty coffee mug and walk back to the bookshop area. "You can't just sit out here drinking. You want folks boycotting the store?" I hand the dark blue mug to Jordan and look around. "Where's the bottle, though? I'll join you. It is Friday, after all. And it's been a really long week. Hard to believe graduation was a week ago tomorrow, and since then we've had a tornado!"

Jordan takes a small drink. "I can taste coffee. But I agree on it being a really long week."

Patty points to behind the sales counter, and so I drop my purse on the couch and walk around the counter. Bending down, I pull out the cork and fill my mug, whose logo has mostly washed off, so I don't know who provided it. "Well, maybe you'll come up with something new to sell in your store.

Coffee-laced wine."

"I don't understand. We're adults. It is legal to have alcohol here, right?" Jordan asks as she takes another sip.

"Legal, yes. Smart for business, no. You just never know when somebody is mad at their mother-in-law, or their husband, and since she can't take it out on them, she starts a boycott of whoever lands in their sights."

Jordan is wearing black pants and a white short-sleeved T-shirt. It fits her perfectly, and even I can tell it didn't come from Target. She stands up, and she doesn't have to struggle out of the chair. She just unfolds, holding her mug in one hand and swishing back her hair with the other. "Thanks for the glass, or should I say, mug of wine, Patty. But I really prefer a wine glass, so I'm going up to my place."

Laney sticks her head in the door. "Carolina, you ready to go?" Then, when she spots Jordan, she comes all the way inside. "Hey, Jordan." She only misses a moment before adding, "Hey, Patty," in the same singsong voice. "Did I interrupt Friday happy hour?"

Jordan looks down in her mug and shrugs. "So, if even in mugs everyone knows we're drinking… never mind. I was just leaving." She picks up her wine glass from behind the counter heading toward the back door.

"How does a margarita sound?"

Jordan stops, then shakes her head before turning around to face Laney. "Sounds pretty good. But I can't go out anywhere. Press is still lurking around, I'm sure. Especially can't be seen out having a good time. Thanks, but no thanks. "

Patty and I just watch. Laney is used to getting what she wants, and what she's wanted all week is Jordan. Laney is fascinated with this celebrity dropped into our midst, and this is the first time since the news story, Tuesday evening, that Jordan has appeared anywhere else than behind the counter at MoonShots. Speaking of lurking, Laney has done her share.

"Oh, no. Restaurant margaritas can't compare to my homemade ones. I have all the makings at my house. We're having a girls' night. Right, Carolina? And it's a perfect night to sit out on the porch and watch the sunset over the mountains. I'm even driving. That's my car parked right there at the curb." While she directs Jordan's sight out the window, she walks to her, takes her mug *and* wine glass, and sets them behind the counter. "I also have some delicious fish tacos all ready for assembly. My daughter Angie is quite the cook." As she adds, "Do you like grilled mahi mahi?" Laney slips her arm around Jordan's arm and starts walking to the door.

Jordan pulls back, but then takes a step forward with Laney. "I love grilled mahi mahi. I'm so tired of frozen meals. Are you sure it's all right? I don't want to interrupt anything."

Laney moves a little faster. "Oh, no. I was just coming to pick up Carolina. And, oh yeah, Patty, too." Behind Jordan's back Laney motions for Patty to get up and come on.

Before I leave my coffee cup behind with Patty's and Jordan's, I finish my wine. Then I find my phone I'd left earlier and was stopping in to pick up. Laney had told me since we missed Cinco de Mayo last week due to graduation, we'd be celebrating it tonight. I left Jackson and Missus in charge of our new guests, ready for a girl's night out.

Maybe *I* should call TMZ.

"Shaw is restricted to his den. He has the Braves on, and Angie made him beef tacos. Doesn't it smell divine in here? Angie, honey, we're home." Laney leads us into the house, across shiny wood floors with wine red rugs. The walls and most of the wood work is white. The woodwork that isn't painted is stained dark-brown. There isn't a curtain anywhere. Big windows with the original glass are open to the crickets and sunset-bruised light. Set on old family property, there are no neighbors to look in the bare windows.

"Hey, y'all," purrs Beau Bennett as we turn the corner into the kitchen. "I'm just watching Angie do her magic. And I took the liberty to have a shot of tequila. Hope there's still enough for the margaritas."

"Of course there is. Beau, you've met Patty, right? Do you know Jordan?"

Beau tips her head and her bangs, ringlets of red, fall across to lie in a line along the side of her face. Like her niece, Brittani with an I, the red hair marks her as a Bennett. However, unlike Bryan's *friend*, Beau's hair is short in back and cut perfectly to lie smooth to the nape of her neck. A good haircut is the best advertising when you own the only beauty shop in town. "Ah, no, we've not met. I don't drink coffee, so I haven't been into your shop. Welcome to Chancey."

I sit on the stool beside Beau. I like her and refuse to let her family connections to my son's heartbreak matter. Much. I say, "Beau owns Beulah Land, the local beauty shop."

Jordan smiles and stretches out her arm to shake Beau's hand. However, her smile is tight and does nothing to take the suspicion in her eyes down a notch. Patty is watching everything from her spot beside the door. Laney acts like there's plenty of tequila, but I'm not sure there's enough in the whole state of Georgia to make these two beautiful, tall divas chill out.

"Here we go." Laney's next words are drowned out by the sound of the blender. On a lower speed, we can hear her explaining she'd mixed the margaritas earlier and stuck the pitcher in the freezer. "Just needs a little blending. Carolina, can you rim the glasses with salt?"

"No salt for me," Jordan says.

"Then you get yours poured first," Laney says as she fills the heavy glass, rimmed in cobalt blue. Beau plops limes in after Laney fills each glass.

"A toast, and then we can go outside. Angie, honey, call me when you're ready for us to eat."

Angie hasn't said a word, but she nods at her mom and sneaks a peek at Jordan.

I ask, "Angie, do you need any help in here?" She shakes her head and again takes a quick peek up. "Have you met, Jordan? I know Jenna and Savannah have met her since they're working at MoonShots."

Another shake of her head, and so I introduce the two. Angie finally looks up and Jordan meets her eye. "Oh, you work at the grocery store. Right?"

"Yes, ma'am."

"I am not old enough to be called ma'am." Jordan's voice is sharp. "Please!" erupts from her, not as a request, but a statement of disbelief.

Angie blinks and then looks at her mother.

Laney laughs. "Oh, don't be silly. It's a term of respect. Not of age."

Jordan doesn't give an inch. "Well, it's rude."

The words Laney wants to say shuffle about on her lips, but she stretches her lips into a wide smile and lifts her glass. "Now, what shall we toast?"

I sneak a sip and then say, "I thought we were celebrating Cinco de Mayo?"

"That we are. To Cinco de Mayo! Wonder what that actually is about?" Laney asks.

Patty has yet to pick up her drink, but she has moved closer to the rest of us. She mumbles, "It means the fifth of May. Some historical date for something that happened in Mexico."

Laney nods and licks a bit of salt from her glass rim. "Sounds about right."

We lift our glasses and then have to wait for Patty to pick

hers up. She is so uncertain, so hesitant, but finally she lifts it up and pushes it towards ours. We take a sip, and the party moves out to the porch.

"If all of you are okay with drinking, I don't understand why it's not okay to have a drink after hours in your own shop," Jordan says as she pulls out a chair.

"Here, Jordan, you don't want to have your back to the sunset." Laney says as she pulls out a chair at the back of the table, facing out. "You are our guest, sit here."

Jordan shrugs. "I don't care. Nature isn't really my thing." And she sits in her original chair, back to the sun and mountains.

Beau, from her perch against the railing, smiles big, and a smirk plays around her lips. Laney looks a bit hurt, and Patty, well, she looks like she always does.

I settle into my chair, facing away from the sunset, and then, since no one else is saying anything, I jump in to make it all okay. "It's just that there's a lot of folks around here who don't drink and don't think anyone else should either."

"But the view here is really pretty. I hate for you to miss it," Laney pushes. She's still standing over the offered seat. Being a gracious hostess is hard to suppress in a Southern girl. Especially when you're intent on becoming someone's very best friend and confidant.

Jordan sighs and settles farther back in her chair. "Really? I've seen the sunset on the beach in Bali, the docks of Santa Monica, and from the peaks of the Italian Alps. I don't believe I'm missing a thing."

Okay, now nobody's smiling. Laney sits down, and Jordan takes a long drink. Just like that, she reduced our world to next to nothing.

Beau shakes her head full of red curls back and rolls her shoulders as if to loosen them. She has on a white tailored shirt and skinny jeans. She's tall and lean even after having four children. She laughs often and big and is usually surrounded with her four little ones, so it's easy to forget she used to model. But with that shoulder roll, she put on her modeling persona. Her eyebrows arch, along with her back, and she seems even taller. "Bless your heart," she says and her accent is still Southern, but echoes Missus' matriarch mode. "Too bad they didn't give lessons on manners along with the plane tickets to those big ol' exotic places."

Jordan looks up from her drink and rolls her eyes. "Whatever. Okay, I'll move my chair around. Don't want to be rude." She sighs again and stands up. Patty jumps up to help her and they get the chair turned part of the way.

We drink and watch the solid gray clouds take over the sunset, which never gets a chance to display any color. (Of course this would hapen, seeing how Laney made a fuss about it, and Jordan was so put out about it.) Laney is strangely quiet and Beau is still in ice mode. Usually those two can be counted on to carry a conversation. Guess I'll have to instead. Sheesh, now *my* Southern hostess genes are kicking in.

"So, Beau, how old are your kids? All in elementary right?"

Beau clears her throat and thaws a bit. "Gabriel is in fifth, and Michael is in third grade. Angel is my only girl—she's in Kindergarten. Only Raphael isn't in school yet. My mama keeps him, and he's only three."

Patty's mouth is hanging open, and her brow scrunched up. "Wait, she says. "Those are all angel names, right? Well, and Angel, of course."

"Yes, they are. I figured I'd keep with the family tradition of picking religious or heavenly names."

"Oh, yeah, I remember." I nod and point at her. "You told me about your aunt's names and why the shop is called Beulah Land, and you turning Beulah into Beau for yourself."

She smiles and takes a sip. "Yes, all that and then Victoria's Secret came out with the angel campaign and I thought that would be appropriate. They always were my favorite employer."

She takes a sip and says nothing else.

This time, Jordan is the one to break the awkward silence. "Victoria's Secret? Guess the kids should be glad they didn't end up named bustier or thong. So, did you work in or manage one of their stores?"

Beau laughs at Jordan's joke, but her eyes don't appear to find it quite as funny. "Oh, no. I modeled for them. It was before the Angels. I did make the covers for three of their catalogs."

"Dinner's ready," Angie says through the open window near our table.

Jordan stands up. "Really? A Victoria's Secret model? That's, um, cool." As Beau walks around the table toward the door, Jordan looks her up and down. "Kudos on keeping your figure. Guess you got married and moved back home? That's nice." (Though it doesn't sound like she thinks it's nice.)

Beau pulls the screen door open and looks back at the four of us. "Oh, I've never been married. I don't really care for men." She looks Jordan up and down and then lets the door fall behind her with a bang.

Patty pushes her chair in. "Then how did she have all those kids?"

CHAPTER 15

"If I have to hear one more time how much better everything is in Chicago, I will kill him and then burn down this house to hide the evidence," Missus says between clinched teeth as she places yellow cloth napkins on the tables covering our deck on Sunday morning, Mother's Day.

Following her, I'm placing silverware on each napkin. It's a beautiful spring day for the first ever Mother's Day brunch at Crossings, and the sky is so blue, it looks artificial. A light breeze makes the weeping willow beside the river sway back and forth. "Well, he and his wife are leaving this afternoon. You know, running a B&B means being nice to people just because they pay you. They don't have to be nice back."

"I must say, I never fully appreciated what you do here. Of course, you're so comfortable in the background you probably have no problem listening to people spout idiocy day in and day out."

"Maybe I don't think it's idiocy," I say under my breath, but apparently not enough under.

"Of course it's idiocy! He's never stopped from the moment they arrived. 'Everyone down here talks so slow and moves so slow.' 'And since when did 'Hey!' become an appropriate greeting for everyone at any time?'" She sighs and puts her

107

hands on her hips. "Of course, I would agree with him on that, except who made him judge, jury, and executioner?"

"Hey. Y'all ready?" Savannah asks as she comes out onto the deck.

Missus looks at her and shakes her head. "What have I told you about that?"

Savannah looks down, missing which particular thing Missus is now donning judge's robes for. "What? This skirt? I'll keep my legs together. For crying out loud, the preacher isn't just waiting for me to not sit all proper, so he can look up my skirt. Besides, there's like a pew in front of me."

Missus tightens her lips, and ignores my daughter, as she struts past her, head high, and goes inside to vent about whatever she feels needs it next.

"I think you look pretty. Don't you think we'll look good sitting together since its Mother's Day? Our colors kind of match," I say as I point down to my navy and white print dress, then to her navy skirt, topped with a green and white shirt.

"It's not the same shade of navy," she dismisses me, then turns to glare at the French doors. "Missus is so aggravating. She's been a real pain this weekend. She came into my room without knocking. Didn't knock at all. She's moving down to the B&B rooms today, right?"

"As far as I know."

Savannah looks around at the tables covered with white cloths, yellow napkins, and waves a hand. "So how long do I have to stay at this thing?"

"Why?"

"Nothing. Will and Anna are coming, so it won't be horrible," she says with a sigh as she folds her arms and goes back inside.

Happy Mother's Day to you, too.

Church on Mother's Day has changed since I was growing up. There are a couple of red boutonnieres signifying the wearer's mother is still alive and a bigger smattering of white carnations or roses pinned to lapels and dresses which signify the death of a mother. "Red to honor, White to remember" is what I grew up hearing. You can see it's a tradition left primarily to the older people in church today. I'd honestly forgotten about it until I saw the flower wearers on our walk from the parking lot. But lack of flowers is not the only change. All women are being honored today, and I like that change. Years ago, a friend announced she and her husband were going to start a family. Back then we all assumed all you had to do was decide, then do it. It was awful to see the sadness in her eyes each time I shared our news of a baby on the way. So, yes, it's a good change.

At the end of the pew sits the newest mother to be, and she's ours. Anna just turned eighteen, and I can't look at her without feeling my stomach swirl. She has no idea how hard this all is. When I look at her I feel sadness in the pit of my stomach, and I try to not look at my son who knew better. I can barely keep from strangling him. If I think long about it, I can't help but believe he took advantage of her. Sure, he loves her. I guess. But she's a kid with no family, no solid footing. I've seen too much to think this can't turn out fine. But I've also seen too much to honestly believe it *will* turn out fine.

Our preacher has a nice soothing, Mother's Day tone, so my mind keeps wandering. Next year this time, there will be a baby in their arms. A baby. A real-life, let see, how old will it be? Five months. A five month old. "Oh, Lord," I breathe out and drop my head. It didn't begin as a prayer, but while I'm here…

"Child, as tiny as you are, you'll be showing in no time. Ain't that right, Shermy?" Gertie Samson booms across the deck.

And even Gertie Samson can't dim the smile on Missus' face. She has Peter and FM on one side, and Anna and Will on the other. Will, my son. Mine. Shouldn't he be at my table on Mother's Day? But the tables aren't large enough for us all to be at one. So I get two of my kids, neither of which is happy about being here. Savannah wants to be at work, and MoonShots being open on Sunday is something I have to discuss with her. Bryan is mad because he was invited to Mother's Day lunch at Brittani's house, and I said no. Who invites another mother's child to their home on Mother's Day? Jackson is preoccupied with work; some derailment is messing up his plans on the job site.

"I may need to go on out there," Jackson says, looking up from his phone. "It's a mess."

"If you have to, you have to," I say as I reach for another croissant roll. But my hand stops mid-air. "Wait. Now?"

Jackson has stood up. "I just said I need to go on out there."

"But, now? You can't wait until we finish?"

He sighs and sits down. "You're right. I have to eat anyway. The food's good. Where did Laney get it?"

"She ordered from a lady who sells full dinners to folks in the area. I might need to get her number, because this broccoli casserole is delicious."

Besides my table and Missus', there's one with Patty, Andrew, and Patty's mom, Gertie Samson. Gertie is all set to move into the Chessie Room after Sunday dinner. Our B&B guests left while we were at church. Patty stayed here to check them out and clean the two rooms a bit, so her mother could move into hers, and so that Missus and FM can move into the bright, airy Orange Blossom Special Room. Patty said she had to stay home from church because she'd promised her mother she'd disinfect her room personally. Gertie is a mountain of a woman, and hard to say no to. Andrew looks to have given up getting on Gertie's good side and is just shoveling massive amounts of food into his mouth. Patty's neck, arms, and face are blotched with red, and she's not eating a bite. Gertie is eating and talking and gesturing at Andrew. When she's not making observations about those seated at the other tables, like how soon Anna will show. The five tables are small and smushed together, so even without Gertie's booming voice, we can hear each family's conversation.

Laney's family surrounds another table, while Susan's fills another. Susan usually takes things in stride, but she's as unhappy about being here as Bryan is. Her mother-in-law asked to have time today with *only* her children, no in-laws or even grandchildren. Yep, my eyes bugged out on that one, too. And even better, all four of her grown children agreed. Susan says the woman thought her four children could do no wrong, until they brought home the people they wanted to marry. Then they were all wrong. So wrong that not even grandchildren could make it right.

So, with just the right amount of chest pain, a lifetime of practice at applying guilt, and a table for six at her country club, she got what she wanted.

Susan and Laney's mother is out of town at her brother's home in South Georgia and she actually took Grant and Susie Mae with her. So that table has only Susan and her oldest daughter Leslie at it. Leslie graduates in a couple weeks and is leaving early to do a special summer session in Athens at University of Georgia. She can't wait to get there, because, you know, no one has ever gone away to college before. (Insert roll eyes prompt here.). Susan is in mourning, and Leslie hasn't a clue. Laney keeps jumping up from her table to see to problems in the kitchen, and Shaw chatters with himself whether she's there or not. Jenna is texting under the table, and Angie is dozing. As hard as it is to believe, Missus' table is the happy one.

CHAPTER 16

And here we sit.

Me and Patty at the Grand Opening of the Book Barn. I'm sitting in the plaid chair. She's sitting on the couch. We have things we should be doing, but we're both just kind of waiting. Not sure for what.

Shannon is in the back of the florist area, arranging flowers at her work table, ignoring us. Where are all the bossy people when you need them?

Patty nods her head and repeats the only line she's had since we opened a half-hour ago at 10 am. "Well, we did it. We opened a book store."

That makes me get up. I really don't want to get violent with my new partner on our first day of business. Behind the counter, I look at everything laid out: our notebook, a calculator, a lock box with change in it. A vase of drooping flowers Shannon gave us to celebrate, but the drooping tells me giving these away wasn't a real sacrifice. "You said your mother is bringing a laptop down for us to use?" I ask.

Patty nods again and stands. "It's an old one, but Ma says it's good enough for what we need." Worrying her hands together, she stammers, "Uh, what do we need it for?"

"I guess to keep a record of our books and so we can keep

track of our deposits."

"We're going to list all of these books in it?" Patty looks around at our half-empty shelves.

"Yes, and then as people trade in books, we'll take them out and put the new ones in. It's important we know if we have a book someone asks for."

"I guess that's true." Patty walks between two of the shelves. "Guess I didn't really think about what it would be like running a bookstore, besides having a bunch of books to read."

That frustrates me to the point of tapping my fingers on the counter because I have to admit I didn't think much about it either. I thought about the books, and keeping the records, but the selling? The waiting for customers? Libraries don't have those problems. "Probably no need for both of us to be here all the time."

From the other side of the third bookcase, Patty says something I can't understand.

"What? I didn't hear you."

She comes toward me, twisting the front of her big yellow shirt. It's a soft yellow, and I can't tell if it's fading, or if it started out this color. It washes her out, and the wrinkles along the front tail from her wringing it don't help either. Yesterday, for Mother's Day brunch, she had on a coral top and a long black skirt, but they were also baggy on her. She's not lost weight since I met her; I just think she likes things she can hide in.

When she reaches the counter I'm still standing behind, she stops. "I need to tell you something."

"Okay."

Her lips don't move, but she's blinking furiously.

"What's wrong? Is it your mom? Andy?" I think for a moment. "Me? Is there something wrong with me?"

She shakes her head, takes a breath, and says, "Andy's moving in here."

"Here?"

"And we're going to sell other stuff. More stuff than just books. You know, he sells a lot of stuff at the flea market. You don't have to be here at all. You know, like… at all."

I'm taken aback by this. "I'm your partner. Don't you think we need to discuss this? And your mother is the landlord. When are you going to tell her about this crazy scheme?"

"It was her idea. I'm supposed to tell you this morning, and they are both getting here…" she looks at the clock on the wall. "…in a minute."

My jaw drops. Unbelievable. "Andy and Gertie? Both of them are coming?"

She shrugs. "Well, in case you get out of control."

The morning's frustrations mount, and I end up yelling, "What do you mean if I 'get out of control'!?"

Patty backs away. "See, I don't want you to get mad like that. Andy and my mom say this is really, well, really just my business."

Trying to keep from yelling, but not doing a very good job, I still shout. "I brought all those books! What about all my work on the store?"

"Mother says she'll pay you for your books, and Andy points out that he did most of the work since he's been here so much. And now he'll be here even more."

I pause. "Wait, you're not just talking about the shop. Andy's moving in here, upstairs, too? Your mother wants Andy to live here with you?" Even though I'm loud, my words are covered a bit by the front door cracking open.

"Yes, I do." Gertie throws wide the front door and comes in carrying a laptop, several books, and her huge brown purse. "He's a keeper, so we might as well start keeping him now. I can see that peckerwood Cross boy was too highfalutin for us. You understand, Carolina, we want you to still keep working here. But we need to entice that Andy with a little more than my daughter's sex appeal. You understand, I'm sure."

Through her speech, she's made her way across the sales floor and now sits the laptop, the books, and her purse on the counter. "Besides," Gertie continues. "Looks to me like you should have your hands full with that B&B of yours. It was plum crazy when I left up there a bit ago. I understand you wanting a place to escape to, and we'll still offer you that. But with me and Andy here, we can handle things for Patty."

"But you'll be going home soon. And maybe Andy doesn't want to manage a book store?"

A big laugh coming in the door announces Andy's arrival. "Of course I want to manage a book store. It's what I was made for."

He comes up behind Patty and gives her a kiss on the cheek. Gertie beams at him, and Patty blushes.

Gertie says, "And you can let me know how much it'll be for Patty to move into my room at the B&B with me."

I haven't felt small since I was in sixth grade and had the mumps. I couldn't eat for a couple weeks and was, for a small window of time, waiflike, tiny, fragile. But standing across from these three, I'm like a soft, new leaf in the wind. Blowing this way and that, no more than a puff from a dandelion. Small, delicate, tiny.

Even my voice has become light. "Patty is moving back to the B&B?"

Gertie slams her hands down on the counter, and I jump.

"Of course!" she shouts. "No hanky-panky until after the wedding. Lucky they only have a few weeks to wait, right?"

Andy puts his arm around Patty and grins. Patty gazes up at him, and Gertie continues to beam at them both. She addresses me, "And they don't have to get married like your boy and Missus's girl did. These are good kids, here."

115

"And just like that, I'm out of partnership with Patty. And Will is being gossiped about by Gertie Samson. Gertie Samson, of all people."

I said I was going next door to get a coffee at MoonShots, but once I was on the sidewalk, I turned the other way. Ruby's feels more like what I need. So here I sit on one of the stools at the back, talking to Libby as she comes and goes, and to Ruby as she cleans up the morning's muffin pans.

"Gertie Samson sounds like her old man," Ruby says from over her sink full of hot, sudsy water. "He always got what he wanted. Some folks even say when he had to leave town, it wasn't due to the sheriff making him, it was 'cause he was done with Chancey and ready for greener pastures."

Libby leans on the counter beside me. "I sure do hate to see you losing your dream of running a bookstore."

I stir a spoon around in my coffee mug. "I don't know if it was really my dream. Just something to do. And, besides, I don't think I was very good at it."

Ruby pulls the plug from the bottom of the sink. She stands up with her hip leaning against the sink and her arms folded. "Did you hear that Moon place was open yesterday morning? Sunday?"

I nod. "Yeah, she wanted Savannah to work."

Libby tsks. "That's not going to go over well."

Ruby twists her mouth and then speaks up. "She wants to order enough muffins from me to send to every church in town next Sunday."

Libby and I match with our widened eyes as the word "What?" explodes from our mouths.

"Yep, called me at home last night. Said she figures folks' convictions will last right up until they get free muffins."

CHAPTER 17

Right there in the front porch rocker where our ghost once sat is the most beautiful man I've ever seen. Honestly? His appearance is more shocking than a ghost. He waved as I crossed the railroad tracks, and by time I get to the porch steps, he's standing and waiting. "Hello, I'm Diego Moon. I need to rent a room. There doesn't seem to be any way to register online."

"Oh, Moon! You must be Jordan's husband." I shake his hand and turn to open the front door. "I hope you weren't too warm out here. Our front door is always unlocked."

"Unlocked?" He echoes incredulously as he picks up his black suitcase from the floor. He then steps over to a hanging bag draped over the porch railing and lifts it, too. "Is that safe?"

When I turn to look at him, I get a whiff of his cologne. He smells better than the Macy's perfume counter at the mall. I smirk. "Safe? If only a locked door would keep these people out." When he stalls, like he might turn around, I add, "Of course it's safe. It's Chancey."

He follows me through the door and into the living room. Thank goodness the room we have open is the Southern Crescent room—the manliest of our rooms. The walls are a rich green, as close to the color of the famous Southern Crescent train as

117

possible. We decided this room should be elegant, as well as comfortable, like its namesake.

As we walk past the dining room and down the hall of the B&B, I give him the spiel for the room. "When the luxury railroad liner, the Southern Crescent, cut from New York to New Orleans in an unprecedented forty hours in the late 1800's, it was the first vestibule train riding the rails in the Southern states. Vestibule meant the cars were connected, and passengers didn't have to pass outside going from car to car." I push open the door, and he steps inside.

"The color of the train cars, and our walls, was picked out personally by the president of Southern Railway in the 1920's, Fairfax Harrison. Mr. Harrison like the two shades of green he saw on the locomotives on a trip to England, so he borrowed it. And here's one last bit of train trivia: the sleeping cars were named for seven distinguished sons of the South from the seven states the train traveled through."

When I finish, I take a breath, and darn it. He has the same magic power as his wife, except it's not Ruby's Café. It's my house he's making look shabby. The dark plantation shutters no longer look like rich, heavy wood. They look like the spray-painted plastic they are. The old wood floor doesn't shine. It has all the sheen of a dirty paper bag. The wingback chair rescued from Missus' attic isn't a family heirloom or antique; it's one stop short of Goodwill. Mr. Moon smells better than the air freshener sitting on the desk beside me. Turning towards him, I push the 99 cent freshener off the desk's surface and into the wicker garbage can behind me.

He is still holding both of his bags and appears a bit stunned.

"Mr. Moon, there are hotels out by the interstate. They're probably not up to your usual standards, but, well, they're not, not this," I say with a wave of my hand.

"No, I'm sure this will be fine. Your home is lovely."

What a nice man, he doesn't sound panicked at all.

Well, not *much.*

He puts down his bags and reaches for his wallet. "How much is the room? Can I reserve it for at least a week?"

I wave his money away. "Oh, no, you can pay when you leave."

"But don't you want to put my card on your books?"

Now he's looking at me, and we're standing close. His hair is so black, it's got blue streaks in it, like Superman's hair in the comic books. His teeth sparkle. Seriously, I'm not exaggerating. They sparkle. I mentioned how good he smells, didn't I?

All I can do is loll my head back and forth, while I stare at him and sniff.

"Madam?"

I shake myself out of the trance. "Oh, no, we don't need your card. I'll let you get settled. My name is Carolina. Just holler if you need anything." Shutting the door behind me, I wince. "Just holler?" I said, "Just holler," to the most beautiful man alive.

"Carolina, I'm holding you completely responsible for this," Missus says to my 'hello' when I make the mistake of answering the house phone on the living room end table.

I say, "Of course you are," and hang up. Then I run upstairs, yelling as I go.

"Okay, Savannah, why are you not at school?" As I was kicking myself for saying "just holler" to Mr. Moon, I came into the living room to find not only the phone ringing, but also Savannah scurrying up the stairs, still in the camisole and pajama pants she sleeps in.

I catch up to her in the upstairs hallway. She has a plate in one hand, and she's running a finger from the other hand in the peanut butter on her toast and licking it. And shrugging. There's lots of shrugging. "Told you. It's just reviews."

"And the reviews are just for the students making A's? Because excusing everyone else would be the only way you and your 'Not A' grades would be excused."

"Mom. I'll go tomorrow. I can get more done here studying than in class."

"Oh, so you've been studying?"

When we hear a car pull in the driveway, we both look toward the front the window. We can't see the car from upstairs, and it doesn't stay long enough for me to go downstairs to see who it is. "Wonder who that is that saw my van here and decided to leave?"

All I get is another shrug and more sucking of peanut butter off her finger. So I yell some more, "I swear, I'd vote for any politician that would make arranged marriages legal."

"Can I go study?" She turns around and heads to the stairs to her room.

"You know I'll know in a matter of minutes who that was just here. One call to whichever of my friends is volunteering at the front desk of the high school."

"Whatever."

I flinch when I even think someone is accusing me of something. How does she stay so calm when she's caught red-handed?

And just who is my local congressman, anyway?

In my bedroom, I unplug my phone where it spends most of its time charging (and not being answered), and dial Laney. "You at the school this morning?"

"Naw, it's reviews. Nobody goes to school on review day. Well, except the A students. They don't know better."

Of course she'd validate Savannah's opinion. I shake that off, for now. "Your girls are home?"

"Okay, maybe I shouldn't say only the A students. Also there

KAY DEW SHOSTAK

are the students who'd rather be at school than home with pain-in-the-rear moms. Needless to say, mine are at school. Unless they're at your house."

"Nope, they're not here. But Savannah is." I sit down on the bed.

"Wait, why are you at home? Isn't today your Grand Opening?"

"Guess it's not my big Grand Opening anymore. I've been fired by Patty and her mom."

"How can you be fired from your own business?" Laney's outrage is palpable, until I realize she's half laughing.

"Well, Gertie owns the building and paid all the utilities. Andy didn't charge us for much of anything, and all I did was donate a bunch of books I needed to get rid of anyway. Besides, it wasn't that fun."

A male voice comes up the stairs. "Um, Carolina?"

I jump off the bed and shout, "Just a minute!" Into the phone, I say, "Gotta go," and hang up on someone for the second time that morning.

Stepping out into the hall, I see Mr. Moon smile up at me from midway up the stairs. "The phone downstairs keeps ringing. Would you like me to answer it?"

"Oh, no. That's fine. I know who it is, and she's just mad because I hung up on her." He walks back down as I descend the staircase. "I had to handle something with my daughter. Oh, you have two of them. Two girls. You might want to look into arranged marriages now."

He smiles uncomfortably, but relief shines in his eyes when the phone starts ringing again and he doesn't have to respond. I dart into the little office off the B&B hall. "Hello, Missus. So what is it I'm responsible for?"

"We can't get the church hall for the wedding reception. And since you have accepted responsibility, I want to know what you plan to do about it."

This woman, I swear. "I have no idea what you are talking about. However, since I know the outcome already, I'll just say it." I spread an arm across the office, as though she can see me. "Have it here."

"Don't be ridiculous. Stay put. I'll be there in ten minutes." She hangs up, and I sit down in the office chair.

From the hallway comes Mr. Moon's voice again. "You're off the phone?"

"Yes." Before I rise from the chair, he's standing in the doorway.

"Can I ask you a question?"

I nod, and he leans against the door way. "Have you met my wife, Jordan?"

I nod. "Yes, she's quite lovely."

"Yes, yes she is. Did everyone here see the news coverage about her?"

His shoulders are held back and his chin high, like he's preparing for a punch. I smile to help him relax, but it seems to just make him harder, his voice, too. "So she is a joke. A scandal here, too, now."

"No, not really! It's not like that. I mean, my daughter works for her. Plus, she had drinks with me and some of my friends Friday night. Not a lot of drinks, just a margarita for Cinco de Mayo. Nobody really believes what they see on TV anymore, right?"

He takes a deep breath. "They do in my world. So, your daughter works at my store? This is the daughter you want to arrange a marriage for?" He laughs and drops his shoulders. "My two daughters are so different, and very young. Carly is sweet and wants to be good. But Francie? I believe arranging a marriage now *might* just be my best bet."

We laugh, and I stand up. He heads back to his room. "I have some work to do, would it be all right if I set my computer up on your deck for a while?"

"Absolutely. And Mr. Moon, Jordan misses her daughters very much."

He doesn't turn around, but his shoulders brace and his head tilts back again. Even his voice is stiff. "She should have considered that before she acted so recklessly."

CHAPTER 18

A light breeze lifts along the front porch as I sit down in the rocking chair Mr. Moon sat in earlier. The heat from the sunshine isn't strong enough to invade the shadows here, but the light is a gentle blue, filled with soft scents of the new grass and leaves and small flowers dotting the lawn and ditch. My lungs can't get enough of the freshness. Nothing is old, nothing is decaying. Everything is new.

Bright green leaves on the maple at the corner of the porch are bigger than they were yesterday, and their little reddish seed pods are lighter. Across the railroad tracks, the woods are thicker, darker. That new shade of green dressing the trees and grass is growing up. Becoming a more serious shade of green. Serious enough to carry through the long, hot summer, but not that serious yet. Kind of like teenage leaves. And not only are the leaves a bit lighter in color, they are lighter in weight, so they dance in the breeze.

I rock and look and breathe. My khakis hit the tops of my feet each time I rock forward, feet which are released from socks. I hate socks and jerked them off when I got home, since I'm no longer a business owner downtown. If you can call Downtown Chancey "downtown." I slipped on my old Kmart canvas shoes and threw my socks deep in my closet. I'll look for them in the fall.

Missus pulls around the curve leading to our road, and her car is only barely visible through the newly thickened woods. I can't help but smile as I can see her disapproval through her windshield as she parks and opens her door. It must be hard to go through life constantly being disappointed by everyone, and everything, around you. She's lost her happy fog of being a great-grandmother already.

She has on a butter yellow pants suit, with short heels in beige. I can't actually tell the color of her shoes from this distance, but I do know they are not white. Not before Memorial Day. She'd rather wear my Kmart slip-ons. Well, no, that would be just as bad. She'd rather cut off her feet. Yeah, that's more the truth.

"Good morning, Missus. Isn't it a beautiful day?"

"It's gone downhill since I left my bed." She sits down in the rocking chair beside me, her beige pocketbook (matching her shoes) in her lap. "What is this I hear about you quitting the bookstore? Is this not your grand opening day? Seems a little early to quit—even for you."

That stings a little. "I didn't quit. I was forced out. They…"

Missus waves her hand in the air like I'm an annoying mosquito. "Enough of all that. I do not really care. Must say I am not surprised. You and that Patty trying to run a business was joke from the start. Everyone knew it. Now, about the wedding."

When my mouth drops open, she holds up her hand. "No, Carolina, I am not joking. Not another word about your tragic career choices. The wedding of our children. It must happen as soon as possible, and now that's ruined. Simply ruined."

She leans back in her rocker, but I notice it stays perfectly still. Rockers, or no rockers, if Missus doesn't want a chair to move, it doesn't move. Her mouth does, though. "I find it interesting that you have no questions."

I rouse myself. "Oh? I'm allowed to speak?"

Missus closes her eyes. "Being juvenile is not attractive, Carolina. Never mind, I will tell you what you need to know."

(Like we doubted that was going to happen.)

"We need a wedding as soon as possible, because, well, you know. The church calendar has no openings the rest of this month and June is filling up between the Church Homecoming on Decoration weekend, which is the weekend after Memorial Day. Vacation Bible School at the end of the month. So, in order to not leave you out of the planning, I thought I'd not put our wedding on the calendar until I talked to you. Then Gertie Samson swooped in and stole it right out of my grasp. June 12. A perfect day for a wedding. And now, thanks to your lollygagging around as usual, it's gone."

"You remember," I say, "they are already married. This is just a, just a formality."

Missus narrows her eyes. "Formality? Oh, you are so obviously *just* the mother of the groom. Why I try to involve you in this is evidence that I try, Lord knows I try, to maintain tradition. Of course they are married, but this is Anna's *wedding*."

I am not rolling my eyes, just in case anyone is wondering. And my voice is not sharp at all. "I'm sure we can find another day."

"Oh, you are, are you? Well, you are wrong. I called you from the church office. The problem events all takes up the entire building with set up and such. VBS, Homecoming, Graduation, and Baccalaureate. We can't even squeeze in for a few hours on those weekends."

"What about doing it the same weekend as Patty and Andrew?"

"Be serious," she snaps. Then she starts rocking. Slowly but steadily, and it's like a train engine building up steam.

"Mrs. Jessup?"

I was so engrossed in watching Missus think that I missed

the screen door opening behind my left shoulder. "Yes, Mr. Moon," I say as I stand. "And this is Missus Bedwell. Missus, Mr. Diego Moon."

When he takes her hand, he bends toward her and kisses the back of it. Missus nods slightly, and I believe there is a slight reddening of her cheeks. "Mr. Moon. My pleasure to see you once again."

"As it is for me. Such a lovely day to spend out of doors. What a pleasant place I chose to open my latest shop."

To see you again? I do a double take. "When did you two meet?"

"When I came to town last month, looking for the perfect location for a special project."

I turn to Missus. "You knew? You knew we were getting a MoonShots?"

She sighs. "Carolina, if you knew everything I have to know to keep this town running as it should, you would crawl right under this house and never come out. Now, I have a wedding to plan, so I will leave you to your guest." She stands. "Unless you've quit the B&B business in the last five minutes."

She walks down the porch steps and to her car while Mr. Moon and I watch.

He shakes his head and smiles at me. "I'm sorry everyone couldn't know, but I've tried to keep a lower profile for this project. I asked her not to tell." He opens the screen door, and I walk in ahead of him.

"How did you find Missus?"

"Oh, I didn't. My mother did. This is actually more her project than mine."

"Then will your mother be coming to Chancey, too?"

He pauses for a moment and lays his hands on the back of the couch, then looks out the front window where Missus' big, dark car is disappearing around the bend. "I don't believe that would be a good idea, Mrs. Jessup. As they say in the old movies,

'I don't think this town is big enough for the two of them.'"

"The foil-covered pan on the stove has the chicken in it. Everything else is on the kitchen table. Just fix your plate and eat wherever you can find a seat," I instruct Will. "FM cooked it all."

"Mmm, barbeque chicken. I'm starving. Where's Anna?" He turns from the chicken with two pieces on his plate and grins. "My wife. Where's my wife?"

My arms are folded in front of me as I lean on the counter beside the kitchen sink. "Outside. She's not hardly able to keep anything much down. She been this sick long?"

Will frowns and sets his plate on the table beside the bowls of food. "Nope. Well, some. Guess it's normal? She says her stomach gets upset easily, even when not, well, you know." Between piled high scoops of potato salad and baked beans, he looks up and shrugs. "Guess I don't really know how her stomach usually is."

"Guess you don't. Enjoy," I say to his back as he balances his plate and a bottle of water while pushing out the back door. Only after the door shuts, do I add, "Nope, you don't know about her normal stomach problems, because you don't even know her."

Gertie lumbers in from the dining room. "Never took to all that eating outside nonsense. Had me a seat in there at a real table. Nice and quiet, too." She takes her plate to the sink and starts rinsing the dishes already there.

I open the dishwasher and load the wet dishes she hands me. "It's like they're playing around with this, like marriage isn't real and hard."

"Yeah, but look at all the folks that did it just the right way, got to know each other. Families knowing each other. Taking lots of time and still end up in divorce."

I sigh and pull out the top rack to load it also. "That's true. Aren't you worried about Patty? She's only known Andy a week or two."

"Naw. She's grown up and all. I had me a chance with a guy real quick-like one time. Think we coulda been happy, but Pa said he had to court me. Like we was back in some fairytale or something." Gertie rinses her hands and then dries them on a paper towel she takes from the holder beside the sink. "Look at me. What fella's going to court me? And I was already twenty-four. He told my pa he'd rather not and he left. So I went to town, found him, and courted the hell out of him." She tears off another towel and hands it to me. "Pa dragged me home, put the fear of God into my fella, and the guy moved on to another job down in Florida."

"Was that Patty's father?"

"Why you want to know?"

"I, um, just figured that's where the story was going. It doesn't really matter."

"You're right. It don't. I'm going back down to the store to do some talking with Andrew about what we should do next. Me and Patty will be back before you lock up for the night."

She leaves the kitchen, and I turn toward the window over the sink. FM and Missus, along with Will and Anna, are sitting at the picnic table. Savannah is at a baseball game, and Bryan is upstairs doing homework. He had baseball practice earlier, and so he's trying to get his homework done so he can play video games with Will. Jackson is out of town, but will be home tomorrow.

After putting a little spoonful of potato salad on a saucer, I join the four around the picnic table.

"Here, sit here," Anna says as she gets up and goes over to perch on the end of the bench next to Will.

Missus moves over to give me more room and clears her throat before she begins talking. "I wondered if we were going to have to come in and find you. We have things to discuss. The wedding is set for Saturday, June 12th. That other wedding will be around noon and our wedding will be in the early evening, which will be lovely. Anna, sit up and listen. Pay some attention, please."

Anna lifts her head off Will's shoulder and smiles at her grandmother. "Yes ma'am. An early evening wedding. We will be there." Then her sleepy eyes open wide. "Oh, Miss Carolina, did Will tell you about his job?"

I look at my son. "You got a job? Where?"

"Connor's Dealership. In Dalton. Sales." He keeps eating his chicken and doesn't look up at me.

Selling cars. He was going to be a lawyer. He wanted to be a lawyer. He was already accepted to law school and now he's going to sell cars. I focus on my potato salad. "So, I guess, Shaw got you the job. It's his and his daddy's dealership, right?"

"Right."

FM nods and starts collecting their paper plates. "Yep, good dealership. Where I buy our cars. Needs some new blood. Well done, son. Carolina, I've got the menus for the rest of the week planned. I'm liking this cooking for a crowd. Hard to be imaginative when it's just me and Missus." He steps away from the table, then turns back and looks down at Anna. "Sugar, what do you feel like for dessert tonight?"

Anna's eyes light up, then she sighs. "I don't know what I could keep down. Maybe some oatmeal cookies?"

Will swallows the food in his mouth and agrees, "Oh yeah, with chocolate chips in them."

Anna shakes her head. "Will, I hate chocolate."

He laughs. "Nobody hates chocolate."

"I do," she says as she pulls away from him then stands up. She sighs again and holds out a hand. "Let's go upstairs."

Will takes her hand and jokingly lets her pull him up. He puts his arm around her, and they follow FM to the kitchen door, which opens just as they reach it. Bryan pops out.

"Okay, Will, done with my homework! Got the Xbox set up."

"Cool, give me a minute." But when he tries to keep walking, he's pulled back by Anna who hasn't moved.

"You're going to play video games?"

"Sure, for a bit. It's been a long day."

"You don't think I've had a long day?"

"I don't know. What did you do?"

Anna doesn't answer in words, but her face and body are saying a lot. Only problem? Will doesn't hear a thing.

FM tries. "So, honey, you want some oatmeal cookies? Sure thing. I'll get right on them. And Will, I can put some chocolate chips in half the batch."

My oldest son grins and holds the door for FM to go on ahead and prods his wife with his other hand. "See there? Everything is fine. You go upstairs and lay down, and I'll come get you when your cookies are ready."

"They are not my cookies," she yells and storms past him and FM and Bryan.

Bryan looks over at FM, "I'll eat hers if she doesn't want them."

Will shrugs. "Cool."

Missus and I groan and close our eyes.

CHAPTER 19

I am bored out of my mind.

FM is doing all the cooking at the house. Matter of fact, he has something that cooked all night in the crockpot that smells delicious. He actually has planned out what he's cooking each night. Missus worked out a cleaning schedule for not only the B&B but the entire house, and, not surprisingly, it works really well. Will is learning his new job, so he has long days. Anna is taking a few college classes online and has taken to hanging out at the library. Savannah and Bryan are wrapped up in the end of school tests and parties. Susan is obsessed with her oldest, daughter Leslie's graduation from Chancey High and the huge party she's throwing for her. Laney, what is Laney doing? She's not been around much. She even took the B&B books to her house so she could do them there. Of course, that may have a lot to do with Missus living here.

Opening the bookstore was supposed to take up all my time, so I cleaned my slate of other obligations. How did I let myself get pushed out of the store so easily? But surely if I'd really wanted to do it, I would've hung on tighter? Surely.

First thing, get up off this couch. Walking through to the kitchen, there's not even papers or stray dishes to pick up. With Missus on patrol, no one leaves anything out. I sit my cold cup of

KAY DEW SHOSTAK

coffee in the sink and watch the swaying of the weeping willow at the bottom of our back yard. A clear blue sky reflects in the river beside it, and I realize I let the spring slide by without visiting my thinking spot. Last fall I spent so much time down there, I kept a picnic blanket folded up to sit on. Of course, that was when I had someone to talk to down there. Never mind that it was a ghost. Or what I thought was a ghost.

Out on the deck, the sun is warm, hot even. Missus decorated the deck with planters of pink geraniums for the Mother's Day brunch, and they still look beautiful.

Maybe I should get into gardening. We've got plenty of space for flowers or vegetables.

In the yard, the dew only remains in the shadows around the deck. The rest of the back hill is covered in sunshine and thick grass, and as I walk down it, I start sweating. Won't be long until there won't be any coolness in the night or early morning air. Twenty-four/seven heat. That's the South—love it or hate it, it doesn't change.

At the bottom of the hill, I enter the shade and privacy of my weeping willow. The whip-like branches are still, and there isn't a single ripple on the water. I know it's flowing, but there's no evidence to point to. There are no bugs chirping or birds singing. Everything is still, and the quiet feels complete as I settle on a bumped-up piece of root.

When Bryan finishes school next week, he'll be a high school freshman. Savannah will be a senior. How did this all happen so fast? Oh, yeah, and by Christmas Will will be a father. Oh, and I'll be a grandmother. And married to a grandfather, which is crazier than anything. How could I get to this point in my life and not know what I want to do? Savannah and her friends talk about what classes they want to take in college, and what they want to be, and all I can think is, "What do *I* want to be?"

Maybe I should take some classes. Go back to school.

Jackson is busier than ever at work and traveling more than

133

ever, too. We're back on the same page, but he won't be retiring anytime soon. And it's not like I would want to go with him when he travels, not to the lovely dirt heaps he usually ends up working in.

I lay my head back against the trunk of the tree and take a few deep breaths to feel how very still everything is.

Boy. That sure can get annoying quick. Everything being so still kind of creeps me out. I jump up, dart out from under my tree, and don't look back. Climbing the hill, my chest heaves, and I really start to sweat.

Maybe I should start working out. Join a gym up in Dalton.

"Hey, FM. What's that cooking?" I ask as I enter the kitchen and go straight to the refrigerator for a bottle of water.

"Morning, Carolina. It's pulled pork for tonight. Cooked a big pork roast all night in the crockpot with a can of Coca-Cola. See, it shreds practically by itself. Just going to put some sauce and stuff on it, and it'll be delicious for supper."

"Well, it sure smells good right now," I say as I steal a little piece of the tender meat. "You really like doing all this cooking, don't you?"

He grins, and his mustache practically meets his squinched-up eyes. "I do. Course, I've only had to do it this week. If I had to fix for a bunch of folks every day, all the time, I might not like it. But, you know, some folks do." He dumps the shredded meat back into the crockpot and starts adding sauces, brown sugar, and spices. The smell only gets better.

"Yeah," I say. "Maybe I should learn more about cooking, get into it more."

"Well, don't do it until I leave next week 'cause I got some more recipes I want to try."

"Promise." I take another drink of my water and cross the kitchen. "I'm going to shower and then head to town. Since I left the bookstore on Monday, I haven't been downtown once."

FM turns to me, big fork raised in his hand. "I noticed that.

134

You seem to be kind of moping around up here. What's the problem?"

I lean against the side of the refrigerator. "I don't know. Just don't know what I want to do. I'm kinda bored."

He shakes the fork, glistening with pork juices, at me. "Enjoy it. Press into it. Listen for that still, small voice. It's a true gift to have realized you have a void in your life before you've gone and filled it up. Take your time. Life'll find you. Always does."

He turns back to his cooking, and I head upstairs. "Hmmm, life will find you." I say it out loud a few times. "Life will find you."

Pulling off my damp tee-shirt and stretchy black pants, I keep saying it in my head. As I stand under the spray of the shower, *Life will find you, life will find you* rolls over and over in my thoughts until... until I stop it with just one more thought.

But, what if it doesn't?

"Hey, Shannon, thought I'd stop in and see how things are going." The little bell on the door rings as I enter the florist. Shannon's head is buried in the flower cooler on the other side of the room.

"Hey, yourself." She stands up and lets the clear glass door close. "So, what's going on? You're not doing the bookstore anymore?"

"Nope, Patty and her mom and Andy are doing it." I walk past her counter and stretch to look past the bookshelves to the painted plywood counter Andy built. "Where are they?"

Shannon shrugs and joins me in the middle area where the two stores meet. "Who knows? And I know you're not working here anymore, but look, the shelves where you had the books?

Look at them."

The shelf we are closest to looks very full of books. Matter of fact they are two rows deep, which means half of the books can't even be seen. Passing that one and moving forward, I see the first two shelves are full of junk. Toys, old dishes, plastic flowers. You name it, and it's there. As long as what you're naming is old, worthless junk.

"This looks awful! What happened to a bookstore or a gift shop? Like with new gifts, I mean."

Shannon sighs. "Andy apparently has several flea market booths he switches merchandise through. Guess this is just another one. Mrs. Samson doesn't even look at it, and Patty says Andy's the business man, and he knows what he's doing. I don't want this place to just look like a junk store. I mean, if it was antiques or something kind of nice, maybe. But that's just ..."

"Junk," we say at the same time.

"Plus, none of them are ever here. Andy shows up with a load of crap, excuse my language, and Patty shoves it on a shelf, then they go upstairs."

She leans over and nudges my shoulder with hers. "Those two spend a lot of time upstairs, if you know what I mean."

"But where's her mother? Where's Gertie? She's left the B&B every day this week early. I assumed she was here overseeing everything."

"I don't know. I've seen her once, maybe, this week. One day she was here at lunch time and brought some fast food from out at the interstate. They sat over there, smelling up the whole place with fried food."

"Have they sold anything?"

She shakes her head while pulling out a broken fern from a bouquet she took from the cooler. "No. Listen, I have to take this over to the Deen's house. Her daughter called it in from North Carolina. Guess it's her mama's birthday. Can you watch things while I'm gone? I'll be right back. I never did hire any help because we were going to watch each other's shops, remember? Well, it's not working out like that. I promise, I'll be right back. Fifteen minutes."

"Sure," I say. "I've not got anything to do."

She pulls her purse out from under the counter and fishes for her keysShe slings her purse over her shoulder and lifts the arrangement of carnations and tiny pink roses into her other hand. I open the front door for her and watch as she crosses the street. The door closes, tinkling the little bell as it does.

All the work I did just last week alphabetizing the books was for naught. They've been shoved on the last shelf in any old order. My library training kicks in, and soon they are straightened out. It wasn't hard—they had been moved in chunks so the right letters were kind of together. Then I made a display of some of my favorite summer reads in the front window. Shannon had cleared a space for us to use, and it still sat empty. On the back of a yellow file folder, I wrote "Great Summer Reads" and tucked it behind the book display. On the junk shelves I found a red plastic sand shovel and then a couple painted wine glasses. The glasses were painted with palm trees and flamingos and looked cute next to a couple summer romances. I took a cheap pair of sunglasses out of my purse and put them on top of a stack of thrillers. With the red shovel, the window looked neat and enticing.

"Hey, the window looks cool," Shannon says as she walks in the door. "Thanks for watching things here. Mrs. Deen was so tickled with the flowers."

"Glad I could help. Doesn't seem fair you're here by yourself."

"No big deal. I was always alone before. And it's not like I'm actually having to sell anything for them."

"Yeah, doesn't look like any books have sold."

A blast of laughter from upstairs makes Shannon raise her eyebrows. "Nope, they're too busy doing something else to sell books."

I dunk my reddening face to grab my purse from under the counter. Thank goodness I don't have to work here and hear about that all the time. "Okay, well, I'm going to go next door. Can I get you anything from MoonShots?"

Shannon lifts up her purple MoonShots cup. "Nope, got a coffee here I've been nursing all morning. Thanks again for your help."

"Anytime. Seriously, just holler if you need me. I've not got much of anything going on right now."

"I'll keep that in mind. Sure helped me out today."

"No problem," I say as I open the door again. Outside, I turn to my left and cross the alleyway to stand in front of a newly cleaned and polished glass, brass, and wood door. Even though it's in another old building, it's so clean and shiny, the MoonShots feels new.

I've yet to get a hazelnut iced latte, and that was always my favorite drink back in Marietta when the weather got warmer. There's not the quaint tinkle of a bell on the door when I open it, instead there is a slight buzz that doesn't interfere with the soft, jazzy music which wraps around me, along with the rich smell of coffee. It truly is like entering a different world, just stepping in here. A wonderful, peaceful world of coffee and peace.

Jordan's head snaps up when she sees it's me. Her blonde hair falls perfectly in place alongside her face, and as it falls, so does her mouth. "So, you met Diego."

"Yes, he seems very nice."

"Is his mother with him?"

"No, he says she won't be coming to town," I respond with a lilt in my voice. It should make her happy to hear that, right? However, her eyes fill with tears.

"Of course not. That would mean she would have to bring my daughters." She takes a deep breath and clears her throat. "Speaking of daughters, can Savannah work Sunday mornings?"

I really want to order some coffee, so I quickly titch my teeth. "Oh, I don't know. She goes to church and, well, I don't think she's going to want to."

Jordan leans on the counter in front of her. "I don't get it. Go to church some other time. My God, there's like some kind of service every day of the week. I see the cram-packed schedules on the boards out front of the churches. God can't be that into a particular day."

"Well, I kind of think he is. You know, Sunday, the Sabbath, and all that."

She wrinkles her perfectly tweezed eyebrows. "Sabbath? Isn't that Jewish or something? I have to find someone that can work. Some of the kids have offered, but their folks freaked out. You're not from here, so I thought maybe you'd be a little more open-minded about Savannah working. But, no, you and your little family go to one of the thousand churches here, too."

"Not really. I mean, some, but Jackson really likes church more than me."

"I'll pay you double if you'll come in and work on Sunday mornings."

"What? I don't know anything about working here." And yet, that smell, that music, how peaceful. It would probably be more peaceful here than at church.

She seems desperate. "I'll teach you. And I'll give you free coffee. Anytime. Please, I'm desperate. Sundays are such a big day for a coffee shop."

"But if everyone is in church, who's going to be buying coffee?"

Jordan smiles. "Come work just one Sunday, and you'll see. I'll give you a flat hundred dollars to work from 6 am until 11:00."

"Really? Okay, put me down for this Sunday. I'll see you at six." I point a finger at her. "And you said free coffee?"

Jordan's smile is big as she steps up to the espresso machine.

"Absolutely. What can I get you?"

I order my drink and look around my new place of employment. All right, FM. Maybe life really does find you.

Chapter 20

"Of course, I knew they'd be moving out!" I say as I throw my hands up in the air. "I just didn't know how much I'd miss them." Those words coming out of my mouth about Missus and FM are cringeworthy.

Jackson is standing in front of a nearly empty suitcase. Behind him are half-open drawers, which are also nearly empty. He looks from one to the other. "Missus was doing our laundry, too?"

"I guess." And the suitcase and drawers aren't the only empty things. The refrigerator, kitchen cabinets, and toilet paper holders are all running on empty. "I was busy and didn't really think about it."

Hard to believe just two weeks ago I was wandering around with nothing to do. Did I mention I'd been busy? Griffin came up and rototilled a big section of our backyard for my new vegetable garden, Sunday mornings at MoonShots are pretty much a given now (besides, I need the extra money to buy gardening supplies), and there are those other times Jordan calls me when she needs help other than Sundays. Most days when she needs me, she finds me next door since I'm giving Shannon a lot of extra time, as Patty and Andrew are *still* busy upstairs. Susan signed me up to help with Vacation Bible School, Savannah and Bryan finished school last week so they are laying around the house needing supervision, and we are having a wedding in only two weeks. A wedding Anna and Will have no time to plan, which Missus is blowing way out of proportion, and which she expects me to participate in.

Then Missus and FM moved out and into their repaired house, leaving me with all the cooking, cleaning, and yes, laundry.

"How long are you going to be gone?" I say as I get up off the side of the bed.

"Only a couple nights, so I guess I have enough clothes to take. But then I'll be cleaned out."

"No problem, I'll start on laundry tomorrow afternoon when I get home from MoonShots and it'll all be done by time you get home."

"It's a pain leaving on Sunday, but they need the time tomorrow afternoon before traffic gets going again on the highway Monday morning. You sure you have to work? I have to leave before noon."

"Jordan expects me. At least you're not missing Leslie's graduation party tonight."

He comes to me and puts his arms around my waist. "We do have to change for the party. Might as well get started now."

"Well, since I have to take these clothes off, might as well," I say and then follow with an exaggerated sigh and a smile. Since our rough patch last winter, we know we can't let too much space get between us. Luckily, we like the no-space thing. And after all, it's not exactly work.

Susan and Griffin's backyard is filled with string lights. They

KAY DEW SHOSTAK

swing from the high tree branches and glow from the depths of the bushes around the patio. The food is set up on their screened-in porch, and coolers of beer, soft drinks, and water sit along the outside of the porch steps. A wheelbarrow full of ice chills the bottles of wine settled in it. Chairs and tables from the church are covered in light blue fabric, the same shade as the dusky sky. Susan entertains frequently, but it tends to be more the spontaneous kind of entertaining. Everyone helps, everyone eats, everyone has fun. This looks more like something out of a magazine.

"Susan, this is amazing," I say as our hostess comes to where we have entered from around the side of the house.

She grins and looks around. "It is, isn't it? I've had such fun putting it all together. You know I don't really plan parties. They just happen. But I wanted this to be special for Leslie. She's such a good kid."

In the corner seating, with cushions and pillows all in shades of blue, Leslie and some of her friends are laughing and talking. Leslie is the serious older sister for not only her siblings Susie Mae and Grant, but all her cousins. She reminds me of our oldest, Will, then I remember how that turned out, giving up law school, having to marry his girlfriend, living with family. But, no, I shake myself. He graduated from college, he and Anna seem to love each other, he has a job. "Oh, reminds me," I say and turn back to Susan. "Will has to work late, but he'll be here straight from work. The dealership is having a big sale. Anna is coming with Missus and FM."

"Yeah, I thought Laney was going to strangle Shaw about the sale being tonight. She thought it would be next weekend for Memorial Day. Did you know Laney got a new job?"

My ears perk up. "No, where?"

"Coming," Susan shouts to Griffin who's yelling for her from the screened porch. "Gotta go, she'll be here soon. Ask her."

Susan whips around, and her ponytail flies straight. She has

143

on a cute red dress with little bulldogs on it. Appropriate for Leslie going off to University of Georgia, but Susan probably actually wore it when she went to UGA. How do some people stay so skinny?

Anna comes up behind me, and poor thing still looks sick. She's having trouble keeping anything down, and I hate that the pregnancy is so hard on her. "Hi, Carolina."

"Hi, honey," I say with a side hug for her. "Still feeling bad?"

She nods. "I had no idea it could be like this."

"Yeah, but surely it'll be better soon."

She nods again then moves toward one of the nearby tables. "I'm going to sit down."

"Can I get you something to drink? A Sprite, maybe?"

She shakes her head and even that bit of motion apparently makes her nausea worse. "No, thank you."

I pull out a chair, examining the swath of blue fabric and bow on the back of the chair, just for the party. "This is too cute."

"Yeah, Granmissus will want us to do them for the wedding when she sees them."

"Where is she?"

"She and FM stopped inside the house to drop off some papers for Griffin. She's found another tourism grant to apply for. She never stops."

"No, she doesn't, and I'm missing that now that I'm having to clean my own house and cook our food and do our laundry."

"Carolina, I'm so sorry. I need to help you more. It's just I can barely stay upright long enough to get my homework done. And now with all this wedding stuff."

"You're fine. You just need to take care of yourself. Let Missus do the wedding."

Tears fill her eyes. "I guess. But it's my wedding." Then she's full out crying.

"Oh, honey," I pull her into a hug and rock her back and forth a bit. "I'll help make her back off. You just let me know what you want to do, and I'll make sure that gets done."

She catches her breath a couple times and then lays her head on my shoulder and mumbles. "I want to do the wedding at noon with Patty and Andrew."

Well, that stops the rocking. "What?"

She sits up and takes a deep breath. "I don't want to have competing weddings and receptions. I want to do it with Patty so we can plan together and just have one big party. I don't feel like being the center of attention by myself."

"You won't," I plead. "You'll have Will."

"That's true, but it would be nice to have Patty beside me, too."

And Gertie. And Andrew's big family. Good thing Missus will never let it happen.

Anna smiles up at me. "Will said you'd help me. He was right. You offering to tell Missus already makes me feel better."

Me tell Missus she has to share the spotlight with Gertie Samson? "Oh no, it won't be good coming from..." And then tears pool in her gray eyes and the dark circles under her eyes deepen until I can't take it anymore. "Of course, honey, if that's what you need me to do."

She hugs me, and over her back I check out the wine bottles in the wheelbarrow ice. Yep, that should be almost enough to make this all better.

Okay, so I didn't need as much wine as I was afraid I would to make things better. When Leslie and her friends vacated the cushiony, corner couches, I settled into the end of one. My plaid cotton shirt and navy skirt are cool and perfect for the warmth of lots of people gathered around on the first of many humid

Southern nights to come.

I have my feet propped on one of the pillowed foot rests, and with only a half glass of wine, I'm feeling very copacetic. Very chill. There's the perfect mix of ages, and everyone seems to genuinely like each other. Inside the screened porch, candles give off a peachy glow, and the food tables are popular. Jackson and a couple of the men are playing corn hole with a group of boys, including Bryan and Grant. Brittani and some of her friends are watching the boys. The boys know they are being watched and the girls know the boys know they are being watched.

As Will walks in from the side yard, I see him scan the party and watch his face relax into a grin when he sees Anna sitting at a table of young couples. He loosens his tie, takes it off, and shoves it into his pocket as he makes straight for her.

Savannah and her group are down at the back of the yard, in the darkest area, of course. I expect before long they'll wander up here and say they are going, well, somewhere. Let's be honest, once a kid can drive, you really can't be sure where they are. You have to hope and trust. After all, they are only months away from being old enough to join the military or get married, all without a parent's permission.

I heard it put this way once: by the time a kid is eighteen, they need to be ready to take full responsibility for their life, because that's where it will reside in a court of law or in any contract they sign. So, that means at sixteen they need to be almost done. Scary, but true.

Susan, in her cute red bulldog dress, is flitting here and there. She waves as she passes by me, and then my little private party ends.

"Are your legs broken?" Missus asks. "That is the only acceptable reason I can see for a grown woman to sit with her feet up like that in public."

With a groan, I drop my feet and scoot back on my seat so she can pass by. She sniffs at the low cushioned seats, but sits down, back still straight, knees locked together and her pocketbook on her lap. "Carolina, we need to discuss the wedding."

Oh, wow, my party really *is* over.

"We will be doing the bridesmaid luncheon at your house, like we held the candidates' tea for the Whitten County beauty pageant. That will be on the day of the wedding at noon. The young men in the wedding party will spend that morning on the golf course, so I will need to ascertain their favorite course. The young women will dress at your home, after the luncheon of course. Beau is lined up to provide hair and make-up assistance. The boys—young men, I mean—can dress at my house and then walk over to the church."

Her face is filled with concentration as she pauses. "That doesn't seem quite right, does it? Anna and the girls should be at my house, her family home, getting ready. And Will and his attendants should be at your house. Oh, yes, then we can have the girls arrive at the church in a horse and carriage." She smiles and nods. "Oh, yes. That is what we'll do. Good idea, Carolina."

I wave my hand at her. "Horse and carriage?! Wait, none of this has been my idea. Matter of fact, that won't really work. Don't you think Anna will want to go to Patty's wedding at noon?" C'mon, I've only had half a glass of wine. You don't think I'm going to spill the truth now, do you?

Missus pulls a face. "On her own wedding day? Oh, I think not. Besides, between you and I, we know what *that* wedding will be like." She shudders. "No, absolutely not." Then she stares at me. "You weren't planning on attending *that* wedding, were you?"

"Yes, I was. I am."

"No, just not possible. And you will share that with Anna, won't you? When she realizes you are not going, she will understand." Missus stands up, all in one swift motion, places her pocketbook over her arm and smooths down her skirt.

My mouth opens, but nothing comes out. This really isn't the time or place to challenge her. She waves her hand, and I see FM turn away, with a clap on the back of the man next to him, from the group he was talking with. Missus steps past me and waits for FM to join her.

"Good evening, Carolina. Hey look, you two are dressed plum alike." And he's right. Missus has on a plaid cotton shirt almost identical to mine, and we both have on navy skirts.

I'm not sure who is more mortified.

Of course, Savannah and her group choose this exact moment to make their exit through the party, informing their parents of where they probably aren't going.

FM is grinning and pointing. "Look, Savannah, your mom and Missus are dressed just alike. We should get a picture."

My daughter looks at me, shrugs, and smiles. "Mom, you want us to get a picture?"

"No," I say, but Missus cuts it all short as she lifts her chin, then turns to leave. FM follows behind her, still laughing.

"Mom, we're going," Savannah says.

"Where are you going?"

"Um, probably downtown. See if Ruby's is open. She said she might be there making pies for the senior picnic Monday."

"Hmm, Ruby's? Well, behave. And remember you are to be home before midnight, right?"

"Of course," she says. She and the rest of the girls have on sundresses or khaki skirts and dressy shirts. The boys wear khaki shorts and mostly collared shirts. They all look so cute and so grown-up.

Jenna plops down beside me on the couch. "Miss Carolina, can you tell my mom I was here, but we're going, uh," she looks up at Savannah, "to Ruby's and whatnot?"

"Where is your mom?"

Jenna flips her mane of blonde waves and curls off her shoulder and leans toward me. "Did you hear about her new job?"

When I shake my head, Jenna stands up, smooths her dress down, and steps past me. "Well, I can't tell you. I promised. Just tell her I'll be home before curfew. Thanks!"

The crowd of sixteen- and seventeen-year-olds meanders through the party on its way to the side gate and freedom. I get up, of course, not as gracefully as Jenna, but sadly, also not as graceful as Missus. That stinks. How did she smooth out the wrinkles in her cotton skirt and shirt with just a single passing of her hands? I'm more wrinkled than Missus' nose when she thinks about Patty's wedding. Okay, that was ugly, but I feel better.

With the teenagers out of the way, I can see Laney's arrived. As she makes her way down the path of pavers she waves at me, then raises and tips her hand toward her mouth. Oh, she wants me to get her a glass of wine. No problem, as I was just on my way to visit the wheelbarrow.

With both glasses, I wander through the people chatting and visiting. Finally, Laney and I meet, and she grabs the glass. "Thank you so much." She pulls me into a tight hug and just as quickly releases me. "Party looks great. Susan did all this?"

"Yes, I did." Susan slips up beside us. "Surprised?"

Laney hugs her. "A bit. You always say *I* go overboard with parties."

"This isn't just a party. It's for Leslie. I can't believe she'll be going away to school in just a couple months. So, did you tell her?"

Susan actually looks mischievous, which is odd. She is the most straightforward person I've ever met. "Tell me what?" I ask.

Laney beams. "About my new job. I'm the brand new manager of Southern Comfort."

Susan is watching me closely, but I don't see why. "Southern Comfort? The alcohol? That's a liquor, isn't it? I think Daddy serves it in his eggnog."

"Silly goose," Laney laughs and shakes her head. "No, over in Collinswood. You know, they got that tourism grant last year?"

"Sure," I deadpan. "The one Missus was so set on that she faked a ghost at my house."

"Well, they are really moving fast, and without my job here on the town council and me promising Mama to not gamble, well, I needed something to do. You kind of helped me get the job, too."

"Me? How did I help?"

"You gave me experience! I feel more than qualified for my new position."

Susan is fully enjoying the show, and I still don't understand. "Did I miss something? What is this Southern Comfort?"

Laney holds up her nearly empty wine glass in a toast and, just like her daughter did earlier, tosses her curls behind her. "Well, its full name is Southern Comfort B&B. And I'm running it."

See? I knew a wheelbarrow full of wine wouldn't be enough.

CHAPTER 21

"The old ladies who clean up and decorate the sanctuary at my church are having a fit over folks bringing these cups to church!" Shannon says. "That's why I have to finish it here."

The sun isn't up, but Moonshots is. Up and running with coffee brewed and more brewing, fresh flowers on the tables, and me a bit short of bright-eyed and bushy-tailed. I'm not exactly blaming the wheelbarrow, but it played a part. However, being here is helping.

There's something I like about leaving the house all quiet and dark, finding the streets the same way, parking alone on the square and then letting myself in the dark front door. Until I switch on the front lights, the only light comes from the back where Jordan is busy. My first duty is turning on the bright lights in the customer and counter area, then I get things ready out front. Fill the cups and napkins and creamers and anything else missed by the teenagers who worked Saturday afternoon. Moonshots isn't open Saturday night here in Chancey. From what I gather, a lot of things are done differently at this store. I'm still not sure why it was even opened.

By time I walk in the door at 6 am, the first pot of dark, rich coffee is brewing and smells wonderful. Before I start cleaning and restocking, I set out the muffins Ruby brings by on Saturday afternoons. This is the only morning there's any food served at MoonShots. (Another oddity of the Chancey store.) Ruby has made an awkward peace with Jordan. Mostly, I think it's because her business hasn't really been hurt. Plus she's selling more muffins than ever.

Shannon brings her troublesome purple cup over to the counter and examines the muffins. "Think I'll take that one. It doesn't look like chocolate. I'm not partial to chocolate this early." Shannon hangs out with us on Sundays after she delivers her flowers for each table.

Jordan pauses from fiddling with one of the machines near me and sighs. "Me either. But that old bat won't let me make an order. We have to take what she has left over from Saturday morning since she doesn't open on what she calls, 'The Lord's Day.'"

Shannon grins and leans on the counter. "Ruby would kick you two ways from Sunday if she heard you call her an 'old bat.'"

Jordan shrugs and pulls on a lever to release some wonderful smelling coffee. She hands me the cup, and I take a long whiff. "Perfect," I say with a look at my boss.

She nods. "It's not hard to make just plain coffee perfect. Best thing about this store stuck in the hills is no one wants the 'fancy' coffees on Sunday morning." She draws out the word *fancy* and adds her estimation of a southern twang to it. "People here think half & half is fancy. 'Just give me whatever ya got in that there carton.'" She shudders, then smirks. "It does make mornings easy here, though."

The simplicity of coffee requests means Jordan hasn't had to hire anyone else for Sunday mornings. I just hand out coffee and give out muffins. Ruby brings us our tray of muffins before she delivers trays to the three big local churches on Saturday afternoons. They're all free, well, to the people eating them. MoonShots pays for them all. Diego calls it overhead; Jordan calls it Diego bowing to hillbillies.

Diego wasn't here even two days on his trip. He and Jordan had a huge fight upstairs, which even though both Savannah and Jenna were working, they couldn't hear actual words. After that, he ran out of town like a scalded dog. Jordan doesn't smile hardly at all, now. And she's losing weight. She no longer looks svelte and stylish, she just looks skinny and tired.

Patty says she doesn't sleep hardly at all. Patty's worried about her, but what can any of us do? She pretty much thinks we're all hicks, and she can't wait to move back to civilization, as she calls it.

So I drink free coffee, eat free muffins, and ignore her. Oh, and get my $100 each Sunday. We get a steady stream of folks starting about six-thirty, all headed to church. Bet it's not just Shannon's church getting fed up with purple MoonShots cups getting left in the pews.

By eight o'clock today only chocolate muffins are left, but that's not a problem as the teenagers are beginning to show up on their way to their Sunday School classes. Savannah and Susie Mae get here first, and both have specialized orders for Jordan to fill. They pretty much ignore me. Jenna arrives right behind them, and being a beauty queen, asks me how I am, tells me she likes my tee-shirt, and smiles a bunch. Being ignored isn't that bad.

Angie doesn't drink coffee, so she just sits with Savannah and Susie Mae instead of coming to the counter, and then Jenna takes the final chair. They take up only one table, but in the space of the next ten minutes, over half the chairs in the shop are pulled around it and filled with their friends. From behind the counter I have a front row seat.

Ricky has his arm around Savannah, and the way he draws circles on her bare upper arm with his thumb looks too possessive. I can't help but smile when she pushes his hand away and then shrugs off his arm. He leaves in only a few weeks for summer football camp at Georgia State in downtown Atlanta. You'd think he'd be looking ahead, but no. It's like he wants to make sure everything in Chancey stays just like it is now. Savannah broke up with him right before graduation, but then got back together with him last week, kind of.

I wish he'd just move down to Atlanta. All this emotion isn't good for keeping distance between young people hopped up on hormones, if you know what I mean. I've already got one out of wedlock pregnancy; we are not having another one.

Laney comes in the door, says hello to a number of folks, and then comes to the counter. "I see you burning holes in my nephew over there. He does seem to have gotten a bit clingy lately, hasn't he?"

"Yes, I know he's anxious about going off to school and making the team and all that, but I don't want Savannah to be trying to make him feel better."

Leaning on the counter in front of me, she joins me in watching them. "You got that right. I know from personal experience, big ol' jock boys like to have their high school honey on one arm and a cute college freshman on the other." Laney turns back to look at me. "Don't worry. I'll jerk a knot in his tail about Savannah. You know I've always got your back."

"Like leaving me to run the B&B alone, while you go build up that place in Collinswood? How does that have my back?"

She shrugs and pats her hair, which is pulled back and smoothed into a classy bun. Her dress is sedate, no cleavage, no tightness across the hips. It's a rather non-descript, gray shirtdress with no waist, very business-like. "Where did you get that dress?"

She ignores my question. "You need to run your B&B yourself. You know that. There's not room for all of us up there telling you what to do. Besides, you only took our advice when we didn't leave you a choice. This is my chance to really see what I can do outside of Chancey."

"Can I help you?" I ignore Laney and greet the person entering the door. I pour another black coffee, point out the leftover muffins on the tray, and hope my so-called *friend* will leave.

Should've known better than that.

"Besides, Leslie leaving for school made me think. Look at them." She points to her girls seated near the window. "They both graduate next year. You and Susan have younger kids. Mine are gone in one fell swoop."

When I look up at her, she tilts her head away from me a bit, but I can still see the tears gathered on the edge of her lashes. Since I met her last year, I've seen her in all sorts of moods, but never sad, never fearful. I've not even known her a year, and yet this shakes me. Her confidence has pulled me into so many things, both good and bad. To even imagine her not being confident? Not being sure she was right?

She turns, never raising her head to look at me, picks up her coffee. She heads across the floor and out the door. That's when I know things are really bad. The world *is* off its axis.

Laney Conner is wearing flats.

155

CHAPTER 22

"Hey, Mom. Anybody sitting here or there?" Will points to the place beside me and, across the booth, to the seat beside Susan.

"Nope, join us." I work to keep the sigh out of my voice, but I knew better than to think with three kids in town, hungry after church, I wouldn't be feeding all three. Four, if you count Anna. Bryan is understandable, but he's easy. He and Grant are fine on their own at a little table for two pushed right up against the front window and only three feet from the Chinese buffet. They'll eat their weight in General Tso's chicken and those sugared balls of dough. Then, they'll go next door to the pet store until we track them down there and say it's time to go home.

Savannah supposedly has this job thing now, so she could, if she truly wanted to, go somewhere I wasn't. Somewhere that doesn't include talking to me, since she obviously wants to avoid talking to me at all costs. But, no. There she is in the booth behind me, sighing and texting and sighing and rolling her eyes and texting and ignoring that Ricky didn't pay for a lunch but he's eating off her plate from the buffet. She's also ignoring me motioning at her to quit filling up her plate for him. As I was contemplating tripping her as she passed with another empty plate, Will and Anna came in the door and straight to the booth Susan and I are seated in.

Susan scoots over, and I do the same, again, trying not to sigh too loudly. Anna slides in next to Susan and Will next to me. When the waitress comes over, Will motions shakes his head no. "We're not eating. Just here for a minute."

He turns to me and smiles big. I smile back and him, then he opens his mouth. "Anna said you offered to tell Missus about the wedding."

"I don't know that I exactly offered..." but as my words dwindle off to end with a question mark, Anna sniffles. "Yes, of course I did. Whatever I can do to help."

Will takes a long breath in and lets it out. "Okay, good. Yeah, that's good. Um, could you talk to her this afternoon? She has a wedding strategy meeting planned for tonight at Peter's house. It's supposed to be a chance to see his renovations, but she's turned it into a planning session. You know how she does." He says all this as he's sliding out of the booth, reaching for Anna's arm and pulling her up next to him so that when he finishes talking he can just wave, say "thanks," and leave. Which happens just as I laid it out. The front door closes with the jingling of a string of brass bells hanging beside it.

I spear a piece of broccoli and lift it to my mouth where I chomp on it like a T-rex.

Susan laughs. "What did you get yourself into now? What's going on with the wedding? From everything I've heard, it sounds beautiful. Right around dusk, like Leslie's party last night. Missus asked to borrow the blue chair covers and table clothes. Of course, *after* I get them dry cleaned.

Can broccoli make you nauseous? Because my stomach doesn't feel so good. "Anna wants to combine her wedding with Patty's at noon."

Susan's mouth opens in slow motion. Her brow creases, and she begins to slowly shake her head back and forth. "Oh, I don't think so." Then it dawns on her what she just heard. "And you volunteered to tell Missus?"

"No, I offered to help Anna with getting Missus off her back, and Anna took it to the next step. Then with the tears always on standby, and the whole constant throwing up thing, how am I supposed to get out of it?"

Susan purses her lips. "You've got to get better at not getting into situations, instead of always having to get out of them. Missus won't have it. She just won't have it. She softened up a bit when she found out about the baby, but now that she's got her great-grandbaby being born right here in Chancey, she's gotten more stubborn than ever. There's no way on God's green earth she'll share her spotlight with Gertie Samson."

I stretch my neck around and happen to see Ricky and Savannah having a major make-out session right there in the next booth. "Cut that out," I hiss. Ricky sits up straighter, but he no longer looks scared or caught. It's like he's grown up in the past couple weeks. Savannah isn't looking at me, but she no longer appears in control of the relationship. She looks like she had completely forgotten where she was. That is *so* not a good look on your teenage daughter.

Susan sees it. I can hear it in her voice. "Ricky Troutman. Go home. Right now. How dare you act like that here."

He slides out of his seat and walks past us with only the faintest nod in our direction. Savannah follows him, then turns back to me. "Thanks for lunch. I'll see you at home." She smiles a bit, but then reaches for his hand. The bells beside the door are jingling again.

Susan and I meet eyes. She says, "I'm sorry. He's my nephew, but he needs to go on to college. He's getting a little too big for his britches."

"Guess in addition to talking to Missus today, I need to have another heart to heart with Savannah. She always seems so in control when we talk about sex, but, well…" I shrug.

Susan waves at the waitress. "Let's get the checks and you

can get on out of here. I'll walk over to the pet store with the boys, and they can hang out at our house. Griffin is going to be on the golf course all afternoon, and Susie Mae has a pool party after softball practice."

We take our bills to the front counter, and as we pay I remember why I texted Susan to have lunch. "Oh, yeah, what's with Laney? She came by MoonShots this morning and looked positively matronly."

"Laney? She wasn't at church today. Said she was going over to the church in Collinswood to make connections for her new job, and then she was making a family dinner for just her, Shaw, and the girls. Did she looked sick?"

"No, she looked like she felt fine. It was her dress and her hair and, mostly, her shoes." I drop my wallet into my purse. "Susan, she was wearing flats."

Susan starts to laugh, then freezes. "Seriously? She's worn flip flops occasionally, but not to town. Real, honest-to-goodness flats?"

"Yes. Nice flats, black leather with a little silver buckle on them. Like something she would buy, if she bought flats."

Susan pushes open the heavy wooden door, and we step out into the afternoon sunshine with the boys right behind us. They head straight for the pet store, and we step to the side in that same direction.

"Okay," she says. "You have your talk with Missus, I'll find out what's going on with Laney, and let's meet at Ruby's tomorrow morning. Around nine?"

"It's a plan. Well, thanks for letting Bryan hang out with you and Grant. I better get home to make sure Ricky isn't there."

We part, and as I get in the hot car, I check my phone for messages. There's only one, a text from Missus telling me about the wedding strategy meeting tonight at Peter's.

Okay, but first to deal with Savannah. Ricky better not be there when I get home.

"Mom, I know what you're going to say." Savannah is rocking on the front porch when I get home. Apparently she's waiting for me to tell her what she already knows I'm going to tell her.

"I'm glad to see Ricky's not here," I say as I step past her to the rocking chair on the end. It's a beautiful early summer day with a breeze, no humidity, dancing sunlight and air so full of fresh smells, it's like sticking your nose in a box of dryer sheets.

"Mom, he's just kind of bored waiting to go off to school. I told him I don't want to date anymore, but then he comes around and he's so cute, and, well…"

She speaks so confidently, until she doesn't, and her voice fades. I watch the doubt crawl around on her face. "Honey, it's called physical attraction. It serves its purpose when you're in a relationship you know you want to be in, but you don't really like your partner at times. Like when you've got babies, no money, and your husband gets on your last nerve. Then that physical attraction keeps you together when everything else says, get out of this."

"Mom," she huffs and looks away from me.

"Just being honest. But it can also get in the way of you getting *out* of a relationship you need to get *out* of. You are letting things go too far. You want to break up with him? Then do it. If you're meant to get back together, there's lots of time for that. Do not have sex with him by accident. Just because he makes you feel, so, you know, so good."

I'm talking fast because she's now standing up. Long, meaningful sex talks with your kids are the stuff of fantasy. You've got to say what you've got to say fast. And really, that's easier for me, too. If I had to think about what I'm saying, or have her look me in the face? I couldn't do it. Just blurt it out and go on your separate ways.

"I'm going inside," she says pulling the screen door open. "And Missus called the house phone. Said you're not answering your cell again." And she's gone. Now, if my heart can calm down from this talk before I have to talk to Missus.

However, as I pull my phone out of my purse and turn up the ring tone volume, it rings. It's her. Great.

"Hi Missus, sorry I missed your calls. Had the volume turned down for church."

"No, you didn't. I heard you get a text in the middle of the sermon. I do not care if you're trying to avoid me or someone else. I will only be avoided if I chose to be avoided. You should know that by now."

And as delusional as that is, it's true. It also makes dashing her dreams of the perfect wedding easier. "Of course, Missus. Now, about the wedding. Anna and Will want to have it with Patty and Andrew at noon. Jackson and I are fine with that." (Well, Jackson will be once I tell him about it.)

I wait, but there's only silence. "Missus? You still there?" The silence continues for a while longer, and then the call ends.

Holding my phone out in front of me, I stare at it. Maybe the call dropped before she heard me. Maybe she'll call back. Maybe she dropped dead of a heart attack. The phone doesn't make a sound. I drop it back in my purse and take a deep breath. Laying my head against the rocking chair back, a smile for the deep blue sky above the trees ends in another deep breath, and another smile. I had both my difficult conversations inside of a half hour.

See, God loves me even if I spent Sunday morning in a coffee shop instead of a sanctuary.

CHAPTER 23

So, Missus isn't dead.

She sent a group text about still meeting at Peter's at 7 pm. Savannah avoided me all afternoon. (A definite advantage to mentioning sex to your teenager.) Will and Anna hung out on the couch watching a marathon of some TV show. I mentioned several times how beautiful it was outside, but they ignored me. So I sat out on the deck and read.

Such a relaxing afternoon has me in a very relaxed attitude, but my cool dissipates as I drive down the hill toward town. The sun still shines, just from behind the surrounding mountains, and that soft blue light that set the scene for Leslie's party fills the air. It's soft and warm and fresh. Missus is right, it would be a beautiful time of day for a wedding.

But don't tell her I said so.

Passing the stores on the main street, I look for lights or people in MoonShots or the florist and bookstore. Lights in the back point out that no one is in either business. With a quick look upstairs I see that both apartments are lit up. I can even see movement in Jordan's. I hoped working with her would cause her to open up, but she seems surlier than when she first came to town. At the corner, I slow down to look inside Ruby's windows. There I can see a person. Ruby is in the back kitchen area. No telling what she's making back there. She sells a ton of muffins every morning, but she also has big side business in pies and cakes and anything you want her to make. For such a small town, where everybody supposedly cooks, she sure sells a lot of food.

Where the street ends at the row of antebellum homes in a wide array of repair and disrepair, I turn right. Missus and FM's home is to the left just a bit. Then two houses past it is the library. They sit right on the square and across from the town park. Peter's house is just off the square, and that is as dire as it sounds.

His front porch faces the side of the last business on Main street, which is a solid wall of old, dark brick. Only a slice of the park can be seen from his front yard. And while his home is as old as the others on the street, his looks it.

There's very little paint left on the warped boards, so it's mostly weathered gray planks. Overgrown bushes crowd up next to the house on all sides, even the front, so the porch is in permanent shadow. I pull up alongside the front sidewalk, and it's evident the town hasn't spent any money to repair the sidewalk off the square. Out of my car and looking back to my left, even with the sun tucked behind the mountains, there is light and airiness in the park and up towards Missus' house. The dark brick of the building behind me, the shaggy, low-hanging trees meeting the out of control bushes, makes it feel darker here. Walking up the front steps and onto the porch feels darker still.

There is no screen, so I knock on the splintered wooden door. Peter pulls it open, but his face looks anything but welcoming and I can hear why. Anna is crying, Missus is preaching, FM is pacing, and Will is… where is my son?

"Where's Will?" I ask as I lay my purse on a pile of boxes beside the front door and head straight for Anna, who is huddled over on the old-fashioned love seat. Peter closes the door, then comes up behind me.

"Mother sent him down to her house for something," he says, following me to the love seat. As I sit down beside Anna, he steps around to stand in front of Anna and face Missus. "Mother, stop this. Anna and Will can do whatever they like. You don't have to come."

Anna jumps up. "Oh, no. She has to be there. She has to be." She pushes around Peter and puts her arms around her grandmother. "You wouldn't not come, would you? I couldn't stand that. Please say you'll come."

Missus melts. Right there in front of us. Her mouth softens, her eyes close, her shoulders relax, and she murmurs into Anna's hair. "Of course, I'll come. Of course."

Peter slumps into the place where Anna had sat. FM walks past us into the well-lit kitchen mumbling about needing some water. The love seat is one of those old ones with wooden scrolling on the back and little arms and it's pretty small, so I get up.

I take the moment to look around and see that the inside of Peter's house has as little life as the outside. Everyone has talked about the remodeling Peter is doing. Looks to me he was just making it habitable, not actually renovating. This house has none of the nice details of his parents'. No thick crown molding, no glossy hardwood floors, no windows with trim worthy of stain or even paint. It's rather bare. Just a room with a staircase to one side. A plain staircase with carpeted stairs and a skinny banister that looks cheap. The windows are small and don't even have a real sill, just a little inch-wide lip.

From what I can see of the kitchen, it appears serviceable. The cabinets look like those you find in a scaled-down model home, oak with shiny brass handles and knobs. The counter isn't granite, just plain butcher-block laminate. Problem is, I know all this is new. He just had the kitchen and living room area remodeled. It is also pretty small, with the kitchen, which is at the back of the house, only a few steps past were we are, and the front door is only a few steps the other direction. And, of course, there are boxes everywhere, as the upstairs is being worked on right now. His house reminds me of our house. Just an old house, but at least ours was habitable when we bought it. No wonder he got such a good deal. Hopefully, the work should be done soon, sounds like he actually has workers upstairs on a Sunday night. That's a good sign.

When Will comes in the back door, then through the kitchen, he holds out to a notebook to Missus and puts his other arm around his wife's back. Anna turns into him. Missus takes the notebook, visibly wiping her eyes. Peter stands up and steers Anna and Will to sit down. The couch is the only place to sit down, besides some kitchen chairs placed around the boxes.

Missus says something about water and joins FM in the kitchen. Peter and I move toward the front of the house. In the corner, to the right of the front door, I turn and look at Peter. He has his back to the staircase, and he runs one hand through his hair.

"Man, that looked like it was going to be awful. Mother was furious when she got here. She hid it until she sent Will off to her house. Then she let into Anna. Caught me and Dad completely off guard."

We both catch our breath, and then a giggle pops out of me. "Can you believe we're actually agreeing to put on a wedding with Gertie Samson?"

He quietly laughs. "It'll be a nightmare. She's impossible, you know."

"Oh, I know. She's living at my house, remember? And we haven't even met Andy's family. Just hearing him talk about them has scared Patty nearly to death."

"At least it's not that far off. We just need to make it as nice as possible and get through it."

We nod in agreement, and then I tip my head towards the upstairs. "You got folks working on Sunday night?"

He looks up the stairs, too.

"Sounds like they're trying to be quiet. Probably afraid they'll get pulled into whatever mess is going on down here." I laugh and then realize Peter isn't agreeing with me and is still staring up the staircase.

"What's wrong?" I ask as I touch his sleeve. "Work not going right up there? I guess it's a good sign they're willing to work on Sunday night, though. Right?"

He finally turns to me and frowns. "Carolina, there's nobody up there."

"But, I hear…"

He nods and lays his hand on top of mine. He draws in a deep breath and closes his eyes.

"I think I might have a ghost."

CHAPTER 24

When I came down at 6:30 and put on a pot of coffee, the house was quiet. Open windows pulled in a soft breeze and a muffled quietness from the lingering fog coming off the river. The only sounds were those of the coffee brewing and the few clanks I made setting the muffins out of the freezer to defrost. Beside them on the kitchen table, I laid out butter, cream cheese, juice glasses, and knives. Then stealing a cup of coffee before the pot was done, I pulled my robe around me and went back upstairs to get dressed.

This trip down the stairs is completely different. The sun is no longer creeping up the backside of the mountain across the river, it's burned off all the fog and now toasts the back of our house. The windows let in heat, and ah, there it is, humidity. It's getting to that time where the windows have to stay closed, and the air conditioning runs 24/7. Even when it feels a little cool outside, the humidity fools you and fills your house with stickiness. Wood furniture feels sticky, the back of your neck feels sticky, and suddenly everybody is getting on everyone else's nerves. See? Stickiness.

Also different from my last trip? The noise level. Closing windows along my path from the living room into the dining room, I find a table full of folks in various stages of dress, eating what looks like a full breakfast (where are the muffins I so lovingly put out?), and drinking coffee.

Will has on his dress shirt and dark slacks for a day at the car lot. Anna has on jeans and an old tee shirt. Gertie is still in her night clothes, which I've become familiar with as she has no problem wearing them whenever and wherever around the house. She has on what must be her favorite, a Hawaiian print caftan. Big red and purple flowers. It's huge and bright and a little scary. We have a couple of railfans coming later this week. I'll try talking to her again about dressing for breakfast, but it won't do any good. I think she's confused that when I say "dressing" I mean not naked. So, maybe I'll just settle for not naked.

"Good morning. Everyone good?" I ask.

Gertie holds up her empty cup of coffee towards me. "Since you're standing."

Taking her cup and mine into the kitchen, the mess hits me in the stomach. Looks like Will and Anna made their lunches to take with them, but then put nothing back into the refrigerator. And someone cooked something, as the sink is full of dirty dishes. When I made coffee just an hour ago, none of this was here. And why is every single cabinet door standing open? Before I can get back to the dining room with my questions (and accusations), Gertie meets me.

"Thanks for the coffee. Speaking of which, you look to be running out, unless I just couldn't find your stash. Kids were wanting some eggs, and since you seemed to be just putting out those day old muffins, I made 'em a real breakfast. Don't worry, I won't put it on your bill." She laughs and nudges me with her elbow. "Get it? Like you should pay me for working here." She laughs at her joke and turns back toward the B&B rooms. "I enjoy staying here. Doing a little work is no big deal for me. I just see what needs to be done and I do it." She waves her hand at me. "No need to worry about it. I'm just glad to help out." Passing the dining room table she takes a small piece of toast she left on her plate and takes a bite of it. Toast, not muffins, which are still arranged on the plate like I sat them out. So if they all had toast that means we no longer have any bread. Guess I have to go to the store.

Before Gertie enters the B&B's hallway, she looks back at me. "Besides, we make a good team. I do the cooking and you do the cleanup. Everybody helping out!"

Anna and Will stand up and take their dishes to the kitchen, but by time I follow them with other dirty dishes from the table, they are already headed through the living room.

"I'm dropping Will off at work and then going on to school." Anna says as she slips on her tennis shoes. She adds, "Savannah ate with us and told us to remind you she had work early this morning." Will is stuffing their lunch bags into their backpacks on the back of the couch.

"And Mom, when Anna picks me up we're going down to the mall to look at some nursery furniture and have dinner. So don't worry about cooking for us." They hustle out the door with their arms and bellies loaded.

Then the house is quiet again. The air conditioner is cooling the sunny downstairs and everyone's been fed. Except for Bryan upstairs sleeping, who will make another round of mess for me to clean up when I get home from meeting Susan at Ruby's.

What did being bored feel like?

"You let them walk all over you," Susan says when I finish telling her about my morning. We're sitting in a booth at Ruby's. "Gertie is staying so long that it's like she's not a *real* guest. Crazy her cooking breakfast, and then expecting you to clean it up."

"Right? I mean, who cooks breakfast for their kids anyway?"
Susan just takes another sip of her coffee.

"You do. Should've known. You cook breakfast for your
kids every morning?"

She shrugs and smiles at me, scrunching her nose in
acknowledgement. "They really like breakfast, and I just use the
same pan I cooked Griffin's eggs in earlier. Not so much work."

I drop my head for my chin to rest on my chest. "Oh, Lord,
you fix eggs for Griffin each morning before work?"

"Well, sometimes it's just oatmeal or toast. Believe me, he'd
think Ruby's muffins were a treat."

"No, he wouldn't. You make oatmeal on the stove and *just
toast* is your homemade bread with your homemade jam on it."

She blinks at me, and I can hear the confusing thoughts
running through her head. *Wait, how else can oatmeal be made?
People eat bread they bought? What kind of containers would
jam come in from a store? Wouldn't labels on jars be kind of
tacky?*

Lifting my head, I give it a little shake. "I am the worst person
on the face of the earth to run a bed and breakfast."

"But people still enjoy coming up to your house, so you must
do something right."

"Yeah, like open the door. Laney's place will put us out of
business in a month."

Susan laughs and then straightens her shoulders. She has
on a button-down, yellow dress shirt tucked into khaki pants.
Her belt is this cute, striped ribbon, like I wore in college. With
her hair back in its usual ponytail, she looks like she's still on
the coed quad. As she clears her throat and lifts her chin, she
reminds me of a kid playing at being an adult. "About Laney,"
she says and her voice is firm. Maybe a bit too firm...

"Is something wrong with Laney? What's going on?"

Susan sighs. "Something's going on, but I'm not sure she

told me the whole truth." She lifts her hand to wave at Libby for a coffee refill. "I went over to the house around five yesterday, and she was cleaning out her freezer down in the basement. You know how beautiful it was outside yesterday and, besides, she doesn't even keep much in that big old freezer. Shaw's daddy was a hunter so when he was alive they had meat in it, but now it stays half empty. Except it sure wasn't empty yesterday. Thanks, Libby."

I drain my cup so Libby can fill it, too. "Thanks, Libby," I get in before she scurries off to the next table. Good to see MoonShots hasn't hurt Ruby's business. "So, what was it full of?"

"Normal stuff. Nothing stood out. But she just seemed distracted. I asked her about the flats, tried to make it a joke, but she teared up. My sister, Laney, teared up."

"Do you think she's sick or something?"

Susan blows a bit on her coffee while shaking her head. "Honestly, I have no idea. Called Mama this morning, but she was headed out to a senior citizens' trip with the church so she couldn't talk. But the only thing Laney would say was that the idea of the girls going off to college had her rethinking things. She wouldn't say what things or even talk about the girls. All she would talk about was the B&B job over in Collinsville and how busy she's going to be."

We both sit and think about it and finally I say, "Maybe she's just growing up."

Susan nods. "Guess so. Griffin said about the same thing, except he added, 'About time.' So, how was Missus? Did you tell her about the wedding?"

"Oh, yeah, Missus. She took it all okay. Not at first, but then Anna cried, hugged her, and begged her to come to the wedding. So it's all good…" I can't help but bite my lip because that's not at all what I want to really talk about.

"Well. That was easier than I thought." Susan has her head

tilted now, and she's watching me. Watching me chew on my lip, squirm in my seat, and shift my eyes back and forth across the tables around us.

"And, uh, Peter? He's good with it, too?"

She's fishing.

"Yep, Peter says its fine with him." Gathering my purse, I pick up my bill to take to the counter to pay. "Well, I guess I better get back up to the house. I kind of left the kitchen a mess," I explain as I stand up. Even looking down, I can feel that Susan's not moved a muscle. She's staring straight ahead and thinking.

Then she blurts out. "Oh, no! Peter started flirting with you again? Please tell me you didn't let anything happen between you two."

I drop back into my seat. "No! No, he wasn't flirting. He just, well, he just…"

Susan leans across the table and grabs my wrist. "You and Jackson are good. You've got to stop this thing with Peter."

"There is no thing with Peter and me. It's his ghost."

Susan lets go of me and sits back. "His what?"

"He has a ghost in his new house. I heard it. Upstairs."

"Another trick of Missus'?"

"No, she couldn't even hear it. She nor FM." Leaning closer, I whisper, "I heard it the whole time I was there. Something moving around upstairs. I mentioned it to the others after Peter told me he thought it was a ghost. Of course I didn't mention a ghost, just asked if they heard something upstairs. Will, Missus, and FM all said no. Anna just looked at Peter and kept her mouth closed. But I think she heard it. You know, she lived there this winter right after he moved in." Leaning back in my seat, I feel so much better. Just saying it makes it not so crazy. "But how funny it is that the guy who played my ghost would have one of his own." I laugh, but Susan just looks at me.

"You know it's not a real ghost, right?"

"Well, but maybe it is."

"Or maybe it's just squirrels living in the attic. That place sat empty for a long time, you know."

"But wouldn't it be fun if it were a ghost? Right here in downtown. There was Missus making up a ghost and she lives just a couple doors down from a real one." Again, Susan doesn't join in on the laughing. She does however roll her eyes.

Picking up her bill, she stands up, and I realize she's angry. "Did it dawn on you that since a ghost got you and Peter close once, he's manufacturing one to get close to you again? Let me guess, he told you not to tell anyone, to keep it just between the two of you?"

"Yeah, but, well, that's understandable."

"Have you told Jackson?"

"Well, no. He's out of town, and well, Peter asked...."

With an arched eyebrow and one hand on her hip, she nods. "Exactly."

She steps nearer to me and puts her hand from her hip onto my shoulder. "Honey, stay away from Peter Bedwell for the sake of your marriage. There's just too much natural attraction between you two." She's sincere, and I nod at her words as I stand up.

Walking to the counter, we switch to talking about the Memorial Day weekend coming up with the opening of the waterfront park.

At the front door we go our separate ways—Susan to her car across the street and me to my van parked on the corner beside Ruby's. I watch her pull away from the square while I fumble with my phone like I'm checking messages or something. When she's gone I tuck my phone away and get back out of my car. Walking fast, I pass in front of Ruby's and walk to the far corner where I turn right and walk along the plain brick wall of the last storefront building. In the center of the short block, I cross the street and notice even in the morning this part of the street seems dark. Up the steps, I enter the porch hidden by the overgrown bushes which block out the light and warmth of the early sun.

It makes perfect sense. We couldn't talk last night about the ghost with everyone here so of course meeting this morning makes perfect sense. And why wouldn't we meet where the ghost actually is?

When I raise my hand to knock, the door opens.

Peter smiles. "Good morning. Hope you're not coffee'd out from Ruby's. And I made us a bite of breakfast. Our friend upstairs has been active already this morning."

See? Makes perfect sense.

CHAPTER 25

"What is wrong with you two?" Shrieking from the back deck makes both boys look at me, but that's about it. Bryan hauls off and throws the clump of clay-laced dirt at Grant and laughs as he dodges the clump coming his way.

Grant has the good manners to wipe his dirty hands down his shirt, adding streaks to the stains already there. He smiles at me, but leaves any explaining to my son. Who just throws another clod straight up and laughs when it breaks apart and rains dirt on him.

Yeah, my vegetable garden. Can't believe Griffin listened to me when I told him to make it bigger. Then, bigger still. He started by rototilling about a six foot by six foot area on Susan's direction. (Apparently I've not impressed my friend with my stick-to-itivness.) But this time I was serious. So, he did another row or two. But I wanted more. Bigger. Lots and lots of vegetables.

Now I have a dug-up rectangle in my backyard about half-a-mile by half-a-mile. Probably not that big, but it looks it. And it's full of clods of clay and rocks, and that's all. Heard of red Georgia clay? Well, if there was a market for it, I'd have it cornered. But you know, there is no market for it.

"I never did like gardening. Don't take you for a gardener,

175

either. Your husband do that?" Gertie moseys out of the kitchen to stand beside me on the deck and joins me looking at the dirt.

Grant and Bryan have moved on around the house and out of shrieking distance.

I sigh. "No, it was my idea."

"You musta been half crazy, or starving to death, to think you wanted to plant something that big."

"I was bored."

Gertie huffs. "What is it with folks thinking they're bored these days? People think they've constantly got to have something going on. Gardens are a real good idea, but you gotta be mighty hungry or really love messing around in the dirt."

"Maybe I'd really love it."

"Naw. You don't have a living plant in the whole house. You got artificial plants around like you're fooling folks. You don't care for being dirty or sweaty. And you don't get that look in your eye when you see plowed-up dirt. Real gardeners get all hepped up about tilled-up soil, kinda like you in a bookstore."

"How are things going with the bookstore?" I ask.

Gertie twists her mouth from one side to the other. "Guess okay. You might need to come back and deal with it. Andy has a junkin' gene, looks like. He keeps bringing in junk to sell. And he sells it, but really making that Shannon girl upset. It is a little, well, junky looking."

"I've got my hands full here with the B&B and my garden."

She grins and lumbers around to go back inside. "I better go. Meeting Missus at the church tonight to do some wedding planning. Figured we'd get some things ironed out before the young'uns get involved." She turns around at the door. "And 'fore you say something about it being their wedding, they ain't paying."

I raise my hands in concession. "I'm sure you and Missus will figure everything out just fine."

"You want to come?"

"No, thank you. Maybe me and Bryan will go down to Calhoun to get dinner and then to Walmart and get some vegetables to plant. I have leftover soup in the fridge if you and Patty want it for dinner."

"Sounds good. I'll let her know."

Instead of shrieking, this time I just yell for Bryan, and he comes jogging from the driveway side of the house. "Want to go get dinner and then go to Walmart for some plants?"

"Sure. Can Grant come?" he asks as he bounds up the steps to the deck, closely followed by Grant.

"Good with me. We'll run by his house and ask his mom. You guys go wash your face and hands."

Passing by me, heat radiates off their skin. Fresh boy sweat plasters down their hair and beads up on their foreheads. Their cheeks look thinner than they did just yesterday. The red circles on Bryan's face remind me of kissing that sweet skin, so soft and warm from a toddler's hard play. But the smell that wafts off him isn't that mix of soap and powder and baby shampoo with an earthiness of baby sweat. No, they stink. Actually stink and as they clod by, the deck shakes. "Put on clean shirts while you're at it," I add. "And deodorant."

Just have to find a place where we can eat outside.

Who knew late May is a little late to start a garden in Georgia? Well, I'm supposing some people know. I got so confused in the garden center at the Walmart, all those little plants look too tender to make it with my clods of clay and then all those pictures of little suns and drops of water on all those little sticks in each plant. Exhausting. And looking at the dirt in the little containers, it's so dark and moist and fine. Finally, I ended up grabbing a bunch of stuff from the discount rack. Figured if it's already going to die, it can come home and die with me.

We ate outside at the Taco Bell and then the boys ran around the garden center while I studied and thought and finally filled my buggy. Now they are in the back seat of the van scrunched over my phone playing some game. The sky is almost purple. There are no clouds or jet contrails to relieve the solid stretch of deep color. Summer, the actual date on the calendar, is around the corner, and the sun is staying up later. The moon is also up, not quite full and accenting the purple sky in a magical kind of way. Taking a deep sniff, the smell of dirt and plants hangs heavier than the smell of boy sweat. Of course, I did threaten the boys with death if they even thought about taking off their tennis shoes, so that helps.

It's going to be a good summer with my garden. I can just feel it.

CHAPTER 26

"They didn't all have labels, but I figured it'd be kind of exciting to see what grows on them."

Anna doesn't seem too impressed with my garden. "But aren't certain things supposed to go together?" She's got on pajama pants, a big T-shirt, and flip flops with which she's made a path through the cool, wet grass. She has a Pop-Tart in one hand and a glass of milk in the other. She's so tiny, I imagine her belly is actually showing, and the idea that it's my grandchild adds to my feeling of Mother Earthiness.

She points with her half-eaten Pop-Tart. "You've gotten a lot done this morning. What time did you get out here?"

"Oh, I had a cup of coffee watching the sun come up over the mountains and have been hard at it since then. So three hours or so. Honestly, I thought all the stuff I bought would cover a lot more area."

Standing back now, taking a couple breaths, I can see why Anna isn't impressed. The ground isn't real level as I just tossed aside the bigger clods and rocks and planted in the holes left behind. I do have a row of zinnias in front and they look good. Well, for flowers from the discount rack. But my grandmother had bunches of zinnias, so I don't think they're that hard. The two tomato plants look a little worse for wear. They are pretty much just lying on the ground. Maybe if I put a clod underneath them to hold them up some. The rest of the plants are kind of in rows. Yeah, it doesn't look that good at all.

"Whoa, Mom. You planted a garden!" Bryan shouts from the deck and then leaps the couple steps. He jogs over to us and is beaming. "Cool. I'll help take care of it like we do at Grant's house."

Oh, this boy of mine. He still likes me.

"Thanks, buddy. I'll sure need some help. Is your sister up?"

He shrugs and starts walking on the clods of dirt in the unplanted area. "What are you going to plant over here?"

"Probably nothing this year."

Anna finishes her glass of milk. "We found some cute stuff for the nursery last night. We went to Costco and saw a good deal on a crib. Granmissus wants us to find out the sex of the baby so she can decorate, but I'm not sure we want to know."

"It's fun either way." Placing clods of dirt for the tomato plants to lie on makes me talk toward the ground, so I speak up. "We didn't know that Will was a boy, but mainly just because they were still making a lot of mistakes with seeing the sex of babies then, but with Savannah and Bryan we found out. Right both times. Plans for you two to move back with Missus and FM still set?"

"Yeah, I guess."

I stand up and look at her. "You guess?"

She stretches one arm, then changes hands holding the empty milk glass and stretches the other arm. "We could move in with Peter. His house is smaller, but he says we can have the whole second floor."

"But, that's where…"

"The ghost is?"

And Bryan is back in the conversation. "Where's a ghost?" He says from on top of a big clod he's been trying to break up by jumping on it.

At the same time I say, "Nowhere," Anna says, "Peter's."

He continues jumping, and I stare at her. "Thought this was supposed to be kept quiet."

She twists one side of her mouth up as she glances at me and then turns toward the house. I follow her onto the deck and into the kitchen.

She runs water into her glass and sets it in the sink, while I get a bottle of water out of the refrigerator.

After a long drink, I lean against the counter and watch as she begins unloading the dishwasher. She's working to not say something. And she succeeds through unloading the entire top shelf. Then as she lifts out the utensil basket she pauses and looks at me. "Peter and a ghost? Isn't that a little convenient?"

Oh. I stand up and tighten the cap on the bottle of water. My face is no longer hot from the morning gardening session; it's heat from the inside. She's thinking what Susan was thinking. "I need a shower," I say and escape toward the stairs.

Going through the living room I pick up my cell phone from the end table beside the couch and see I have a couple unread texts. One from Jackson saying he'll be home Thursday afternoon, one from Savannah saying she has work today at noon and for me to wake her up at eleven, and one from Laney. Laney's begins with a string of exclamation points, and when I open it, I see all caps. Not a good sign. WHY WERE YOU SNEAKING IN AT PETER'S YESTERDAY?

Want to bet she's not going to buy the ghost story either?

Not that it's exactly a story. I think he really has a ghost there. But it is a little weird that he told me not to tell anyone, and here's Anna talking about it. That slows me down and causes me to not continue up the stairs but to turnaround and go back into the kitchen.

"Okay, so yes. I went over to see about the ghost," I say to her back.

She turns around and puts a hand on her hip. "You know

Peter likes you, right?"

"As a friend. That's all."

"Okay. Whatever. But we are thinking about moving in with him."

"Your grandmother won't be happy."

"That might be good enough reason to do it."

"Really?" I sit bowls from the dining room table into the sink. Apparently while I was outside, folks had cereal for breakfast. "You mad at your grandmother now?"

"Not exactly mad, but she really doesn't like Patty. Or at least doesn't like us having our wedding together." Anna sits down at the kitchen table while I finish loading the dishwasher.

"Missus is used to getting her own way." Wiping my hands on the dish towel hanging on front of the oven, I shrug. "Hate to tell you, but she's not going to change. People like to think you get softer and nicer as you get older. From what I see, your personality just intensifies. If you're nice, you get nicer. If you're a pain, you become a bigger pain."

Anna stands up and sighs. "I thought everything I could ever want was right here."

She turns so she doesn't see me close my eyes. This is what I was afraid of. Missus, Chancey, a home, and a family all wrapped up in a neat little bundle. A bundle that now has my son tied up in the center. I open my eyes, and she's gone. Hearing her trudge up the stairs, I can't help but feel such sadness. This is a hard way for a girl to grow up.

The fresh pot of coffee I made after Anna went upstairs is now an old pot of coffee smelling up the house. Waiting for it to brew, I sat down on the couch and fell asleep. So much for getting an early start on the day.

"Savannah?" I say to noise in the kitchen as I stumble in to dump out the burnt coffee.

"So, now you're awake? I told you I needed to get up at eleven." She's leaning against the counter eating a cup of yogurt.

"I guess I have to go to work with my hair wet, now."

"Oh Lord, it's 11:30? You look fine. And what's wrong with your alarm clock?"

"I'm helping Jordan today, that's why I'm going in late. I won't get off until four and then I'm going straight to the baseball game. You do know we're playing for a spot in the championship, right?"

"I guess I heard that. Where's the game?" I don't look at her because I can sense rolling eyes on the horizon.

"Here. Everyone's going. I've got to go to work. So, anyway, don't look for me until late. If we win, I'm sure Ruby's will be open. Besides, now that I'm working and school is out we should probably get rid of my curfew."

She says all this as she collects her purse and keys and heads out the front door. Half following her, I see a note laying on the couch beside where I was sleeping. It's from Bryan.

"Going swimming with guys."

I completely slept through my son writing me a note and leaving it beside me. Oh, yeah. This up-with-the-sun-gardening thing is *so* me.

CHAPTER 27

"Over here!" Laney shouts at me when I get out of my car and head toward the baseball stands. Turning, I see a group of ladies in folding canvas chairs at the edge of the fence.

Laney and Beau are the only ones I really know, but I wander up to them.

Beau grins and hands me a red Solo cup. "You need a chair? I've got an extra one."

"I figured I'd just sit in the stands. What is this?"

"Just a wine spritzer. The principal frowns on alcohol in the stands, but down here he leaves us alone." She introduces me to the other two ladies, both whom I've met before but whose children are grown, so I don't run into them much. They both work outside of Chancey.

"Didn't you get my text this morning? You know, the one in all caps? Isn't that supposed to imply its importance?" Laney growls at me.

Beau closes her car door after retrieving a chair for me from her back seat. "That must be some kind of hangover for you to be that grouchy. Here you go, Carolina."

She points me to my chair and then sits back down in hers. A long foul ball comes to our fence, and we all watch the players run to it.

I tilt my head toward Laney. "You're hungover on a Tuesday?"

"What about it?" she spits and then raises her eyebrows at me. "My text? Peter?"

Not liking her attitude, I adopt it. "What about it?"

"Fine. Ruin your marriage. I don't care." Laney stands up. "I'm going to find Susan and sit with her."

Beau just stares up at her. "Maybe you should just go home and get a good night's rest. Without some wine to chill you out, you're not much fun." The three of them laugh, but Laney stalks off.

I'll finish my wine spritzer and maybe go find her later. I don't remember her ever being hungover. Especially not on a weekday. And this late in the day? Something's not right, but I'm sure Susan can handle it.

As I wait for Beau to put her chair in her backseat, I hold mine and watch the folks leaving. We lost the game. Badly. No championship for Chancey this year. Everyone is moving slowly, but apparently Ruby's is open anyway as several people mention seeing that they hope to see me there as they pass. Funny that a year ago I didn't know this little town even existed. Much less envision a command performance at Ruby's.

"You going to Ruby's?" Beau asks as she reaches for my chair.

"Yeah, I meant to catch up with Laney during the game, but once we got to talking about books... well."

Beau closes the car door and opens her front door. "You really should come to our book club. I don't know why I didn't think of inviting you before. Everyone's mostly like Ruth and

Mary Ann, a little older than us. But neat ladies. I'll forward the email invite to you."

"Okay. So, just a minute. Laney told you she was hungover?"

"Yep, I handed her a glass just like I did you, and she practically threw it back at me. Listen, I've got to go. My kids are at my aunt's house having a pizza party. I know she's ready to get rid of them. It was fun to hang out. Drive safe."

I step closer to the chain link fence and wave as Beau backs out, her red hair blowing around her face from the open window.

Something wasn't right about Laney and being hungover, and now I know what was bothering me. Savannah was over there until late. At least that's what she said. She and Jenna and Angie were watching movies with some other friends. Laney was drinking enough to have a hangover with a house full of teenagers? She and I definitely need to talk about this. Probably not a good idea to talk about it at Ruby's with the rest of the town there, but we are going to talk, and sometime soon.

Wouldn't you know it? The only spot open to park near the square is right in front of Peter's house. Without the slightest turn of my head, I get out of my car and never look to my right or behind me. What? Peter's house is right there? Why, I never even noticed.

The sidewalk is old and worn, initials carved in decades ago are barely readable. Air softened by humidity feels comfortable. There is no chill at all. My zippered jersey jacket is open and falling off my shoulders. Beside Peter's house—I'm in the safety zone so I can look to my right—is another old house. A young family lives there, and I step around a tricycle on the sidewalk. The house looks worn and comfortable. Not run-down like Peter's, but not perfect like Missus' and FM's. Along the sidewalk, irises reach up to me with pointed, pale-green leaves and light purple flowers and perfume from my childhood. Purple irises abound in the South, but especially in my home state of Tennessee, where they are the state flower. The smell is sweet and more like perfume than something in nature. My Aunt Darla had a whole yard full of them. Apparently they are easy to share, because I remember everyone saying they got theirs from her. Hmm, maybe some irises in my garden would take up some of the empty space.

I cross the street and walk past the closed repair shop and an empty building with dark windows. At the door to Ruby's, I look inside before opening it. It's pretty full, and I can't help but laugh thinking how this place scared me last fall. How threatening all this seemed. How I didn't feel I belonged. One of the coaches of Bryan's team pushes out the door and says "Hello" as he's leaving. He holds it open for me, and I step inside. Susan is at a table with the preacher, who is also her boss, the preacher's wife, and the music minister from church. She waves at me and points to the other corner where I see Bryan and Grant with a bunch of other friends. She gave them all rides from the ballfield. Waving at Bryan, I catch his eye and wave a five dollar bill at him. He darts through the crowd and grabs for it.

"Hold on. You can talk to me for a minute, I haven't seen you all day. You had fun swimming?"

"Yeah, c'mon, Mom." He reaches for the money again. "Didn't the game stink? We're all staying in Matt's barn tonight, okay? They have a new calf."

Over his head, I look for Matt's parents, and his dad gives me a thumbs up. I nod and smile back at him then look down at my son. "Do you need me to bring you some clothes? Or a toothbrush?"

"Naw. I'm good. Mom, the money?"

I hand it to him, and he rushes back to the crowded booth.

His group travels like a pack of puppies, and I know they'll show up on my front porch probably tomorrow wanting to camp out by the lake. Will and his friends did the same thing, but I remember a lot more video games and hanging out at the mall than camping and barns. Savannah isn't here. As a matter of fact, there are no teenagers here.

As Libby passes by with a full pot of coffee, I lean towards her. "Have you seen Savannah?"

She sighs and puts a hand on her apron-covered hip. "That girl up the street? The coffee lady? She opened up, too, tonight. All the teenagers are up there. Ruby is fit to be tied. Special openings were supposed to be just for here. At least that's what Ruby thought with that painted on schedule on the other place's door. You got a cup?"

"No, not yet. I'm headed back to the counter. But thanks." At the counter, I pull out another five and then slide onto one of the spinning stools there. The seat is old leather and the chrome is shiny for something so many decades old. Libby comes around the counter, grabs an empty cup, pours it full, and sits it in front of me.

Ruby walks up behind her. "Get you a piece of pie, Carolina? Or you going up to that other place for some of that fancy stuff she's serving now?"

"Oh, no. I'm definitely here for some of your pie. Whatever you suggest."

"Sure you don't want a croissant? Or that spinach and cheese thing? I don't know who's making those la-dee-da things for her, but it better not be anyone who ever wants another piece of my pie." She narrows her gaze at me.

"Me? You think I could cook anything Jordan could sell?"

"Lord, no. Everyone knows you cook only cause you have to keep your kids from starving. But you do seem to know what folks are doing, and your daughter is over at that place all the time. Plus, ain't you working there on Sunday mornings? What do you know?"

"Nothing, Ruby. I promise. I didn't even know they were serving food."

She turns to the rack of trays behind her and when she turns back to me she has a small plate in her hand and is shaking her head. "Your daughter doesn't talk to you?"

And hoping to be given the piece of pie, I don't roll my eyes. "Nope, she feels I'm on a need-to-know basis and she's determined I don't need to know much." Yes, I know other mothers and daughters share every special little thing that happens in every single day. Yes, I wish Savannah talked to me more. Yes, I feel ashamed and accept all responsibility. Now, can I please have a piece of pie?

Ruby sets the plate down and hands me a fork. "Count your blessings. My Jewel won't shut up. Even now that she don't live with me, she has to call and tell me every time someone looks cross-eyed at her. Or when her husband don't flush." Over her shoulder, she yells back at me, "Don't ever complain about your kids not talking to you. It's highly overrated."

After a couple bites, I'm in love. Her pies are straight from heaven. I have no idea what this pie is made of, some kind of berries. The crust is so good and buttery. With the hot coffee, it's about perfection.

"Mine was chocolate."

The last piece of crust sticks in my throat as I hear Peter's voice from beside me. He sits on the stool and swirls it around so he's facing me.

"I bet it was good. This is berry of some kind."

"Looks good. Save me a bite."

I swivel my head to look at him. His eyes are literally twinkling. "Just joking. I know the old crows here would really be cawing if you start feeding me from your plate."

"Peter, it's not funny. Even Anna got onto me. Folks here don't get us just being friends." I pick up the last piece of crust and put it in my mouth. Not so much because I wanted it, but in fear he'd pick it up and eat it if I left it. When I look back up at him, I can see in his eyes he knows what I'm thinking.

And he thinks it's funny.

His eyes suddenly shift behind me. "Mother. I didn't think you were coming tonight."

I turn a bit on my stool to see Missus standing next to me. "Is this something you two cooked up?"

Again, someone accusing me of cooking. Although I don't think Missus means in the kitchen. "So now Anna and Will might not move in with us, but settle for that shack you're trying to fix up?"

"Mother, it was just an idea," Peter says. Then with the twinkle back in place he adds, "Carolina checked out the second floor last night and thought it was fine. Didn't you?"

"Of course it's fine. But I didn't know any—"

"You two are always cooking up something together. First the ghost up at your place, Carolina, and now this."

"Wait, the ghost up at my place wasn't my idea. That was you. All you."

She waves her hand at me. "My great-grandchild will be sleeping under my roof. Make no mistake about that." She crosses her arms before whirling around and dismissing us both. Ruby comes up and leans on the counter behind me.

"Well, looks like y'all have been put on notice. No more fooling around."

Peter just shrugs and raises his hands in innocence. I scoop up the change laying on the counter and shove it in my jeans pocket as I stand and shake my head at Ruby. "No tip for you. And maybe I will start going to Jordan's. Lots less crowded down there, I bet."

I meet Susan coming in when I open Ruby's front door, and I ask, "Want to walk down to MoonShots? I hear the older kids are all down there. Grant and Bryan are spending the night at

Matt's, and his mom and dad are back there in the booth."
We both wave at the boys and at Matt's mom and dad, then
walk out the door and down the sidewalk. She pulls down the
sleeves of her shirt, she's always freezing. Must come with
being so skinny.

I ask, "Did Laney catch up with you at the game?"

"Yeah, she sure was in a bad mood."

"Yeah, I caught a bit of that before she went looking for you.
She told Beau she was hungover."

"Hungover? Really? She did seem like she didn't feel good."

"But weren't the girls all over there last night late? Would
she drink that much with them there?"

Susan stops. "You're right. And I talked to her around 10:30,
and she sounded fine." We continue walking and then slow as
we survey the insides of the book and florist shop. Shannon
has little lights left on in her side, but the book side is dark and
cluttered. Like a junk store, which is what Gertie said. Then as
we reach the windows of MoonShots we stop again and look
inside.

There are a couple tables of teenagers, but they don't look
to be having that much fun. Of course, it was their friends who
lost the game earlier. Susie Mae is there, but Savannah and
Laney's girls aren't.

"Looks like the younger high schoolers," Susan says. Then
she turns to me. "Hey, I have an idea. Let's go check out Laney's
new B&B tomorrow. You free?"

"Absolutely. That's a great idea."

"Maybe it's not as wonderful as she keeps telling us it is.
Maybe that's why she's so grumpy."

"Speaking of grumpy," I say with a nod inside the coffee
shop, "look at Jordan."

She has her blonde hair pulled back in a little ponytail, but
it doesn't look as smooth and polished as it used to. Her face
has lost the polished look, too. She's still beautiful, but her face

pulls downward, helped along by her mouth. The crispness which made her stand out is gone. She looks tired.

"Oh, fudge, we've Chancified her," I say.

Susan bends her head toward me. "And what does that mean?"

"You know, made her normal. Tired, grumpy, frazzled."

"You're saying that's how we are?" Susan looks for a moment at her reflection in the window, then focuses on Jordan. "Yeah, you're right. I didn't think it was possible for her to look normal, did you?"

"Guess not. I figured she was like Laney and would defy the odds to stay looking good."

"Now I am getting worried about my sister. She has gotten frumpier lately, hasn't she?" Susan turns toward me. "And if you ever tell her I said that, I'll deny it to the moon and back."

As a group of kids leave, we hold open the door as they mumble hello's to us, and then they head across the street to the park. We enter into the brightness.

"Mom, can Carrie spend the night?" Susie Mae asks before the door even closes behind us.

"Sure, if it's okay with her mom."

"It is," the girl beside Susie Mae says without even looking up from her phone. "I just texted her."

Susan looks at the table and then leans to look in her daughter's cup. "I'll be heading home in a just a minute. You want to ride with me or get a ride later?"

The girls glance at each other and shrug. "We'll go with you."

While they talk, I wander to the counter. "Hey, Jordan. So you're selling food?"

She stands with one hand on her hip and even her slump is no longer stylish but looks like any normal tired person. Of course, she is still 5'10" and supermodel thin.

"I guess you can call it food. It's not very good, not like the fresh pastries we can get back home. And what's up with being open at odd hours? The kids working today said if Ruby was opening we had to. I didn't make more than a handful of sales tonight. What a waste of time."

Susan looks at the pastry case as she walks up. "Were those frozen?"

Jordan doesn't answer, just starts ringing up the register. "Time to close."

Susan and I make eye contact, and we both frown. Jordan looks even more beatdown up close.

"Wanna take a ride with us tomorrow?" Susan asks, and I know she's doing it as an olive branch. "Kind of a quick road trip?"

"Really?" There's a bit of a spark in the young woman's eyes, and she stands taller. "I'd love to get out of this place. This store. This town. It's dead here once the kids go to school in the mornings. This was a stupid place for a MoonShots. We're losing our ass—" She breaks off when Susan's and my eyes widen. "Oh, that's right. No cussing either. God, this place is a nightmare." She closes her eyes and holds her hand up to us. "I know. Gosh. Gosh, this place is a nightmare." She lifts the money drawer out of the register and takes it back to the safe.

"Really?" I whisper to Susan. "We're taking her?"

Susan scrunches up her nose. "Well, it seemed like a good idea for a minute."

Jordan stomps back toward us. "What time? You want to just come by here? Get a coffee for the road? I'll get someone to fill in for me, or maybe I'll just shut it down. Not like Diego would see a difference in the receipts."

"Ten?" Susan says looking at me. I nod, and she swivels back to Jordan. But Jordan has walked to the end of the counter and headed toward the few kids sitting at the table where Susie Mae and Carrie still are.

"I'm closing, kids." She picks up the cups and napkins and doesn't even glance at the startled faces. The kids don't waste time leaving.

"See you at ten," she says as she dumps the garbage in the can beside the counter. She pauses at the light switch long enough to turn off the overhead lights and leave us in semi-darkness. She ignores us as she continues closing down, and with a quick look at each other, we join the kids milling around on the sidewalk.

Susie Mae looks behind us. "Jordan kicked y'all out too? She's in a bad mood lately. Kinda glad I didn't get a job here now."

I turn the opposite way from them, and Susan calls out to me, "Where are you parked?"

"Oh, down here. Everything was full when I got here earlier."

Susan scans the few cars left near the square, and then I see her realize where my car is. "Parked at Peter's?"

"It was the only place."

Susie Mae turns to walk backwards, and I can't see her grin in the dark, but I can hear it in her words. "Mr. Peter has a crush on you!"

Susan just waves her hand at her daughter and gives me a 'told you so' look. Okay, I couldn't actually see her look, but that is her specialty.

Chapter 28

"Do we have to take these backroads?" My perch in the back seat of Griffin's little car is fine, except my stomach is queasy from all the swoops we're making.

Susan glances over her shoulder. "They can truly only be considered back roads if there is a bigger road to take. This is the highway between Chancey and Collinswood, no back road at all."

"Reminds me why I never go home to Illinois. Not the curves or hills, but the nothingness. Hard to imagine there could be this much nothing." Jordan stretches her legs as much as she can, but even in the front seat, there's little room. "This is your husband's car, you said?"

"Yeah, he needed my van to pick up gardening stuff when he's down in Marietta this afternoon." Susan tilts her head towards the backseat. "How's your garden coming, Carolina?"

"Okay, I guess. Got some stuff planted, so just wait and see now."

As we swoop around another looping curve of grass and patches of tiny purple, yellow, and white flowers, the conversation lags. We sip our coffees in their purple MoonShots cups and don't talk. I watch the play of the sun on the hills and trees. The morning air was mild as we gathered at MoonShots, but by time we left the store, the morning shadows and mildness were gone. You can practically hear everything growing. Okay, enough quiet.

"So you just closed the store. Is that really going to be okay?" I ask the front seat passenger.

Jordan doesn't seem as eager to relinquish the quiet, but since Susan (I'm sure) also wants to hear the answer to my question, no one says anything. We just wait her out.

"I've done everything Diego wanted," she says. "Everything. Moved here without complaining, much. I haven't called him or the girls. Only talked bad about his mother when no one was around. Haven't gotten drunk, or been on TMZ after they got tired of hanging around after the tornado, or screwed around, or gotten together with my friends. Everything. Yet has he forgiven me? Let me talk to my daughters? Given me any idea of when I get out of this prison? No. Nothing. Nada. So why should I keep jumping through his hoops?"

"Sounds like he holds all the cards," Susan says.

"Yep, every damn one of them. Oops, sorry for saying 'damn.' Bless my heart."

I speak up from the back seat. "You can't bless your own heart. But, you know, Diego seemed nice when he was here. He's probably just hurt and worried about the girls. And you."

Jordan sighs. "I know. That's why I agreed to everything. You ladies won't understand this, but until you think you're losing everything, you don't really know what you have."

Susan dips her head to meet my eyes in the rearview mirror. "We might know a bit more about that than you think." She looks back at the road. "Simple places don't always mean simple lives."

"Well, New York is anything but simple. I know there are dozens of beautiful women throwing themselves at him, and here I am stuck in the boondocks. You saw how gorgeous he is."

From the backseat, I agree. "I think he's the best looking

man I've ever seen. Can I ask you what you could possibly have seen in another guy? I always wonder that when some beautiful celebrity gets cheated on. If someone like Halle Berry can be cheated on, how does *anyone* stand a chance keeping a man?"

Jordan shakes her head. "I have no idea. It just gets out of hand, and before you know it, you've gone too far."

Susan brakes the car, and we slide to a stop at a red light in the middle of nowhere. As the sound of the motor fades, a silence fills the car, and I remember sitting at the winery last winter with Peter. All the times it could've gone further. And Jackson with Carter all day when she was so unhappy in her marriage. What seems so real and visible suddenly appears fragile and susceptible.

Susan clears her throat as the light turns green, and she accelerates the car. "My lies almost ruined my relationship with Griffin. We're still working on it. I wasn't cheating with another man, but keeping lies for my daughter was a type of cheating. I forgot Griffin was supposed to come first."

"Hey, that's like something Diego said when he was here," Jordan says as she sits up straight. "That he had to take some of the blame, as he'd not put me first. Said he wanted to change." Her voice falls, and she sits back slowly.

"Well, that sounds good," I prompt as she doesn't continue. "What did you say?"

She pulls in a deep breath and lets it out slowly before answering. "I called him a liar and told him he was just trying to play the saint."

And the silence is back.

"I don't understand wanting to stay in someone's house,"

Jordan whispers. "Especially their old house."

Susan shushes her, adding, "Remember who you're with," and she motions at me with her shoulder.

"Yeah, but yours is about trains. Don't understand that either, but it's at least a reason."

We found the Charming House B&B and are now standing at the front door. We've rung the doorbell, tried the door knob, even peeked around the corners to see if there was anyone in the side yard.

Jordan pushes past Susan and bangs on the door with her fist.

"Jordan! Stop that," I say as I pull her back and away from the big wooden door. "You're going to knock it down."

But she does get results. The door opens. Flies open actually. And an old man sticks his head out of the door. "What's going on? I was coming, takes a bit to get down the stairs."

"We're sorry," Susan says. "We weren't sure if you were open."

"You lookin' for a place to stay? We got one room that's ready." He looks us over. "But y'all'd probably want separate beds. Only got one bed in that room. Drat, that Mrs. Conner, she's supposed to have gotten us up and running by now. Y'all come on in."

He turns inside as he motions for us to enter. We look at each other at the dratting of Laney and follow him into the dark room.

He goes to a big, old-fashioned desk with lots of cubby holes and starts shuffling through the stacks of papers there. "I can't make head nor tails of all this. Probably best if you ladies just go find somewhere else to stay."

Susan pats his arm, but before she can say anything, Jordan steps up. "When are you supposed to open? Can we just take a look around? We're not interested in staying right now, we're checking out places for an event later this year."

He looks up at her, and as she shifts her weight to lean on her other hip, she flips her blonde hair and tilts her head to more pointedly fix her eyes on his.

"Oh, yes, ma'am. No problem with that. Just follow me." He leads us back into the kitchen, which is dark, because there are curtains pulled on the windows. "This was all my wife Jean's dream. Move to the mountains and open a B&B. Who knew it would be so much work?" We follow him up a narrow set of back stairs. At the top, we walk down a wide hallway as he points out non-descript bedroom after non-descript bedroom. The only one available, and fully furnished, is just as non-descript as the others but with furniture and bedding. At the end of the hall, we are still following him as we come down the front staircase.

Back at the front door, our tour is complete, and he's not mentioned Laney again. Just his wife, but I can't tell if his wife is alive, or sick, or what. So finally, taking a page out of Jordan's book, I just ask.

"She's over to the hospital to visit Mrs. Conner. Mrs. Conner, that's our manager, took sick. She's not gotten much done round here, and then this morning she flat out faints right there in the living room." The man shakes his head. "We ain't ever going to open."

Susan gasps and turns for the door. I motion for Jordan to follow her outside. "Which hospital?"

"Oh, the one out at the highway. It's that new place. Highway toward Chancey."

It clicks, and I remember passing a medical place, so I shake his hand and rush out. Jordan is in the back seat, and Susan is in the passenger's seat. They've left the driver's door open for me. I slide in and put on my seatbelt.

Susan has her phone out. "I don't have any messages. I'm calling Laney's cell." She points me in the right direction, but when she says, "Laney?" I hit the brake and pull to the side of the neighborhood street.

"Laney, where are you?"

We can hear Laney's voice as she talks and talks. I'm turned halfway in my seat looking at Susan, and Jordan is pushed up right behind Susan's seat. "Okay, then you better go. See you later," Susan says. Then she hangs up the call, and her hand holding the phone falls to her lap.

"What did she say?" I ask. "Is she okay?"

Susan grits her teeth. "She's at work, she said. They have workmen at her B&B, and she's having to direct their every move. She can't talk right now because she's expecting an inspector there any minute."

Jordan flops back in her seat. "And you just let her get away with lying? This place is lousy with people not saying what they really mean."

"She said nothing about fainting? Or going to the hospital?"

Susan shakes her head. Then she points at the stop sign ahead of us. "At the corner, turn left. Let's go downtown and check it out. I think there's a soda fountain in an old drugstore where we can get a sandwich."

We find the drugstore. It smells like medicine underneath, but over that is the smell of cooking. Frying butter, mostly. There are stools along the soda fountain, and a few tables sit up right next to the drugstore aisles. It's early for lunch so we have our choice of seats.

We sit at one of the tables, and the girl behind the counter is there before we get settled.

"Here's today's lunch menu. Can I get you something to drink?" She hands us handwritten sheets of paper. Jordan tells her water, I agree with that, and Susan orders a Coke.

Jordan never looked up at the girl, and so she's read the entire menu by time the girl heads off to get our drinks. "Grilled Cheese, Grilled Cheese with Ham, Ham and Cheese Sandwich, or," she flips the paper over, "nope, that's it."

We laugh as we look at the back and see that that truly is the entire menu. "This is worse than Ruby's," I say.

When the girl brings our drinks, she explains. "Our cook

retired last week, and so the owner is just trying to muddle through until we find someone. Luckily everyone likes her grilled cheese pretty good. And there's nowhere else to eat until you get near the interstate."

Jordan says she'll take a grilled cheese and ham, Susan asks for the same, and I just take the plain grilled cheese.

"So, what do you think is going on with Laney?" I ask.

Susan flings her hands off the table a bit. "Who knows? Probably dieting again and hasn't eaten anything in a couple days. That's how she always lost weight for pageants. She sounded just fine. Hope she's not sick."

Jordan takes a sip of her water after examining the glass for smudges and dirt. "Not sure how her B&B is going to go. This place seems deader than Chancey and not nearly as cute."

"I agree. Too many convenience stores and no real downtown area. And comparing our B&B to that one…" I grimace. "No way. It's too cluttered and dark. Smelled dingy, too."

"Knowing my sister, she's bitten off more than she can chew, and she doesn't want anyone to know," Susan says. "That's partly why I didn't call her out. No reason to rub her nose in it."

Jordan grins. "Plus, she'd just lie some more."

I raise my water glass to clink it with Jordan's. "Ma'am, you are figuring out the South just fine."

Our waitress drops off three bags of potato chips and then lifts plates from the bar behind her, and we see why the menu can be so limited. The bread is thick, and the cheese is, too, gooey and glistening. The ham on Susan and Jordan's sandwiches is not from a package. I bite into my sandwich, and the crispness of the outside gives way to soft, homemade taste. This may be the best grilled cheese I've ever eaten.

We don't talk as we all three eat. We ummm, ahhhh, and shake our heads in wonder. By the time, we finish there isn't an empty seat, and the room is buzzing.

"Everything good here?" the girl asks as she walks past the

end of our table. We nod as she says over her shoulder, "When you're ready to pay, just tell the man at the register up front what you had."

"This lady could make a fortune in Manhattan." Jordan wipes her hands and drops her wadded napkin onto her plate. "Guess we should make some room for those folks." A line had formed through the drug store.

"Looks like she's making her fortune here, and she doesn't have to live in New York," Susan says.

Jordan blinks at Susan in disbelief. "Do you people not know that most of the world would give anything to live in New York City? Get out of these little towns like this?"

Susan steps to the counter and pulls out her change purse. "I love little towns like this and like Chancey."

"You get it, don't you, Carolina?" Jordan asks as she turns around to me, where I'm trying to stay out of the conversation. "Don't small towns make you feel suffocated? Like trying to live in a box? Or instead of a box, more like a cage?"

I shrug and step back to pick up a package of gum as the cashier shows up. We pay, and as I'm the last one to leave the store, I think about it. How do I feel about small towns? Funny, I used to know for sure that I hated them. I'm not so sure anymore.

Huh. Funny.

Chapter 29

A warm car, full stomach, and more silence meant a little dozing for me in the back seat on the way back to Chancey. As we are looping around the final curves into town, I fully wake up and sit up straight. The way Jordan's head is leaning, I think she's napping, too. Susan smiles at me in the rearview mirror. Pulling my phone out of my purse, I see that Patty has called me a couple times, so I call her back.

"Hey, what's up?"

"Can you come to the bookstore?" she asks.

"Sure. We'll be there in a bit."

"Who's 'we'?"

"Me, Susan, and Jordan."

"Jordan's with you? We thought she'd run off."

"Run off? Where would she run off to? Why were you looking for Jordan?"

Patty doesn't say anything for a bit, then with a sigh, says, "Bring her, too. Jordan, not Susan. I mean, Susan can come if she wants, but you don't have to bring her. But bring Jordan. Okay, bye." And she hangs up.

Jordan is awake. "Who's looking for me?"

"Patty, I guess. Probably folks wondering why MoonShots was closed."

She pulls at a crick in her neck. "Yeah, maybe it wasn't a great idea to just close it like that, but I had to get away."

Susan pulls the car up to the square and pulls into an angled spot on the side. We gather our purses and climb out of the little car. MoonShots being dark looks strange. Funny how quickly I've become used to it being there, clean and well-lit. As we near the bookshop, we can see people inside, but the afternoon sun makes it hard to see more than just shapes. Susan pulls open the door and steps back for me and Jordan to enter.

"Maaaaamaaaa!" squeals burst out, and Jordan is hit with a little body. Looking up there is the cutest toddler headed our way also. She's also squealing, but not in real words. Susan and I edge in behind Jordan, who's now bent down and wrapped around the first child. The toddler reaches them and is enfolded in her embrace.

Patty meets me and Susan as we move around the huddle and into the store. Stepping away from Jordan and her girls squeals, we hear crying. Patty grimaces at me, then moves to the side so I can see the couch in the bookstore. Anna sits there, huddled over and sobbing. Patty just shrugs and grimaces again, so I go over to sit beside the young woman. It's rather noisy and confusing, but as the little girls calm down, Jordan brings them over to the sitting area. She hesitates when she realizes Anna is crying.

"Oh, what's wrong?" Jordan asks as she sinks into the chair across from us and the girls arrange themselves in her lap.

Anna shakes her head, but doesn't look up. Patty and Susan move to stand behind the couch. Patty is wringing her hands, and Susan is looking at her phone.

"Patty," I ask, "What's going on?"

"Anna and Missus got in a big fight about the wedding. Big fight. Momma just went to talk to Missus."

Oh, no. Gertie doesn't exactly talk, she more demands, belittles, then dismisses. Not sure that's going to go over well with Mrs. Shermania Bedwell. But it's hard to worry about that while looking at Jordan. It's as if her daughters have pumped her up, like air does an inflatable bouncy house. Everything about her looks full and alive. I grin inwardly. Diego will know she needs to be with her girls when he sees her like this.

Susan is still scowling and typing on her phone. Patty sits on the arm of the couch and pats Anna's back. My arm is still around her, and her crying has quieted. In the excitement of seeing their mother, the little girls hadn't noticed Anna at first, but now they are staring at her with sober faces. So, I interject, "Girls, have you seen your mommy's apartment?"

The oldest one shakes her head for both of them. I lift my arm from around Anna and stand up. "Hi, I'm Miss Carolina," I say as I bend and offer a hand to the little girl with long, blonde curls.

She lifts her chin and extends her hand. Jordan prompts her. "Say 'hi' and tell Carolina your name."

"I'm Francie. This is Carly. She's still a baby."

Carly tucks her little round face into her sister's back. All that's left poking out is her brown hair, held back from her face with a blue ribbon. Francie leans back against her mother, making Carly pull her head out.

"Hi, Carly. You both sure are pretty. Want to go see your mommy's apartment?"

"Yeah, girls. Let's get up," Jordan says as she pushes out of the chair, and the girls stand on the floor at her feet. "Where's your daddy?" she asks. The girls just shrug, and Jordan looks up at Patty, who, being about as helpful as a couple toddlers, shrugs also.

Francie looks at the floor, but Carly grins up at her mother and yells, "Cici!"

Jordan returns her grin for a moment, then her grin slides away. "Cici?" She bends to look at Francie and works on refixing her grin. "Francie, honey, Cici is here with you?"

Francie tucks her lips together and nods. Carly bobs up and

205

down and yells "Cici, Cici," over and over. Jordan stands back up, looks down at herself, then back up at Patty. "My mother-in-law brought the girls?"

Patty nods, and Jordan steps away from her daughters. "Look at me. I'm wearing yoga pants, yoga pants for God's sake! I should've known she'd wait until I was at my breaking point and then swoop in. Oh, no. What was I thinking?"

Carly's bops have stopped, and both girls are still, staring at their mother as she melts down and keeps backing away from them. She's halfway to the back door, when she seems to have remembered them. "Patty, watch the girls. I have to go change." She turns and dashes toward the back.

She's almost to the door when I catch up with her. I grab her upper arm and pull close to her. "What is going on? You haven't seen your daughters in weeks, and you're going to change clothes and leave them down here? Don't look back at them right now, because you are kind of crazy. You need to calm down, go back in there, and take care of your children. To hell with this Cici person."

She shakes off my hand, takes a deep breath, and then looks around. I also turn and see that Susan has pulled Francie and Carly back into the chair and onto her lap. The brown and blonde heads are bent together watching something Susan is showing them on her phone.

Jordan's smirk, the one she graced us with plenty when she first arrived here, is back. She pulls herself up and looks much more than just several inches taller than me. "My children are fine. Now, I need to get dressed and go meet my mother-in-law." She jerks away from me. "I may be crazy, but if she finds me in yoga pants with a ponytail out in public, my life is over. I will never get out of this hell hole." She pulls open the back door and says before it closes, "Tell Susan thanks. I'll get the kids later."

When I turn around, Patty is motioning me over to the counter on the florist side of the shop, where Shannon is standing, watching the show.

"Patty, what is going on here?" I demand.

"Well, that Cici lady showed up with Francie and Carly about half an hour ago. She came in here because she wanted to know why MoonShots was closed. That's when we thought Jordan had run off. Then she left the girls here with me and Shannon and Mama, like Jordan just did, and about that time Anna came running in crying about not doing the wedding at all. That she was sorry she ever came here in the first place. That's when my mama stormed out of here headed to Missus's. And all I could think to do was to call you. I sure am glad you were close."

Her relief is evident. And scary. What does she think I'm going to do? Shannon is busy arranging ferns in a piece of green oasis and listening. Anna is still on the couch, but she's mesmerized by whatever the girls are doing on Susan's phone and she's no longer crying. Susan sneaks a peek at me and widens her eyes for that moment our eyes meet.

Before I can think of anything to do, Anna gets up and comes over to where we are standing. She leans back against the counter, watching the girls and Susan. "How old do you think the littlest one is?"

Patty answers, "Think Jordan said she's two."

Anna rubs her belly, only a little mound. "So before I turn twenty I'll have one like that?"

Her fear comes through her words, and I slip my arm around her waist. "Not like that, but yours. Yours and Will's baby. But that's a ways off, it'll be tiny first, and you'll be so in love with him or her, you won't have any room to be scared." Of course, I don't tell her that size has nothing to do with how hard a baby is. Okay, another lie. Sue me.

"Maybe this is why the wedding is so hard to get together. Maybe we're not supposed to be married, or have a baby. I can adopt it out and everything goes back to normal, right?" She first looks at Patty, who, remind me to kill her later, simply nods.

I don't give her a chance to look at me. I flip around in front of her. "No, you need to just, um, you need to go home. No, you need to…" Looking around, my glance falls on the steps to Patty's apartment. "You need to go upstairs. Lie down and rest." I push her toward the stairs. "Patty, go get her settled, and then you come right back down. Wait, Andy's not up there, is he?"

"No, he's off at an estate sale on the other side of Dalton."

"Good," I nod. "You two go on up. Anna, we'll talk about all this later, but now you need to rest."

As they walk up the old staircase, I text Will to call me, and then put the phone in my pocket. I smile at Shannon, and she laughs. "Things sure weren't this interesting before the bookstore moved in."

"Glad we can provide free entertainment for you," I say.

Susan lifts the girls off her lap and stands up as I approach her. She turns off her phone before sliding it into her jeans pocket. "Sorry, but I have to go. Staff meeting at church. I'm already running late. Bye girls, I'll see you later." I watch her dart out the front door and look back down to big eyes and solemn faces.

"Are you girls hungry? Let's go get a muffin." Usually I wouldn't take off to another location with children I've just met, but I honestly don't think anyone will care.

Besides, I need coffee, and I need chocolate.

CHAPTER 30

The spinning stools at Ruby's are a hit. Francie twirls hers from one side to the other, in between drinking her milk and eating the muffins Ruby supplies her with. Carly is too small to hold on by herself, so she rides on whoever's lap she can beg herself. Of course, with that big grin and dark brown eyes, it's not too hard to find an available lap.

Savannah stuck her head in long enough to see that me and the girls were there and to say she'd been sent to find us by Jordan when she arrived to work at MoonShots after school. Ruby's isn't usually open this late in the day, but everyone's talking about the showdown between Missus and Gertie that took place on Missus' front porch earlier. As with all other area happenings, Ruby says if people are going to be hanging around talking, they might as well be buying her muffins and coffee.

So far, the most seemingly accurate portrayal of Missus vs. Gertie is from the leaders of the Brownie troop which was meeting in the gazebo at the time. For their last meeting before summer, they gathered for a picnic in the park. As soon as their little charges got picked up, the two leaders headed straight to Ruby's with the full story.

The two women are young and cute, and accented by their shining eyes, glossed lips, and loud whispers, we get the story.

Apparently, Missus wouldn't invite Gertie inside her house. They couldn't rightly hear what all Missus was saying, but Gertie, who is loud anyway, was yelling most of the time. What it boiled down to is that Gertie and Missus must've not liked each other back when they were in school. Their argument left the topic of the wedding real quick and moved to their daddies and, believe it or not, whether Missus stole the Miss Whitten County beauty pageant. (At this point of the story, my stomach got a bit upset because FM flat out told me he threw the pageant for Missus. He was one of the judges, and he fell for his future wife there. Even told me that Missus' daddy gave him money to throw it.) Those of us too new to Chancey, or too young to remember, can't imagine Gertie being in a beauty pageant, but Ruby assures the whole restaurant that Gertie Samson was a stunner. "Long red hair, full-figured like a World War Two pin-up, and that husky voice that says she just got out of bed," she says with a nod.

At this point someone brought up the picture (a life-size picture I should add) of Missus in her crown and sash, which is front and center of FM and Missus' front hall. It's hideous. Nightmare hideous. Even worse than looking at it is how proud the two of them are of it. They point it out and make you comment on it. So, since we can all see how Missus looked, and now hear how Gertie looked, it's not hard to imagine that someone cheated on Missus' behalf.

After almost an hour at Ruby's, the little Moon girls are ready to move on from muffins and spinning stools and so am I. "C'mon, girls. Tell Ruby 'bye' so we can go find your mama and grandma."

Francie lets herself off the stool and reaches for my hand. "No, we can't call Cici 'grandma' or *abuela*. It's not allowed."

Carly grins and shakes her head like her big sister is doing. "No no no."

Ruby has brought me wet paper towels to wipe off the girls'

hands and mouth, so I'm bent down doing that as the door opens again. I hear Carly shout, "Cici!"

Great, couldn't she just stay in MoonShots? Like we don't have enough Queen Bee juice flying around town with Missus and Gertie in full attack mode. I wad up the wet paper towels in my hand and straighten up to greet Diego's mother. I know what she looks like from the news stories after the tornado and the media's discovery of Jordan.

"Hello," I say. "You must be Mrs. Moon."

"Sentora. Mr. Moon is my deceased husband. Francie, Carly, come with Cici." She doesn't reach out a hand to them, but simply turns around and walks toward the door. Both children follow her. Behind them, we all share questioning looks. Okay, some are not questioning, just down right judgy.

"Ma'am?" I say, as I walk along behind the girls. She doesn't turn around until she's at the door. Her granddaughters stop and stand beside her. I hold out my hand. "Hello, I'm Carolina Jessup. I was watching Carly and Francie for your daughter-in-law."

She looks past me to the counter. "Are you also the one that allowed them to eat here?"

"Well, yeah. They had a muffin and some milk."

With an exaggerated sigh, she says, "Of course they did. Francie, did you ask as I've taught you?"

Francie bows her head. "No, Cici."

I reach down to touch the bent blonde head. "She was a perfect little lady." The girl and I exchange smiles.

Cici's voice is ice cold. "A perfect little lady who probably just drank whole milk. Possibly straight from some cow tied out back. And I'm sure the term 'gluten free' means absolutely nothing here."

Uh oh.

"Now you just wait a cotton-pickin' minute," Ruby says from behind the counter.

I reach behind Cici and pull open the door. "Let's go," I say. And I push them out the door. By time the door shuts behind me, Cici has started down the sidewalk. Francie has taken Carly's hand, and they are following their grandmother. I catch up and take Carly's other hand. I'm rewarded with a big grin, and it hits me like it did Anna this morning. We're getting one of these!

We march past the bookstore/florist, and I only see Shannon inside. I don't know where Patty and Anna are. At Moonshots, we follow the first Mrs. Moon inside.

Jordan has regained her previous polish. Her hair is slick and hanging on either side of her face. Her makeup is perfect; even her lips are lined, like you see in a magazine. She has on black pants which end in beautiful black pumps with a red sole—which means designer something, right?

Jordan stands beside the end of the counter where the new pastry case sits. She has perfect posture, and her aqua blue blouse wraps around her slim body. The color matches her eyes, which a quick look confirms to be as cold as ice chips.

Carly pulls away from our hands and runs, clapping, to her mother. Jordan smiles at her and softens her gaze. She pats her younger daughter's brown curls. The baby is itching to be held, but no one picks her up. However, she doesn't make a fuss. Just reaches out to lay her little dimpled hand on her mother's pant leg. Francie and I join the two of them, but the older girl doesn't say anything. She just stands beside me, watching. Watching everything.

Jordan, still patting Carly's head, says, "So I see you met Carolina. She's the owner of the local bed and breakfast."

Mrs. Sentora turns to look at me again, this time up and down. Jeans, bushy hair, a polo shirt, and slide-on tennis shoes apparently don't impress her. "So that's who you are. My son enjoyed his stay at your establishment, but I believe he may have oversold its attributes." She turns back to Jordan. "Where is the closest *good* hotel?" And I am not making up her emphasis on the word "good."

Savannah, who's been wiping tables around us, steps up to the older woman. I see attitude in the whip of her hair, the drop of her shoulders, and the lift of her chin. "Why don't you stay here, in Jordan's beautiful apartment upstairs, and Jordan and the girls can stay at my family's *establishment*?" Good girl! I didn't raise a self-appointed princess for nothing.

Once again, Mrs. Sentora does the up and down, but apparently finds Savannah more appealing because she actually smiles a bit. "Excellent idea. I know every cent my son put into the apartment, so it must be livable."

So, is she saying our B&B isn't livable? I'm now with Ruby on waiting a cotton-pickin' minute, but before I can say anything, Diego's mother has walked behind the counter and left the room. Again, not one word to these beautiful girls standing here, left waiting for instructions.

Jordan looks at her daughters. "Francie, you and Carly go with Mrs. Jessup, and I'll be there later."

Excuse me, what?! "Jordan, are you serious? I have…" Then I see the girls' reflections in the shiny counter. No grins, no laughter, just waiting. Waiting for someone to send them on their way. "What a great idea!" I say as I look down and pull their hands to face me. "We'll have such fun!"

They both light up and dash toward the front door.

I follow, and my heart is breaking. They don't say goodbye to their mother, they don't even look her direction.

They are learning the lessons taught to them well.

213

"I've been put on nanny duty," Savannah says at my frown when she comes in the front door not long after Carly, Francie, and I got to Crossings. She usually doesn't get home for a couple more hours from work.

"By Jordan?"

She falls down on the couch. "Yep. Sent to help you out even though I don't really like little kids. Susie Mae wanted the job, but for some reason Mrs. Sentora, the grandmother, likes me."

Not surprised. Don't they say royal blood outs, like the princess feeling the pea under the stack of mattresses? Or birds folding their laundry if the princess happens to be poor and has to do it herself? Peasants are to be used for things like stacking mattresses and filling bird feeders.

"Where are they?" Savannah asks as she looks around for her charges.

"Taking a nap in the Orange Blossom Special room. I laid down with them and read them a story. They went out like a light. So, you really don't like kids?"

"Not really." She leans up and kicks off her tennis shoes. "What are you supposed to do with them? I mean, I don't hate them or anything, but they seem kind of pointless to me."

She stands up and walks barefooted into the kitchen. She's

been home maybe all of three minutes, and she's left her shoes, pocketbook, jacket, book bag and probably a bunch of hair (teenage girls shed worse than dogs) in her wake. Maybe she has a point about kids.

"Jordan say when she'll be getting back here?"

"Oh, yeah." She comes back into the living room as she opens a Little Debbie oatmeal pie. "They're going to eat supper up here."

"Who? The girls?" I think I hear something from the B&B area, so I stand up.

Savannah nods, but adds just as I'm stepping out of the room. "And Jordan and Cici."

"What?" I lean back into the living room. "But I don't want them all eating here. What would I cook? Who invited them?"

She shrugs and takes another bite. "Nobody, I guess. I get the feeling Cici doesn't wait to be invited." She reaches for the remote control and turns the TV on.

Turning back towards the B&B hall, I remember. "Wait, you go check on the girls. You're getting paid. Besides, I have to think about supper now."

In the kitchen, my brain is as frozen as all the food I'm staring at. I have to cook for me and Savannah and Bryan, so I can just add to that. No need for anything fancy. But corndogs? Sandwiches? Grilled cheese? Fish sticks? None of that will work. Oh, I know. Breakfast for dinner.

There's two pounds of ground sausage in the freezer, plenty of milk for gravy, and an extra-large bag of frozen biscuits. Everybody likes breakfast, right? As I sit the sausage out on the counter to begin thawing, I try to think of who all will be here. If I invite Gertie, she'll make the gravy. She makes amazing gravy, as we found out back at Christmas. And Will or Anna need to stop by the store and bring home another dozen eggs.

As I move around the kitchen, I realize I'm smiling. I'm kind of happy. Not sure why, but not going to fight it. Then Savannah shrieks, "Mom!" from the B&B hall.

She meets me in the dining room. "The little one pooped. It's on the sheets." She shudders and gags. "It's so gross." She turns and heads straight for the bathroom at the end of the hall. "You get them," she says as the bathroom door closes.

I turn right and the girls are sitting in the bed, looking up at me. Big eyes and solemn faces. They look scared to death. I roll my eyes and grin. "That Savannah, she's just a big baby, isn't she? Scared of poop."

Carly grins and shouts, "Poop!"

Francie shakes her head and frowns at her little sister. "We don't say words like that."

I walk to the side of the bed Carly is sitting on and put my face next to hers, so we are both looking at her sister. I whisper, "Poop, poop, poop." Carly giggles and whispers the same thing.

Francie thinks for a minute, then half-laughs. "Carly is a poop monster."

Carly frowns, but I tickle her under her chin and ask, "Are you a poop monster?" We all laugh, and then Francie sees Savannah standing at the door. Sounding more like her grandmother than ever, she demands, "Are you scared of poop?"

Even Savannah has to laugh at that. I take Carly into the bathroom as I give instructions for Savannah to strip the bed, which really didn't have anything but a tiny stain, and for Francie to bring me Carly's bag from the living room.

Clean and fresh, the tiny girl is a perfect bundle of snuggles as I carry her into the kitchen. I think examine the B&B calendar in my head as we pass through the B&B hallway. The Southern Crescent room is open, but only for one night. Tomorrow we have a couple coming who are staying in that room through the weekend, so hopefully Cici will be headed back north because the Orange Blossom Special room is also booked out.

Responding to my texts earlier, Gertie has arrived and is changing clothes in the Chessie room, which she now shares with Patty. Now, that Patty's apartment above the bookstore is Andy's bachelor pad. Gertie has her hold on the Chessie room until after the double wedding, which is why I have no problem asking her to come make gravy.

I set Carly in one of the kitchen chairs, and she immediately scrambles up to her knees so she can see into the bowl of eggs Francie is stirring on the corner of the table. It's a big bowl, with only three eggs in the bottom of it. Someone here knows how to keep a little one occupied without too much risk.

Patty is slicing sausage patties and laying them in a frying pan on the stove. Moving to look out the French doors to the deck, I watch Anna peeling apples and entertaining several bees. She looks as if she doesn't realize the bees are there, she's thinking so hard. Somehow, I don't think she's focusing that hard on peeling apples. Poor thing.

Will makes a racket as he comes in the front door with a grocery sack in his hand. He lifts it toward me. "You texted me to pick up eggs?"

I meet him at the couch, take the bag, and say, "I need to talk to you. On the porch." I put the bag with two cartons of eggs beside Patty on the counter. "I'll be right back."

A wave of heat hits me as I open the front door. "Wow, it feels even warmer than it did earlier."

My oldest pulls at his dress shirt. "I'm not sure how I'm going to handle the sweat on the car lot this summer. I was soaked through by time I left at five. It was church night, so the dealership closed early. What do you need?" he asks as he sits in the farthest rocking chair, the one from which you can see the train bridge and the river.

I sit down next to him. "Anna was distraught this afternoon. Did you talk to her?"

He squints. "Yeah, some. Guess her grandmother was really getting to her. But she's fine now."

"Really? She's fine?"

He shrugs, dismissing the question. "Yeah. So, it looks like there's a crowd for dinner. Who all's coming?"

"Jordan, and her mother-in-law is in town with Jordan and Diego's little girls. And Gertie and Patty. Gertie's making gravy." I shake my head and get back on topic. "You know, Anna seemed to be upset seeing Jordan's littlest one, Carly. She's a toddler. Honey, Anna's had to deal with a lot all of a sudden, facing becoming a mother."

"Mom, quit worrying. She's fine. She's tough. Believe me, this is what she's always wanted." He stands up. "I've got to get out of these clothes, and I'm starving." The open door lets out the smell of sausage cooking before he finishes talking, and he's gone before I can say anything else.

"Everything's fine, and I'm starving." Sounds like the title for a bestselling Husband Manual. I think of the sub-title grimly, as I stand from my rocking chair: "How to never have sex again."

Anyone surprised to learn Cici thinks biscuits and gravy is disgusting? Or that she'd never seen gravy that color? Gertie was just as unimpressed with my frozen biscuits. Anna didn't get the apples cooked enough and put in too much cinnamon and no sugar, so they weren't really edible. She went crying upstairs. Jordan declared the entire meal unsuitable for her girls to eat as she pointed around the table: starch, starch, fat. Starch, starch, fat. Her own version of duck, duck, goose, I believe. She gave the girls scrambled eggs only and that was okay until Francie remembered that eggs are baby chickens. She then also cried. Carly then cried because, well, she's two, and the only one with a valid excuse, in my opinion. Will, Savannah, Bryan, and I ate well until Jordan barked at Savannah that she wasn't

being paid to sit around stuffing her face when the girls needed
to be bathed and put to bed.

Cici then demanded that that was Jordan's job, that since
she obviously couldn't run a coffee shop, her contribution to
the Moon family was only the children. Yes, she used the word
"only" when referring to her granddaughters, as though they
were an afterthought. Luckily, they were crying, so they didn't
notice.

Jordan left with the girls in tow. Savannah shrugged and got
up to follow them saying, "I'll give her a hand."

Still at the table, Will pushes another piece of sausage into the
middle of another biscuit and nudges his little brother. "Let's go
finish our video game." He juggles his dishes in his other hand
and dumps them in the sink, somehow without breaking them.
Bryan chugs the rest of his glass of milk, carries his dishes to
the sink, then follows Will downstairs where they've rigged up
a TV and game system in the basement.

Gertie gets up from the table. "I did most of the cooking.
Lets me out of cleaning." She also takes her plate and sets it in
the sink to join Will and Bryan's before heading to the living
room. She groans as she settles on the couch. The dulcet tones
of the TV soon follow.

Cici looks around the table and kitchen. "If I may ask, are
there any apples that were not destroyed in the making of that
mess?" She points with her nose, which luckily is quite pointed,
at the full bowl of dark brown apples. "An apple would hold me
over until I get back to town to get something to eat."

Patty shakes her head. "Mrs. Moon, there ain't nothing to
eat in town. Unless you're talking about that frozen pastry stuff
in MoonShots. I don't even think Jordan has any food in her
place. She's not real good at shopping."

The older woman closes her eyes. "I should take my
granddaughters right this minute and leave this place. It's really
not fit for… never mind. I'll go, I'll go to say good night to the

girls and then someone can give me a ride back downtown."
She does not take her plate to the sink or even push her chair in.

So, it's Patty and me for clean-up duty.

Hopefully, no one is surprised.

CHAPTER 32

"They left yesterday. Ordered some big black car from Atlanta, which pulled up in front of MoonShots. Cici instructed Carly and Francie to climb in, then she joined them, and the car drove away. That's what Savannah told me last night," I say into the phone to Laney. "Did you even get to see them? Where have you been?"

"Duh, in Collinswood at my real job. Everything over there is really coming together."

"Really?" I ask, because I can't believe Susan hasn't told her we went over there, so it's hard to say anything more.

"Yes, really. It's beautiful, and I'm loving it."

"How are you feeling?"

Then she bites my head off. "Fine. I feel fine. Why? Do you think I don't look fine?"

I sigh. "Hey, I've got to go. Guests are coming out of their room. And I think you look fine, it was just a simple question," I say and then hang up before she can accuse me of anything else.

Our new guests are coming out of their room, but I do have a couple seconds to think that I don't really know if Laney looks fine, because I'm trying to remember the last time I actually saw her. Also, it wasn't a simple question. I mean, her employer had to take her to the hospital, for crying out loud. Of course,

I'm not supposed to know that.

"Good morning," I greet our guests. "Did you sleep well?" The couple are both young, mid- to late twenties. The husband, Brad, points to the coffee pot. "Can we help ourselves?"

"Sure," I say, "but let me pour you the first cups. And there are muffins from Ruby's, a local bakery. Cream and sugar are there on the table, too."

His wife, Deena, takes a saucer from the stack and pulls it in front of her. "They look delicious. You said yesterday Ruby's is downtown? But she's only open in the mornings?"

I nod. "Unless she wants to open some other time, but that's purely on her schedule. We also have a MoonShots, and there's a Chinese restaurant out by the grocery store. We usually suggest going into Dalton for dinner. And feel free to use our refrigerator if you want to buy any snacks or drinks. We're pretty casual here."

"Good morning," Anna says coming into the kitchen. "Sorry to interrupt."

I smile. "Anna, this is Brad and Deena from South Carolina."

Anna pours herself some orange juice from the pitcher on the table. "Are there enough muffins for me to have one? I'm running a little late for class."

"Oh, are you in college?" Deena asks. "Are you a freshman? You hardly look old enough to be out of high school."

"Yes, I'm a freshman. Just taking some summer classes to get my feet wet."

Deena laughs. "Enjoy every minute. Campus life is so much fun." She nudges her husband who's taken the seat beside her, facing the outside doors. "Even though we're from the same town, we didn't start dating until we ran into each other at a frat party when I was a sophomore, and now here we are about to be parents!"

My back is to the table where the three of them sit. I lift a wooden spoon out of the container beside the stove and pretend to stir the pot sitting and drying on the stove. Oh, and I listen. Deena bubbles over. "We're here this weekend to tell our families. They don't know we're even coming to Decoration. They are going to just die!"

Brad stands up. "But first, we're going to explore around here and watch for trains. Miss Jessup, can we take our cups out to the front porch?"

"Sure," I say as I turn around. "And congratulations on the baby! When are you due?"

"Around Christmas," Deena glows. "Won't that be fun? I'll work until Thanksgiving, and then I'm quitting to work at home after the baby comes." She smooths her shirt down. "Silly, isn't it, but I can't wait to start showing more." She looks at Anna. "I know you think I'm more than silly. When I was young like you, I couldn't even imagine wanting to be married, much less having a baby, and gaining all that weight. But, one day…" She beams at Anna. "Have a great day at class, hope we can talk more. College is a blast."

Brad and Deena walk out the front door, and Anna stands up. "How old do you think she is?"

I bite my lip. "Deena? I'd think around twenty-seven, twenty-eight?"

Anna picks up her notebook and purse. She has only taken a bite of her muffin, but she walks away from the table and into the living room.

"Honey, don't you want to take the rest of your muffin to eat on the way? You're going to be hungry."

She turns to look at me, and there are tears in her eyes. "I'll have a ten-year-old when I'm her age. No fun college years, no fun job, no surprising family with the welcomed news. This really is a mistake."

"No, honey," I say as I head her direction. By time I get to her, she's at the front door. Raising her shoulder, she keeps me from hugging her.

"I have to go. I'm late," she says pushing open the front door.

The door closes, and I watch her get in her car, turn it around, and pull across the railroad tracks. Jackson will be home tonight, and we need to talk. Maybe he can get through to his son that Anna is really struggling here. I don't know who can get through to Anna. I'm too close to this. Maybe Laney or Susan. Or wonder if she'd talk to Peter.

Poor thing.

Back through the quiet house, I go into the Orange Blossom Special room and take the sheets off the bed where Jordan and the girls slept. The room is at its best in the warm sunshine. All the white makes me cold in the winter, but as the days warm up, this room feels like a garden. The sunlight picks up the orange trim on the kitschy map blanket of Florida with its bunches of oranges and bright green leaves. The trellis of white silk orange blossoms around the window mix with the green outside and look like they've stolen in through the windows. The lime green rugs we only added last month are perfect in brightening up the dull wood floors. I pull the blinds all the way up and let light fill the room before picking up my armful of sheets and heading to the basement.

"Oh! I didn't know you were down here."

"Hey," Bryan says as he twists back and forth helping his car on the screen do whatever it is he's wanting it to do.

I know talking to a boy playing a video game is a sure waste of breath, so I just go to the washer and start putting the sheets in. Eventually he either wins or loses, not sure which, but he lays back on the old couch and tosses the controller beside him. "Hey Mom, those people. Brad and that girl?"

"Deena?"

"Yeah. They said they're here to decorate? Our house?"

"What?" I pull the knob to start the washer and step over to the end of the couch. "They're not decorating anything. Well, not that I know of. They have family here, and they're going to tell them they're expecting a baby. It's a surprise."

"Yeah, and they said they're going to do it at the decorating thing."

"Oh, Decoration. Um, it's a thing where you go to where your family's buried, and you clean the tombstones and pull any weeds, then put nice flowers or wreaths on the graves. I guess that's why they call it Decoration. It's a Southern thing. Memorial Day was the holiday for the North after the Civil War. The South decided to do it the next weekend. I grew up going to where my mother's family is buried up near Chattanooga. Guess that's why Deena and Brad know their families will be around."

He picks up the controller. "Okay, just wondering."

"You want some breakfast? There's muffins left over, or you want some eggs?"

Shaking his head, he falls back into his game, and I'm dismissed. I can't believe he'll be in high school in the fall. I know how fast high school goes. With Will, I had trouble believing he'd actually been there for a full four years. It just flew. Savannah will be getting her senior pictures taken this summer, and all of her friends will be figuring out their next steps. Waiting for college acceptances, stressing out over grades, looking for real jobs.

Bryan—sprawled on the couch playing video games with his bedhead and sleepy eyes, wearing Atlanta Falcons pajama pants and no shirt—is an endangered species. Only found in this isolated habitat. Care and feeding provided by a specialized worker with a lifetime appointment.

My heart swells, and there's a catch in my throat. How did I ever get so lucky to get this job?

CHAPTER 33

"When I left here back in the winter, I told my wife we were coming to stay some weekend." The tall man speaking isn't wearing his usual dark suit, but his shirt is still starched, his khakis aren't wrinkled, and his shoes look dressy casual.

Jackson reaches out to shake his hand. "It's a real pleasure to have you both here, Mr. Reynolds."

"Oh, no. Call me Frank, and this is my wife Teresa." His arm fits around her comfortably, and they look like they could do those ads where an older couple is sitting in a pair of bathtubs watching the sunset and, well, you know.

I shake their hands after Jackson. "Please have a seat while I get the wine and some snacks."

Mr. Reynolds made this reservation at Crossings months ago, once the opening of the water park donated by Mountain Power was set for Memorial Day weekend. Apparently, everything to do with getting the power plant up and running went as smoothly as promised. Because it sits up on the bend of the river far from town, and with all the construction traffic using a road built just for it out along the railroad, folks in town haven't seen much of the activity out at the power plant site. However, we have kept up with progress on the waterfront park, and the kids, especially, can't wait for it to open. Mr. Reynolds, as president of Mountain

Power, has overseen this project from Atlanta, only staying with us that initial weekend back in February.

"What can we carry out?" Brad and Deena step into the kitchen from the B&B hallway.

"Oh, thanks," I say. "This tray is ready, glasses are already on the table, and that bowl of grapes can go. There's a pitcher of cucumber water already out there. Is that okay with you, Deena?" It's my first Friday Afternoon Wine and Cheese at Crossings. The evening shade on the deck makes it possible to sit outside even if the day's been warm. However, I'm imagining we'll have to move our Friday Afternoons inside soon due to the coming heat.

Jackson holds the door for Brad and Deena to carry the tray and bowl out, then steps inside the kitchen. "What can I get?"

"Take the wine in the chiller, and I'll bring out this one to open first." I step up to the door he's holding open, and he leans down to my ear.

"You look beautiful tonight. You've done magic with this place."

When I smile up at him, I see he means it. He truly thinks I'm great. And beautiful. Heat flushes my face, and I roll my eyes and smile even more. "Come on, we have guests."

The warm sky is a lavender backdrop to swallows and bats darting after bugs way above our heads. When the air stills, there's a chill deep inside it. Then before it can settle, a warm May breeze blows it away. Like shooing a fly out an open car window, the heat is sending any lingering coolness back up north. The heat is king now, and there will be no more nights sleeping with windows open. No more grabbing a sweater on the way out the door. No more socks or hose or boots until September. Actually, in September it won't be cold enough for socks or hose or boots, but Southerners feel the need to bend to fall fashion. And just sweat it out.

Gertie and Patty have gone back to South Georgia for the

weekend for a wedding shower. Patty has never mentioned much of anything about back home, but apparently someone there wanted to throw a shower for her and Andrew. Gertie's absence coinciding with my first Friday Afternoon Wine & Cheese at Crossings is a sign of how pleased God is with me. That can be the only explanation, right?

With the sky losing its last tinges of lavender to a darkening blue, our first Wine & Cheese Afternoon has faded to early evening. "This has been delightful, Carolina," Teresa Reynolds says as she reaches for her husband's hand. "However, we do have reservations for dinner. We don't want to keep our guests waiting, so I believe it's time for us to leave."

Jackson stands. "Of course. And we'll see you tomorrow at the opening."

Frank shakes Brad and Deena's hands, as they also come to their feet. "And even though you're not from this area, hope you two will come tomorrow, too. Plenty of food to go around. A caterer is coming up from Roswell, I hear."

"We just might," Brad says. "The church we grew up over in Canton is having a big picnic tomorrow, but not until everyone has been to the cemetery to clean it up. That's when we plan to show up and surprise everyone."

As we all walk into the house, Will and Anna come down the stairs. Jackson introduces everyone, and Deena looks at me when she hears Anna is our daughter-in-law. Then when Jackson explains that they recently surprised us with their news of us being grandparents, Deena and Brad both look confused. Anna just stares at the floor.

Before I know what's happened, Will has invited Deena and Brad to join him and Anna for dinner at the Chinese restaurant, then a walk downtown, and coffee at MoonShots. The four of them are out the door even before the Reynolds, and in a matter of moments, the house is quiet again.

Jackson has his arm around me and leans over like he's

looking down the front of my shirt. "So, Mrs. Jessup, what are the two of us doing for dinner?"

I grab hold of his hand and take him into the kitchen, where I open the refrigerator and pull out a small cutting board covered with plastic wrap.

Jackson takes it and starts reciting what it holds. "Salami, ham, turkey, and peppers. Looks delicious."

"Can you also carry this?" I ask, holding out a loaf of fresh Italian bread. He takes it and then watches as I consolidate the cheese we had outside onto a plate with some grapes and sliced pears. Lifting that, I turn to face him. "We could eat this down here, but we have champagne upstairs on ice."

He grins. "Upstairs? Like, in our bedroom?" His grin only grows when I nod.

Turning toward the living room and the stairs, he pronounces, "I'm a huge fan of Friday Afternoon Wine & Cheese at Crossings. I might even like this more than the trains."

Chapter 34

While I've been keeping up with the progress of the waterfront park, Jackson hasn't. He's astonished. "Last time I was out here was for the Easter Egg hunt," he says, climbing out of the car.

The morning sun slants across the parking lot, and the hair on my arms lifts, responding to the humidity. There isn't a cloud or a breeze in the state today. "I'm glad they decided to do all this early. It's going to be hot today."

"I can't wait to swim out to the docks!" Bryan says. "Wait'll you see it all, Dad."

Bryan has on his bathing trunks, waters shoes, and a tee shirt. We're all dressed casual and comfortable. I have on a light blue sundress, and Jackson is wearing shorts and a knit golf shirt. He and I don't plan on swimming today. Or maybe we'll go home and come back in our swim suits.

"I smell bacon," Jackson says. "Are we eating first?"

"I'm not sure. Susan has been pretty quiet about the whole thing. I think she's preoccupied with Leslie going off to college in the fall. I'm not sure how she even got put in charge of this."

"There's Laney and Shaw," Jackson says, and we turn to walk in their direction. Bryan has wandered off to where the teenagers are standing together. Leaving the parking area, we follow pine straw-laden paths through the shade of the woods. When the pine straw ends at an expanse of thick green grass, we stop to get the whole effect.

A pavilion spreads along the river bank. It's open in the middle, and through it, we can see the water and swimming area. The grassy shore hosts picnic tables and grills. On the ends of the pavilion, there are closed-in areas for bathrooms on one side and a concession stand on the other. Over to our far right and left, there are smaller covered shelters with more picnic tables.

"Wow, you and Bryan were right!" Jackson says. "This is really something." As we walk closer, we can see the wooden docks out in the water.

"And there's a zipline out past that dock. See it?" Even though I'm pointing to my right, my eyes are searching the crowd. Laney and Shaw are no longer in front of us. Susan said something last week about Laney not looking good. She's right. She looked disheveled, or maybe she really is sick. When I get a glimpse of her, I pull on Jackson's arm and lead him into the pavilion.

The stone floor and high ceiling of the pavilion make the temperature drop as we enter, helped along by several ceiling fans. Now we can see the tables set up with chafing dishes, and lots of folks in white dart around setting things up. We can also see the area beside the lake where there is a microphone set up with a few chairs in the audience. As we say 'hello' to folks, steady tapping on the microphone gets our attention.

"Hello?" says the emcee, a representative from the power company. "Can you hear me? Good. We'll begin the presentation in a few minutes and following that—yes, it will be short—we will eat. Have another cup of coffee and start gathering in this area so we can begin shortly. Thank you."

I nudge Jackson. "Let's go see how Savannah is doing with the coffee station. I could use another cup."

At one end of the food tables, we see the familiar purple

cups, and our daughter working along with a young man and Jordan. We pick up cups of black coffee, and then step to the area with the cream and sugar.

"Good morning. Things look busy here," I say.

Savannah doesn't even glance my way. "Coffee and morning. Who'd have thought we'd be busy?" Gotta love having a teenage daughter.

Jordan steps back from the counter. "It's insane is what it is. I still can't believe I agreed to it. What is it about that Missus woman that makes it impossible to say no to her?"

Jackson laughs as he stirs his coffee. "If you figure it out, let my wife know, won't you?"

Jordan still wears the sheen of her mother-in-law's visit. Her hair is perfect once again. She has on her black sleeveless turtleneck and long, tight black pants.

"We enjoyed having you stay at Crossings Wednesday. The girls are adorable," I say.

Jordan doesn't answer me, just goes back to work. Jackson raises his eyebrows at me, and we step away. He asks, "Did y'all ever figure out why her mother-in-law even came here? From what you said, it doesn't sound like she felt bad about Jordan and her daughters being separated."

"It had nothing to do with the girls. I really felt like nothing ever has to do with the girls with Jordan and Mrs. Sentora. Diego seemed to like Francie and Carly more than either woman does."

Pausing at the edge of the crowd, we watch Mr. and Mrs. Reynolds make their way to the front. They got up and left early this morning, as he said they still had some things to work out for the grand opening. I'm not sure what they would've been working out, as it looks like everything was all taken care of. If Susan is in charge of something, there's no need to worry about anything being left out.

Jackson bangs my arm with his elbow. "Is that Griffin and Susan up there with the Reynolds?"

"Yeah. Boy, they sure are dressed up! Even the kids." Griffin and Grant both have on suits, and the girls are in Sunday dresses. Susan is wearing a black and white dress that looks very expensive. It also looks like a bit much for opening a park. "Do you see Laney?" I ask.

Scanning the crowd, I finally see Laney toward the back. Now, I can see for sure that she doesn't look good. She seems faded, like she doesn't have on makeup, which we know is not a possibility. Her hair is flat, and her dress looks too big for her. Baggy even. "I see her," I say to Jackson and head in her direction.

She's too busy looking up front to notice me coming. But when she does see me, she turns to leave. I grab her arm. "Wait. Hey, I wanted to see you."

"Well, now you've seen me," she snaps. "Happy?"

My mouth falls open, and I'm brought up short by how mean she sounds. "Laney? What's going on?"

Her chin becomes as solid as stone and her lips, lipstick-less lips I should add, press together, forming more unmovable flesh. Her crossed arms pull in even tighter, and her eyes bore into the folks gathering around the microphone. Shaw comes up behind her, and his smile at me is half-grimace, half-nothing. He lays a hand on his wife's shoulder, but she shrugs it off.

"Welcome to the opening of Chancey Waterfront Park," Mr. Reynolds booms. He talks about how well the town and his company have worked together. He welcomes numerous folks in the crowd and each of the people standing up front with him. Except Susan and Griffin. Although they are standing closer to him than anyone else, he doesn't mention them. Until the very end.

"All this," he spreads his hands towards us, "is due to the hard work of Mrs. Susan Lyles, and I have the honor of announcing this is only the first of many events Susan will be planning, as she has agreed to accept the position of Park

Events Director. A position funded by Mountain Power, I might add." When the crowd begins to applaud, he holds up his hand. "Not yet, wait just a minute. That's not all the news about this wonderful family. Along with opening this magnificent park, and introducing the Park Events Director, I also have the delightful duty today of announcing the newest addition to our company, Mountain Power, Executive Vice-President Griffin Lyles." He holds out his arm to Griffin, and directs him to the microphone.

I don't believe I was the only one in the crowd who gasped in surprise, but I know for a fact, Laney was the *only* person there that burst into tears, turned, and ran towards the parking lot.

"No, I didn't get to talk to her," I answer Jackson's questioning look. "Shaw chased after her and stopped me. He said she wasn't ready to talk to anyone. And she was wearing flats again, so she was faster than usual. Let's go congratulate Susan and Griffin."

Walking through the crowd, we hear the rumble of surprise. Tipping my head close to my husband's, I ask, "Is this something Griffin is qualified for? I don't know that I even know what he does."

He dips his head down and runs two finger around his lips, pulling his chin down. "I'm not sure I know either. He always made it sound boring and, well, boring. Think I assumed he was an accountant somewhere. I knew he worked in Dalton, but not long hours, right? Didn't he always seem to be around? And all the committees he's been on with the city take a lot of time."

"Well, maybe that has something to do with it. He does know the city and the area."

"Congratulations, Griffin!" We laugh and greet him with

hugs. "Susan, you, too. Two new jobs." I look in Susan's eyes and try to hold her gaze. "I had no idea. Why didn't you say something?"

She shrugs and darts a look at Griffin. "It's really been up in the air. They offered this to him a few weeks ago, but it just came together in the last few days." She turns a bit away from Griffin and Jackson. "It seemed almost too good to be true, honestly. Griffin really doesn't talk about work much. He has his MBA, but we never wanted to move from Chancey, so jobs like this seemed out of reach. Then when they also asked me to be event director, it seemed like the perfect time for a change all around."

I can't resist hugging her. They both look so happy, so polished. So out of place and out of the ordinary. In just a flash, they don't look like the perfect small town couple, they look like they belong back in Marietta or Atlanta.

As we pull apart, she seeks *my* gaze. "You have to know, you gave us so much courage. We saw the way you and Jackson changed your lives, and it made us both antsy." She crushes me to her again. "Thanks."

Jackson's hand at my back says we need to move on as a congratulatory line has formed behind us. Then Susan pulls on my arm.

"Did you see Laney? I know Shaw was here."

"Uh, I think she was here. But I think she had to leave or something."

Susan frowns. "Maybe she's still not feeling well. She had some kind of virus earlier this week, which really wiped her out. She won't talk to me, but now that this shindig is done, I'll have more time to concentrate on her. Go get something to eat. The grits are amazing."

People are seated at temporary tables and the permanent picnic tables. The sun on the water gives a glow to everything, and Jackson and I head straight to the food line. We chat with those around us as we wait and fill our plates. Seated with some folks we know from church, I marvel at how this has all happened so fast. Last year this time, this park didn't exist. Matter of fact, along with the nests of snakes removed from the riverbanks, a nest of drug dealers were sent packing off to jail to make way for the park.

Last year this time, we didn't know any of these people, including our now daughter-in-law. This time next year, we'll be grandparents. The baby will be, let's see, six months old. It'll be a real part of our lives. Savannah will have graduated, and Bryan will be a quarter of the way through high school. It's been a good change being here, but I'm still not sure I can say I would do it all again.

I hope Susan and Griffin know what they are doing. Changes can be rough. But really, how much of a change are new jobs? It's not like a new town or school or friends. Maybe she's just excited and exaggerating the big moves, but she does know what she's talking about when it comes to these grits. They are amazing.

"Carolina, I have you down for deviled eggs," Missus informs me of this as she walks behind my seat at the picnic table. Of course, she says this when my mouth is full of grits, so I turn over my shoulder while swallowing and raise my eyebrows and shoulders in question. But all I see is her back as she walks away.

Standing, I wipe my mouth, and say, "Excuse me," but she doesn't turn. Missus has on a salmon-colored, stiff cotton dress with short, cuffed sleeves. I follow her up to the pavilion and catch her just inside the shade of the high wooden-beamed roof.

"Missus, what was that about deviled eggs?"

She turns to me and gives me that look up and down she feels serves as a greeting. I picture her getting along swimmingly with Mrs. Sentora. "What is it, Carolina? You don't want to make deviled eggs? I tried to give you something you could not possibly have questions about."

"Of course, I don't have questions about deviled eggs, per se. Just why you've assigned them to me?"

"Who should I assign them to?" She looks to her right where Jordan is just leaving the bathroom. "Should I assign the deviled eggs to Jordan?"

Jordan stops. "Devil what?"

"Missus wants to know if you'll make some deviled eggs?"

"Don't be ridiculous, Carolina, she's not even in our family. Ignore her, Jordan. You are free to go."

Jordan strikes a pose, like a model at the end of the runway. Hands on hips, head tilted up, and just a tad to the side. "What in the world are deviled eggs? Oh, wait, are you talking about those nasty things my *grandmother* used to make?" Jordan's cheeks never look so sculpted as when she's looking down her nose. "She actually had a plate specifically made to hold them. Please leave me out of any conversation, or event, which involves those nasty things." Her long strides, in her tight black pants, take her away from us before either of us can express our dismay that her grandmother only had *one* deviled egg plate.

Missus smirks. "She resembles a granddaddy longleg the way she stalks about on those heels in those tight pants. I do not believe I would fit in in New York." Her attention comes back to me. "Now, what is it you are yammering on about?"

I draw in a deep breath to consider the correct question. "Where should I take the deviled eggs for which I have been made responsible?"

"Oh, yes, I see. You are quite right in that it will be too hot to have them at the cemetery all morning, and with my house being repainted, you obviously know to not bring them there. So, either have them in a cooler on ice or bring them to Peter's before church. I'll make sure he leaves his front door unlocked." She has so graciously explained all this while all I can think about is putting a stick underneath that thick coil of pearls around her neck and then twisting it so they tighten, and tighten, and… "Wait, the cemetery?"

"Yes, with everything going on for the wedding I wanted to get the food assignments for the Decoration lunch next Sunday out early. It's such a shame my entire downstairs has to be repainted since the painters incredibly used the wrong color. But Peter's house will just have to do." She perks up. "Unless you are offering your home? It would be nice for all the relatives to see your side of the family's house. Actually, that is an excellent idea." She turns away and starts walking, her voice carrying in the wide open pavilion. "I'll leave it to you to work things out with Peter. After all, *I* am doing *everything* for the wedding."

"What are you doing?" Jackson asks as he comes up behind me.

"Hosting the Decoration lunch for Missus' entire family, apparently. And making deviled eggs. I love Will and Anna, but I'm not sure I love them enough to be a part of Missus' family."

He puts his hands on my shoulders and sighs.

"Oh, and get this, Jordan thinks deviled eggs are nasty. No wonder she's so skinny and unhappy."

CHAPTER 35

"So, how did it go? Telling your parents and everyone about the baby?"

Jackson and I are sitting on the front porch when Brad and Deena arrive back to Crossings. We came out to enjoy the sun setting behind the mountains, but the sun has long been gone and our wine glasses have long been empty.

Deena beams. "Just like we imagined. They were all so happy and surprised to see us, but nothing like when we pulled that tiny Georgia jersey out of the bag."

Jackson gets up and motions her to take his chair. Then pulls over the other two rocking chairs as she sits down. "Can I get you anything?"

Deena shakes her head. "No, I am exhausted. Cannot wait to get in bed, but I did want to apologize for yesterday morning. I didn't realize Anna was your daughter-in-law. Or that she's expecting. I always know how to stick my foot in my mouth."

I reach out and pat her arm. "Oh, no, you were fine. It's all so new to us, and I think it's just now hitting her how hard it is going to be. But they have a great support system here."

Jackson rocks forward and leans his elbows on his knees. "We didn't know they were dating. Or when they ran away and got married. We're having a commemorative ceremony here in a couple weeks. Lots of changes for all of us. So, don't worry. You're not the first, or last, to not know what to say."

She gives a little smile. "We had a really fun time with them last night. They both seem to love Chancey. I can't believe they've neither one ever lived here until this year."

"Probably why they still love it," I say.

Brad laughs. "We love our families, but knew we needed a little distance. All the questions and worries. That's even why we stayed here this weekend. Unless we do things by surprise, someone finds out first and feelings get hurt. Being a couple hours away works great. But, hey, since they've never gotten to live around family, maybe it'll be different for them."

Jackson and I lock eyes and he mouths, "Missus," just before he rolls his eyes.

Deena stands up. "I need to go to bed before I fall asleep out here and you have to carry me in," she says to Brad as she reaches out for him to take her hand. "We're going to pack up and head out in the morning to go to church with our families, then we'll head home from there. So we'll be out of the way early."

I stand up and give her a hug. "Where do y'all go to church?" I cannot believe that jumped out of my mouth, but you can tell they are from a small town in the South because they don't bat an eye.

"Collinswood First Baptist," Brad says. "We started dating in the youth group."

"Oh, I was there this week. Not at the church, but Collinswood. A friend of mine is running a B&B over there. Right downtown, The Charming House?"

"Oh, yeah, the Charmings lived there for years. Cute name, isn't it, for a B&B? I heard the house finally sold. How's it going?" Deena asks.

I pull a face. "Hard to tell. Lot of work to do, and my friend is being pretty secretive about it all."

Jackson pulls open the front door and motions for us to walk in. He says, "Carolina thinks the owners might've bitten off more than they can chew. Was it always rundown? Did you know the previous owners?"

The couple looks at each other. Brad answers, "When we were all kids, but they moved away, like a lot of folks did. Not much of a reason to stay in Collinswood. After Miss Johnson passed away, all the drive to fix the town kind of died with her. She pretty much ruled the roost there."

"Probably like our Missus," I say, then explain, "she's Anna's grandmother."

Deena stops and turns to me. "You know, Anna and Will mentioned her. If she's like our Miss Johnson, that explains a lot. Things go her way or no way, I bet."

Jackson and I both nod.

Brad clears his throat and tries for a light-hearted laugh. "Guess that explains the problems with the wedding. Hope they can, well, work it all out without killing the old woman."

"Oh, it probably won't come to that," I laugh.

Deena slaps at her husband. "He shouldn't have said that. It's just, well, that's how Miss Johnson died. Two of her grandkids killed her."

Brad interjects, "Allegedly."

Jackson and I stare at them. Jackson asks, "Allegedly? Are they in jail?"

Denna shakes her head. "Nope. Not enough evidence. She fell down a flight of stairs, and the only other people in the house were her two grandkids. Their parents were out of town, and she took it upon herself to stay with them even though they were in high school. She always, always knew best. Drove everyone crazy, but especially her family."

"Are they still in the area? What are their names? Johnson, I guess?" I ask as I shiver and step closer to Jackson.

Brad licks his lips. "No, um, it was Mrs. Johnson's daughter and son-in-law's house." He stares at us, and Deena suddenly says, "Well, goodnight. It's been great staying here."

They walk on toward the B&B hall, but they've only gone a couple steps when I say, "Wait. I know the last name, don't I?"

Jackson looks down at me, "You do? Who?"

"Charming."

Deena smiles and shrugs. "Yeah, sorry."

Just as they turn back towards their room, the door behind us is thrown open. I scream and Jackson yells, which causes the Reynolds to both yell.

Behind them, Bryan and Savannah push inside. "What's going on?" they ask.

I take a deep breath. "Nothing. Y'all just scared us. So, everyone's home all at one time it looks like."

The Reynolds had taken Susan and Griffin out tonight. Savannah and Bryan spent the day at the park, where we also went back and hung out in the afternoon. It had been a long day for everyone, and we all look it.

Bryan heads upstairs after saying the waterfront park is the "coolest place on earth."

Savannah jingles her keys, and says she's going back out, but she'll be home before midnight.

Teresa and Frank turn down Jackson's offer of a glass of wine or anything else and trudge off to their room.

As doors shut around the house and settling-in sounds fade, Jackson and I sit side by side on the couch.

"Today's been a good day, I think," he says.

"Gertie and Patty will be back tomorrow. I have to sit down and get Anna to talk. I have to help her handle Missus with this wedding."

"How crazy was that story Brad and Deena told us about that Miss Johnson?" Jackson says. "To be accused of killing your own grandmother?"

I nod. "When we were driving out of Collinswood, I

remember thinking that they needed a Missus to get them together. Town seemed so much sadder than Chancey. Didn't seem at all like a place Laney would choose to work."

He stands up and then pulls me up beside him. "Well, we can't fix any of these things tonight, and I'm exhausted." We head up the stairs and then I remember the wine glasses we left outside. "You go on up and brush your teeth. I'm going to get the wine glasses."

On the front porch, there's no light except from the bit of a moon over the river. I step out into the grass to see the stars. *Lots of changes for everyone around us.* I turn Jackson's words over in my mind. Susan said our moving here made them feel "antsy." I don't know that I like making people feel antsy or unsettled. I know I don't like everything changing. If we hadn't moved here, would Will be getting ready for law school, instead of getting ready for a baby? Would Susan and Laney still be happy with their normal lives? Would Missus not be on this kick to fix up Chancey if there wasn't a B&B for visitors to stay in? Would Patty not be living in Chancey and not know Andy and not be getting ready to marry a virtual stranger?

How interesting the way things interweave. But, it's too late to wonder about any of that. I walk back up the porch steps and pick up the wine glasses. Then I realize something—everything I'm doing today will impact lots of people's futures. Just like our decisions last year to move here, all the decisions on the bookstore, the weddings. It's enough to make you too scared to do anything.

You never know when you might make someone want to push you down a flight of stairs.

Chapter 36

"Well, I think it's the girls getting ready to leave for college," I say to Susan as we walk out of church. Rosebushes line the sidewalk with light pink blooms. They fill the space with a rich scent.

"Maybe. You know I don't get hurt easily, but to have her leave without saying anything to Griffin about his new job? I'm sorry, that's just rude." Susan shakes her head. "What are y'all doing for lunch?" She holds her hand up to shade her eyes as she looks back up towards the church building.

"I think we're going to the Chinese buffet. It makes everybody happy, and it's quick. You?"

"Maybe we'll join you. Yesterday was so busy I didn't get anything put together for dinner today. I'm so glad I told Jordan I couldn't work today. There's Griffin. Let me check with him." She heads back towards him, except on the outside of the rosebushes.

Taking a couple steps to the shade beside the road, I look down toward the back of the library and the row of houses that face the square. The new construction on Missus' and FM's house can be seen best from back here. They added an upstairs deck for Will and Anna's room with a double set of French doors. Of course, Missus already has it lined with flowers; there is a table and sitting area. It's perfect. Except, except… such a feeling of sadness comes over me when I think of Will. It'll go away when the baby comes, right? He seems happy, and Anna is sweet. They decided to get married, and he's a grown man who can make his own decisions. He's smart, and if that's what he decided, I'm sure it's going to be fine.

"Oh, hey, you can see our deck from here. I didn't realize that." Will joins me in the shade.

"Hey, you." I chuck his shoulder. "You weren't up when we left, although we did leave a little earlier than usual to get Bryan here for the Memorial Day ceremony with the veterans."

He nods. "Anna didn't come, so it was easy for me to get dressed and get here."

I'm surprised by this information. "Oh, she seemed to be feeling better this morning. She got up to say goodbye to Deena and Brad. I know because I saw her then."

"Yeah, she and Deena really hit it off. They're both due like the same week."

I nod down toward their new deck and home. "So, when do we get to see the new place? When will it be ready for you to move in?"

Will shrugs. "Anna's not getting along with Missus, so we're kind of dragging our feet. I haven't even seen it all done yet."

"Let's fix that," Missus says and makes us both turn around. "Come have lunch."

"Oh, we have plans, I think. Will, you can go."

Will tips his head and grins, blond hair falling into his eyes. "Now, Missus, you know I can't see it before Anna." He reaches out a hand to her, which she leaves hanging. "How about Anna and I come over one night this week?"

"Yes, that will do. Carolina, you and Jackson, too. Tomorrow night for dessert and coffee at seven." She looks away from us and back up the walk. "Finally, the pastor is done talking to every Tom, Dick, and Harry that wanted to shake his hand," she says as she steps away from us and on to her next target. "I will see you both tomorrow."

"Son," I sigh as I take hold of his arm and look up at him. "Are you sure living with her is going to be all right?"

"Of course!" He acts like this is no big deal at all. "So, Dad said you're going for Chinese? Can I tag along? I'll bring Anna some soup and a couple eggrolls. I'm starving." He backs away and waves, then yells toward the kids gathered in a group on the lawn, "Bryan, want to ride with me?" Bryan and Grant look to Grant's parents for a minute, get the approval nod, and then dash across the front lawn of the church toward Will and his car.

I walk along the road in the same direction and see Savannah waiting at our car. She has on her purple MoonShots shirt with black shorts. We haven't let her work Sunday mornings, so she walks over as soon as church is over. Usually, she leaves so quick we don't see her.

"What's up?" I ask at the same time that she asks me, "Did you hear? There's a picket at MoonShots."

"A picket? Like, protestors?"

"Yes." Her blue eyes shine with excitement and a little bit of fear. "Jimmy texted me, and so I wanted you and Daddy to drive me down there."

"Hey, what's up?" Jackson calls as he gets near our car.

"Savannah wants a ride to work because the store has picketers."

"No way. What is there to picket in Chancey?"

"Who knows?" I say. "Get in, let's go see."

The car is hot, and as soon as we close the doors, we roll down the windows. Savannah is in the seat behind her daddy. As we drive down the street beside the library, we can hear voices, like a chant. Sure enough, there are about a dozen people walking in a circle on the sidewalk and road out front.

Jackson makes the left turn which takes us in front of the library and Missus' house. As we prepare to turn right onto Main

Street beside the park, the chant seems familiar.

"It's the Lord's Prayer," Savannah says.

She's right. The people are walking in a circle and saying the Lord's Prayer in unison. One person holds a sign saying, "Keep the Sabbath."

We pull into an angled spot, and at the same time, from the other direction comes a news van. *Great.*

We watch as the news van parks and empties. The camera man is only a couple spaces away from us, and as he takes a few minutes to set up his equipment, the dark-haired anchor jogs across the street and walks up to the protestors.

Savannah dials her phone and then says, "Jimmy. There are news people outside the store. Tell Jordan." She pauses, and we can hear through her phone as the boy yells to Jordan. Savannah adds, "No, they don't have the camera shooting yet." She hangs up and opens her car door. "I've gotta go help."

"Wait," Jackson and I say in unison, but she's already following the reporter's path across the street. We see Jordan look out the front door and then watch as she opens the door for our daughter to dart inside. The camera man is filming now. He approaches the front door where the reporter waits with the man holding the Sabbath sign.

"Now what?" Jackson says.

"Wait, I know. Call Will. Tell him to come to MoonShots right now."

As he dials, I call Susan and tell her to come, too. Andy comes lumbering across the street and waves at Jackson but comes to my window. "Hey, Miss Jessup. You see what's going on over there?"

"Yeah, Savannah just went in to work. We're going to go inside and see how things are right now. A show of support for Jordan. Others are coming." As I open my car door, he scoots back from it. I tell him to call Patty. "She'll want to come down and support Jordan, too."

He nods and chews on the inside of his lip. His hands remain plunged in his baggy jeans pockets. I hold out my phone to him. "Want to use my phone? And I don't care if she's upstairs, and you were upstairs. Is that what you're worried about?" He weaves around a bit, pulls one hand out of his pocket to take my phone, but doesn't push any buttons or open his mouth. He just holds the phone looking down at it.

Suddenly he jerks up his head. Then I hear it. Heels coming down the sidewalk behind me.

"What is the meaning of this?"

"Guess it's a picket. Of Moonshots," I say as I turn around. From my time working in the library, I know there's the Snow Queen in Narnia and the Red Queen in Alice in Wonderland. And, now, the Blue Queen of the Southern Mountains. She's wearing a light blue skirt and jacket, crowned with silver blue hair, and the sparks flying out of her eyes are an electric blue. Andy now actually has a reason to be a mumbling, bumbling idiot. I'd be terrified too, but I'm thinking I'm not Missus' target this time.

Halleluiah.

"This is not permitted in Chancey. We are not that sort of town. You," she points at Andy who is still holding my phone, "call the police."

She turns from him towards me and takes a step closer. I step away from her and into the street. She has on those white gloves, and I've seen the damage they can do to mere mortals. "Carolina, where are you going, and why are you here?"

Jackson had left me to deal with Andy, and now from the still chanting picketers, he calls my name and causes me to turn that way. I can hear him because the praying is softer while their leader is being interviewed. With a smile back at Missus, I walk across the street. Behind me, I hear the heels, so I walk faster. Shoot, Andy still has my phone. I look to my right where I left him. "Andy, bring my phone when you come inside. Call

Patty." It's like talking to a bump on a log, though he's usually a ball of energy. He must not be a morning person.

Closer to the picketers, I realize no one looks familiar. We've not lived here long, but I've come to expect that I know someone pretty much everywhere I go. They are all dressed for church, looks like. Nothing fancy, but not working clothes. One of the ladies is talking to Jackson, and as I come up, she smiles at me and sticks her hand out.

"You must be Mrs. Jessup. So nice to meet you. I've heard all about you."

"Wow, Jackson isn't usually that fast of a talker," I match her smile, but my eyes dart to my husband. Why would they be talking about me?

He closes his eyes for just a moment and shakes his head just the tiniest bit, takes a deep breath, and says, "Carolina, let me introduce you to Mrs. Taylor."

"The police have been called," Missus says as the heels joins us.

Mrs. Taylor nods her head and says, "We expected that might happen. Are you Mrs. Bedwell? Anna's grandmother?"

Missus catches the words almost out of her mouth and replaces them with, "Do I know you?"

Jackson speaks up, "This is Mrs. Taylor, Andy's mother. The gentleman at the microphone is Reverend Taylor, Andy's father."

Missus, Andy's mama, Jackson, and I all look to the other side of the street where big old Andy stands, still holding my phone. He lifts his other hand in a small wave, but stays on that side of the street.

So he must not be all that stupid, right?

"Who knew they'd take such offense when they don't even live over here?" Yes, Andy was finally dragged across the street where he stands in the midst of the crowd.

"Son, we're not offended. The Lord is offended," Reverend Taylor explains. "We understand the citizens of this town are not allowed to speak their mind about this establishment being opened on Sunday morning, so we stepped in to give them a voice."

Andy lowers his head and then looks away.

Jackson asks, "Why do you think the town isn't allowed to speak its mind?"

"Well, son, isn't that want you said?" asks the big man with the gray suitcoat on. His red hair isn't as bushy as Andy's, and it's plastered down with perspiration. His face is flushed, but not in anger. Just the hazards of being a big, pale man with red hair, wearing a suit coat, shirt, and tie, standing outside the last weekend of May in Georgia. Matter of fact, Mr. and Mrs. Taylor seem like the kind of people who never get upset. Not your average picketers.

Now Andy has attracted the full attention of the church folk, the reporter, the sightseers, and Missus. Still looking away, toward the street, he starts talking. "Maybe, but it was just to, to well. I don't know. Sometimes I just talk too much, maybe?"

The reporter steps up to Missus. "Mrs. Bedwell, we met during the tornado coverage. Is this true? Is there a campaign of silence in Chancey?"

"Don't be ridiculous. We support all business. And all churches. Interview over." She pushes aside his microphone with one gloved hand. As she steps to the door of MoonShots, she seems shocked that my husband has not stepped up to open the door for her. When he finally arrives to do his menial duty, she steps into the shop, but not before turning to find me in the crowd. "Carolina, you and that young man and his parents are to come inside. No cameras."

I look at Andy and his still-smiling mama and say, "The queen has spoken. We don't want to add a beheading to all this fun, do we?"

Andy hands me my phone as he shuffles by me. "No, ma'am. A beheading is not a good idea."

We are barely in the door when Will, Bryan, and Grant come in carrying brown paper bags with grease spots coming through. My favorite kind of bags. Will holds them up and announces, "We packed up some food and brought it with us 'cause you said to hurry, and we were starving. Dad, I told the China Palace people you'd take care of it later."

Susan and Griffin are right behind them. Susan pushes past all the guys and comes up to me. "We ran into Will and them as they were leaving China Palace since we had to run into the Piggly Wiggly first. What's going on?"

Jordan is behind the counter. "You can't bring that food in here. What kind of hillbilly brings outside food into another store?"

Savannah whips her hair around and faces her boss, hand on her hip, chin lifted—normal teenage girl stance. "Those pastries you serve are awful. They all came here to help you, and it *is* lunch time."

Wow, the pastries must be bad if Savannah, who loves beyond words generic Pop-Tarts and dollar-store snack cakes, thinks they're awful.

She comes from behind the counter and joins her brothers in digging through the fragrant paper bags. With an eggroll in hand, she jumps up to sit on the counter. "Chill out, Jordan. This ain't New York."

Will high fives his sister, then sits down to the plate of food he's put together from the open containers.

Griffin has a plate and hands one to Jackson. "Don't worry. While we were there, I paid half the bill. Told them to add whatever they had ready to the takeout so none of us would starve to death." Louder he announces, "Folks, there's plenty."

Pretty soon it's a party. Coffee goes pretty well with Chinese food, we decide. Outside the picketers continue praying, and Missus is beside herself. "Stop eating. Stop talking. This must be resolved this very minute. I will not have my town disparaged by you out-of-town do-gooders. Jordan, as the manager and owner of this establishment, you must see this has to end."

Jordan shrugs. "I hear this isn't New York. What do I know? Except this is the most business I've had on a Sunday since we've been open. I may hire them to come march around outside every Sunday."

Andy stands up, hitching up his saggy blue jeans. "I'll take care of it. Mom, Dad, sorry I misled you. You know how I go on sometimes. Can I ask Mr. Stanley and them to stop marching around and praying out there?"

The reverend just nods and waves a hand at his son. He apparently didn't understand Missus saying, "Stop eating" as he has an eggroll sticking out of his mouth.

Missus steps up to the reporter, who comes in when Andy opens the door to go out, and passes her hand over the bags and boxes of food. "This isn't a fit lunch. Please come have lunch with me and my husband, and we will give you a tour of the repairs and renovation to our home after the tornado."

Invitation given and acceptance assumed, she heads to the door. Griffin is seated closest, so he jumps up to open the door. Without a single look back, she leaves. The camera man scoops up two crab Rangoon appetizers, wraps them in a napkin and tucks them in his pocket before grabbing his equipment.

The reporter hesitates, grumbling, "I feel the story is here. Not at some old lady's house."

Camera man, already moving toward the door turns back and grins. "Buddy, you're going to want to see this house. It has a life-size portrait right in the front hallway that's perfect for a haunted house. Plus the old lady's a hoot."

After a couple guffaws, he catches his words and cringes. "Oh, sorry, folks."

Grant, with all the world weariness a thirteen-year-old carries, answers for all of us. "Man, no worries, we've all seen the picture."

CHAPTER 37

Jackson being in town means I get up early and we have coffee together before he leaves for work. We started this when the babies came along, and it was the only time we could find for just the two of us. I can be a morning person when I really try. Jackson makes me want to try when he says, "This is my favorite part of the day. Sitting here in the quiet with you."

Dew covers everything this time of year, so we'd stuck the chair cushions in the kitchen last night. They are dry, and the standing dew around us on the table, the deck railing, and the grass is picking up the sunshine as its beams find their way through the trees. The hazy fog draping the tops of the mountains dissipates first in the growing light. We sat down in half darkness, now in the distance, tops of the trees are touched by golden light. We watch it move down the tall pine trunks as we drink our coffee. This might be my favorite part of the day, too, if it weren't so early.

He refills my cup as he give me a goodbye kiss. I'm going to make something in the crockpot for dinner so we can eat early enough to get to Missus' for dessert at seven. It was good to get to meet Andy's parents yesterday. He finally admitted he never called Gertie and Patty, which is why they didn't show up for the impromptu lunch party. I also found out Andy's dad is doing the wedding. Both weddings he said, but when he said that, Andy wouldn't meet my eye. Sounds like a little more exaggeration. Anna stayed upstairs all day yesterday. She wouldn't even come down to eat. Will heated up her lunch and took it to her. I don't care if you do have a husband and a place to live, being pregnant at eighteen has got to be terrifying. Shoot, it was terrifying for me at twenty-three. Maybe I can get her to open up to me later. Although on Mondays Will drives her to school and she stays there all day. This Maymester thing she's taking means concentrating a whole semester of work into one month.

As the sun hits the lawn, the bugs pick up. A low buzz of summer background music. I've got a full day of cleaning to do. Although our next guests don't arrive until Friday, so I really don't have to do the cleaning today, right? The meal for the crockpot is one of those that comes already put together in a bag, frozen, so that should take all of five minutes. I lean up to look over the railing at my garden. Nothing there looks like it needs picking or whatever else you do with gardens. It's helpful that I'm not so good on identifying weeds. Amazing how a day can just open right up with a little creative thinking.

"Hey Mom." Will comes out to the deck holding a cup of coffee.

"That cushion is dry. Your daddy was sitting on it."

He sits down and takes a sip of his coffee.

"How's Anna feeling?"

"Good, I think. She just needs some time alone. I guess she's not used to so many people around."

"Yeah, I can see that. Plus, you know, having a baby is scary."

He frowns and shakes his head. "Naw, I don't think it's that. She's real happy about having a family."

"How about you? How are you feeling about having a family so soon?"

He picks up his coffee and holds it in both hands as he looks over it toward the river. "It's a change from what I thought I'd be doing. But for some reason it feels really right. Like this is what was supposed to happen. Anna and I are going to be real happy. I just feel it."

"That's good, I guess. She's lucky to have you."

"She's different from the girls I always dated. You know, the real confident, sporty girls? The ones in charge of everything. It's like I met her, and she needs me. But, I need her, too, because I like who I am with her more than with those other girls."

I sit up. "Wow, you really have thought about this."

He grins at me. "Yeah. Prayed a lot too, and that's helped."

I feel like I've kept pushing this whole situation away. Not thinking about it. Afraid if I looked too closely it would all fall apart and leave a baby, a young mother, and my disillusioned son all spinning out of control. At least out of my control. It never occurred to me that someone else could be in control. And he prayed about it? Well, that's interesting.

He stands up. "I left Anna upstairs in the shower and I told her I'd bring her coffee up. I think I'll be taking the last of the pot. Want me to make more?"

"No, I'll make some in a minute. So we're still going to Missus' at seven tonight, right?"

"Yeah. I'm excited to see our place. I think Anna's getting more excited, too." He opens the kitchen door and laughs, then shakes his head "Missus still scares Anna."

Which leaves me blinking in my chair. He finds it funny to be scared of Missus? I'm not sure if he's praying or just drinking heavily.

By the time Anna and Will leave, Savannah is up and eating cereal on the couch watching a sitcom rerun. Bryan has stumbled through, grabbed a box of cereal and a banana, taking both downstairs to play videogames. The only thing he managed to communicate was that he and the guys were going to the waterpark at noon if I can give them a ride.

"What are your plans for today?" I ask Savannah when she turns off the TV. In the living room, she's stretching and completing her wake-up routine. Stretching means I can actually talk to her.

"Nothing. Work."

"You don't usually work on Mondays," I say.

She shakes her head and explains. "Going to go with Miss Laney over to her new B&B. She's paying me and Angie to help her clean."

"It's kind of creepy over there," I say.

That got her attention. "You've seen it? What do you mean 'creepy'?"

"Yeah, me and Susan and Jordan went over last week. It's dark. Big and dark. You know our guests this weekend, Brad and Deena? They grew up in Collinswood, and apparently an old woman was murdered there."

"No way! That's awesome. Is there a ghost?" she asks, but then she pauses. "Wait. Like a long time ago, right? Not recently, right?"

Lord help me, I can't resist. "I don't know. Felt like it happened recently as creepy as that place was." If a mother isn't going to strike some notches in her teenage daughters' over-confidence, who will?

"Oh, wow. Wonder if Angie knows about it?"

My pride brings a smile, and I'm well into unloading the dishwasher when I realize Savannah is quiet. Right up until she's standing behind me saying, "Miss Laney wants to know what you and her sister and Jordan were doing in Collinswood. Wants to know if you were spying on her?"

Oh. "Well, we just took a ride over there. There's this place that has amazing grilled cheeses. I need to get dressed." I'm out of the kitchen before I realize I still have a clean bowl from the dishwasher in my hands. I sit it on the end table beside the couch and hurry upstairs. Shoot. Susan's going to kill me.

In my room, I shut the door, unplug my phone from the charger, and start dialing. "Hey Susan. Want to go to Ruby's? Okay, great. See you there in thirty minutes. Oh, and Laney knows we went over to Collinswood. See you soon. Bye."

Now, what to wear?

CHAPTER 38

"Laney was ticked. She called right after I got off the phone with you," Susan says before I can even sit down.

"I'm not sure I even knew it was really supposed to be a secret that we went over there."

Susan channels her inner Missus and cocks an eyebrow at me. "Really?"

"Okay, I didn't mean to tell Savannah. I was messing with her about maybe there being a ghost. Did you know about the woman dying there?"

Susan sighs as she waves at Libby. "I didn't put two and two together at the time. Charming House just seemed like a cute name for a B&B. Plus, everything at the time she died was about Mrs. Johnson. She was a big deal. The funeral was huge, I remember. Our church's ladies took over a bunch of food for the funeral dinner. My kids were all small, so I didn't go, but I made a cake, I think."

I peer out the window onto the square. "I wonder if people will want to stay somewhere a person died. Or was murdered. By her grandchildren. Did Laney say if they're going to play up that part of it? Like a murder mystery thing? Hey, Libby."

Sitting our colorful fiesta-ware cups on the table, Libby welcomes us and pours our coffee. "Isn't the waterpark the greatest? We took Forrest over there after church and had a picnic. I saw your boys. They were having a great time, too."

"Cathy and Steven go with you?" I ask. Steven is a teacher at the high school and has a roving eye. I don't trust him as far as I can throw him. Therefore, I try to keep track of his movements.

"Well, Cathy did. Steven is busy with that summer play he's directing over at the playhouse in Dalton. Says he's going to be getting some our Chancey actors and actresses involved."

Both my eyebrows and Susan's are through the roof. "Over my—"

Susan speaks over me. "Which are the good muffins today?"

"Oh, you're going to love the blueberry streusel one. It's got mandarin orange in it, too. You each want one?"

We nod, and she takes her coffeepot off to fill other cups on her way to the back.

I lean over the table and hiss, "There is no way on God's green earth that Savannah is going over to Dalton to be in any play Stephen Cross is involved with."

"Has she mentioned it?" Susan asks.

I take a minute to think back. It's so hard to remember what all kids say, isn't it? "I don't think so. But it's good to know so I can be ready if she does. So, Laney and Collinswood. What did she say?"

Susan settles back in the booth cushions. "It was strange. She was mad, but then she got all sad." She leans up and whispers, "She started crying, but then she hung up real fast."

"Crying again? Laney?" We're interrupted by delivery of our muffins, and as we open them and spread butter on the halves and take first bites, we concentrate on them. The muffins are delicious. Sweet streusel crumbs with cinnamon on top and inside, big juicy blueberries. Tiny flecks of orange add to the appearance, but add even more to the taste.

After a swallow of coffee to clear my mouth, I ask, "Maybe she really is sick?"

Susan sighs again, and I know she's been thinking the same thing. "That's what started her crying. I didn't say we knew she'd been to the hospital. Didn't want her to know we know she lied about that, so I asked her how she's been feeling. Said maybe she's coming down with something. But she said she's definitely not sick."

"She looked sick on Saturday. And then she ran off like that, and didn't come to church yesterday."

Susan picks at her food normally when she's eating, but I watch as she picks without eating anything she's picking. Just making little piles of muffin crumbs. "What?" I ask. "What are you thinking?"

Another sigh, and she looks up at me. "This feels so weird to say. Really impossible actually."

"What? Tell me."

She half-smiles and shrugs. "I think Laney's jealous."

I laugh. "Yeah, right. Laney? Who in the world would Laney be jealous of?"

Susan frowns. "Me. Me and Griffin."

You know how hard it is to pull back a big, old grin and swallow it? How it causes your breath to stack up in your throat and leaves your lips nothing to do? Well, that's what I'm doing while my friend stares at me.

"Yeah. Maybe." I lift a hand and turn to look for Libby. I don't even know if I need more coffee, but I've got to do something to hide my astonishment. Susan thinks Laney is jealous of her. Apparently Will isn't the only one drinking.

By time Libby refills my half-empty cup, I've got things under control. "Yeah, that's true. Laney could be jealous. What made you think of that?"

Susan pinches some crumbs between her finger and thumb and puts them in her mouth. Watching her, I realize she's got lipstick on. And mascara. Her hair is in the ever-present ponytail, but it looks more intentional and not just jammed back there while she was driving. She has on jeans, but with a blouse, not a T-shirt or even a golf shirt. Wait, what's going on?

"My sister has always had to be the center of attention, and maybe she's not now."

"You look nice," I venture, "makeup and all. When do you start your new job?"

She smiles, and I see I've asked the right question. "Yes, my new job. Maybe Laney's jealous of that. And, well, of Griffin's new job."

"I can see that. She was upset at the announcement. But, still, that seems awfully petty. Even for Laney."

"I agree, but it's all I can think of. And I start my new job next week. Luckily we have a summer intern at the church, so he'll take over the stuff there and I can concentrate on the park. And Laney being jealous will blow over. She'll get onto some new thing and be the best in the world at it, and everything will be all right again. Speaking of the church, I've got to get over there for the staff meeting." She scoots out of the booth then goes back to the counter to pay for her coffee and muffin.

Libby comes by, but I wave off more coffee. "No thanks, but can you pack me up, oh, four of the new muffins? Just leave them at the counter, and I'll be there to pay in a minute."

Finishing this particular muffin, and resisting finishing Susan's, I check the weather on my phone. Thunderstorms are forecasted for today, tonight, and tomorrow. Looks like the rain won't start for a couple hours, so hopefully I'll get home in time. I finish my coffee, do not touch Susan's muffin, and slide out of the booth. At the back counter I'm paying Libby when Ruby comes up and stands beside her.

"That girl, the Yankee coffee girl?"

"Jordan?"

"Yeah. What's her story? I mean, I know all about her screwing on the beach and it getting filmed, but is it right she has kids her old man is keeping her from seeing?"

262

"I guess, yeah. You met her husband. Diego."

Ruby's eyes bug out. "That's who she was screwing around on? Law, she's not got the brains God gave a goose. But that's no nevermind. Although, now I'm not so sure I want to help her out."

I'm shocked. "You're thinking of helping her out? How?"

"She needs some food to serve over there. She wants me to make some up-north kind of stuff. I mean, it's just recipes. How hard can they be?"

"You don't think it'll hurt your business here?"

Ruby wraps her wiry, muscled arms around herself and pats herself on each upper arm. "Well, I didn't say I'd make them good."

"Really?"

"Naw. You're right. Folks'd know I made it, wouldn't they? But I do feel a bit sorry for the girl. I didn't put it together that the looker was her husband. I did meet her mother-in-law, and she's a cold one, I tell ya. My mother-in-law was like that. Thought I wasn't fit for her prince, so I gave her the prince back. Never did think I did right by all that. I should've fought more. Guess that's what I want the girl to know. Don't let no old woman mess up things with your man."

Libby and I nod at her wisdom. Then Ruby slaps the counter. "You tell her. You tell her for me. Tell her I'll make whatever it is she wants me to make. Us girls gotta stick together." Ruby slaps the counter one more time, turns around, and walks back toward the cooking area.

"Ruby. Wait, why should I tell her what you want to say? Just call her." But Ruby is done. She doesn't look back at me, just waves her long arm in the air.

Libby turns to me and shrugs.

"Okay," I say. "Give me a muffin to take to Jordan, too."

Libby slips one in another, smaller, bag and hands it to me. "This one's on the house."

With my two bags, I step out into the windy, humid air and turn left on the sidewalk. My hair whips around my face, and pulling open the big old door of the bookstore/florist is near impossible with the wind holding it shut.

"Whew. At least it's not raining," I say as Shannon pulls the door shut behind me. "Thought I'd bring y'all some muffins." Gertie and Patty are standing behind the book counter, and Andy is just coming down the stairs from Patty's apartment. He hesitates when he sees me, but I yell, "Hey, Andy. Sure was nice to meet your folks yesterday." He slowly walks on down the stairs.

Gertie looks from him to me. "Your folks? How did Carolina meet your folks when you been telling me they're just too busy to meet me?"

See, worth buying muffins, wasn't it?

Patty comes from around the counter, and I hold the bag of four muffins out to her. "Shannon, there's a muffin in there for you, too."

Shannon and Patty sit on the couch, each with a muffin in hand. Gertie has come out to meet Andy on his way to the couch. "Your folks, son?"

He shrugs and maneuvers around her. "They were just in town. Carolina ran into them."

I plant my hands on my hips and squint at him as he makes his way to the chair facing away from Gertie and then reaches into the bag for a muffin. "Ooh, blueberry. These look delicious. We should think about asking Ruby for a muffin wedding cake. You know how people are making their cakes out of a pyramid of cupcakes? We could do muffins."

Apparently, he needs a little help from me to answer his future mother-in-law. "Since you have the minister all figured out, Andy, you're moving on to the wedding cake? Gertie, at least you know you'll get to meet Rev. and Mrs. Taylor at the wedding since he's officiating."

Patty chews her mouthful of muffin, but her mouth is still half full when she puts it together and mumbles, "Your daddy is a preacher?"

Andy cocks his head and scrunches up his face. "Didn't I tell you that?"

Patty shakes her head. "Guess it don't matter none. Just seems funny I didn't know."

Gertie has moved to stand over the chair her future son-in-law is sitting in. "Funny is one word for it. Just hope it's the *only* word for it."

"Andy?" I say trying to get him to fill them in, but he just looks at me and grins, so I do it. "And you'll get to see them in the Wednesday paper. Wouldn't surprise me if they are on the very front page."

Shannon blurts, "Oh, the picketing! Were they with the picketers?"

Gertie and Patty wait. And wait. And wait. Finally, I can't stand it. "Andy told his parents that everybody in Chancey was against MoonShots being open on Sunday mornings, but that the churches were being kept quiet by, well, by whom, Andy?"

He lifts his shoulders and says, "Missus, I guess. Don't know I really said by who."

Gertie looks even more confused. "But why?" She sits down in the chair next to his.

He shrugs again and continues eating.

Patty is watching her mother, when Shannon gets up, brushing crumbs from her hands. "Thanks for the muffin, Miss Carolina. That was delicious." At the end of the couch, she stops. She has on a pale yellow jumper that shows off her dark hair and fits her short stature. She firms up her shoulders and places her hands on her hips. "Andy, it's not funny you talking bad about Chancey. We've been real nice to you. Now for your folks to think we're bad and don't like MoonShots. Well, you just better never do anything like that to *our* business. You've already made it look like a junk store."

And like she's just walked in, Gertie looks around her. Her gaze settles on the junkier aspects of the place and then about the time Shannon gets back to her counter in the flower store side, Gertie's eyes stop on Andy. "Son, me and you got some talking to do."

Patty leans forward. "Mama, don't you mess this up for me."

"We're just gonna talk," Gertie says, still staring at Andy who is happily eating his muffin. She repeats, after she turns her head toward her daughter. "Patricia Louise, we're just gonna talk." Then she looks up at me. "'Preciate the heads up, Carolina. And the muffin. I'll take it from here."

With a nod at her, and a glance to see if Patty looks mad, I turn around.

My work here is done. Now on to next door. Shannon shakes her head at me and grins.

Apparently there's a lull in the wind, and as I push open the door, it opens easily. Too easily. I pile out and would've fallen into a heap on the sidewalk, if I hadn't ended up in Peter's arms.

"Hey there," he says as he stands me up. "You okay?"

"Yeah, door seemed to just give way. Sorry about that."

"No problem. You headed home?"

"Nope," I hold up the small bag. "I've got a muffin for Jordan."

"That's where I'm headed," Peter says, and he extends his arm out for me to lead the way.

We fight the wind down the street to enter the coffee shop. It's so quiet, smells heavenly, and is blessedly cool. For some reason the humidity doesn't seem to invade this place like next door or Ruby's. Probably some new age insulation that also keeps it from smelling like an old building. It smells new, and like coffee. This place makes me miss our home back in the suburbs, again. Nothing else here in Chancey reminds me of Marietta like this place. Old buildings can be beautiful to look at, and connect you to the past, but they might just be overrated. Unless you have the bucks to completely redo them and make them seem like new.

Peter wrinkles his nose at me. "This place feels artificial. Doesn't it?"

We are so on the same wavelength, just going in opposite directions. Why is that so evident now? What if I'd... well, I didn't. I didn't.

"You here for coffee or to see Jordan?" I ask.

"Both. You?"

"Just Jordan. I've had my fill of coffee today. Probably had enough for the entire week."

"Yeah, me too probably, but I'm not going to let that stop me. I'll take a regular with cream and sugar," he says as we approach the counter. The store is empty, but the pastry case is full. I step closer to it as Peter asks Jimmy if Jordan is around. I don't jerk my head when he says he has an appointment with her, but I do frown. From what I hear, that wouldn't be an odd expression when looking in this case.

"They don't look that bad to me. Of course I'm not a real connoisseur of fresh baked goods," I say.

Jimmy, whom I met yesterday during the siege, wrinkles his nose at me, and whispers, "They just don't taste right. I told her to put in a rack of Little Debbies, and she'd do better. She got kinda mad."

"I didn't get mad." Jordan strides out of the back room and around the counter. She has on a royal blue dress and matching heels. The dress is simple, but probably cost an arm and a leg. It's form-fitting with ¾-length, tight sleeves. Her eyes look a softer, deeper blue next to the dress, and she has on pink lipstick that adds to her fresh look. I kind of miss the black. This looks almost approachable. Oh, and she's approaching Peter.

"Can I help you, Carolina?" the smiling lady asks. She and Peter look really, really good together. Now I notice that he's wearing gray pants and a dress shirt. His beard is trimmed and his hair smoothed back. What is it with everyone in Chancey looking good this morning? I did not get the memo.

"Um, here. It's a muffin from Ruby. She says she'll help you out and do whatever you need her to do."

"Just give it to Jimmy," she says as she and Peter exchange a look, and he nods at her.

I hand the bag to Jimmy and turn back toward them. Peter sips his coffee, and they look at me. No, they're waiting me out. They want me to leave. Okay. They can't make me leave. It's a public place.

So I turn towards the door and leave.

Seriously, like I'm going to ignore the unspoken directions of a couple of well-dressed, good-looking people? Please. Do you even know me?

CHAPTER 39

"My garden and just everything is going to burst out all over when this rain stops," FM says as he holds out a hand for our wet raincoats. We left our umbrellas on the front porch.

Jackson apologizes, "We tried waiting for a break in the rain, but there just wasn't one."

"No problem at all." FM shakes Jackson and Will's hands and then gives me a quick hug. He waits for Anna to struggle out of her jacket, and then he gives her a tight hug. "Darlin', it's so good to see you. Your grandmother just couldn't wait for you to get here tonight."

Anna doesn't smile. She hardly said two words on the drive here. And none of us really know her, even though we are now related to her, so we don't know if this is normal or if should we be worried. Will isn't worried, but that's not really surprising. He's just not a worrier.

"Can we go on up?" Will asks, one foot already on the bottom stair.

"No, you may not. We are having dessert first," Missus says as she comes through the kitchen door. "Welcome, everyone. Let's move into the parlor."

The men step back for her to go through and then motion me and Anna to go ahead of them. Missus sits on a rose-colored settee in front of a coffee table on which dessert plates have been set. They each hold a piece of cheesecake, a strawberry, and a drizzle of chocolate. She has a silver coffee service on a tray with china cups. "Anna, sit here beside me. Carolina, there," she says as she points me to the chair directly across from the settee. "Men, sit wherever you are most comfortable, after you get your coffee and dessert. By the way, its decaffeinated coffee since it's late."

She pours coffee for everyone and hands out plates of cheesecake.

"No, thanks. I don't like cheesecake," Anna says.

"Of course you do. Everyone likes cheesecake," Missus says. "Now about the wedding."

Anna takes a small sip of her coffee and sits back, leaving her plate where Missus sat it on the table in front of her.

"You will all be glad to know the music for the wedding is set with the string quartet we decided on and a pianist from Kennesaw. He's quite good, plays for the Atlanta Symphony Orchestra occasionally."

Will is busy eating. Anna is busy not eating. So I ask, "Who is the 'we' you're talking about?"

Missus picks up her fork. She slices off the tip of her cake and lifts the fork to her mouth. She chews, swallows, take a sip of coffee, and finally looks at me. "What is it you want to know, Carolina?"

"I'm just wondering who decided on a string quartet and a pianist."

She clears her throat and looks at her granddaughter. "Anna, did you want to help select the string quartet or the pianist?" Getting no response, she looks to my son who is lifting the crust end of the cheesecake to his mouth, with his fingers. "Will?"

He pauses. "Oh, no. I don't care." Then he pops the last

piece in and grins.

I try again. "What about Patty and Andy? What kind of music do they want?"

"What kind of music do you think they want?" She scoffs. "Any input they would be allowed to have, would most assuredly be inappropriate. Carolina, I understand your sympathies for democratic principles, but this is a wedding. My first wedding in Chancey since my own. There is a certain way it must go. I feel inviting you here, to my home, and letting you see the plans should be adequate to calm any fears you might have. Your son and my granddaughter seem quite willing to leave everything in my hands. Not that I'm complaining, you understand. It is a joy. A joy to bear this family's responsibilities."

"Is Gertie happy for you to bear her family responsibilities, too?"

"Gertie Samson will not ruin this day. She will not." Missus stands up. "Everyone ready for the tour?" She steps around the coffee table, but as she comes in front of me, she stops. "I will send you an email detailing the rest of the arrangements. If you feel Gertie needs to be informed, that is your prerogative. Feel free to get some of her father's moonshine, sit out on the porch, and go over everything, detail by detail. You might have to explain some of the bigger words, but that is your choice." And she walks out of the room. "Follow me."

FM tries to smile at me. "It's all made her a little crazier than usual," he whispers. "I'll work on her."

Jackson offers his hand to Anna and helps her up from the low settee. "Come on, Anna, let's go see. You know your grandmother can be over the top, but she loves you. Right?" His last word comes out rather weak, and Anna looks as weak and unsure as he sounded. And so very tired. Will walks out to the hall, but waits beside the newel post of the staircase. Anna goes to him, and he hugs her to him.

"It's going to be all right," he says as he kisses the top of her head.

On the second floor, Missus is turning on lights. FM pats his granddaughter's back. "She's so excited about y'all living here. It's real nice up there. You're going to love it." Anna smiles at him and they start up the stairs.

Jackson and I bring up the rear, and as we do he studies the steep, old-fashioned staircase. "Well," he mutters to me, "if staircases were your weapon of choice, looks like this one would do the trick."

CHAPTER 40

All the chores I put off yesterday are waiting for me today, but at least the rain has stopped. And FM was right. Everything is bursting out. My garden might be a problem. It's a mess. Everything is climbing on top of each other, and there are these shoots (which I hope are some kind of vegetable, but I have my doubts) that grew four feet last night. Okay, since I really haven't been down here to look at the garden at eye level, they may have already been three feet tall, but needless to say, they are almost as tall as me.

We enjoyed our coffee on the deck, and after Jackson left, I refilled my cup, rolled up the bottoms of my pajama pants, and ventured barefoot into the wet grass of the backyard.

Jackson has been very tolerant of my garden. I can't say he was happy to see so much of the grass tilled up, but he's tolerating it. Or maybe just ignoring it. What's getting harder to ignore is that we can't just mow the part I didn't plant. You can't mow tilled up ground. That really never dawned on me. So, behind the ten feet or so which I planted, there's another twenty feet of weeds, clumps of dirt, and more weeds.

The sound of a car door out front makes me turn around. I walk through the yard to the corner of the house and then up the side yard to the front. Seven on a summer morning is early for any of the kids to be up, or at least to be outside. At the big maple tree on the front corner of the house, I look up on the porch, and there is Susan looking in my front window.

"Hey."

She jumps. "Oh, you scared me. I knew Jackson was in town, so I figured you were up. What are you doing out here?" she asks as she jogs down the porch steps.

"Just wandering around. You've got coffee?"

She raises her travel mug as we walk back the way I'd come. She has on long jean shorts and those plastic gardening shoes, so she doesn't think twice about walking through the wet yard. By now my pants have fallen out of their folds and are dragging in the dewy grass.

"What are you doing wandering around this early?" I ask.

She doesn't answer, and we continue walking in silence. Crows call to each other, and the chirp of bugs in the trees provides a relaxing undercurrent. One tone, like the sound of a fan, or white noise. And I can smell everything growing. Green, if green has a smell, smells like this. Water, dirt, freshness. "Love how it smells out here," I say, taking another deep breath.

As I start up the deck steps, Susan continues past them. "Show me your garden."

"Compared to yours, mine can't really be called a garden," I say to her back.

She says, "Tomatoes, lots of tomatoes. Some kind of squash? Zucchini or yellow squash?"

I shrug. "Don't look at me."

"Hold this," she says as she hands me her coffee. She bends down and begins pushing and pulling at the plants. And true to my fears, she yanks up a couple of the really tall stalks.

"Darn, I was hoping those were just doing really, really well."

"They are. They just aren't anything you want in a garden." She stands back up and reaches for her coffee cup. "Tell you what. I'll come over tomorrow morning, and we can clean this

up a bit. See all those little yellow flowers? Those. And those."
I nod.

"Well, those are all going to be tomatoes, and these are going
to be yellow squash. Those over there, I'm not sure what kind
of squash that is." She takes a sip of coffee and looks out to
the expanse of weeds. "So why did you have Griffin plow up
all that?"

I'm at a loss. "I was bored. Thought I wanted a garden. And
why have a garden at all if you can't have a big one. How hard
will it be to turn it all back into grass?"

She laughs and shakes her head. "Won't be awful, but won't
be easy."

We turn toward the deck, but then she stops and looks back
at the garden. "Wait. Wait a minute." She swivels to face me.
"Okay, here's why I came up here this morning. We're moving."

"What?! Leaving Chancey? But you just got your job, and
Bryan will be lost without Grant. And your family. Where are
you moving to?"

"Slow down. We're not leaving Chancey." She walks toward
the steps and climbs them without answering any of my other
questions.

As I join her on the deck, I see Will in the kitchen. Looks
like he's packing a lunch and he doesn't see us out here. Too
absorbed in the music leaking through closed windows and
doors from inside. Susan and I watch him for a minute, then
she walks to the railing and leans on it. "We bought a house up
in Laurel Cove."

"Laurel Cove?" *Luxury homes on the side of the mountain,
filled with people from Atlanta who want the quaintness of
Chancey, but wouldn't dream of living here.* That isn't a slam
on Laurel Cove; it's actually how they advertise. Most of my
negative thoughts about Laurel Cove came from the mouth of
the woman standing in front of me. "But you hate Laurel Cove."

"Not really. I mean, it's beautiful, right?" She pushes away from the railing and moves to sit at the table. "Maybe I didn't like it because I knew we could never afford to live there."

"Ohh, the new jobs." I sit back down in the chair I began the morning in.

"Yeah. It will be nice to have a new house. No more uneven floors or sticking doors or coats of old paint to deal with. And we have a pool."

"You already have a house picked out?"

"Hey, Mrs. Lyles. Didn't know y'all were out here." Will steps out onto the deck, coffee in one hand, toast in the other. "Congratulations on the new house."

How does he know?

"Thanks, Will. How did you hear?"

"At the dealership yesterday. Mr. Conner was talking about it." Will takes a bite of toast and heads to the door. "Gotta go get Anna up. Bye. Mom, we'll be home earlier today, in time for dinner."

"Okay." Last night we didn't see him and Anna until we went to Missus' and FM's. The door closes and the music from inside fades. I turn back to Susan. "So, you have a house picked out?"

"Yep. It all happened kind of fast. When the job came up for Griffin, part of the package included moving expenses. Except we didn't need to move. But in the contract there was all this money for closing costs and stuff, which made it seem like a good idea to at least think about it. That's where we went with the Reynolds Saturday night. They're buying a house up there, too."

"Really? They didn't mention it."

"No? Guess they were afraid folks would ask about us buying a house, too, and they understood we wanted to let folks know."

"But it's a done deal?"

"I guess. Something about the power company owning property up there and, well, yes, it's a done deal. We signed the papers Sunday afternoon."

"Wait, so you knew yesterday morning? You didn't say anything at Ruby's."

She taps her fingers on the table and looks down the hill toward the river. "I started to, but you found it rather funny that Laney could be jealous of me and Griffin. Plus, I didn't have much time due to the staff meeting."

"Well, Laney being jealous does make more sense now." Laney and Shaw Conner are people who know they belong in Laurel Cove. Susan and Griffin Lyles are not.

She stands up. "I need to go. Just wanted to let you know before you heard elsewhere."

"I'm happy for you guys," I say as I rise and walk around the table to hug her. "It's a big step, and if I can help with whatever, just holler."

She smiles as we hug, and then she tilts her head at me as we pull apart. "Well, now that you mention it. The new house, along with being built on pure rock, doesn't have space for a garden. Maybe I can help with yours? That's one thing I hadn't even thought about until last night. You know I have to have a garden. And then this morning—" She opens her hands toward my back yard.

"Yes. Oh, yes. That would be amazing! I now love the idea of you moving. One hundred percent behind it." I laugh and hug her again. "This way you can't get too high-falutin' and forget about us little people."

We walk into the house. She leaves out the front door while I go upstairs to get rid of my soggy pajama pants. Funny, I always imagined these little towns stayed the same, nothing changed from year to year. But we've not been here a year yet, and it's just change after change after change.

At the top of the stairs, Will dashes out of Savannah's door. "She's not up there."

"Who? Savannah's not in her room?"

"No, I mean, yes, Savannah's there, but Anna's not." He

looks around, and I notice every door on the floor is open, including my bedroom, his and Anna's room, the bathroom and even Bryan's door.

"Anna's gone."

CHAPTER 41

"I slept in Bryan's room last night since he spent the night at his friend's. Anna wasn't comfortable, and she wanted to sit up and read. I took my clothes in there, too, and got dressed in there this morning. I just came up to wake her, like I told you. I thought it was good she was able to sleep in."

Savannah comes down from her room and joins us in the hallway. "Were you just upstairs asking me if Anna was in my room? What's going on?"

Will repeats, "Anna's gone." He shakes his head. "She's not here."

His sister moves past us and down the stairs. "Probably just down at Missus' or Ruby's, right?" She opens the front door. "Yeah, your car is gone."

"The car is gone? She really went somewhere?" Will isn't good in an emergency. He's a thinker, a planner. Steady as the day is long, but not a fast mover. Luckily, his sister is.

"Ruby, hey, it's Savannah Jessup. Have you seen Anna this morning? Is Missus there, or has Patty been in?" She listens while Will and I join her at the bottom of the stairs.

"Okay, thanks, bye." She hangs up. "No Anna, but Patty was there earlier and Missus is outside on the sidewalk talking to FM. Want me to call Missus?"

"Let me," I say and, being Savannah, she can also read minds.

"You'd call her, but you don't know where your phone is, right? Here use mine."

"My phone is somewhere," I mumble as I dial.

"Hey Missus, it's not Savannah. It's Carolina. Has Anna stopped in to see you this morning?" When she says no, I shake my head at the kids.

Will takes a deep breath and goes into the kitchen, saying, "Mom, I need your keys. Where's your purse?"

Missus is shooting questions at me, and I can overhear FM shooting questions at her. I jump into their questions. "There's no need to get all upset. She's just not here. But she's obviously somewhere. We just have to figure out where that is. I've got to go. Y'all go to the bookstore and check with Patty." And I hang up.

Savannah grabs her phone from my hand and runs up the stairs, shouting at her brother. "Don't leave without me. I'll be dressed in two minutes."

Will comes out of the kitchen and hands me my purse. "I can't find your keys in this. You'll stay here, in case she comes back?"

"I guess. But aren't we getting ahead of ourselves. She maybe just went for a drive. Or to get something to eat. Being pregnant is confusing and, well, hard."

Will's dark eyes are scared, and he keeps licking his lips and running his hands up and down his arms. "Yeah, I bet that's it. I'll get my wallet and phone. I need to call work."

In the bottom of my purse I find my keys and my dead phone. Maybe she's tried to text or call me. But when I plug it in on the kitchen counter, nothing comes up. By the time I've called Jackson and explained everything to him, the kids are back downstairs and heading out the door. "Wait!" I call after them. "Check Peter's, too."

Will has calmed down, and now he's thinking. "Yep, I thought of that. We'll get on the way, and I'll make a few calls.

She might've gone to school, even."

Down on the sidewalk, Savannah grabs her brother's arm. "Wait, is her phone off? What do you get when you call it?"

He walks past her, shrugging off her hand. "She forgot it. It's upstairs still plugged in."

Savannah drops her hand and looks back at me. "She didn't take her phone?"

Now, *I* often forget to take my phone with me out of sheer forgetfulness. But if someone under twenty doesn't take their phone, it's not because they forgot it.

It's because they don't want to be found.

All the things I didn't get done yesterday have all been done in record time today. The kitchen sparkles because I was tied to that area while my phone charged. Now it's in my pocket as I make trips between the B&B rooms and the washer and dryer downstairs. Usually I hang the sheets on the line, but I don't get a good signal out in the backyard. So, everything had time to wash, dry, and I've made up the final bed with clean sheets. Still no one has heard from or seen Anna.

The police have been notified and are looking for her, too. Of course, the police looking isn't really official due to the whole 48 hour missing thing. However, one benefit of living in Chancey, a call from Missus *makes* things official. But there don't seem to be any leads. She just drove off. We don't even know when that was. Last anyone saw or heard her was when Will left their room to sleep in Bryan's around 11:30. Now folks are running out of places to look.

Savannah and Will are at the campus right now. Security has searched for her car there, and they are on the lookout for her, but I think Will just needed something to do. Missus and Peter are doing a good job of rattling cages at the police station, and while the Atlanta media isn't interested yet, they are wanting to be kept up to date with any developments. Right now everyone is calm; most likely this drama will all be over any minute. Any minute. Yep, any minute. Then the next thought is, *But this is how every missing person case starts.*

Through the living room window I watch a car pull into our drive, and my heart jumps until I realize its Laney. She pulls several bags from her back seat, so I open the front door and hold it for her. "Figured y'all needed some food. Didn't really want to bring it because you know we're going to be a laughing all about this mix-up just any minute now. But, well, food is always good."

The bags are from a BBQ place out in the country. She puts them on the table and then heads back out again. "I've got a gallon of sweet tea, too."

When I open the door for her to come in, she just hands me the gallon of tea.

"No, I've got things I need to get done. Anna will be back soon, I'm sure of it," she says all this as she's walking down the sidewalk, and when she gets in her car, she never looks back at me. Just wiggles her fingers from the steering wheel before she turns to cross the tracks.

"Now that was strange," I say as I move things to make room in the refrigerator for the tea. Making sure my phone is in my jeans pocket, I go upstairs to look in Anna's room one more time.

There is still nothing there to tell me anything. Her purse is gone as well as her tennis shoes. The clothes she wore last night to FM and Missus' are gone, so we know what she's wearing. Her school books are stacked on the dresser, and her backpack is in the corner. She didn't take her duffel bag or any of our suitcases. Car doors outside make me run out to the hall and down the stairs. At the bottom, I meet my kids, all three of them, along with Jackson, Peter, and FM coming in the front door. Jackson hugs me, and for the first time I feel like crying. "Hey there. Figured we'd all come back here to put our heads together. I took the rest of the day off. Laney told Savannah she was bringing some lunch by."

"It's in the kitchen," I say and reach out to hug FM.

He mumbles in my ear. "Why would she do this? She has to know she'd scare us all half to death," he says. "You've not heard from her either?"

"No, just been here waiting. I'm sure she's off thinking, and she'll be home soon."

"Yeah," he agrees with a nod. "You know she plum forgot her phone. I'm gonna strap it to her wrist when she gets home."

Peter tries to grin at me over his father's head. "Hey, Carolina." As FM wanders on into the kitchen, Peter lowers his voice and says to me and Jackson. "It worries me she didn't take her phone. She's been upset lately, didn't you think so? She wouldn't say much of anything over the weekend, when we were at the house. And I know she was not happy with Mother. What was going on in her head?"

Jackson tightens his lips and shrugs. "No clue. She was awfully quiet last night."

"Yeah, but I just thought once we got past the wedding, and they got settled back down in your parents' house everything would be fine."

Peter nods. "Mother says she loved the renovations."

I grimace at that. "Well, I don't know that she 'loved' them. Like Jackson said, she didn't say much of anything all night."

It occurs to me that one Mrs. Shermania Bedwell is not with us. "Where is your mother?"

Peter sighs. "She's at the house. We kind of got into it. She thinks this is all because she didn't take a strong enough hand with Anna. To quote her, 'Let her roam around town and move here and there. Her wedding being turned into a Gertie sideshow.' She seriously thinks she's been too laidback."

Jackson rubs the back of his neck. "She was anything but laidback last night."

"Really," I agree. "She was downright dismissive anytime I asked even a simple question. We just have to find Anna and let her know we aren't going to stand for her grandmother acting like that anymore."

Peter takes a step toward the kitchen, but turns his head to speak only to me and Jackson. "And I'll move heaven and earth to get my house ready if they would rather live with me."

"With the ghost?" I stammer.

Jackson looks exasperatedly from me to Peter. "Please tell me you two haven't started this ghost thing up again."

Peter moves on into the kitchen, and all I do is shrug. "Are you hungry?" I ask as I move past him. Just as I reach for one of the tubs of barbeque, Will's phone rings.

He looks at the number, shakes his head and frowns to say he doesn't recognize it, but still answers. Suddenly he stands up. "Okay. Okay. That's fine." He listens for a bit and then adds, "That's good. Tell her I love her. Thanks." As he pushes the end button on his phone, the air leaves his body, and he sinks back into his chair.

"She's fine. That was Miss Linda from the cafeteria at school. Not here. Athens. At UGA. Anna's with her."

He takes a long drink of his sweet tea and grins. "She's fine. Oh wow. I can't believe how relieved I am."

Jackson had moved behind him, and now he places his hands on his oldest son's shoulders. "She went all the way to Athens?"

Peter nods. "She's mentioned Miss Linda. She went to her church before her mom died. Is she the lady that got her the job in the cafeteria where you met her?"

"Yeah, but I didn't have Miss Linda's number or anything. I'd called a couple of the girls that were here last fall to keep an eye out for her, but I didn't really think she'd go there. Not great memories with her mom dying and all."

Jackson pulls his keys from his pants pocket. "Want me to drive you over, and you can drive back with her?"

Will leans back, lifting the two front legs of his chair off the ground. "No, she's staying over there a few days, apparently. Miss Linda says she just wants to be by herself and think." He straightens up, and his chair bangs on the floor. He looks at the table. "Doesn't want to talk to anyone."

No one says anything, then Will says what we are all thinking. "But guess that mostly means she doesn't want to talk to me, huh? Probably means she didn't just forget her phone, right?"

Savannah bumps her big brother with her shoulder. "She's tired and confused. Less talking will probably be good for her. Just let her have some space."

Bryan, mouth full of barbeque and bread, adds his wisdom. "With girls, if they don't want to talk, best to just not talk."

As we laugh, we also reach for our phones to spread the good news. Will picks at his plate, then stands up and stepping around his father, opens the back door.

"Let me," I say as I move to follow him outside.

Blue sky stretches without a cloud to break it up. The green of the grass and leaves attempts to match the sky's dominance. It's a two-tone world with the spring colors gone and the dryness of summer not a reality yet. Will stands in the grass at the bottom of the deck's steps. When I close the door, he turns to see me and smiles, saying, "I'm just so relieved, yet..."

I pat his back and put my arm around his waist.

"When I kept telling people she was missing, I'd say 'Anna's missing,' but then at work or up at the school I'd have to say, 'My wife is missing.' I don't think I've said 'my wife' so many times in the entire time we've been married."

"Honey, you've not been married that long. And you had no time to get used to it before you were married."

"What if we made a mistake? Anna's been so sad lately and

wondering that. Maybe we shouldn't have gotten married."

"It's a hard choice, but before you found out about the baby, did you think you wanted to get married? I mean, we didn't even know you were seriously dating."

He walks away from me and down toward the garden. He stands there looking out to the river. A small breeze ruffles his hair, and I wait. Then as I'm waiting, I realize what I'm really doing. I think I'm praying. And realizing that, I lean into it. Let it happen. Okay, so I'm praying. Me, by myself, no one leading me or making me or any of that. My eyes stay open, and I can feel love pouring in the direction of my son standing ten feet away from me. Then I feel that same kind of love surrounding me. Okay, so this is praying. Peace. A feeling of acceptance. Okay.

Okay.

He turns around to me and he's grinning. "Yeah, you know what, I think I did want to be with her her before the baby. I did. I knew at Christmas. Watching her with everyone else, all the kids from school and Savannah's friends and our families all being here. I remember thinking she was the only one I wanted to hang out with when things got crazy." He walks to me.

"And when I went back to school and she stayed here. She's who I wanted to talk to. I don't think I knew I was falling in love, but I couldn't see anyone else." He hugs me extra tight. "Thanks, Mom. I've got to go call Miss Linda. Whatever Anna needs to do is fine by me. She's my wife, and I'm here for her." He jogs up the stairs and yanks open the door, then slams it behind him.

Me? I'm left with all that blue and all that green and that prayer thing.

I'm a pretty lucky woman.

CHAPTER 42

"So why is Peter hanging out at MoonShots?" Savannah asks as she drops her keys on the kitchen table and ambles over to where I'm mixing a batch of brownies.

"I didn't know he was. Here, hold the pan for me to pour this in."

She sticks her finger in the batter and licks it. "Jordan's still married, right?"

That makes me raise my head from my work. "You think it's romantic? Jordan and Peter?" Then I remember the blue dress. After scooping the last of the batter into the pan, I pick up the bag of chocolate chips. "I did see them together recently. All dressed up. Sprinkle some of those marshmallows on top, too."

With the extra chocolate and marshmallows spread out, the pan is ready for the oven. I'm not really a good cook, but I'm a darn good enhancer. Fluffer. Add-to-er. Buttered crackers, potato chips, toasted pecans, or chocolate chips and marshmallows. Throw any of them on top of what you're making and it looks like you know what you're doing. Fake it 'til you make it. And if you're good enough at faking it, you never actually have to make it. (This is where I'd put a winking smiley face if I was typing.)

Savannah takes a handful of marshmallows out of the bag

before putting the wired tie back around its opening. "What's all this cooking for?"

She's talking about the big pot of eggs boiling on the back burner, the brownies, of course, and the platter of boiled chicken breasts. I pick up the platter and take it to the kitchen table as I explain. "It's for Missus' family reunion after Decoration Sunday. We are officially in the family now, since Will and Anna got married."

"And this Decoration is the thing out at the cemetery, right?"

I sit down at the table and begin shredding the boiled chicken. "Yep. I've been assigned deviled eggs, brownies, and the chicken for Missus' chicken salad casserole. She doesn't trust me to make her casserole, just boil the chicken. She probably thought she was insulting me. But I refuse to be insulted with less work."

Savannah slides into the chair across from me, one leg tucked underneath her. She still has on her deep purple MoonShots shirt, and it brings out the dark area under her eyes. She has an olive undertone in her skin like me and my father. It gives us under-eye circles when we're tired, but also lets us tan without burning. Nothing is all good or all bad.

"So, Jordan and Peter?" she asks. "They were all dressed up? Where were they going?"

"I don't know. It was one morning last week. No, wait, it was this week. Monday morning." I sigh and shake my head. "Anna missing on Tuesday made this week seem like forever, but it's only Friday."

We neither one say anything, but we're not actually silent. Finally I ask, "Have you talked to her? Or has Will said anything?"

She gets up from her seat and pulls a banana off the bunch in a bowl at the other end of the table. "No. I told Will to tell her she could call me, but she hasn't. Will says she's fine. You?"

"No. Missus hasn't talked to her either, but FM has. He said she'll be home this weekend for Decoration."

She eats her banana, I shred chicken, and the clock on the wall ticks.

Folding the banana peel up to throw away, she asks again, "So, about Peter and Jordan?"

"Why are you obsessed with Peter and Jordan?"

She shrugs. "I don't know. He comes in and just kind of sits there and drinks coffee. Jordan comes out and sits with him, but they don't talk loud enough for us to hear."

"Us?"

"Well, whoever's working. It seems odd to all of us."

"But not in a romantic way?"

"Mom. He's way older than her. He's like fifty, right?"

"No, he's only forty-five."

"You say only because you're forty-six."

"How old is Jordan?"

"She's almost thirty," Savannah says, wrinkling her nose.

"Really? I guess I thought she was older than that. Not that she looks older, but she's had a career and the kids. Have y'all heard anything more from Diego or his mother?"

"I guess he wasn't too happy about his mother coming down here like that. He was overseas, and she just came down to rub Jordan's nose in everything, apparently. He's coming down soon, and Jordan says he's not leaving without her."

"I know she's ready to get home to the kids."

"Whatever." Savannah has lost interest and stands up. "This is Ricky's last weekend before going off to school for the summer semester, so we're going out tonight, probably out to the lake with some others." She throws the peel into the garbage and moves toward the door into the living room.

"Is he excited?" I ask.

"Not really. He needs to build up his legs, they've told him, and so he needs to work out a lot, and he also has almost a full course load, so he can take a light load in the fall."

I can feel in the air that I have maybe one more question. Kind of like at a news conference when the President starts moving away from the podium and one more question gets thrown out—and answered.

"Are you going to miss him much?" I don't turn to face her, acting like it's thrown off the top of my head. Just sitting here deboning chicken and passing the time. Her not saying anything catches me off guard. She's really thinking about it. Maybe they're more serious than I was thinking. "It's understandable if you miss him. You've been dating him almost a year…" I say as I look over my shoulder.

And she's not there.

The life of a mom. Unheard or ignored, it's all the same.

Chapter 43

"Maybe this means next weekend will be nice for the wedding," FM says, looking out the front windows as folks come scurrying across Crossing's front lawn, bowed under umbrellas and carrying assorted dishes and bags.

We woke up this morning to steady rain. The kind that doesn't blow or drown, just doesn't stop. The skies are heavy gray, and the Decoration picnic has moved inside. Food sits on every available flat surface. Will and Bryan put up the beach canopy on the back deck, so we could put the coolers of ice and gallon jugs of iced tea out there. Jackson went with some of the other men to at least unload the new pea gravel to put on the family plot. It's a raised area in the cemetery where all of Missus' family is buried. The entire area is covered in small white pea gravel and Decoration Day is mostly made up of putting that down and raking it around the head stones, then setting out new plastic flower arrangements. They won't be raking the gravel today, but the truck the gravel is in needs to be emptied out, so they'll dump it and folks will come back later in the week with rakes and the flowers.

FM rocks back and forth a bit. "So, what do ya think about Anna moving in with us until the wedding?"

"Really, I think it's a good idea. This whole thing has been

so off-kilter from the beginning. They need some time apart."
I look around to make sure no one is in hearing. "But you do
think there'll be a wedding?"

He shrugs. "Anna came back with this real determined streak.
More like her grandmother than ever, and she won't say a word.
Missus is right put out. Not happy at all. But no one's told me
there won't be a wedding. What's Will think?"

"Psh, he doesn't want to stir the pot, so he's not even asked
what's going on. Just says that Anna's back, and since they're
already married, it doesn't bother him if there's another wedding
or not. Gertie may kill all of them, and then we can just do a
big ol' funeral."

"You two might want to help out instead of standing there
watching it rain," Missus demands from the dining room.

FM cuts his eyes at me. "Think she means us?"

With a giggle, I turn around and curtsey to Missus. "Yes,
ma'am." Of course, like with Savannah, I assume people remain
around to hear me, but I'm mistaken. She's already turned back
to the table, directing placement of, well, of everything.

Missus was an only child, but her parents both came from
large families, so most of the people are her cousins and their
families. Everyone is excited to meet me and Jackson and Will,
but Anna is the star. I wonder how many are here just to see the
unknown grandchild of the family's matriarch. Anna found a
backbone in Athens, along with a pregnancy glow. Her tummy
is rounding, but she's also standing taller so, she looks much
bigger than before. While in many ways she's prettier than
before, I miss the softness. It's like she came back girded for
battle and hardened. But maybe that's just me. And, honestly,
armor isn't a bad idea if you're going to move in with Missus.
She moved in there last night and told Will to stay here with us
until the wedding. Yeah, you know as much as I do.

When Jackson comes in, he motions to me that he's going
upstairs to change out of his wet clothes, and with everything

in the hands of the ladies who've been doing this dinner for decades, I follow him.

"Hey there," I say as I close the bedroom door behind me. "I bet you're drenched."

He's in the bathroom, and he sticks his head out. "Yeah, but we got it unloaded. Me and Peter did most of it since we lived close enough to go home and change. Things good here?"

I sit on the bed. "I think so. Missus is large and in charge. Will and Bryan have been huge helps. Set up the canopy on the deck and put up the card tables and little side tables in the basement, too. Figure mostly the kids will eat down there. Stinks about the rain."

"Wasn't it weird in church this morning with everyone sitting with their families?" he asks as he takes a golf shirt off the hanger in the closet. "I mean, there were a lot not with family there, but interesting to see the different groups of people."

"Well and even the dinner downstairs. Strange to not have Grant running around with Bryan, and Savannah not having a friend, or Ricky, in tow."

"He leaves tonight, you know."

"Crazy how things change so fast. This time next year Savannah will be getting stuff ready to move off to college herself."

Socks in hand, my husband comes to sit beside me on the bed. "And we'll be down to only one kid." He pulls on his socks as he shakes his head.

"Did you ever think about how we would be a part of a new family when the kids got married? I know I didn't."

"It happened so fast with Will and Anna. Maybe if we'd had more time we would've thought about it. But yeah, all of them downstairs. And church, being told by Missus we were to sit with them."

"And whenever Savannah and Bryan get married, that's more new family. Guess with us never living near our families, it just didn't dawn on me. Speaking of which, have you heard from your mom about the wedding?"

He nods. "Yep, she's coming. Glad we saved the B&B room for her. Shame your folks had the cruise booked this month. But not a shame Dad and Shelby had the book tour already scheduled. I never heard from Colt, but that's not surprising."

Colt is Jackson's younger brother who has never married. It's hard to nail down where he'll be—unless it's football season. Since he's a high school coach we can look at the team's schedule and know where he is every Friday night. Now that Etta's coming, he may actually show up. Jackson's other brother Emerson with his wife and their three daughters are going to be here for the wedding and then continue down to the Gulf Coast for vacation. They live in Virginia, and we don't see them often. They have hotel reservations in Atlanta the night of the wedding, so no worries on putting them up.

"If Colt shows up, we can put him in Bryan's room. Gertie is in her room, your mom in the Orange Blossom Special room, and Anna's friend from Athens, Miss Linda, in the Southern Crescent room."

Jackson lays his hand on top of mine. "Enough stalling. Time to go downstairs. Besides, I'm starving, and I can smell the food all the way up here." He starts to stand up, but I pull him back with a tug on his hand.

"Do you think Anna's happy? She seems different since she came back."

He sighs and looks at me with one side of his mouth tightened. "I honestly don't know. Peter asked me the same thing. He thinks she's different, too. He says it's like an armed camp over at his folks' house. No fighting, but Anna and Missus at odds."

"But I don't want my son to live like that," blurts out of my mouth before I can stop it. "He doesn't deserve that. Not to mention the baby. The baby definitely doesn't deserve to live in an 'armed camp.' I'm having real trouble being happy about this wedding. Everyone at church and downstairs congratulating me and smiling and I'm heartsick. Plain old heartsick."

Jackson wraps his arms around me and lays his head on my shoulder so that I can lay my head against his. When he pulls away after a minute or two, he smiles at me. "But, honey, there's nothing we can do. Will is a grown man. A grown, *married* man." He stands up and pulls me up beside him.

Thinking of my son living with Missus makes me cringe and lean in for another hug. Against my husband's chest, I say, "Well, I just want you to know. If in the next few months Missus gets pushed down her staircase, I'll swear on a stack of Bibles it was a ghost. A very *friendly* ghost."

CHAPTER 44

"They didn't want a rehearsal dinner. Said it repeatedly. No, we don't need anything like that. Just a small wedding, just for the memories." My muttering to myself almost keeps me from hearing the phone answered on the other end.

"Hello? Hi, my name is Caroline Jessup, and I'm trying to find a venue for a rehearsal dinner this coming Friday night. Yes, I know it's last minute. Do you have something or know of a place that might?

"I have no idea how many. You tell me how many you can fit in and that will be the number we have. Sure, I can hold." Closing my eyes, I stretch my neck and try to slow my breathing. All that calmness is for naught when the memory of Anna asking me about the rehearsal dinner last night pops up. Again.

Everyone was pretty much gone from the Decoration Day stuff, and those of us left in the house were busy washing and putting away dishes or picking up stray napkins and cups. The guys were out back taking down the canopy and putting the coolers away. The rain had kept right on up throughout the day and was still doing its thing. The sun never made an appearance and it got dark early for a late spring day. As the house got darker, the house got quieter, until it was only me and Missus in the kitchen. Anna had been upstairs taking a nap, and the first we knew she was downstairs was when she called to ask one of us to bring her some iced tea. Did I say, "Ask"? Okay, good. Missus ignored her, but I pulled out one of the glasses I had just dried and filled it with ice and tea, then carried it into the living room. She was on the couch, wearing her gray dress from church and the dinner. In the gray light, she looked so peaceful with her shiny hair laying on her shoulders, rested eyes, and a pearl necklace adding to her own glow. I sat the glass down and then took a step back. "You look beautiful today. That gray is a good color on you, especially with your eyes."

"Thank you," she said. "It's been a long day. So many people to meet. I wanted to ask you about the rehearsal dinner. Will is hopeless, he said he didn't know anything and keeps forgetting to ask you."

I paused. "I thought you didn't want one."

She laughed. "Wasn't that silly of me? Of course we should have one, don't you think? A chance to be with just the family. Andy's family is having theirs in his father's church fellowship hall. I think a restaurant would be more fun, don't you? Would be nice to have some wine for everyone, and good food. But I don't want to keep you from your cleaning in the kitchen. Wherever you decide will be fine. The rehearsal is at six." She laid her head back and closed her eyes, without ever taking even a sip of her tea.

Heart racing, I walked back into the kitchen and leaned against the counter. Missus dried the plate in her hands and put it away. Then handing the damp dishtowel to me, she looked in my eyes and said, "Welcome to my world."

"Mrs. Jessup?" The voice on the phone brought me back to reality. "Yes, our upstairs private rooms is available for this Friday evening. It only holds up to forty people. I can send you an email with our contract, menu, and other information. We need a credit card number to reserve it. We can do that now, or would you like to look at the contract first?"

"Let me take a quick look at the contract, and I'll call you right back, okay?"

I unplug my phone and rush downstairs to the B&B office and computer. Gertie is sitting at the kitchen table and waves at me as I pass. "I need to talk to you, Carolina."

"In a minute. I need to do something first." In the office, I take care of everything for the rehearsal dinner. Missus suggested this restaurant, and I've heard Peter rave about it so I'm sure it's suitable, and the contract looks fine. Luckily, the Italian Bistro can handle everything we might need or want. Of course, what *can't* you get handled with a good credit card number?

Back in the kitchen, I pour a cup of coffee, offer a warm up to Gertie, then sit down across from her.

"Didn't think y'all were doing a rehearsal dinner," she says.

"Yeah, me either. Up until Anna decided she wanted one last night."

"You think it's being pregnant that has turned her into Miss High & Mighty?"

I shrug and shake my head as Gertie continues, "Or do you think she's just like her grandmother and been hiding it all this time?"

My only response to that is to take a sip of coffee and scream in my head, "Please, God, No!"

"Anyway, wanted to talk to you about what all you said about the bookstore when you came in, and wanted to talk about Andy."

I remember being in the bookstore, but that seems like a million years ago now. "What exactly did I say about the bookstore? I mostly remember telling you about Andy's parents and the picketing."

She shifts herself around and rests more fully on her arms. "Yeah, there was all that, and believe me, I'm not looking forward to the rehearsal dinner at their church. I'm afraid they're going to turn it into a church service. His dad is already not happy about the ceremony being over here in your church. We pretty much just said Missus made us do it. Surprising how that stops people from complaining."

That makes me grin. "I'll have to remember that."

"Shoot, you're the one I learned it from. Seems nothing 'round here's your fault. Anyway, you made me see the light about how Andy boy was turning your bookstore into a junk shop. Lord knows, Patty will let him do whatever he wants... and no comment on that being how she got a marriage proposal so fast... I'm talking about the business here. You know, I am a businesswoman first and foremost."

Like a kid trying to figure out which present to open first on his birthday, my mind dashes between all she said. I do *not* blame everyone else! *My* bookstore? Patty letting Andy do whatever he wants. No, never mind, that one I *don't* want to unwrap. Okay, picked one. "*My* bookstore? You kicked me out, remember?"

"So you never wanted to run the bookstore?"

"Of course, I did. I started it, didn't I? You—"

She eases back in her chair, moving her folded arms from the table to her chest. "There you go. Wasn't your fault at all, was it? You know, you could've told me to go jump in the lake."

"It's your business. You pay the rent. You get to decide who works there," I argue as I stand up and walk to the sink to set my coffee cup in it.

"But you sure didn't fight me about it, did you? Girl, you need to decide what you want and then go get it. Don't believe I've ever seen the likes of someone with more opportunity and less gumption in my life. Makes you think God's surrounded you with pushy people just a-hoping you might one day push back. Well, I gotta go get dressed and get down to *my* bookstore." She stands up then pushes her chair up to the table.

I keep my eyes focused out the window over the sink and wait to hear her door close down the hall.

How ridiculous. God surrounding me with pushy people,

so I'll push back. For crying out loud, that's crazy. With a tilt upward of my head, I stare at the light blue morning sky until a sigh escapes. "And just when I was beginning to like you."

Chapter 45

"Well, at least now we know there's going to be a wedding," I say with a sigh. It's Wednesday morning, the week of the wedding. Finally, the rain has ended, and after cleaning all day yesterday, Crossings is ready for Jackson's mom, Etta, and Miss Linda from UGA.

"That's true," Laney says. "So, tell me what's going on with Anna staying at Missus'? Aren't they already married? Why would she move in there earlier than need be?"

"Laney, come down to Ruby's. I've been sitting out here on the steps of the gazebo talking to you for fifteen minutes already. I'm starving and want to go inside. You can't be that busy if you can talk to me all this time."

"Then never mind. I'll talk to you later. I have work to do." And she hangs up on me.

Susan is busy with her new job, and Laney says she is, too. But I'm not quite buying that Laney was at work. She seemed more than ready to chat on the phone forever. Oh well, there'll be someone to sit with in Ruby's. At the very least, I can sit at the back counter and talk to Ruby and Libby.

Whoa. In the middle of the street that thought stops me. Why do I want someone to sit with?

Back in the suburbs, I used to eat alone a lot. Take a book

or a magazine and never have any fear of anyone bothering me. People don't bother you if they don't know you. Here? Everybody knows you. And they don't think twice about sitting right down at your table. How have I come to expect, and maybe, *maybe*, even enjoy that?

My steps are slower and I consider not going into Ruby's, but going down to MoonShots. It's a different crowd there (if you can call empty a crowd), and Jordan doesn't do idle chatter. But I didn't even bring a book with me. Wait, when did I start going out without a book in my purse?

The bells overhead laugh at me as I push open Ruby's door. MoonShots coffee may be better, and soft music can be heard due to less talking, but have you noticed how many skinny people are usually there?

"Hey, Carolina. Ruby was just asking if I'd seen you," Libby says as I enter.

Scooting around Libby, I spot the mayor's wife and a couple other moms of young kids. "Looks like y'all have a morning off."

Betty smiles and takes a deep breath. "The Presbyterian church is continuing their Mother's Morning Out this summer. Just one day a week, but that's better than nothing. Carolina, do you know Jenny and Tara?"

"Just from when I worked at the library. Good to see you again. You too, Betty. Enjoy the rest of your morning off."

At the next table there are more familiar faces who smile and say "hi," but I don't stop to talk as Ruby is at the back counter making a big "come here" sign with her arm. She has a cup of coffee poured and a muffin sitting on a green plate in front of her. With the hand she's not waving me in for landing with, she's pointing at the muffin and coffee.

"Hey, Ruby. This for me?" I pull my phone out of my front jean pocket and sit it on the counter. These shorts from last year are a little tight. Probably shrunk in storage.

302

"Who else? Coffee black and a bran muffin. You look like you need to lay off the chocolate ones for a bit." Okay, in MoonShots, they may all look down their skinny noses at you in judgement, but they usually don't say it to your face.

"Ruby!" Libby says. "Be nice."

Ruby shrugs her bony, pointy shoulders in her droopy tank top, but you don't hear me saying anything, do you? "Sorry, Carolina. At least you don't yo-yo up and down like that make-believe beauty queen Laney Troutman. You seen her lately? Wow." Ruby jumps when Libby sits the pot of coffee down hard on the counter burner behind her. "Oh, okay. Everyone looks amazing. Everyone in Chancey is ravishing and thin. And sweet, everyone is sweet as sugar, right? Come to think of it, the thinnest one around is that snotty Yankee girl. Guess you can't have looks and manners."

Libby rolls her eyes and then pokes Ruby in the back with her elbow as she passes. "Didn't you want to talk to Carolina about something other than how unattractive her friends are?"

"Yeah," Ruby looks over her bare shoulder at her employee. "That's why I asked you if you'd seen her."

Libby rolls her eyes again and walks out from behind the counter. "Well, there she is."

Ruby watches Libby start the rounds of refilling coffee cups. "Sometimes I think I need to hire some young person who would appreciate this job more."

"Right." I take a sip of coffee. "You've obviously not hung out with any young people lately. What did you want to ask me?"

"Did you tell that Jordan I'd help her out?"

"Yes. That very same day." Hmm. The bran muffin is not bad after all.

"She hasn't said anything to me. And you're sure you told her?"

"Like I just sat here and lied to you?"

"No, I guess not. But I'm kind of excited about trying to

make those new things she was talking about. Been looking up recipes for biscotti and scones and even strudel. Good to try new things every so often." She turns to the door at the sound of its bells jingling. "Here comes your friend. Wonder if she knows her sister is turning into Shamu?"

"Ruby! Behave," I instruct in my best librarian voice before turning around to greet Susan.

"Savannah said you were here. I called the house looking for you." She reaches out and picks up my phone. "Yep, ringer turned off."

"Oh, forgot I did that. What do you need?"

Her eyes are shining as she sits down. "Have you talked to Missus?"

"Not since Sunday night, why?"

"We're going to do it. We're going to hold the reception for the weddings at the Lake Park. And I'm in charge."

"What? Isn't it at the conference place in Canton? Thought Missus had that all wrapped up."

"I convinced her to unwrap it. It'll be my first major event. The weather is going to be perfect, and so I talked her into it."

Ruby makes a harrumphing sound. We both look at her, and her eyes are definitely not shining. "Never known Shermania Cogdill Bedwell to be talked into anything."

And there goes the shining of Susan's eyes. "But…"

"Not saying it's not a good thing, just don't fool yourself that it wasn't what she wanted all along. Want a muffin?"

Susan turns to me. "You think it's a good thing, right?"

"I guess. I didn't know the park was set up for private events like this."

"Well, we're closing early. I'm going to put up all kinds of those little white lights, like I did for Leslie's graduation party. The caterers said it was no problem. I do have to go order the chairs and tables and stuff, but that's not a problem, right?"

I shrug.

Ruby shrugs.

Susan stands up. "I've got to go."

"Wait, is that all you wanted with me?"

"Mostly, but also to say congratulations on the bookstore. Heard you're back in charge. Talk to you later," Susan says as she backs away from the counter. Then turns and scurries out the door.

Ruby takes a couple steps back, into the baking area, then comes forward to lean on the counter in front of me. She holds a chocolate muffin. "You didn't even know you were back in charge over at the bookstore until she told you, did you?"

"No."

"Here, you might as well have some chocolate. You are now in charge of Andy and Patty, and Gertie is your boss, so a few extra pounds are the least of your worries."

CHAPTER 46

Not only can't I find anyone to sit at Ruby's with me, what could be a fun road trip to check out the Italian Bistro for the rehearsal dinner is just me. Alone. All week I've tried to get someone to go with me, but they all have these so-called jobs—which are really cutting into my social life. Etta won't get here until tonight, and tomorrow being Friday, and the date of the rehearsal dinner, it's now or never. So, alone it is.

Apparently, I also have a job now. I got out of Ruby's yesterday without seeing anyone from the bookstore, and I avoided seeing Gertie this morning before I left. So, no bookstore updates yet. However, I have to risk talking to Gertie and stay at home at some point to deal with the mess in the B&B's office. All of the upcoming guests at Crossings are associated with the wedding, so the disorganization doesn't really matter, does it? I bet Laney has Charming House running smooth as fresh peanut butter. She's really good at organization and keeping everything straight. I always thought she was just dropping in and messing around, but apparently she was actually doing stuff, real stuff for Crossings. I miss her messing around now.

So, a road trip seems perfectly logical. Funny how those swooping curves *out* of Chancey make me so happy. Sunglasses on and window open with the radio up loud on a classic rock station doesn't hurt either. We're supposed to have a beautiful stretch of weather after all that rain we got. Once I get to the interstate, or four-lane as everyone in Chancey calls it, I roll up my window and turn the radio down a bit.

Near Canton, my exit, the new shopping centers and restaurants surprise me. It looks more and more like Marietta every time I come here. Construction took a break during the recession, but the pace has picked up again. And it's all so pretty. Mature landscaping accents parking lots and signs that are only a few months old. Old brick, which probably isn't brick at all, makes the buildings appear substantial. Signs are tasteful and substantial, well, they would be if the stones making up the signs were something other than styrofoam. At the first red light off the interstate, I get a glimpse of a hillside of apartment buildings. Lots of customers to keep all these shops and restaurants open. Instant customers. Instant buildings. Instant happiness. Hmmm, I don't remember being this cynical before we, um, before we moved to Chancey. Could being surrounded by bricks that were in place before the Civil War have jaded me for my beloved suburban beauty?

Shaking off my doubts at the first traffic light (hanging from a brass and black pole with acorn-sculpted finials and baskets of purple colored petunias), I take a deep breath and a quick look at Google Maps on my phone.

Missus mentioned the Italian Bistro to me Sunday night in the midst of my panic about a last-minute rehearsal dinner. She said since it's a favorite of Peter's, she'd checked it out for the reception, but decided it wasn't big enough. She said it would be perfect for the rehearsal, and that it wasn't too far from Chancey.

The farther I drive, though, the less things look new. Just as things begin to look not only not new, but a bit shabby, my Google Maps guide says to turn. Then the shabby turns into old, but not bad old, just real. Like real wood and brick and stone and actually matured, in-place, landscaping. Not drawn out on paper last month and planted, full-grown, this month. At least that's how it is on one side of the road. The other is undeveloped and for sale, according to the string of large signs I pass.

My final turn is into a parking lot fronting a string of businesses, and the one on the end nearest me is my destination. Cars fill the parking lot as its right at lunch time. I didn't think about calling first to get a tour. They offered one when I made the reservation, but I didn't set anything up. At least I can get lunch and maybe things will clear out.

It's pretty non-descript on the outside, but even from the sidewalk I can smell garlic and roasting meat. It's hard to believe we used to live surrounded by restaurants like this. I completely took that for granted. Now my knees practically weaken at the idea of a new place. I have to admit, the idea of no one knowing me adds to the knee-weakening. (Another thing I took for granted.) When the door opens, I'm in a small, busy area. It looks more like a store than a restaurant. There are a couple metal tables, a refrigerator case with salads, meats, and cheeses. There are shelves around the other walls and tasteful displays set all around. Then I realize it *is* a market. The Italian Shoppe says a big sign, and then I notice the sign for the restaurant over another door. I go to it and pull.

The smells intensify, and the light dims. A sign says to seat myself, so I step into the room to locate a small, empty table. I survey everything around me and smile at the swooping staircase up to an open area. That's our room. The one at the top of the stairs, the lady had said. Missus was right; it is perfect. After lunch, I'll ask to go up and look around. A row of small tables near the stairs is my destination, and I'm passing occupied tables when suddenly Peter is sitting right in front of me. Next to Jordan. They look very cozy, except for that startled look on their faces. Startled? Guilty? Either works.

Peter is dressed up again, hair pulled back neatly, white dress shirt with a tie loosened around his neck. Jordan is back in black, wearing a sleeveless dress with a high neckline. Her hair is loose and brushes the tops of her toned shoulders. Peter's arm lies on the back of her chair, and their plates are pushed together, as well as their glasses.

"Carolina," they both say, but they look around behind me. They even make me look.

"Who are you looking for? To see if I'm alone? Well, I am. Jordan, you're married. Peter, she's married and has kids."

"Yes, I know," Peter says as he stands up next to me and then puts his arm around me. "Let me explain."

"Get your arm off me." My face is hot, and I'm confused at him standing so close and trying to put his arm around my back. As I push away, he stays right with me, and when I bump into a lady at the next table, she complains. I try to turn around, but Peter bustles me back toward Jordan. What in the world?

Jordan has her head bowed and her hand across her forehead. Good, she looks embarrassed. To free myself of Peter, I step toward Jordan. "You need to remember stunts like this are why you are in this 'godforsaken place' as you call it. You have two little girls that miss you. And Diego misses you, too." Now, I turn on my one-time friend. "Peter, I'm ashamed of you. I'm leaving now, and I won't say anything because, well, there's the wedding and the baby. And I already have too much on my mind. Peter, you need to come home, and Jordan, you need to go back to New York." This time I'm able to leave Peter at the table and dash back out the door to the shop and then outside.

Savannah was right. *Peter and Jordan.*

What are they thinking? In the van, I sit and wait to calm down. Maybe I overreacted. But no, they were sitting together. And had been sitting together while they ate. They looked very nervous to see me. Why did Peter keep trying to hold onto me?

Guess he didn't want me to leave until I promised not to say anything. And I thought he liked me. That's laughable now. And embarrassing.

As I pull out of the parking lot, my stomach grumbles. Darn, that food smelled delicious.

CHAPTER 47

It's my favorite time of day in what is quickly becoming my favorite place to spend it. There isn't even the smallest ripple on the water. Unlike at our house, the water here forms a lake to the side of the river. The constant movement of the water at the house, even when it's slow and sluggish, changes things. Also, along the river, the water's edges are mostly inaccessible banks of red clay and tree roots. Here at the lake park, the smooth expanse of grass and pine needles slides right into the water. In the swimming area, it's met with a beach of sand, but here, off to the side, the tall pines are reflecting in the still water at their feet.

Luckily, the drive home from the restaurant provided time for my anger to subside, helped along by a hamburger and fries from McDonalds. (Like a good credit card, they fix most anything.) I arrived back at Crossings just minutes after Etta's arrival. My mother-in-law is a happy sort, and even more happy since she's moved to the beach. Bryan apparently carried her bags to her room all the while expounding on the new Lake Park. I got home just in time to put my stamp of approval on the plan to pick up a pizza and eat dinner there.

Now that we've eaten, Etta is watching all of Bryan's tricks on the diving board from a lawn chair at the edge of the beach.

Jackson and Savannah are also swimming, and I have wandered off to watch the lavender sky reflect on the still water. Being around the end point, the splashing of my family isn't disturbing the mirror-like water here.

The air is as still as the water, and while substantial, it's not heavy with heat like it will be soon. There's a softness to the air and light. Just on the edge of darkness, my eyes see more clearly than in the light of day, farther and deeper. And my breath slows and deepens. Today sure didn't go as planned, but I do think the rehearsal dinner will be great at the Italian Bistro, so that was accomplished. Thinking of Jordan's girls brings a sigh, but that's her decision. And maybe, well, maybe it wasn't what it looked like?

Squeezing my eyes shut, my headache digs deeper. I can't let this ruin this weekend. Peter and Jordan are adults, and I don't want him. I'm happy with Jackson—it was just so abrupt seeing them there. Wait. Stop thinking about them.

Rolling my shoulders, I breathe deep and smile at Etta's laugh. My kids have such great grandparents. My eyes pop open. Wait, I'm going to be a grandparent. Like, really soon. And then the park looks different. I see myself in the water teaching a little one to hold its breath before easing him or her under. Or me, sitting in the lawn chair blowing up water wings, while a bouncy tot urges me to hurry.

Guess I knew this would all happen, but I don't remember ever thinking about it. I never had time to wish for a grandchild or plan a child's wedding. I've always found it hard to live in the moment. I seem to have no problem spending time regretting passed moments or worrying over future moments. But this moment? Very hard to focus on, don't you think?

And now the moments are flying. I keep finding myself blinking my eyes and shaking my head, but my vision doesn't clear. And while I'm doing that—another moment passes. And another.

Turning around, I tune in. Jackson meets me to walk back as I rejoin my family and the others enjoying the summer evening at our new park. He rubs his wet arm against my shirt sleeve. At first I push him away, then I laugh, lift his arm, and lay it around me, on my shoulders.

"I'll get you wet," he says. But I hold onto his hand and snuggle into him.

"So? How perfect is this?" I say. "I'm glad your mom is here."

"Me too. Hope the weather is this nice for the reception on Saturday."

"Yep, but all that matters is right now, this very moment. How about ice cream on the way home?"

Jackson kisses me and laughs. "I don't know. Think we can talk Bryan into it?"

"It's so cool, Meemaw! It's an old gas station, but they sell ice cream. Good ice cream. The ladies are like you."

Savannah swats at her brother. "Shut up. They're not like Meemaw."

Bryan shoves a stiff arm at his sister from his place in the back seat of the minivan. Etta and Savannah have the two middle-row chairs. "They are too like Meemaw, nice and funny."

My daughter and I make eye contact as I look over my shoulder. The ladies at the gas station are known for a lot of things. Nice and funny are the gentlest, and least used, descriptors.

Miss K and Miss G man the cash register at the gas station across from the high school. Right beside the cash register is an ice cream cooler that holds six tubs of ice cream. And it's good ice cream. The two tubs closet to the register are always vanilla and chocolate. The other four rotate depending on the ladies' whims. You never know what will be there, and they never apologize for an errant choice. Often the adults are left ordering what we don't want, because a new flavor can only be bought when that tub is empty.

A string of old picnic tables lines the blacktop on one side. Behind them is a grassy patch of weeds. Parking is on the other side of the gas station lot. It's not exactly laid out for safety, with everyone moving across the area for pumping gas, but everyone knows what the deal is and just tries to be careful. It took me some getting used to, since in the suburbs everyone is preoccupied with safety and signs. To allow people, especially children, to figure something out on their own is considered neglect, if not full-out abuse.

We park, and everyone goes inside because, unless you want chocolate or vanilla, that's the only way to know what's available. Bryan gets to the cooler first and asks for a cone of pink bubblegum, then turns to the newspaper stand. Now this is a feature you don't find everywhere. Newspapers that list out the recent area arrests, with mugshots and everything. Miss G and Miss K read each one cover to cover as soon as it comes in and are conversant on every single legal indiscretion, but most especially on the more colorful ones. So Bryan, knowing the drill, places his order, then, while he waits, bends to look at the front of the most recent arrest paper.

"D'ya see the one about that boy that tried to rob the Krystal through the drive-up window? Stuck his hand in to grab a wad of cash, but the girl at the window was a-thinkin' and she just pulled that window lever. Got holdt of him good and tight!" The Misses look and sound alike, big and country. Miss K has long white hair she always wears in a scrappy braid that trails down to a wisp. Miss G has red hair, but not a natural red. More like mercurochrome red. Think fake fire. Miss G is the one telling the burglary story, and she moves onto other local crime stories of note as she rings up our total.

Etta chooses butter pecan, and Jackson tries red velvet. I like chocolate with nuts or fudge, but the other two choices are the pink bubblegum Bryan got, and orange and vanilla cream. While I'm deciding, I'm distracted by the drive-thru robber story, and at the end I just point and nod to Miss K, who is standing over to the side, holding my empty cone. Whatever I get will be fine.

Miss K bends into the ice cream case and comes back with a scoop of orange and white. As she stands up, she give a little swing to her head to make her braid fall back across her shoulder. "There you go." Pushing the ice cream down into my cone, she takes her time, then finally handing it to me asks, "So, how was that Italian place? Go there much?"

"What?" Even though I've got my fingers on my cone, she won't let go. I look up, and she's staring at me. "Um, The Italian Bistro? We're having the rehearsal dinner for our son there tomorrow."

She nods, but still won't let me have my ice cream. "But today? Looked like things got exciting."

Now I might not want my ice cream. My stomach doesn't feel that great. "Today? Um, why?"

Lifting her hand away from my cone and backing up, she raises her eyebrows. "You should know."

Jackson has paid and he, his mom, and Bryan are near the door when Savannah comes in. "Here she is," Jackson says. "Hers is the extra one I paid for."

"Thanks, Dad," she says as she holds the door for him, Etta, and her brother to leave. When the door closes, she comes to me, and I notice she doesn't look in an ice cream frame of mind.

"What's wrong?" I ask while preoccupied licking the drips running onto my fingers.

"You and Peter. I thought that was, was, well, nothing. What were you doing today?"

Mid-lick, I glance back at Miss K, who looks like one of those huge old Galapagos turtles with their heads extended out as far as possible. Not surprisingly, it's extended in my direction. "Today? Me and Peter?"

She then holds up her phone three inches from my face. "You are on TMZ. They have video."

"Video of me? Doing what?" I hold out sticky, orange fingers toward her phone, but she jerks it away.

"Yeah, you and Jordan fighting over Peter in some dark restaurant."

See, this is why staying in the moment is highly overrated. Some moments suck.

CHAPTER 48

"Well, at least you're the one being cheated on instead of being the one doing the cheater," Laney opines the next morning. "And you look pretty darn good in the video."

"I'm not either. There is no cheating. Where did they come up with that story?" I ask, as we walk up the sidewalk along the downtown shops. Missus is hosting a bridal tea this morning for both Patty and Anna. Last I'd heard, Patty wasn't invited, but then after Anna came back home from her stay in Athens, Patty *was* invited. Gertie, too.

I have on a silver-blue skirt and short-sleeve, white blouse. Laney is wearing a caftan. It's a nice caftan, rich jewel tones and a silky material, but still a *caftan*. Her hair is as large as ever, glossy black and curls that stay where they belong. Susan won't be here this morning as she's come up with some issues about moving the reception to the park, but nothing she can't handle, she's assured us all. Etta begged off saying she wants to reserve her strength for the rest of today's festivities.

We cross the street and walk up the sidewalk, where the thick green and white leaves of FM's *hostas* are all crowned with light purple flowers on the ends of thin, single stalks. They bob in the morning breeze and dart at our knees. The small front lawn is crisp and perfect, edged in old bricks. On the gray and salmon porch, turquoise pillows and cushions adorn the wicker furniture. Big ferns in hanging planters, still wear glistening strings of water droplets from their morning watering. It's hard to believe that a few short weeks ago, this house had a tree lying on it. .

Laney steps back for me to go up the porch steps first. She gathers the long skirt of her dress out of the way.

"That's a beautiful caftan," I say, watching her face for any reaction.

She only sighs as she motions for me to walk on ahead, then asks, "And why can't you ask Peter how TMZ got it?"

"One, because he won't answer my phone calls, and two, I'm scared to be anywhere near him. I guess what all the celebrities say is right: the paparazzi are just everywhere."

She laughs as she joins me on the porch. "Seriously, Carolina? The paparazzi?"

"Well, how else do you explain it?"

She just shakes her head, and we both turn when the front door is opened. Missus looks at Laney, and her eyebrows dip; then she looks at me and does a slow head shake. "What in the world have you dragged my son into now?"

Laney's caftan comes in handy as an invisibility cloak when she fluffs it out and breezes in the door between me and Missus, grabbing my hand and pulling me in her wake. "We want to say hello to everyone. Thanks, Missus."

In the formal living room, we find the other guests, along with the guests of honor. Patty looks scared to death, Anna looks bored to death, and Gertie looks pert near death.

This should be fun.

Laney leads us to the girls and then pushes me towards the seat next to Gertie. "I'm sure this is reserved for the mother of the groom. Or is Andy's mother sitting here?" Laney asks. Patty's shrug is tight, Anna's is loose, and Gertie closes her bloodshot eyes and shakes her head.

The lady I remember from the picketing waves at us, "No, I'm right here."

So I sit down in the seat Laney chose for me.

Gertie opens her eyes, barely. "Hi, Carolina."

"Are you okay?"

"No. No, I'm not. Guess you know I got in late last night. Hope we didn't wake you up."

"I didn't hear you. You said, 'we'? You and Patty?" (Funny, but I already know the answer to the question. You probably do, too.)

Gertie snorts. "Not much left you can get arrested for in most states, but I believe doing what I was doing last night with your own daughter might just be illegal in all fifty." She snorts-laugh again and looks more alive. "Did you see Bill this morning? He was still sleeping when I pulled myself out of bed for this tea rigmarole thing."

Savannah is here helping serve along with Jenna and Angie and Susie Mae. Bryan spent the night with a friend we ran into at the ice cream store, so at least this stranger, Bill, Gertie picked up, isn't in the house with my kids. Just my mother-in-law. "So," I say. "Where did you meet this Bill?"

She pushes her hair back with both hands and takes a deep breath. "Oh, we go way back. He lives up on the mountain where my family used to live. We get together every so often. You know I needed a date for the rehearsal dinner and the wedding, of course."

"Of course." How could I have forgotten there are social expectations which simply must be followed? For crying out loud. I do feel a little better that she didn't just meet him last night out at the Chili's at the four-lane. "Maybe I should let Etta know he's there," I say as I pull out my phone and text her.

Missus calls us all to attention and makes the introductions. In the midst of her hostessing duties, my phone dings, and she scorches me with a look. When she looks away, I read the text from Etta. "Yes, I know. Delightful man. I made him breakfast."

Risking another fiery look, I whisper to Gertie. "Etta made him breakfast, so he's up." I smile when she looks at me, but my smile falls when she stands up.

"Gotta go." With her long legs, she steps over and around those of us between her and the door. In the hall, with no one in her way she makes even better time, and when the heavy door slams, our tea cups shiver in their saucers. Now, I'm getting lots of hot looks. From everybody.

"What did you say to her?" Savannah asks.

Am I the only one that hears the judgement in that?

"Me? Nothing. I mean, nothing except that..." Okay, there's no way to explain what I said.

"She wasn't feeling well at all, bless her heart," Andy's sweet mama says. The last and only time I saw her was at the MoonShots protest Sunday morning, a week ago. She's a little thing, even when she's not standing next to her huge husband and son. She's wearing a raspberry colored dress, hose, and smart little heels, holding her tea cup in one hand while her other is folded lady-like in her lap. She lifts that hand to pat Patty's hand and repeats, "Bless her heart."

Patty just melts. It's stunning to watch someone who has had so little kindness in their life receive kindness. Makes me love Andy's mama and realize that more than anything I want Patty and Andy's marriage to work out. And while I've been all caught up in Will and Anna, I'm reminded that this is a real wedding for Patty and Andy.

"Yeah, she wasn't feeling well at all, honey," I say and smile extra sweetly at the big, uncomfortable girl.

Patty grins back at me, her nervousness gone. She even laughs a bit. "Hate Momma's not feeling well. I just figured she was racing back to Bill if he's out of bed. She can't never get enough of that man."

Well, then, there's always that.

"Can't help but appreciate Gertie getting us out of Missus' little tea party early," Laney says, as we step off the front porch and into the midday sunshine. It blasts the sidewalk and makes the hosta flowers hang their heads. When summer hits in Georgia, you know it. I dig in my purse for my sunglasses, and Laney swirls her caftan to make a breeze.

At the main sidewalk, Laney turns left instead of crossing the street.

"Where are you going?" I ask as I follow her.

"Peter's."

"Why?" I'm still with her, but I can peel off to cross the street at any time.

"To find out what in the world was going on yesterday. Don't you want to know if he's having a fling with Miss New York?"

"I do, but I don't think we can just ask him."

She stops and turns around, hair and caftan both in full motion. "Of course we can. We're his friends. Besides, something else is going on."

But when we get to his house, there are only workmen around, so we finally cross the street and head to our cars. "I feel like I haven't really talked to you in forever," I say as we pass Ruby's. "We haven't been out for coffee in a long time."

"Yeah, well, you know… with the new job and all," she says.

"How are things going at Charming House?"

"Okay, I guess. It's not like working up at Crossings with you and Susan, or even Missus. They don't let me have control." She steps off the sidewalk behind me toward her car. "And you know how much I like to be in control."

I laugh, but she doesn't join in. By time I realize that and stop to look at her, she's in her car with the door closed and the engine starting.

My car is across the street, but as I look for traffic, I see Jordan outside of MoonShots on her phone. Couldn't ask Peter, but there's no reason not to ask Jordan. At least, none I can think of in the half-minute it takes to walk up to her.

"Hey, got a minute?" I say when she ends her phone call.

"Sure. I need to go upstairs and change shirts." She's pulling at her knit, long-sleeved shirt. "You can come."

We walk back into the building, and I nod and speak to the young man behind the counter. Jordan just passes through and then pushes out the back door with me in her wake.

"You don't have a way to get upstairs without going outside?"

"Nope, but it's not really a big deal." We climb the metal stairs, and at the top, she points to one of the chair on the covered deck area. "Wait here. Be right back."

There's no breeze, and the heaviness of the air feels like real weight. I wipe the back of my neck with my hand and sit back in the chair. After all that hot tea—only Missus would serve hot tea in June in Georgia—a glass of water would be lovely. I step to the glass door and look in. I don't see Jordan, so I slip in, grab a glass out of the wire strainer and fill it from the tap. As I'm leaving, I hear the bathroom door open, but I've had time to sit back down and drink half the glass of water before Jordan comes out.

"There, that's better," she says when she does. "How do you people survive down here with this heat? It's absolutely suffocating."

"You get used to it."

"Thankfully, I don't have to."

"You're leaving?" I ask.

She nods. "One way or another. Listen, sorry about you getting caught up in that yesterday. The story was so obviously full of holes that it only made it to the show's website, and it's even been taken down from there now."

"Do they follow you everywhere?"

"Who?" she says from near the stairs. She hasn't sat down since she came out.

"The paparazzi? They were obviously there yesterday following you I assume."

"Oh, no." She looks down the stairs and away from me. "That was something I set up on purpose."

"What? Why would you do that?" I stand as she starts down the stairs. "Jordan, what's going on?"

She only shakes her head and keeps walking down. At the bottom, she turns around and watches me as I descend. She smiles, but looks so smug. "Don't worry. It doesn't matter now." She opens the door and holds it for me to go inside. I do, and then I hear the door close behind me. But no Jordan. Okay, guess we were done talking.

Chapter 49

"It's not like they used your name. Or even Peter's. Maybe she was trying to make Diego jealous?" Jackson is buttoning the cuffs of his shirt and is turned away from the bathroom door where I'm standing. He turns when I clear my throat, then says, "Look at you."

"Like it?" When I went shopping for a dress for the wedding, I found a perfect dress for an evening out, on sale. When Anna wanted a rehearsal dinner, after the initial panic, I realized I already had the perfect dress. It's a deep plum and sleeveless, except for little piece of gauzy material that drapes down off my shoulders. Its low cut, just enough, and has a flare at the tail of the skirt, at my knees, to make it feel fun and princessy. Already this summer, I'm appreciating the short haircut I got in the winter, even if it was forced at the time. And with my neck and shoulders bare in this dress, the haircut looks even cuter. Plus I did some fluffing of the spiky parts.

Jackson holds me and puts his lips on a very sweet spot just below my ear. "You look amazing."

"You know there's nothing with Peter, or anyone else, right?"

"I do. And it was fun you reminding me, again, last night when we got home. I should probably drop TMZ a thank-you note." He growls and pulls me tighter. "Maybe you can remind me again later, when you have to take off this dress."

"I'm serious, it was scary how far apart we got. We can't forget that it can happen so quick."

He pulls back to look at me. "And I am serious, I will need frequent reminders."

I smack his arm, kiss him, and pull out of his arms. "Let's go. Hope Bryan and Savannah are ready."

Opening our door, Savanah jumps a bit. She was just getting ready to turn onto the stairs after leaving her room. "Your dress looks good, Mom," she says, but she's not looking at my dress as much as she's studying our faces. She takes a deep breath and smiles. "You both look good."

Jackson steps back for me to follow our daughter down the stairs. "It's a big night out for the Jessups, isn't it? Bryan, you ready?"

"Yep, down here. Will left and said he'd meet us all down at the church."

Jackson tosses his keys to his youngest. "Want to start the car, get the air going?"

Bryan not only catches the keys, he doesn't even look that excited. "Sure, Dad."

I'm left on the bottom stair with my mouth hanging open. "Jackson. He's not old enough to start the car."

Jackson grins. "Sure he is. Will was doing it earlier than this, remember?" He goes out onto the porch.

Guess I do remember, but Will was the oldest, and I was ready for him to grow up. Bryan is the last one. In the kitchen, I transfer my driver's license and favorite lipstick into my ancient little black purse. Savannah is drinking a bottle of water and leaning against the counter.

"Mom, I'm sorry for jumping on you about the video on the internet last night. I know it was just a mix-up."

"Thanks. I tried to talk to Jordan about it today. She said it was something she set up? She also said she's leaving."

"Great, she'll probably just leave MoonShots hanging, and I won't have a job now for the summer. Just great. Hey, Meemaw, I like that skirt."

Etta has on a yellow skirt and royal blue, short-sleeved sweater. "I don't know if the colors work, but it was the best I could find. Anything I wear, I'm still a little round grandma. Soon to be a little round great-grandma." She winks and puts her arm around Savannah's waist, then asks me, "Is the other lady that's staying here coming tonight?"

I hang my purse on my arm. "She's coming to the rehearsal dinner, but not the rehearsal, and then will be back here to spend the night. The car should be cooled down if we're ready to go."

Savannah tips her head to look down at her meemaw. "So you're not upset about them having a baby?"

Etta nibbles her lip. "I'm not saying it's going to be easy or that it's the best way to start out a marriage, but I've been around long enough to know that a baby doesn't care if the world it's coming to is ready for it. It just comes and turns that world upside down. Ready or not."

Rubbing in a dab of hand lotion, I watch the two of them walk through the front door. It's hard to believe, but the baby Anna is carrying will one day tower over me like Savannah does her meemaw.

Isn't life a bit startling?

CHAPTER 50

I've never been to a double wedding before. It's hard to focus. The act of shifting my eyes and thoughts between the two couples competes with the act of staring, open-mouthed, at Will. How can my son be this grown up? I have the same feeling which engulfed me when we were leaving the hospital with him as a newborn—shouldn't somebody stop this?

Anna doesn't look happy; Will doesn't look happy. Then I look over at Patty and Andy, and they are practically delirious. Savannah serves as Anna's maid of honor, and Jackson is Will's best man. Gertie and Andy's older brother serve in the same duties for Patty and Andy. Bryan is the usher, and him leading me to my seat has so far been my favorite part of the day. The whole day. Our morning was rough. But, I shouldn't be surprised after last night.

Rehearsal was chaotic, as most wedding rehearsals are. Between nerves, weariness, anticipation and that first mix of all the family—times two for this double wedding—it's a recipe for chaos. I hoped the drive to Canton, to the Italian Bistro, would calm everyone down.

The venue was perfect for a warm summer night. A balcony right outside our private room gave us a place to spread out to, and watching the setting sun over the mountains was magical.

Wine flowed, and although Anna and Will didn't seem to be speaking, no one focused on it. Anna's friend, Miss Linda, from the UGA cafeteria, turned out to be a delightful older woman who had taken Anna under her wing. But even Miss Linda's best attempts left Anna more removed and Will drinking more wine. Missus spoke loudly, then even louder still as she tried to salvage the party. Peter spent more of the evening downstairs than up—avoiding me, I assumed, since we didn't exchange a word all night.

No one thing stood out as bad; it was just one of those nights where everyone is awkward and uncomfortable. Jackson kept close to Will's side as a best man should, but Will didn't want to talk. Finally, we were able to leave. I don't think Will and Anna even said "good bye" to each other.

Miss Linda was sitting out on the deck in the half-light of dawn when I finally gave up trying to sleep this morning and came downstairs.

"This wedding is a mistake. Not the marriage, this wedding," she said when I sat down. Before I even had a sip of coffee. Thanks, Linda. "Anna has never sought attention, and here she is in the center of it all."

"Well, it'll all be over soon." See? Before coffee I'm no help at all.

She pats her hand on the table. "As soon as it's light, I'm going down to her grandmother's house to tell her to just let the other couple get married. Will and Anna can head out of town for the night, move into their place with Missus, and start over on Monday."

"No wedding?" I asked. "But we have family coming, and well, it's already today. Just a couple more hours. Plus, we've already had the rehearsal dinner."

"And that went well, don't you think?" she said, looking at me from over her glasses.

She had a point there. "But won't it be an even bigger mess

with cancelling?"

"Maybe," she said. "But we don't know just how big a mess the wedding will be, right? But them leaving and then Patty and Andrew having their wedding, well, we know what that would look like. Right? Those are the odds I'd go with. Cut and run."

"But what if they regret it?"

She turned to look at me. "Carolina, there is no good solution. We only have two bad situations to choose from."

"I think they've already chosen."

She threw up her hands and laughed. "They've chosen? I've only met Anna's grandmother once, but she doesn't seem entirely reasonable."

"You're right there."

"And, honestly, Carolina, you and your family have not pushed back on anything. Anna has a tyrannical streak, maybe from her grandmother, and you and your husband, along with Will, let her get away with it. She ran your poor son around tonight, and he let her."

"But that's not the Anna we got to know last fall. You don't think it's just the emotions from the wedding and her being pregnant?"

Miss Linda sighed. "I'm sure that's some of it. But, honey, her mother was a mess. Clean by the time I met her, but depressed and sick. Anna has to have a backbone of steel to have come out of that as well as she did." The older lady with the red hair streaked with silver pulled herself out of the chair. "I'm going to get dressed and go down to see her. I'm supposed to be having breakfast with her this morning anyway. We're going to Ruby's. Didn't I see a place named Ruby's on the square?"

"Right. And thanks. We'll talk to Will, and we'll back whatever they want to do."

And we did talk to Will. And Will talked to Anna. And Missus talked to all of us. We talked and talked some more. All the while getting ready for the wedding. And now here we are.

It hurts too much to watch Will and Anna, so I'm focusing on Patty and Andy.

Gertie and Bill are actually a cute couple. They remind me of Patty and Andy: big and country, settled. Not a lot of mystery or sophistication to get in the way. Andy's parents are also happy, and watching Andy's tiny mama treat Patty like a princess, can't help but make me smile.

Everything turned out pretty. Gardenias are the main flower, so the sanctuary smells amazing. Sunshine illuminates the stained glass windows along the sides of the sanctuary and infuses the light inside with depth and color. Savannah is wearing a light blue dress she wore to homecoming last year, but she actually looked better at homecoming. Her smile was more genuine then. She spent the morning relaying messages between her brother and Anna.

Savannah is the first in the procession to walk back down the aisle, with the rest of both wedding parties behind her. She smiles at me and her daddy. Only we would notice the weary lift of her eyebrows and crookedness of her smile. Behind her, Will and Anna look like one of those old-fashioned pictures where people don't smile. Or maybe they look like snarky models, who refuse to even pretend they're happy. Patty and Andy bound down the aisle, arms tightly intertwined and pressed into each other.

Okay, that's over.

Bring on the party.

Chapter 51

Hugs are not always my favorite. Especially those people who hug you and don't even know you. They just hug everybody, including their bug exterminator.

And excuse my French, but these hugs today suck.

It's an absolutely perfect day at the lake park. Perfect. Light breeze, low humidity. Trees draped with white lights, which become more pronounced with every inch the sun sinks in the sky. Tables draped with ivory clothes and twines of ivy. Gardenias float in shallow bowls of water, and the string quartet sends lovely music to ride throughout on the breeze. Susan has brought in tables and chairs to fill the pavilion and even scattered some along the lake. There's a picture station next to the water with an old wagon to climb up in or just lean against. *Southern Living* could do a country wedding shoot here.

But about those hugs. My friends hug me lightly, and then pat my back. They speak softly and smile weakly. More like hugs at a funeral than a wedding. The head table has seating for only the newlyweds and two of their attendants with their dates. Gertie and Jackson both begged off sitting at the head table. Left it for the young people. Savannah is back toying around with Ashton now that Ricky has left for college, so he's her date, and on the other end are Andy's brother Luke and his wife. Speaking of *Southern Living* magazine, the two newlywed couples look like Before & After. You know, those stories of couples before they lost weight, or went through marriage counseling. Where before they look bad, like they want to run far, far away, and then after, where they look as happy and loving as Patty and Andy... Who'd believe both couples just got married?

Laney hugs me, again, and this time I push her away. "Stop hugging me. They're fighting, not dead."

"Okay, grouchy. I've got to say, my sister did a really great job with this."

"It's beautiful. Hard to enjoy, but beautiful. But tell me, why have you seemed to have such trouble with her lately?"

She dismisses the question. "Just stuff going on. Look at the girls. Can you believe they'll all be going off to college next year?"

Savannah and Ashton are in their seats at the head table surrounded by some of their friends. "I like that Angie is going softer on the black eye-liner," I say.

Laney laughs. "Yeah, me too. Figured it was just a phase—no, I *prayed* it was just a phase. She's still in love with the black hair dye, but then so am I." She pats her dark hair. "So, the rest of us can sit wherever we want? Guess I'd better go stake out a seat. You've got all of Jackson's family to sit with, right?"

"Yep, Etta is ecstatic to have all three boys together. You met his brothers, right?"

She nods and then grins, "That younger one, the football coach..."

"Colt?"

"Yes, he's one good-looking young man. And he's not married?"

"No, he eats, lives, and breathes football. He's quite a bit younger than Jackson and Emerson. He's not forty yet."

"You and Emerson's wife get along?"

"Okay, I guess. She's just so into the girls."

Laney smirks. "As are the boys here. They are beautiful girls."

"Yeah, they are. We don't see them much. I think the only reason they're here today is they were going right through here on their way to Destin. But it's made Etta so happy."

"Well, I'm going to go find a seat. Talk to you later."

Looking over the crowd, I notice Jordan. Wonder what she's doing here? When she sees me, she starts my direction. "Hey, Carolina. Everything looks great."

"Thanks," I say with a questioning look.

"Yeah, what am I doing here?" She shifts from one hip to the other. She's wearing a sleeveless dress, soft pink with a black belt tightened to show off her tiny waist. Her hair is in a low bun, and she has on high heels. "I told Diego I'd be here. He's, ah, he's coming to see me."

"About the video?" I ask.

She shrugs. "Maybe. I just wanted him to see I've made friends here. That I've really tried."

"Okay. Fine with me if you stay." Then I turn and see an unmistakable head of blue-black hair. "Oh, look, there he is."

She whips around and dashes off to meet him. How does she walk in high heels on these pine needles?

I follow her, until I see that Diego looks mad. Really mad. Then I see him looking past her to the rest of the crowd, most of whom are now watching him. He's not been loud, but his presence really made an entrance. Then he sees who he's looking for. "With him?" he says, loud enough to carry to those of us nearby, and then he pushes past his wife, headed straight for Peter.

Peter holds up his hands. "It's all going to be fine, Diego. You know its better this way."

Diego struggles to hold his voice down. "You think you know what's better for my wife?"

"I didn't say that..."

"And behind my back." Then he turns behind him and points at Jordan. "Together you planned all of this." He catches sight of me and steps in my direction. "Dear Carolina, you have been a good friend. I do not know what there was between you and this Bedwell person, but he is not to be trusted."

"Nothing! There is nothing. Was nothing." I practically shout as I step to Diego, then remember where I am and lower my voice. "This is a wedding reception. Maybe you should leave."

Jackson has met me at Diego. "That's a good idea, Mr. Moon."

"He's taking everything from me. Do you know this?"

Peter apparently has had enough. "Are you serious? I didn't take anything away from you! You threw it all away. We're just trying to help you out now."

Throughout the crowd, I see cringes and skepticism. I must admit, probably the same looks appear on my face. "Peter, she's his wife. They have children."

"Exactly. Now she can go home."

Okay, scratch that. Replace skepticism with confusion. "What? You and Jordan aren't, I don't know, like, together?"

"Yes, but only as business partners. The rest, well, the rest was for this idea, this plan. You honestly believed she and I were a thing?" He shakes his head and rolls his eyes to the heavens. "Everyone, *everyone* knows a MoonShots can't make it in Chancey. It's a joke. It's losing money hand over fist. Right, Jordan? Right, Diego?"

Jordan nods enthusiastically; Diego only manages a tiny lift of his head. He grabs hold of Jordan's arm and pulls his wife to his side and tips his head close to hers. Then, in a quiet voice, says, "Please explain."

She bends her head to his and talks softly. Peter takes a deep breath and says, just as softly, to me and Jackson, "It was all about his ego. A place he could punish Jordan, but that's done now. Jordan and I figured out a solution. A place like the market of the Italian Bistro, a few tables, some homemade foods and treats, picnic staples, gourmet food. We worked it all out, but Diego wouldn't give us the time of day. He let his anger get in the way of a good business decision. So, well, we made sure he'd come down here by setting up that video. You showing up was never part of the plan."

"How could it have been? I only decided to run up there that morning."

Jordan lifts her head and puts a hand on Diego's shoulder. She speaks a little louder, so those of us surrounding them can hear. "It was only business with me and Mr. Bedwell, I promise. The video was just to get you down here, and well, to get some free publicity for Peter and his new shop. Diego, I will never hurt you like that again. Our marriage has to work, but it can't when we are so far apart. Let me come home."

Diego spends a few moments looking at his wife, then around at the crowd. He takes her hand and says to me and Jackson, "My apology for intruding like this. I do let my temper get away with me sometimes. We will go now, but as it looks like we are going to be doing business here in Chancey, we will see you soon." He drops Jordan's hand and steps toward Peter with his hand outstretched. "My apologies to you, Mr. Bedwell. Excuse me, I meant partner." The men shake hands, and then Diego walks back through the pavilion with his wife.

Susan steps up and welcomes everyone, then she explains how the buffet lines will work. The service people begin taking off chafing dishes lids, and the smells waft to us. It's been a long, exhausting day, and no one has to be begged to get a plate and get in line.

Even Anna and Will seem to enjoy the rest of the reception. They aren't really talking to each other much, but fighting gets old eventually. Besides, once you're married you know you can pick the fight back up any old time.

A small dance floor in the center of the pavilion becomes a

fairytale. The white lights in the rafters glow down on a scene of two brides dancing with their husbands. The soft lights of the sky skim across the lake, and we all take a deep breath or two, full of good food, cake, and wine.

"Susan, come sit down for a minute. You've worked yourself to a frazzle and done an amazing job," I say as I push out the chair beside me.

"Yes, you did, my dear sister. Sit down. No one will fire you," Laney adds.

Susan grins and sinks into the white wooden chair across from her sister and next to me. Her bottom no sooner hits the seat than Missus barks, "Susan Lyles."

She starts to jump up, but Missus lays a hand on her shoulder. "Stay there, I believe I'll join you." Missus lifts a white cloth napkin from the chair next to Susan. "Did I hear correctly that you are moving up to Laurel Cove?"

"Yes, ma'am, that's correct."

"Hmm. I'm not sure how I feel about that."

Laney leans up. "It doesn't really matter. My sister and her husband have worked very hard for everything they have. They deserve the biggest, best house in the whole world."

Susan not only blushes, her eyes get shiny. "Why, Laney! Thank you. I wasn't sure you were happy for us, for me."

Laney shrugs. "I wasn't. But no surprise. I like being the center of attention. But I guess if I have to share it, might as well be with you."

"Lots of changes," I say watching the dance floor, where Anna has her head resting on Will's shoulder as they sway. "This time next year, Missus, you and I will have a baby to play with."

"Me too," Laney says.

Susan frowns, "You talking about their grandbaby?"

"Nope, getting one of my own."

All of us can't help the reflex of looking at the bundle of high school kids, with Angie and Jenna at the center. Susan goes pale,

and I lean up. Missus swallows and lifts her hand to her throat.
Susan finally asks, "Jenna? Angie?"
Laney smiles and answers, "Nope. Me. I'm due in August."
And I don't really remember much after that.

Don't miss...

Next Stop, Chancey
Book One in the Chancey Series

Looking in your teenage daughter's purse is never a good idea.

After all, it ended up with Carolina opening a B&B for railroad buffs in a tiny Georgia mountain town. Carolina knows all about, and hates, small towns. How did she end up leaving her wonderful Atlanta suburbs behind while making her husband's dreams come true?

Unlike back home in the suburbs with privacy fences and automatic garage doors, everybody in Chancey thinks your business is their business and they all love the newest Chancey business. The B&B hosts a senate candidate, a tea for the County Fair beauty contestants, and railroad nuts who sit out by the tracks and record the sound of a train going by. Yet, nobody believes Carolina prefers the 'burbs.

Oh, yeah, and if you just ignore a ghost, will it go away?

Chancey Family Lies
Book Two in the Chancey Series

Holidays are different in small towns. You're expected to cook.

Carolina is determined her first holiday season as a
stay-at-home mom will be perfect. However...

Twelve kids from college (and one nobody seems to know)
Eleven chili dinners (why do we always have to feed a crowd?)
Ten dozen fake birds (cardinals, no less)
Nine hours without power (but lots of stranded guests)
Eight angry council members (wait, where's the town's money?)
Seven trains a-blowin' (all the time. All. The. Time.)
Six weeks with relatives (six weeks?!?)
Five plotting teens (again, who is that girl?)
Four in-laws staying (and staying, and staying...)
Three dogs a-barking (who brought the dogs?)
Two big ol' secrets (and they ain't wrapped in ribbons
under the tree, either)
And the perfect season gone with the wind.

Derailed in Chancey
Book Three in the Chancey Series

Should she jump?

When the train is headed for disaster, the engineer can jump out, right?

Carolina knew moving teenagers from the Atlanta suburbs to a small Georgia mountain town was a horrible idea. She knew opening a B&B was an even worse plan. She can't see around the next curve, but...

Should she jump?

Oncoming headlights aren't only aimed at her family, the town of Chancey is being set up for a collision that could change everything. And as that unfolds, Carolina's husband Jackson is smack dab in the middle of it all, his hand on the throttle, going full steam ahead.

Should she jump?

Would you?

The Chancey books are available in both print and ebook on Amazon.com

You can find out more about Kay and her books
on her web-site, kaydewshostak.com

Prosper Community Library
700 N. Coleman St.
Prosper, TX 75078
(469) 219-2499

CPSIA information can be obtained
at www.ICGtesting.com
Printed in the USA
LVOW11s1821251016

510212LV00004B/935/P

9 780996 243063